BROUHAHA

Ardal O'Hanlon is an accomplished actor, comedian, and writer best known for his leading roles in *Death in Paradise* and *Father Ted*. He is also the author of the critically acclaimed novel, *Talk of the Town*. He lives in Dublin.

ARDAL O'HANLON

Brouhaha

HarperCollins*Ireland*

HarperCollinsIreland
The Watermarque Building
Ringsend Road
Dublin DO4 K7N3
Ireland

a division of
HarperCollins*Publishers*
1 London Bridge Street
London SE1 9GF
UK

www.harpercollins.co.uk

First published by HarperCollinsIreland in 2022

3 5 7 9 10 8 6 4 2

© Ardal O'Hanlon 2022

Ardal O'Hanlon asserts the moral right to be identified as the author of this work

A catalogue record of this book is available from the British Library

TPB ISBN 978-0-00-852962-8
HB ISBN 978-0-00-854737-0

Typeset by Palimpsest Book Production Ltd, Falkirk, Stirlingshire

Printed and bound in the UK using 100% renewable electricity
at CPI Group (UK) Ltd

MIX
Paper from
responsible sources
FSC
www.fsc.org
FSC™ C007454

This book is produced from independently certified FSC™ paper
to ensure responsible forest management.

For more information visit: www.harpercollins.co.uk/green

For my children, Emily, Rebecca and Red,
whose humour, resilience and companionship
were such a boon during the great Uncertainty

Between thought and expression lies a lifetime.
Lou Reed, 'Some Kinda Love'

PART ONE

Kevin goes to work

'Did I snore last night?'

'Not really, love. Sure, wasn't I awake anyway?'

Kevin, balancing the tray in one hand, picked up a cup of tea with the other and placed it on Sheila's bedside locker next to a plate that was decorated with two slices of toast, which were neatly quartered, buttered and smeared with a thick-cut marmalade, the thickest cut available to man. There was also a probiotic yoghurt-type drink, as prescribed by one of Sheila's bridge-club friends, and a selection of pills on a saucer.

'Thanks.'

'Don't forget your tablets!'

'Do you know, I think I'm feeling better today?'

He'd heard that one before.

'That's great, love.'

'I might get up.'

Kevin left the tray on the floor and got back into bed himself with a cup of tea. He'd had his porridge downstairs and his own fill of tablets when he was feeding the baby.

'Philip Sharkey is home,' he said, chancing a glance at his wife of twenty-two years, twenty-three this coming December.

'Oh?'

'I might go and see him today. So I might.'

That was the last thing Sheila needed to hear. She returned the cup to the bedside locker, shuffled down under the covers and turned her back on him, leaving Kevin staring at the wall, not for the first time, at the surreal painting of the head of a sweeping brush that doubled up as theatre curtains. It had been copied more than competently by Sheila, in happier times, from a book of Russian poster art. He often tried to imagine what scenes unfolded behind the bristly drapes, as he finger-brushed his own bushy moustache.

Over the past few days, Kevin, no flies on him, had sensed a tension in the town thanks to Dove Connolly's poor decision to blow his own head off. It wasn't just the act of self-harm itself, the pointless splattering of blood and bone and brain all over his bedroom wall, that was the issue, unsettling as that was. In so doing, poor Dove had spread panic amongst the townspeople, raising all sorts of ugly questions, reviving all sorts of rumours, and inviting all sorts of unwelcome attention upon them. In Kevin's mind, there was method in Dove's madness. Showing a shocking assertiveness for possibly the first time in his life, and the last, says you, Dove blew the lid off the whole town.

Tullyanna was famed for its extra-wide Main Street. It was said to be the widest in Europe. A handy feature to have when there were so many people to avoid. Which was all very well except, in what was a smallish border town populated by just three thousand pinched faces and all of them secretive, you were never quite sure who exactly it was you were supposed to be avoiding.

The sun was out for once – out of curiosity, says you – a provocation to the innately furtive natives on this headsore summer's day.

As a cop, Kevin couldn't deny that he was excited by the macabre turn of events. To his shame, he was energized by it. With Dove's best friend, Philip Sharkey, showing up unexpectedly, there was a curiosity in the air. Kevin could almost hear the clicks of sheds being unlocked and shotguns being loaded, or was that just the cogs in his mind finding purchase again after years of inertia?

He got dressed, in his best suit, now a size too big, polished his shoes and walked the half-mile or so to the garda station, as he did most days, in his familiar slow-weaving side-to-side stride. He passed both graveyards without incident, surprised by how quiet the dead, of all denominations, were this morning. The lake, to his right, was still, a lone fisherman – Herman the German, Tullyanna's only tourist in living memory – finishing a croissant before casting his first line of the day. They were both startled by the cat-like screech of a shabby-looking bird that rose high above the old monastery on the other side of the lake, a buzzard, bejaysus, if Kevin wasn't mistaken. He'd heard they were back. At the old railway station, now a builders' providers, he took a left to go up Church Street past the Gothic Revival Catholic church, a towering edifice of sparrow-picked limestone from which he was currently barred.

Up through the town he ambled, election posters jostling for position on the telegraph poles, wrought-iron baskets hanging from street lamps and shop doorways, bursting with all sorts of floral effusions, lobelia, at a guess, geraniums, as you would expect, trailing fuchsia, petunias, begonias, busy lizzie, all the old reliables and, of course, clematis, at the behest of the Tidy Towns committee, who had a good feeling this year, as they did every year, fair play to them, their efforts to paper over the cracks dogged and admirable and, fingers crossed, not entirely futile.

By all appearances, Tullyanna was a fine market town, dominated on one end of the Main Street by a substantial cut-stone courthouse in the classical style and on an incline at the other end by the deceptively humble Protestant church. The thoroughfare itself was flanked on both sides by handsome three-storey townhouses, all now host to shops and hairdressers' and pubs, some of the premises sadly shuttered given the times, yet many of them gaily painted in lime-greens and pinks and powder-blues, with contrasting quoins, as if nothing was amiss.

He turned in to the shopping centre for a fortifying coffee and a hunk of Victoria sponge. Antoinette's was one of only two units (of fourteen) defying the slump and remaining open. His eye was drawn to a large mural on the wall opposite the café, painted by the late Dove Connolly. Dove had been commissioned by the proprietor of the shopping centre, Dinky Murtagh, in a fit of munificence some five years ago, during more prosperous times, to reflect Tullyanna in all her glory. Although it featured prominent landmarks – the churches, the old mill, the new meat plant – and characters, contemporary and historical, Dove's quirky, some might say satirical, some might even go as far as to say *esoteric*, tableau was not to everyone's liking. Indeed, some of the more, shall we say, Hogarthian caricatures – Dinky himself was depicted with frog features and bulging pockets – and more libellous inferences were painted over within minutes of the unveiling. It was rumoured that Sandra Mohan, or multiple allusions to Sandra Mohan, were hidden, *Where's Wally?* style, within the mural. One notable absence from the painting was Philip Sharkey.

Kevin was planning to call on Philip later in the day, after work, a fondness for him and a protectiveness towards him not in any way lessened by time. This was, mind you, despite Philip being now a fully grown man, the smooth edges roughened, a determination about him, as Kevin had noted last night at Dove's wake, that was nothing short of *intense*.

Only Philip could help him now. Philip would know better than anyone why Dove might have died. Philip, Kevin knew rightly – and it was a sore point, every bit as nagging as his pancreatic pain – had never told him the full story before he skedaddled thirteen years ago. Perhaps now he could regain the younger man's trust.

'Lovely day,' says Cathy of the Cakes, without irony, presenting him with his treat, the highlight, by a distance, of his morning so far.

'Thanks, Cathy.'

He took a seat alone, stirring four illicit lumps of sugar into his coffee. The coffee cup was square in shape, an affectation too far. He'd have to be careful. And him dressed to the nines on such an auspicious day. The sniggering started at a nearby table. Young fellas at a loose end on their school holidays.

'Well, Kojak.'

'Heal me!'

He ignored the wisecracks, knocked back the coffee and left the shop. Mercifully, although it was a warm morning, there weren't that many people about. As he approached the station – a former RIC barracks, its striking limestone façade dressed in the rusticated fashion – he observed a number of gardaí, holding onto their hats, hurriedly getting into two squad cars and haring off in the direction of Dundalk.

'What can I do for you, Kevin?'

It was young Pádraig O'Loinsigh at the desk. He could hear the old hubbub in the dayroom beyond.

'You can buzz me in, Pádraig, for a start.'

'You know I can't do that, Kevin.'

'C'mon now, stop your messing. I have work to do.'

'Kevin, I'm sorry, but you know the rules. Only serving officers allowed in the station. Do you want to do the traffic?'

O'Loinsigh offered him the hat. He looked at it, a regulation beat officer's cap, peaked and well-worn, and his face dissolved in a mixture of horror and sadness. The truth was, and it was a truth that was tough to bear, and sometimes he bore it and more often he didn't, that Detective Sergeant Kevin Healy, one-time winner of the Walter Scott Medal for Valour, was no longer a serving member of the force.

He had retired or, more to the point, had been forced to retire more than five years ago due to his various health issues, issues not limited to the usual anxiety and depression. In a pitiful coda to a glittering career – well, glittering apart from the glaring failure to nail anybody in the Sandra Mohan case and the complete absence of anything resembling glitter – Kevin was indulged by his former colleagues who, with the blessing of the District Commissioner, allowed him to direct traffic at a busy intersection on the Main Street. This he did, to pass the time, while under medication, willingly and with good humour, and with extravagant gestures to match, possibly inspired by Jacques Tati, the French clown for whom he had a reverence. To the amusement of some, and the heartbreak of many, he helped to alleviate a well-known bottleneck in the process, until such times as clarity returned and the extent of his humiliation dawned on him again.

'We're busy, Kevin. A body! Out by Derrykeen. Battered, by the looks of it.'

'Who is it?'

'I'm not at liberty to say, Kevin, you know that.'

The young officer took a swig of Lucozade.

'Even if I knew, I couldn't tell you.'

He drained the bottle, burped, *excuse me*, and turned his attention to a young woman clutching a passport application, yet another would-be emigrant in a rush to get away, badly in need of a signature by a competent, *compos mentis* pillar of the community.

Philip gets out of bed

Philip didn't like getting out of bed, and who could blame him? Mind you, he didn't like lingering in the bed either.

Although now aged thirty, his childhood bedroom was still plastered with the posters given to him by his uncle Francie – Francie McNally the barber, who'd gone out of business when the new unisex salon arrived in town back in 1994. They were black-and-white pictures – Blu Tacked ironically to the wall in a fit of mischief by his fun-loving former self – a collage of headshots of moody men with pursed lips advertising all sorts of styling products. Posers, you could say, if you were the judgemental type, with high, back-combed hair suggesting everything was going to be cool. The corners of the posters curling outwards suggested otherwise. Nothing stayed cool forever, not even in Tullyanna.

'Philip!'

He ignored his mother, and him blowing smoke rings towards the ceiling, the Os dissolving into question marks. Why did he put the posters up in the first place, and why didn't he take them down? He put them up because it was funny. Well, at the time it seemed to himself and Dove, the town's resident iconoclasts, that it was funny. Glorifying hair models instead of footballers, as many of their friends did. It was a small and private and probably useless *artistic* gesture, a Dadaist-style protest somewhat out of time and place, Tullyanna not, of course, being the Weimar Republic between the wars. Albeit a place, some would say, equally corrupt and just as volatile. And it was every bit as 'funny' and subversive to leave them up on the wall, for posterity, not that Philip found much to laugh at anymore, not now that his best friend in the world was dead. Dove was dead. And it was all his fault.

Philip smiled. They were the *sensitive* kids, himself, Dove, Sandra, Paddy Mathews, Deirdre. In the High School, people hated them because they name-checked obscure bands and shared a copy of *Last Exit to Brooklyn*. Between them they hoovered up the five copies of *Howarya!*, the music and social affairs magazine, that arrived every fortnight in Kennedy's newsagent. In hindsight, they probably deserved a certain amount of opprobrium for smoking Gauloises and growing their fingernails long and maybe, just maybe, acting a bit superior. *Feeling* a bit superior to the boggers, and the hard men, and the unassuming mainstream Joes whose only ambition in life was to own their own car. Sandra, who taught them all to think bigger, made her own clothes, for God's sake. Dove had been drawing his own comics since he was five years old, always full of the jokes, and deeper meanings to those in the know.

'Philip, love!'

'Jesus!' says he, a little too loudly, perhaps, as she rounded the door.

'Don't Jesus me. Charlie O'Dowd's at the door.'

'Is he?'

Although he might have sounded surprised, that wasn't a surprise. The only surprising aspect of it was that it had taken them three full days before they made contact. Very considerate.

'Do you have to smoke in bed?'

'I do.'

She stood there in the doorway, the arms folded, not entirely unloving and not entirely unlovely herself, the bouffant hair-do immaculate, immutable as ever, a constant at least in an ever-changing world. Philip knew she was worried about him, and she had every right to be. Drizzling sweat, the lips chapped, he hadn't budged since he'd arrived home for Dove's funeral. At six foot four, he was too long for the bed. No doubt she thought he was overdoing the brooding. The conversation, since his return, was not sparkling, their exchanges brutally short.

'Well! Are you going to get up? And see Charlie?'

It was Uncle Francie who had introduced him to fly fishing. And to hash. Although he loved the smell of the barber's shop – the pomades, the hair tonics and gels – and the sleepy-quiet within, the intermittent chit-chat and the snip-snip, and the buzz of the buzzing thing – the trimmer – he had no intention of following his uncle into the trade. He didn't do foregone conclusions. He liked to confound expectations (usually to his cost) and avoid predictability (with all too predictable results). Like a lot of dreamers, Philip had wanted to sing in a band, a notion – to the average onlooker – that was never realistic. Number one, he didn't have a great voice – alarmingly higher than you'd expect. Two, he was slow to sing in public, needing a good feed of drink to get him going, by which time basic coherence would be the issue. And that's being kind. And three, he might not survive the coming weeks if, as widely suspected, his motive in coming home was to stir up trouble.

He stubbed out his cigarette and straightened himself up, still stiff and sore after his exertions the previous week in New Mexico. The room was smaller than he remembered. The bed was saggy. Some of his toy soldiers were still on the window-sill. Dove, he recalled, had a vast collection of men, thousands of them, in all shapes and sizes, from every army and every era in history. After school, they'd commandeer the musty 'parlour' in Dove's house. After dividing up the soldiers, the boys would carefully arrange them in elaborate formations on the floor and on top of the television set and the mullioned bookcase and along the back of the couch. You might end up with a coalition of Roman centurions, American GIs, a skiing division of the Red Army and maybe a few Subbuteo men to make up the numbers. It wasn't a complicated game. Once the legions were in position, you'd take turns throwing cushions at the rival confederacy. Whoever knocked over the most soldiers won. All that groundwork, all that discipline, all those hours of painstaking preparation undone in a moment of madness. The story of the world. No matter how much he tried to regress, to sink deeper into the bed, to disappear, he always woke up in the present, aware of who he was and what he had done and what he had failed to do.

No snob, Philip, he never minded sweeping the barbershop floor of a Saturday teatime, or the few quid in his pocket, or the bottle of McArdles or two that Francie produced at six o'clock sharp to kickstart the weekend. And he learned to judge a man by his hair, a useful knack to have in an uncertain world, peopled by men skilled in the arts of deception. And so, you won't be surprised to hear, Philip in his carefree youth kept a lock of each customer's hair. On handwritten cards he bullet-pointed their significant character traits and awarded them marks out of ten. And he stuck the hair samples and the cards into a scrapbook that, as far as he knew, was still under the bed. Stooping to see would have been beyond him in his current state. Although something of a 'joke', presumably, another 'arty' stunt, it was a database that might or might not come in handy to future generations of genealogists and documentary film-makers trying to make sense of what happened the summer he skipped town.

Joanne reads the death notices

Joanne McCollum had inherited her father's habit of, first thing every morning, scanning the death notices in the national newspapers. Unlike him, she didn't use a magnifying glass, which made his big, watery eyes bigger and more watery.

'You're fierce morbid altogether,' said Welly O'Boyle, throwing his gym bag on the floor. 'You shoulda been an undertaker.'

'I'd take great pleasure in sewing your gob shut for a start,' she replied drily.

'How's himself?' he whispered, directing his thumb at the door to Carson's office.

'O'Boyle!' Carson screamed from behind the door.

'He's in flying form. Enjoy!'

Welly, vigorously giving the two fingers on both hands to the bellowing voice, slouched in to see Carson. Joanne turned back to her papers in the *temporary* offices of the *Northern Chronicle*. They'd been seven years now in the *temporary* offices, above a butcher's in the middle of Mullinary. The county town. It was seven years since work had stopped on Carson's wet dream – a *'fuck-off, state-of-the-art'* premises on the ring road – when the builder went bust. Sales were chattering away in another room, their work cut out for them now that the country was broke. Joanne was not looking for anyone in particular. It was a morbid pastime to be sure, not, however, unrelated to her own profession.

She, fascinated by violent crime from an early age, wrote the court reports, amongst other things. Luckily for her, there was no shortage

of material these days, a fierce thirst for blood coming over the populace all of a sudden. For years – nine, coming on ten – Joanne had
beavered away, happy enough, for the *Chronicle*. Not the worst paper
in the world, despite the cramped working conditions and Carson's
foul temper. Dutifully, she turned up week-in week-out in draughty
courtrooms and at accident black spots, writing half the paper some
weeks, not that she got any credit for it. Not that she was looking for
credit.

It's just, and there was no getting away from it, a lot of people didn't
take her *seriously*. It wasn't anything Aisling and Anjali, her housemates, said. They both had *real* jobs in the pharmaceutical factory out
the Armagh Road. Last Sunday, they'd asked Joanne to go for brunch
in the new place in town.

'The Bunch of Thyme.'

'Jesus, I'd love to, but I'm doing the camogie.'

Joanne was reporting on an under-16 match that day. It was her
job. Besides, she liked camogie. She remembered reading the match
reports when she was a child, the joy of seeing your name in the local
paper. Your photo. The pride. She *believed* in what she was doing. Its
value to the community.

It was the way they smiled. She liked them. They were her friends
but, it's just, they couldn't help being patronizing. They didn't have to
say it, but she knew. *Real* journalists were people who wrote for national
newspapers and appeared on lunchtime radio at the weekend discussing
weighty affairs of state. *Real* journalists didn't stand on the sidelines
of a pitch or shivering outside the council chambers harrying county
councillors – their toupées on backwards – as they hurried, *no
comment, no comment*, over to the pub.

They were grand, Aisling and Anjali, with their endless takeaways
and their quiet satisfaction at selling record amounts of arthritis medication worldwide. Not taking anything away from them. But they just
didn't get it. As far back as she could remember, she was obsessed
with the 'news'. The more macabre, the more she was drawn to it.
Even as a pupil in the small two-room primary school in Drumahair,
she used to rush home every lunchtime to read her father's *Independent*.

Not just the headlines, she devoured the whole thing, cover to cover, the sports news, the business pages, even the small ads. Joanne always knew the price of hay.

Like many a funeral-going sociologist – half the country's population in her estimation – she liked to test her mental powers on these poignant memorials.

From these tiny biographies, reading between the lines, you could sometimes divine the cause of death. Well, Joanne could. Died *peacefully* was grand. Nothing out of place there. Or, *after a long illness*. Okay. But died *unexpectedly* was a different story. Or *tragically*. You'd want to know more, wouldn't you? She'd come across died *eventually* once, a clue, perhaps, to some outstanding frustration of the bereaved. You could conjure up the life that was led – *a confirmed bachelor* or *a tireless raconteur* – and work out who had the most to lose and the most to gain by the passing away of the dearly beloved. There was poetry to be cherished in the surnames of the deceased – Byrne and Carroll and Murray – and there was poetry, too, in the names of the townlands in which they perished. Castleblayney and Dundalk and Aughnaboy. She kept an eye out for Drumahair, *the Ridge of Two Demons*, so as she'd have something to talk about to her parents next time she saw them.

There was darkness as well as poetry. The cute placenames were sometimes synonymous with shame, for a wholesale Cromwellian slaughter or the brutal mundanity of a fistfight outside a chipper on a Saturday night in which a Byrne or a Murray might have lost an eye, incidents forgotten by everybody except Joanne, of course, who had a head for detail and an empathy for the underdog.

She'd written up more than her fair share of stories about brutal, senseless small-town violence based on the cases she covered in the Circuit and District courts. As a teenager, she'd hop on Molloy's minibus with her friends of a Saturday night and travel the twenty miles to Tullyanna to Shadows, the legendary nightclub. *Where love stories end!* as the joke went. Having gone to secondary school in the Loreto convent at Tullyanna, she would have known a lot of the heads there. At Shadows, she'd witnessed, up close, first-hand hidings meted out by chronically shy and gentle souls, fellas too shy to ask a girl to dance, their demons let loose by spirits and, who knows, the movements of the moon? At first, she was shocked and repelled by the brutality and the *routine* nature of it all. Later, well, she became *inured*, curious as to where the impulse was coming from.

Nobody had died in Drumahair over the past few days, she was relieved to see, jigging her leg up and down and exhaling smoke through full-ish sardonic lips.

When she was fifteen, she read a feature in one of the Sunday papers about a girl called Maeve who'd died of an overdose somewhere in Leitrim and she seven months pregnant. Nobody knew of her secret at the time. And nobody knew who the father was. The whole affair was a source of shame to the town, well, to the priest, the gardaí, the doctor, and the respectable people of the parish, who blatantly covered up the facts. Who were they all protecting? And why? And why couldn't Maeve confide in her friends? That's when Joanne decided in her head to become a journalist.

'Hey, Joanne, go easy, will ya?'

It was Welly again, beside her at the 'news desk', back from his bollocking for being late. He was wearing the same knitted jumper, with the purply-green colours of a pistachio nut, he'd worn every day for as long as she'd known him. The whole office, in fairness, was rocking on its rickety floor with all the jigging she was doing.

'I can't fecking concentrate here.'

'Make the coffee, so.'

He got up obediently, the chair screeching on the bare boards.

'C'mere, do you have any idea why the swans in Muckno are dying? Do you care, Joanne? Because I don't. I *hate* swans. Carson, the narky bollox, wants me to go down there. Thinks it might be diesel.'

She laughed. A lively, impatient woman, by any standards, Joanne had a throaty laugh and a torrent of formidable hair. She blew a stray curl from her face as Welly, an amiable Donegal man, wittered on.

One name suddenly caught her attention. *Connolly, Dermot (Dove). Of Tullyanna.* Ah yes, Tullyanna. *The Hillock of the Boggy Pool.* She was more than familiar with that parish, and not just because of her convent education in town and a few formative trips to Shadows. Joanne had spent some quality time there in 1999, investigating the story of Sandra Mohan on what was the fifth anniversary of her disappearance. A sudden coughing fit, caused by holding her breath too long, brought her to her feet. A brief wave of nausea rose and fell in her gut. She gagged.

'You alright?'

'I'm grand. You just need to wash that jumper.'

'Heresy, Joanne. You don't wash wool.'

He handed her the cup of coffee.

'Thanks.'

She drained half the cup to liven herself up for her first big job of the day. An interview with Rita, the local country music queen. She was actually looking forward to it.

'Jesus, Welly, did you wash your socks in this?'

'There's gratitude.'

O'Boyle wasn't the worst. The floor listed towards the window that looked over the Diamond. A forty-tonne lorry passed, rattling not just the window but the very walls. For three months, on and off, she'd stayed in a B&B in Tullyanna while researching the feature she'd written for *Howarya!* It was entitled, 'Small Town, Big Secret.'

Joanne replayed that seminal experience in her head. Although very content with being a rookie at the *Chronicle*, she had taken it upon herself, with Carson's blessing, to discover once and for all what had happened to Sandra. For Joanne, it was a big deal. She had known Sandra personally, not well, but had known her all the same. She would have been doing her Leaving Cert when Sandra, a precocious, cheeky child, was going into first year. They would have been in the choir together when the president visited town. Joanne, a prefect, had a distinct memory of scolding Sandra for giggling her way uncontrollably through an otherwise earnest rendition of 'Spancil Hill'. There was always *something* about her. Or maybe that was just Joanne projecting in hindsight.

And so, on behalf of the people of Tullyanna, although not everyone appreciated her good intentions, she submitted, unsolicited, her story outline to *Howarya!*, determined to place Sandra front and centre of the case. Not as a 'missing girl', as the papers had it at the time, or as a lost child of the recession, but as a person in her own right. To her amazement, the maverick magazine with the social conscience, the bible, the style guide for rural youth with uppity notions – people like herself – accepted her proposal and, after many months and multiple drafts, ran with the piece.

Joanne, in her idle moments – and there weren't many of them on a short-staffed regional newspaper – would have preferred to be a novelist, relatively anonymous but treasured by her discerning readers, she mused, taking the piss out of herself, exquisitely charting the subtle class and gender vagaries of the day from a quadruple-glazed seaside home. She would have preferred to be Edna O'Brien. But she didn't have the confidence – the gall? – or the patience to write novels. What she did have, as her mother used to say, was *mettle*. And, as a regular in the courthouses of Monaghan, Cavan and Dundalk, she had rosy cheeks and a *métier* in the reporting of true crime.

When she first heard about Sandra going missing, Joanne was still in college in Dublin. DCU. Doing her master's in journalism. Perhaps it didn't have the impact on her then that it had later. But it – the disappearance, the perfunctory-at-best investigation that followed, the lack of curiosity on the part of the townspeople as time went on – nagged away at her. She found herself constantly thinking about Sandra, keeping an eye out for her in pubs and clubs in Dublin, recalling every encounter she'd ever had with her. The time she had to 'mind' Sandra's class when Miss McCabe was out sick and Sandra, off the top of her head, reeled off all fifty states of America in alphabetical order. Joanne spent a lot of time with the first years that week. Sandra stood out for a number of reasons. She seemed – all too regularly – to *forget* her lunch. One day, Joanne discreetly offered her one of her sandwiches. And Sandra took it. And, afterwards, in the corridors, she wouldn't look Joanne in the eye. It was always at the back of her mind, after she got a job, to write something about the mystery. *Do* something about it. About Sandra. She felt *obliged* to resurrect the story. Two things. She got emotionally involved. And she might have got it wrong.

Aged 30. Died abruptly at his home. That was a new one, *abruptly*, even to a seasoned obit-expert like herself. She looked up from the paper.

'Died *abruptly*. What do you think that means?'

Welly stuck his tongue out and let his head loll to one side. Joanne nodded grimly. She took a last sip of coffee and flicked her cigarette into the dregs.

'Classy bird,' said Welly.

She could be an awful cliché sometimes. Such a hack. She knew that better than anyone.

Playing killer

Charlie O'Dowd's hair was dyed black and arranged in a sort of quiff. That's all you need to know about Charlie.

'I heard you were back.'

'I am.'

'Where were you? England or America or one of them places?'

'Aye, one of them places.'

Any amount of them places, in fact. You name it, Philip had been there and he had done it, the whole lot – steel-fixing, oil-rigs, tunnelling through the Earth's crust with a crew from Donegal – and he'd the bruises and tattoos to prove it. Trawlers, too. A lighthouse in Newfoundland where he learned to be alone; and to sing without fear at the top of his voice. He was a big man, unafraid of hard work and hard knocks. And none of it was any of Charlie's business. In fact, the less anyone knew, the better.

On the footpath outside his mother's house, he paused, a fidgety O'Dowd in a lumberjack shirt tucked into his turned-up jeans, watching him closely. Philip took a deep breath, inhaling the familiar smell of pig slurry that emanated from the farm next to his house, a smell that had always washed over the town. He personally didn't attach any symbolic meaning to the smell, although who knows what effect such immeasurable amounts of methane and ammonia could have on the average human brain.

'C'mon,' said Charlie, indicating their direction of travel with a toss of his head, as if Philip was in any doubt.

It goes without saying that he shouldn't have come home. He hadn't *planned* to come home. If it wasn't for Dove, he might never have come home. *Suicide, my hole*, says he to himself. But here he was, come what may. He'd had glimmers of happiness in the previous decade or so. In Hanoi, apparently, he'd shacked up for six months with a woman whose heart he won in a karaoke bar. Sally was her name. Despite his protests, she waited on him hand and foot while he recuperated from a broken leg. He never asked her what she did for a living. She never asked him what he was running away from. *Sing, handsome man, sing!* And he sang, with bravado, leaning on his crutch, *Are you lonesome tonight?*, bare-chested, in a wavering alto-baritone-bass. It was at times like that he was able to forget about his friend Sandra Mohan.

He'd liked Sandra more than he'd ever admitted to anyone. It was when she turned up at a party in Una Doyle's wearing a dress she'd made for herself out of empty crisp bags that he was first taken with her. She must have been collecting the bags for months for the sake of a one-off gag that fell apart within minutes. It was the way she made little figures out of cotton buds. It was her boldness. It was the exaggerated way she turned her head and fluttered her eyelashes at whoever was speaking, to make them feel like they were being heard. Even if she was being semi-ironic. It was the putdowns. The speed of thought. It reminded him of the film *The Omen*, the way the devil boy Damien answered questions before they were even asked. The truth is, he was afraid of her too. Shy and tongue-tied at the time, he couldn't keep up with her. He couldn't take the gratuitous insults when she was drunk. The cruelty. Anyway, Dove got there first, for all the good it did him.

Sally was never cruel. He loved her in a way, the language barrier notwithstanding, and paid the rent. Without the verbals, it was an uncomplicated arrangement. Equality issues aside, he enjoyed being spoiled, although he was all-too conscious, when sober, of the great injustices of the world. The iniquities of history. The imbalance of power between the sexes. And the races. But he was rarely sober.

Occasionally, when the mood took her, she'd walk on his back. Up and down the spine, she'd walk with the balance and grace of a ballet dancer, expecting nothing in return. Never once did she say, '*It's your turn to walk on my back now.*' To the best of his knowledge, an Irish woman would rarely walk on your back unsolicited, or indeed solicited, without lengthy negotiations in advance and a quid pro quo of some sort built into the arrangement, not that he'd ever actually asked anybody to do such a thing, not knowing that it was even a thing, not being aware of the disarming pleasure to be had from that particular ministration until he met Sally in gung-ho Hanoi at the turn of the century. Anyway, with the old demons getting restless and the leg on the mend, he upped sticks and left – the very idea of *happiness* appalling to him – not without huge regret to add to the deep pool of regret stagnating in his guts.

The head still; the jaw, unshaven, firm; the blue eyes fixed straight ahead; he missed nothing to his left or right. It was as if he'd never been away. On his left, he passed the low-slung warehouse with the curving corrugated iron roof the colour of blue, behind which the river ran, and the rats too, where he and Dove had smoked Uncle Francie's hash and once found the body of a dead man. The building was now a grain store, the huge sliding door of which they'd used as goals in soccer matches that seemed to last all summer long. At twenty feet by twenty, even someone as uncoordinated as Dove never failed to score.

On his right stood the same few houses – O'Neills', Raffertys', McCabes' – albeit with extensions now, and porches too. The gardens were untended, for fear of being accused of showing off, Philip supposed, showing off being a crime in those parts worse than murder – well, the murder of a teenage girl anyway. And they wouldn't be tended until the next religious procession passed through the town, which, at a guess, wouldn't come around 'til March. Lace curtains were still the veil of choice through which the neighbours watched Philip being escorted to his fate by Charlie O'Dowd.

Sally had had his son, or so he was told by O'Donnell from the Inishowen Peninsula. He was a well-known nuisance who, surprise surprise, turned up in Perth some months later, where men not cut out for hairdressing in a humdrum town flocked for work. Although O'Donnell was a liar, he had a great head for heights and as such was tolerated by the other steel-fixers, not all of them known for their tolerance. *I swear to God*, he says, *and hope to die, he's the spit of you, the absolute spit.* A highly unlikely scenario, decided the ever-impassive

Philip. His relationship with Sally had been perversely chaste and he was far from divine. He had stared at the weaselly Donegal man as they'd squared off on a six-inch metal beam high in the southern sky, and was briefly tempted to push him to his death. Or to jump himself. At the pivotal moment, his legs turned to jelly, the old vertigo returned – in the nick of time, says you – and he decided to move on, if you could believe everything you were told. Mind you, a bolthole in South-East Asia or in Western Australia, or in *one of them places*, might come in handy one of these days. Very handy indeed.

'Have you got a smoke?'

Some things never change. Philip offered Charlie a Rothmans and Charlie took it, completing his image – rockabilly mark II, circa 1983 – as if nothing had happened in music or fashion or in Charlie's life since Shakin' Stevens had arrived on the scene, after many a false start, to enjoy a remarkable career in the charts. Charlie, who would have been all of nine years old when that particular hip-swivelling role model was in his pomp, was nervous, not up to the task of divining Philip's intentions. They walked on autopilot – Charlie unnerved by Philip's silence – the short distance towards JJ's, election posters, many of them featuring an all too familiar face, festooning the windows and telegraph poles of the town.

As they walked towards the town centre, the bells of both churches, Catholic and Protestant, rang out, comparing notes in a spirit of ecumenism, *gong gong gong gong gong gong*, six gongs in total, only slightly out of sync now that the Troubles were over and the Peace Process was in full swing. The sky blue-silvered. Rain threatened. Philip's T-shirt billowed in a cooling breeze. Men of a similar age as Philip and Charlie, and men slightly older than them, silently left their homes, singly or in pairs, and were drawn, inexorably drawn, to the same rendezvous point, namely JJ's bar on the Main Street. Some were married, some weren't. Some were balding, some grey. Some were more resolute than others in the face of Dove Connolly's passing and Philip Sharkey's unlikely return from afar.

'Where are you going, hi?'

Philip gave Charlie a spare-me look and took an unscheduled left into the shopping centre. There he stood in front of Dove's giant mural for the first time, ignoring the whining beside him.

'We're going to be late, boy.'

He wasn't expecting it to be quite so impressive in scale, or so humorous. They say you could recreate a mythic Dublin from the pages of *Ulysses* and a mystical Belfast from the lyrics of 'Astral Weeks'. Well, in that vein, between the viaducts of *his* dreams, Dove had managed to recreate for the ages an alternate, surreal version of Tullyanna.

'Bit of a looney, ha?' says O'Dowd.

'Yeah.'

It's like Dove was talking directly to him. There were references to stuff nobody else would get. The waving firefighters on the fire engine were straight out of *Blue Velvet*. A hot-air balloon soared away from the town hosting, among others, their mutual friend Paddy Mathews and, Philip burst out laughing, a local historical figure by the name of Hugh Begley who was transported to Australia on the good ship *Hyderabad* in 1849 for stealing a hen. The implication was that these were the lucky ones who managed to escape the town. (Mind you, Paddy Mathews only got as far as Navan, where he taught geography at the Mercy.)

'What's so funny?'

Philip pointed at the representation of Fergal's Gym. In it, a character very like the skinny O'Dowd beside him was lampooned as a barbell, the outsized quiff and brothel creepers the weights, being held aloft by Fergal Coleman himself. And, if his eyes didn't deceive him, Philip could just about discern . . . was that a swastika in the figuration of the weights machines? Knowing Dove, it probably was.

In JJ's, now run by Latvians, or maybe Lithuanians, they assembled around the pool table, the lads, their eyes cast down, in the back room, a room that hadn't changed one bit in about forty years, probably the only room in the whole of Tullyanna that hadn't been entirely transformed in that frenzy of garish reinvention and cheap credit known as The Boom. It was still a shrine to lost causes. There were eight of them in all, well, seven now that Dove was dead, although he was there in spirit, a ghost shaped by their collective exhalations, at peace or in agony above the table. It was hard to tell what was what with the undead. A pair of young fellas scarpered sharpish, two solids and one stripe still un-sunk, never mind the black, in no doubt whatsoever that their time at the table was well and truly up.

Fergal Coleman, one of the older men present, in his mid to late thirties, chalked the cue squeakily, sending shivers up Philip's spine. Fergal, looking at Philip amusedly, stretched his neck to the left and to the right and loosened his shoulders as Charlie racked the balls. He was a candidate in the upcoming general election, a fact that Philip was struggling to process, naturally remembering him in a very different guise. His teeth were straight and a shade or two whiter now. The necktie was an anomaly. Fergal did a full circumference of the table, the lads standing back, watching Philip watching the performance. Although he had developed a paunch, the paunch became him, and he moved smoothly, the feet barely leaving the ground. Then, and only then, spake Fergal.

'We'll say nothing,' he says, breaking violently, the cue ball flying off the table and heading straight for Philip's head. Philip caught the ball in his hand and calmly placed it on the heavily patched baize. 'We'll have a nice game of killer,' Fergal the Candidate continued, lifting his pint of Kaliber non-alcoholic lager. 'We'll drink to the Dove. We'll go to the wake. And then we'll see.'

'To the Dove.' He lowered half a pint and wiped his mouth with the back of his sleeve.

'To the Dove!' came the refrain in various tones, ranging from quiet conviction (Philip himself) to sneering insincerity (Charlie O'Dowd). They all lowered different amounts and all, with the exception of Philip, wiped their mouths with the back of their sleeves. He, as usual, his wits about him, was alive to the vagaries of body language and the tendency of like-minded individuals to mirror each other's movements, especially when they were in a jam and in need of mutual reassurance. And even though his mouth could have done with a good wipe, he restrained himself, allowing the far-too-fizzy beer to dribble down his chin. He wasn't like the rest of them. And never would be.

His inaction was noted by the others. It wasn't the specific failure to wipe his mouth that bothered them. They studied him carefully but couldn't quite put their fingers on it. It was more of a general feeling that something was amiss. They were all vaguely aware of some typical Sharkey sin of omission, some tribute unpaid, some conformity unobserved.

'No hard feelings.' Fergal Coleman offered Philip his hand.

Philip kept his hands to himself. Coleman nodded. The others nodded. Philip braced himself. Coleman glanced over at Macker, who glanced at O'Dowd, who went immediately to the jukebox and put on the Prince song 'When Doves Cry'.

Coleman handed his jacket to Lonergan. For about thirty seconds he danced, all the while looking at Philip. Forward and back, he moved, and side to side, all the limbs in fluid motion, hinging and squatting and tossing his head like a horse, everything bar a backflip. He was energetic and remarkably agile for a candidate in the upcoming general election. When he was finished gyrating, he put his jacket back on.

They took turns, the lads, trying to pot a ball, Tullyanna's finest, the names, for the record, in alphabetical order, Fergal Coleman, Tommy Courtney, Lorcan Lonergan, Macker, Charlie O'Dowd, Philip Sharkey, and Stephen 'Omar' Sheriff, the banter at a minimum. If you potted a ball, you stayed on the table. If you missed, you were eliminated from the game. Some were pool wizards (Charlie and Macker), their finesse unimpaired by the tension in the room. Others were rattled and barely able to hold the cue (poor Tommy C). All of them, the skilled and unskilled, the nervy and the cool, remembered well the last time they were gathered in JJ's and what had transpired later on that night.

Philip, as it happens, won the game, potting each ball emphatically, the echo resounding like gunshot. There was general surprise and a few grudging grunts of admiration. They looked at each other. No doubt about it, he *had* changed. His stance, his cueing action, his dead eye had all greatly improved. Coleman patted Philip on his back.

'Good man!'

Fog on the window

Detective Sergeant Kevin Healy sucked on a fruit pastille as he sat in his car outside the late Dove Connolly's house, the tears rolling down his cheeks. The fog on the car windows on this damp August evening blurred his view of the comings and goings – the story of his life, says you – and there was nothing on the radio to comfort his broken heart now that his favourite presenter, Dessie Desmond, had been dumped in favour of playlist conservatism. Kevin was distraught. And tired. So very, very tired.

Healy wasn't much of a sleeper at the best of times. He didn't blame his pancreatitis, the pain, although currently acute, a familiar one. Ever since he was shot, at close range in the abdomen, it was a pain that came and went. The shooter, a man in a balaclava who objected to Kevin blocking the door of the Blackhill post office with his car while he was trying to escape with a bag of money, came and went too, a key-holder to his subconscious.

Nor did he blame Sheila's snoring. That had been a source of disharmony between them for some years now, not helped by his little joke that it was like sleeping with a Massey-Ferguson 125. *A smallish tractor,* he'd pointed out, in an attempt at conciliation. *A collector's item.* His son, Shane, had a good laugh at that one. A Massey 125. Good old Shane! Sheila lay beside him at night wearing a chin strap that didn't really help with the snoring or the harmony in the home. It didn't become her, reminding Kevin of the masked raider who shot him in Blackhill.

It had all been so *casual.* As Kevin tried to extricate his gun from his holster, the first robber slid over the bonnet on his backside and ran to a waiting souped-up Nissan Sunny. The second robber to exit the post office – one of only a handful of buildings (pub, shop, three or four private dwellings and a tiny primary school) in the weirdly deserted village that morning – stopped at the car door and watched Kevin fumbling for his gun. Their eyes met. The man had every opportunity to run but didn't. He *chose* not to run. Almost certainly smiling behind the balaclava, he rather slowly raised his gun and pointed it through the open window. '*Not your lucky day*,' says he. After calmly shooting Kevin, as if that wasn't bad enough, the man stood there for a while, looking into the car, despite, you would think, the urgent need to get away, to observe the consequences of his action. To watch Kevin bleed.

Wide awake, night after night, year after year, staring at the ceiling, his wife Sheila's vocal emissions unladylike and unceasing, Kevin occasionally fantasized about putting her out of her misery, putting a pillow over her face, say, or pushing her down the stairs. Or just dropping the television on her head. That would be hard to explain. *Eh, the telly fell on her, officer, three times in all, as I was trying to move it to a better vantage point, do you see, to get a better look at the* Late Night Poker *and the* Bonanza *repeats*. Or, as night wore on, and the snoring got louder, and his imagination became more feverish, he would explore the possibilities of inducing in her a bout of pneumonia that, with her notoriously weak lungs, she mighn't survive. Or hypnotizing her into walking towards a lake.

Would he sleep better or worse if she was dead? That was a conundrum he mulled over now and again, but never seriously. What was he truly capable of, if push came to shove? If a mild-mannered man like himself could even briefly and, let's be clear, *frivolously* contemplate the murder of a beloved wife, a woman he not only loved *and* wanted but *needed* more than air, what was any man capable of? He often looked at her, fondly, in her ludicrous mask, the murderous inklings quickly subsiding, He didn't feel guilty (or bad) for having such thoughts. After all, he'd make a full confession in the morning when she'd ask him drily, '*How did you kill me last night?*' And no harm imagining the myriad ways to kill somebody, if it might help to solve a puzzling case or, God forbid, if he ever got around to writing a murder mystery himself. Besides, he had far more troubling thoughts that were not as easy to share, even with soulmates like Sheila.

Years ago, when they were first married, they'd lie awake together, his arm around her, and her full of the questions. She wanted to know everything about his work, every detail, no matter how mundane. That was when he was at his happiest, he supposed, his love for her and his love for police work indistinguishable, the conversation flowing seamlessly between them, incorporating crime – grotesque and petty – and police procedures and everyday trivia, interrupted by beans and toast with Tabasco sauce and the odd bout of love-making, nothing wild or fanciful. But all that changed after Sandra Mohan went missing. Everything changed, most notably his luck.

Naturally, Ciara's going away was another sleep-inhibiting issue preying on his mind. His daughter was probably somewhere over Kazakhstan by now, if his calculations were correct. But the truth is there was always something niggling away at Kevin, always something just out of reach, some idea or wispy thought that could never be articulated, which, he felt certain, if ever grasped, would explain everything he needed to know. He knew rightly how Tantalus himself must have felt – if only he could get his hands on the juicy grapes. Mind you, Tantalus was a woefully misguided character who cooked his own son to please the gods – making a dog's dinner out of a god's dinner. He made a mental note to run one that one by the Doc. His old friend the Doc would love that one. But what was *he* being punished for? His own son, Shane, remained *uncooked*. Just how had he offended the gods? The answer was just there, within reach, if only he could sleep on it.

He was after saying goodbye to Ciara at the airport that very morning. They were not the only father–daughter combo at the gate to leave volumes unsaid and voids unfillable. Australia! He couldn't believe his little girl was gone. After all the humming and hawing about what to do with baby Paul, and all the agency work she'd managed to secure in the previous months, he was sure she'd stay, defying the dire economic conditions of the day and the exhortations of her more adventurous friends. One by one, they took the plunge, and once Ciara had made up her mind, no amount of prayer (on his part) or emotional blackmail (his wife, Sheila) was going to persuade her otherwise. She was always a very stubborn girl. Sheila couldn't face the airport, or, Kevin feared morosely, the rest of her life without Ciara. Somewhat in denial, she had spent the morning at the hairdresser's getting a colouring treatment that Kevin, decorated detective that he was, failed to notice when he got home. He needed to pay more attention. He knew that.

There was still Shane in the house, a good lad, tall and thin, probably on his fourth bowl of Frosties now before bedtime, a divil for the Frosties, Shane, studious enough in his own way, about to enter his final year of school, and sporty too, thank God, a reliable if not over-physical half-back on the Tullyanna minors; and there was the baby too, of course, Ciara's baby, Paul. Naturally, she'd wanted to bring him with her but, Jaze, how would that work? Sheila, in fairness, put the foot down, putting her own woes to one side so as her daughter could have some sort of a life. It was only for six months.

Before parting, Kevin had handed Ciara a thousand Australian dollars in cash that he couldn't afford and a walnut, a charm he'd carried about in his coat pocket and rolled between his fingers when he was thinking, which is what he spent most of his time doing. He'd been rolling it for a good while now, ever since it was forced upon him by an old man in a snowstorm on the Camino de Santiago, a charm to which he had become attached and even, in some way, although not a superstitious man, *dependent*. It was a charm he missed now as he left the car, the Sacred Heart on the dashboard, the rosary beads dangling on the rear-view mirror, fat raindrops falling, the sky a bloodclot blue, to pay his respects at Dove Connolly's wake.

A better place

Although Dove had, by all accounts, shot himself in the face with his father's legally held shotgun, the family insisted on leaving the coffin open. Why, people wondered? Despite the best efforts of Duffy, the undertaker, Dove was a grisly sight. Duffy himself was furious, a state he couldn't conceal as he rushed around performing the niceties. It was a thankless job that wouldn't reflect well on his morbid enterprise, especially now that he no longer had the monopoly in the town. They'd be questioning his expertise, and he a third-generation mortician. Why, oh why? That was the first question they asked on entering the bedroom where Dove's body was laid out instead of the more obvious question, *why the fuck did he shoot himself? Or who the fuck shot him?*

'Why would a grieving mother allow such a thing in her own home?' Philip overheard a woman whispering to her companion.

'A warning to others who might be . . . like-minded, Carol.'

'God knows, there's no shortage of them out and about.'

The two women blessed themselves and had a good gawk around the room.

Others would see the physical damage itself, the theory went, and the emotional effect it would have would make them think twice. That would be a generous interpretation, Philip thought, knowing the Connolly family, as he forced himself to look at Dove, trying to picture the winsome face his friend had sported before the likes of guilt and hard drugs ravaged his mind. He stared for a good long time, failing to bless himself or touch the hand of the corpse or even shed a tear, according to eye-witnesses well-versed in funereal protocol. It was some mess, alright.

Philip had always liked Dove, loved Dove, so-called because of his dark hair and swarthy Spanish Armada complexion. *Dubh* was the Irish word for black, so everyone naturally enough called him Dove for the craic and the name stuck. Looking around the room, the nosier mourners could see for themselves that he'd been a talented artist. Although he sold himself short, it has to be said, by sketching for the most part in the genre of lurid fantasy, inspired by Celtic mythology, and he enamoured with the apparently big-breasted goddesses of yore.

Balubas, he called them, Philip remembered. Breasts, in Dove's scatological lexicon, were known as balubas, a name borrowed from a Congolese tribe best known, in these parts at least, for decimating a platoon of Irish soldiers during a UN operation in 1960, a reference that would have been lost on Dove himself and indeed most of his generation for whom 'balubas' was just a catch-all word, the etymology irrelevant. It could also mean 'mad' or 'extremely drunk and possibly rowdy', as in, *Oliver Reed was balubas in the pub last night.* Indeed, it was often used to describe the state of Dove himself after a typical night out from about the age of fifteen onwards. Dove was regularly balubas before Sandra disappeared, never mind afterwards. Not only an illustrator, Dove had also been a useful guitarist with an interest in Jethro Tull and Horslips and other seventies folk-rock outfits whose flute-heavy recordings he inherited from his brother, Gerry Junior, now a successful accountant in Toronto. The mutual ambition they'd had, Philip and Dove, to form a band and play in Dublin's Baggot Inn – a surprisingly modest ambition for two hotheads, but a pledge nonetheless sealed in pinpricks of adolescent blood – was never going to be realized.

Philip had known Dove's parents well, Gerry and Dee, proud people, in hardware, now bent beyond hope.

'Sorry for your trouble.'

Townsfolk queued to comfort them in a corner of the kitchen with that old reliable platitude. The kitchen, a poky afterthought in an otherwise spacious house, was claustrophobic.

'Sorry for your trouble, Gerry. Deirdre.'

Someone, some creative genius, attempting originality, deviated from the formula, the time-honoured, foolproof mantra, and said to the bereaved couple, within Philip's earshot, 'Well, at least he's at peace now.' If looks could kill. What possible peace had Dove achieved and him in Limbo at best, having left Gerry and Dee bereft and the whole town in shock, and Philip a man possessed, as well as bereft and in shock, although you wouldn't know it to look at him?

Immediately realizing his own stupidity, the man, who Philip learned was a school-teacher above in the convent, who should have known better, added by way of mitigation, 'He's in a better place.'

While it may well have been true that Hell was a better place than Tullyanna, it was not the right thing to say to Gerry at that moment. Dove's father made a barking noise like a seal, which stopped dead the soft chatter on the ground floor. Mortified by his own stupid banalities, the teacher ran out of steam and hurried away from the house, hopefully having learned a valuable lesson or two.

They looked as if they were trapped, Dove's parents, backed into a corner by the community's good intentions. At first, Dee didn't recognize Philip, who in his youth must have spent as much time in her house as he did in his own, a chatty, carefree lad, cheeky, with a thirst for tea, and well able to hold his own in mixed company.

'Sorry for your trouble. Sorry about Dermot.'

It must have been his voice. Her crumpled, papery hand gripped his and a light momentarily flared in her eyes. The crowd melted away and the years rolled back and a trace of a smile appeared on her face.

'Philip. It's yourself!'

Now that Philip was here, surely Dermot (she never acknowledged the name Dove) would bound down the stairs, two at a time, humming the theme tune to *Hawaii 5-0*, and kiss her on the cheek, and this nightmare would be over? The last time Philip stood in her kitchen was *that* night, you know, in the summer of '94, when Dermot's girlfriend disappeared. Disappeared off the face of the Earth. Dee had heard them coming in. She'd never really liked her. Sandra. God forgive her, but it was the truth. She remembered them throwing on a burger and changing their clothes and leaving the house again. She failed to pass on those little details to the gardaí when questioned a few days later.

Gerry accepted Philip's outstretched hand as if it was a wet rag. According to one bystander, and him almost choking on a second slice of the exceptionally dry and bland sponge cake in circulation at the wake, a storm crossed Gerry's face. It changed colour dramatically from its default ruddy to a violent puce, taking in some of the more unlikely blues and purples along the way. It was only thanks to a deep-seated civility, bred into him by generations of shopkeepers, and perhaps a late-developing devotion to Our Lady of Fatima, that prevented him from clocking Philip with the nearest heavy object. Gerry was always regarded as a straight man, in business and in morals, but like many a straight man before him, he was now in danger of straying from the righteous path. His dealings with God and man, hitherto square, were all of a sudden under increased scrutiny by a panel of expert people-watchers comprised of nearly everybody in the town, and them holding their breath while they eagerly awaited a long-overdue, in their opinion, fall from grace. There were few spectacles as satisfying as the sight of a self-righteous prig falling off his high horse.

The Connollys were proud people and had nothing to hide. They had done everything they could, and more, to help their son over the years, what with the counselling, and the rehab, and the jobs. Nobody could argue otherwise. Money, they showered on him. They had welcomed him home, with open arms, no bones, after his wife Claire and the children left him, and had installed him in his old room, with the vast record collection and the colouring pencils. They had done everything possible for the lad except, of course, for keeping the shotgun under lock and key. It wasn't as if Gerry asked his son to shoot himself in the head. No, Gerry felt strongly, it was the right thing to do, to leave the coffin open. It was right to shock people, to let them share the Connolly family horror, the horror of this world, the world they had all conspired to corrupt, in contempt of God and his mercy and his love.

'Don't mind Daddy.' Gerry Junior interrupted Philip's thoughts in his pseudo-Canadian accent and his intact face and his incongruously well-cut suit. 'He's not himself,' he said as he tried to stall his late brother's children, the twins, from going up the stairs to view their father's corpse. Claire, Dove's wife, was nowhere to be found, under sedation elsewhere, consumed by guilt – her guilt at how relieved she was that Dove was dead.

'I have something forya,' Gerry Junior said, 'remind me to give it to ya, eh, after I deal with these monkeys.'

Philip was trying to avoid the cop, Healy, a heavy, slow-moving unit in an anorak, with a combover, stuffing his face with cake and taking it all in. Philip slipped out the back for a fag, where he was identified, correctly, by some of the more astute members of the party as one of the chief mourners.

'Well, Philip. It's great to see ya. Welcome home.'

'Ah Paddy.'

'Terrible news.'

It was floppy-haired Paddy Mathews, camper, if anything, and certainly more at ease with himself than when he last saw him.

'I hadn't seen him for about a year. To my shame. He wasn't in a good place, Philip.'

Paddy told him that Dove wouldn't even go for a pint. Rather, they had stayed in Dove's bedroom, chatting. Dove was pacing the room in a clockwise fashion, touching the same objects on each circuit.

'It was weird. The television. The chair. The picture of the Last Supper, you know the one, it's very good, with him in the middle and all his musical heroes, Frank Black, Gram Parsons, I didn't know the rest of them.'

'No Depeche Mode then.'

'Very funny.'

Philip didn't know the painting at all. It certainly wasn't on Dove's bedroom wall now. He wondered who was Judas.

Paddy went on to say that Dove had been spouting conspiracy theories, too, the usual ones, about 9/11 and Diana's death and even the moon landings.

'What moon landings?' says Philip, deadpan, a flash of his old fun-loving self to the fore in the comforting presence of a childhood friend.

'What? Ah, stop your messing.'

'There isn't even a moon,' he added, before the current reality caught up with him again. 'Poor Dove.'

'Yeah. He was talking gibberish. He thought MI5 were after him, and MI6, and the soldiers, all blaming him somehow for Princess Diana's death. It was crazy. Crazy stuff altogether.'

They both looked at the ground for solace. Nothing there to help the situation, not even a flagstone inscribed with a reassuring platitude.

'It was really sad. And then he started looking at me funny. And he clammed up. Like I was *spying* on him or something. I didn't know what to do. And that was the last time I saw him.'

Hovering on the edge of hushed conversations within, Philip had picked up bits and pieces about Dove's life, not all of it, as his chat with Paddy would suggest, irredeemable. He'd held down jobs, the most notable and lasting of which, not being cut out for hardware, was in the four-star Drumlish Castle hotel, where he was a waiter and where he met Claire, an efficient receptionist but no great judge of men. Still a suspect in the mysterious affair of Sandra Mohan, Dove continued to drink heavily throughout their courtship and marriage. With such a thirst, along with the various medications prescribed to him and on top of his partiality to hash, it was no surprise that he slipped from time to time into the black swamp, a feature of the town all too familiar to many of its residents. It was during those staycations, some would say, that he produced his best paintings, many of which he sold on Sunday morning forays to Dublin's Merrion Square, where he was remembered fondly by his fellow artists for his ready smile and the inexhaustible supply of fudge he stole from the hotel kitchen. Unschooled in fine art – unless you included the efforts of their old art teacher, Miss King, or Daphne as they called her based on a close resemblance to a character in *Scooby Doo* – Dove had his own distinctive style, influenced by comic books, Pop Art and the hyper-real paintings of Robert Ballagh.

Philip was surprised and gratified to hear that Dove played, too, on and off, in a band that covered punk and New Wave classics, genres he had pooh-poohed in the past, and that the surfacing of his old charm was not unheard of, even after he started dabbling in heroin.

As Paddy drifted off, Philip took out his phone and listened back to a message he'd received from the Dove not three weeks ago. If only he'd answered the call at the time – the first communication in any medium he'd had from his closest friend since he left the country all those years ago, since he, let's call a spade a spade, abandoned Dove to what was always a dangerous, solo crusade. But he wasn't in the habit of answering his phone to unknown Irish numbers.

'*It's Dove.* (Long silence, very long silence.) *I found her.* (Heavy breathing, sobbing.) *I found Sandra. I can't talk now . . . on the phone. You know yourself.* (Whispers.) *They're after me.* (A flicker of the old Dove.) *You're still a bollox but you have to come home.* (And then, mimicking Philip's mother, winding him up by slipping in the irritating pet name she called him.) *Come on home, Pippy love, I found her.*'

Defender of the snails

Philip, the eyes closed, leaned back against the pebble-dash wall, the cool, moist air a relief as an aggressive rosary reared up inside in the kitchen. He'd listened back to the same message many times. Granted he knew next to nothing about Dove's recent life. Yeah, the mental health clearly wasn't the best. The heroin probably didn't help with the perspective. But would he have taken his own life if he'd indeed 'found' Sandra, whatever that meant, if he had such a momentous discovery to share? Would he have playfully mimicked Philip's mother with a shotgun in his hand?

'It was m-m-my fault.'

Tommy Courtney materialized, stuttering, from the darkness, his thin, drawn face guarded by a pair of outsized ears, the lobes stretched like King Tut's to accommodate some spectacular outsized ear jewellery. He stood in front of Philip, swaying slightly.

'I sold him the smack.'

Tommy was a shadow of his former self, his freckles no longer cute, his mop of orangey-red hair now lifeless, a stranger to shampoo, his pallor not helped, if rumours were true, by him dining exclusively on a diet of frozen meat discarded as out-of-date in the lane behind the new Lidl.

Within, the prayer continued, faster now, having already gone up a gear, *Hail Mary, full of grace*, vroom, *the Lord is with thee*, the mourners in unison, on fire now, building up a nice head of steam, the prayerful heads buried in cushions, the faithful lost in the repetition, in the rhythm, the mumbling call-and-response routine

38

mercifully numbing their grief. It was an incantation that had every chance of raising the dead.

'He knows where she is.'

'What's that, Tom?'

'The m-m-m-Mohan girl, he knows what happened.'

'Who knows, Tommy?'

Detective Sergeant Healy was looking out the window, his docile, moustachioed face concealing a restless brain, as Philip well knew, having been football-coached by him long ago, on the minor team, and been subject to his pioneering ways. Sometimes they trained while blindfolded. Sometimes they watched nature films, mainly featuring shoals of fish. Once, in advance of an important match against Clontibret, a new system was imposed upon them based on the movement of the planets and orbiting moons, Philip being one of the planets, not an easy concept to absorb on a Sunday morning after a night out on the piss. These radical developments in an otherwise primitive sport were frowned upon by the politburo that ran the club along traditional, no-nonsense, *take-the-ball and-the-man* lines.

Philip was, of course, subject to Healy's brainy interrogation methods after Sandra went missing too. His was a softly-softly, somewhat patient line of questioning that, Philip recalled, involved a spin in the car, and a bag of chips, and, somewhat controversially, a blindfold. Ah yes, the old reliable, a Healy motif, you could say, disorientating to be sure and of questionable legality, but no sweat to Philip, who was always comfortable in the dark. Despite what people thought, Philip did not know exactly what happened to Sandra Mohan, then or now. He did not know whether she was alive or dead but, by Jaysus, he had his suspicions, and he was determined to find out.

Tommy clearly wanted to enlighten Philip further, but before he could unburden himself fully, he was startled, not by Healy's curious face in the window, but by the arrival in the back garden of Fergal Coleman, Lorcan Lonergan and Charlie O'Dowd. Tommy fumbled for the naggin of generic vodka in his pocket, having rightly assumed it would be a dry wake, no flies on Tommy, as the men approached, the rosary now in extra time, driven sadistically by Gerry Senior.

St Paul, pray for us, St Dymphna, pray for us, St Martin de Porres, pray for us, many of the congregation getting restless now, even the holy Joes, *St Maginus, pray for us,* whoever the fuck he was, *St Serenus the gardener, pray for us,* as opposed to who, St Serenus the mechanic? The invocations were interminable, surely Gerry was making them up now at this stage, to make them all pay, and pay, and pay, *Great Uncle Bulgarius, pray for us, Sacha Distel* . . .

Tommy skulked away backwards, into the murk, muttering to himself some feverish prayer of his own. He wasn't the only one who slipped away at Coleman's appearance.

'Have you got a smoke, Sharkey?'

'Sure, Charlie.'

Coleman declined the offer of a cigarette.

'They're bad for you.'

That was good coming from Coleman, who winked, lest the irony was lost. Although only five foot eight and avocado-shaped, you always felt he was looking down at you. It might have been the hooded eyes, roving, alert, blue eyes deep-set in a large fleshy head. It might have been an optical illusion.

'We're all very sorry about Dove. Nice guy and all that. May the devil make a ladder of his backbone.'

Philip nodded, not at all sure what that meant, and whether it was a blessing or a curse.

'Over-fond of the sauce. And the whatnot, ha? But a nice guy. Wasn't he, Charlie?'

'The best,' says Charlie, sucking on the fag for all he was worth, as if he was hoping to find something in it he'd never found before, some sustenance, spiritual or otherwise.

'Powerful turnout all the same. It's a good town. We look after our own.'

They all nodded and looked down at the ground. Charlie squashed a snail underfoot. Coleman gave Charlie a dirty look, an unlikely defender of the snails.

'Relative of yours?' Philip inquired of Coleman, nodding towards the flattened mollusc.

There was a brief hiatus, a stoppage in time, into which many possibilities poured, before Coleman stooped down and picked up the snail between his thumb and forefinger. With his other hand he untucked his shirt and then he rubbed the snail on his belly.

'The old dermatitis,' he said, throwing the snail into the hedge. 'Good for acne, too, did you know that? And healing *wounds*.' He rubbed his hand through his buzz-cut hair, like a disappointed father.

'How is the mother, Philip?'

'She's grand.'

'Good. She must be happy to see you.'

'Happy enough.'

'She'll miss you.'

'Not so sure about that.'

'She will. You were always a mammy's boy. Only codding.' He winked again, to underline the fact that he was, indeed, only codding.

'I'm staying, Fergal. I'm staying in Tullyanna, it being such a good town.'

Charlie had a sudden fit of the coughing.

'Sorry.'

Fergal Coleman absorbed this information. His award-winning muscles, once plumped on steroids, were now, if not exactly flabby, in a state of slow deflation, the stately and not unflattering transformation still ongoing within the confines of an incongruous suit.

This much Philip knew. He was now the owner of a gym, Fergal's Gym, and a white van with the legend *Fergal's Gym* printed on the side of it in big red letters. Fergal was also the proprietor and chief security officer of a security company called Coleman Security. Clearly a horse of a man, he also found the time to preside over Coleman's Taxi Service. A respectable businessman now, by all accounts, he was married to Teresa and a fun-loving father of four lovely girls, each of them with her own pony. His wife gave riding lessons, free to the children of the less-well-off and for a fee to the merchant classes.

Now, despite having a previous drug conviction, he was a county councillor representing the fast-growing political wing of a former paramilitary outfit. Indeed, he was standing for the general election and tipped to win a seat on an anti-austerity ticket in a fit of post-crash contempt for the established parties. Hence the suit. And the concerned expression on his face. Despite what people said about him, his was a friendly face, quick to crease in a smile. His whole body rumbled when he laughed, which was often. But he could do sincerity too, as well as any man. In fairness, he was effective in addressing the needs and wants of his constituency. Didn't he lead the picket, for example, against the closure of a local hospital, restraining in the process some of his more exuberant followers who were jostling and spitting at a septuagenarian sitting minister? A great man for the pickets, Fergal! There was a supply of blank placards in a corner of the gym, in readiness for every cause going. Didn't he even organize a convoy of trucks for the Gaza Strip? He had to twist a few arms here and there to personally wrest the merchandise from the tight-fisted burghers of the town – the boxes of Daz, and Fruit 'n Fibre, and Wagon Wheels – from men unmoved by the plight of the Palestinian people, or any cause other than the bottom line, especially now in straitened times.

All this information was freely available. Philip, stewing in his own juices in the bed, had gleaned much of it from his mother and the local paper since he came home.

Most notably, according to Fergal's cheerleaders in the local press, Coleman had single-handedly cleansed the town of anti-social elements. That was a good one. With some of his own more memorable tattoos now partially erased, he bore little resemblance to the violent gangster who once threatened to kill Philip, and Philip but callow at the time, and he convulsed with rage and confusion and vengeful thoughts. Fergal, he remembered, threatened not just to kill him but to kill him stone dead, which was presumably worse than just being killed, if he didn't leave town and never come back. They say he had a green-, white- and orange-feathered Phoenix tattooed on his penis, with all that implied. Philip didn't quite believe it. He did remember the three Celtic goddesses sexualized on his breastbone, Banba, Ériu and Fódla, and a dagger on his thigh. Of the one on his neck – the coordinates – there was barely a trace.

Now he was back. And Coleman and his coterie were intimating in no uncertain terms, right there in Connollys' back garden, that the threat had not entirely gone away. Unless Philip was sorely mistaken, they didn't want him digging up trouble, not now on the eve of a potentially historic election, not ever.

But Philip hadn't come home for the good of his health. Although not a man susceptible to signs and portents, Dove's 'suicide' was a clear summons as far as he was concerned. If he was ambivalent about the phone call, if he had fatally dithered, unsure about Dove's meaning and Dove's motive, afraid, in all fairness, that he was being set up, news of Dove's shocking dispatch, by his own hand or with assistance, was an unignorable gong. A normal person, Philip presumed, didn't think absolutely everything that happened everywhere was somehow connected to them. The Rwandan civil war was hardly his fault, but once or twice it occurred to him that he could have done more to stop it. (Write a letter? Become a mercenary?) Objectively, there wasn't an awful lot he personally could do about the demise of the bees. He knew that. But he'd learned the hard way that a soul, tormented, was exposed and sensitive, infinite in its capacity to absorb more pain.

The tragic death of his friend *was* all about him, no two ways about it. If it was suicide, Dove's cry for help was specifically directed at Philip. He was sure of it. If this was his way, the only way, to get Philip home, the desperate final act of a sick man, then so be it. It was an entreaty, loud and clear, that he could not refuse. Too late to save Dove himself, but he would honour the dead man's wishes. He would find out once and for all what happened to Sandra, even if it meant following Dove to the grave.

The rosary over, or at least in abeyance, the kitchen cleared quickly. The exhausted congregation fell over each other trying to reach the garden for a much-needed gulp of air. Fergal smiled at Philip, put his hand on his shoulder.

'Okay, my friend. If you need anything, let me know.'

Their short conference was interrupted by the exodus from the house. Gerry Junior was amongst the survivors of the rosary, and him carrying a plastic SuperValu bag that he handed over to Philip.

'Hey, Phil, Dove wanted you to have these.'

'Thanks.'

Gerry looked at Philip, smiling gormlessly like he'd been doing all evening, before moving off to mingle. Coleman flashed a look at his team. O'Dowd tried to X-ray the bag with his busy eyes.

'You the heir to the fortune?' enquired Coleman.

'Well, he was his boyfriend, in all fairness,' quipped O'Dowd.

Philip, unfazed – the temper well under control – took his leave and moved back inside, not incurious himself about the contents of the bag.

'Let sleeping dogs lie, Sharkey,' shouted O'Dowd in the parting.

Lorcan Lonergan, Coleman's director of elections, and not one to miss a trick, took advantage of the exodus, ushering some of the mourners towards his candidate, who bent a sympathetic ear to hear their more secular prayers.

Street angel, house devil

O'Boyle grudgingly made a move for Lough Muckno.

'Fucking swans. If I don't come back, tell my mother I love her.'

'You sure about that? She might die of a heart attack.'

'Good point. Say hello to Rita.'

The newsroom was quiet, apart from Devlin – or the 'sports department', as he was known – who had the intensely annoying habit of verbalizing every word as he typed it. Carson, as per usual, was berating somebody down the phone in his office next door. Sales were outside having a smoke.

The deceased man, Dermot Connolly, was *very sadly missed by his parents Gerard (Snr) and Deirdre, his brother Gerard (Jnr), his loving children, Marshall and Cliff.* He had talked to her in desperation, in the absence of anyone else who'd listen to him. The fact that he was an avid reader of *Howarya!* no doubt helped her case. Without his contribution, *Howarya!* would probably not have commissioned the piece. That long overdue 'evisceration' of small-town Ireland didn't do her any favours among her old school friends. Nor, more importantly, did it bring Sandra back to life. Or even back into the front of people's minds. Mind you, it was a right skewering of the pieties and proprieties of Tullyanna and, by extension, Drumahair and all the other pretty border towns where young girls went missing. For all the stir it made.

Joanne, at the time, had *visualized* the reaction her piece would get, the consternation it would cause, using a technique advanced by Mickey Nolan, the Capel Street self-realization entrepreneur to whose classes, books and dietary supplements she'd briefly subscribed after she'd left college. *Visualization,* she quickly learned, was one big pile of shite. Joanne, determined to get a full refund from Mickey Nolan, wrote a tongue-in-cheek letter to his headquarters, a full-size poster of a gurning Mickey in the window. God, she was naive in her youth.

While the article ruffled a few feathers right enough, and one or two prominent columnists – the usual suspects – wrote hand-wringing articles about what a shame it was – girls going missing and all – bottom line, Sandra wasn't found. And *nothing* was done.

Joanne remembered 'Dove' Connolly as a scrawny, nervous kid, by then about twenty-two years old, hand shaking like an old man with Parkinson's. The top button of his plaid shirt was closed, a detail she'd held against him. Having no real interest herself in something as frivolous as fashion – apart from scarves – she couldn't imagine why somebody who was still *grieving* for his lost girlfriend would go to the trouble.

He told her Sandra was like a wild horse. Of course he did. *You'd think you were getting somewhere and then she'd bolt, not before kicking you in the face.*

Joanne re-read the article on her laptop. Devlin, old school, tank-topped in a shirt and tie, was getting carried away in the corner, rhapsodizing about the county team who'd just made the All-Ireland semis.

'Having . . . shown . . . tremendous . . . grit . . . Joanne, another word for *grit*?' he shouted over to her, his clumsy hands hovering above the keyboard.'

'Spunk,' she offered, knowing full well he'd ignore her.

'Very good. Having shown tremendous . . . *gumption* . . . throughout . . . the . . . campaign.'

Next door, Carson, a breeder of prize Collies, was now ordering special dog food from the Netherlands. She could hardly bear to read it again.

> *What did you love about her?*
> *Everything.*
> *Could you be more specific?*
> *What do you want me to say?*

What do you want to say?
She was beautiful. I don't know. I'm not comfortable with this.
Have you ever been in love, yourself, Joanne?

Joanne remembered that she'd been thrown off-guard at the time by Dove's defensive question, and had been slightly stumped for an answer. Had she? Probably. Sean Canning in DCU, if push came to shove, who was on the debating team with her and liked the Joni Mitchell song 'River'. He was, as they say, too nice. And now that she thought of it, if anybody was to ask her again, there was Colm the guard in Mullinary. She liked him a lot until she found him trying to crawl into bed with Aisling and Anjali, and her after arriving home exhausted, having just interviewed the residents of Mullaghduff whose lives had been upended by the sudden appearance of a huge sinkhole in their estate. She still saw Colm on the street and at football matches. Not a bother on him.

We're not talking about me, Dermot.
    It's not one thing. It's . . . she was . . . she is . . . I can't describe
it. It's everything. Her face. Her eyes. Her . . . the way she carries
herself. Like she knows where she's going.

Boys. Boys. Boys. If they're not putting women down, they're idealizing them. She *was* pretty. The last time Joanne saw her, as fate would have it, was the night Sandra disappeared. For a laugh, Joanne had brought some of her college friends down to Tullyanna for the 'Arts' festival.

'Well, Joanne, remember me!'

She didn't recognize Sandra at first on the crowded Main Street, the Don McLean tribute act in full swing on a trailer behind them in the Market Yard. She was thin and heavily made up, bluish blusher accentuating her cheekbones, a little creeping plant painted over one eye.

'It's me, Sandra. Sandra Mohan. You were always very good to me, Joanne.'

'Sandra! Of course. Hi!'

They hugged like they were old friends.

'How are ya? My God, you look amazing.'

47

Sandra beamed up at Joanne, her smile lighting up the town. Her eyes were a little dilated and she was slurring slightly, but not in an especially alarming way. Besides, her parents, Tom and Carmel, were jiving furiously beside her, the sweat pumping out of them.

Dove's story? As far as she was concerned, it didn't stack up. It just didn't.

At first, she thought he was covering up for his friend, Philip Sharkey, something of a dark horse, who'd absconded a few years before she arrived to set the record straight. It wasn't a big town, but she had no clear memory of Sharkey. Did Dove himself, with his curly red hair and his boyish chin fluff, have it in him to kill a person? Joanne was of the persuasion that all men, even the best of them, were capable, in extremis, of extreme violence. Especially when they were high on that traditional hooch of hormones, alcohol and whatever was in the air. And there was always something in the air. Especially in midsummer in a small country town. As she well knew.

It was during the second abortion referendum in 1992 when Joanne briefly and spectacularly fell out with her own father. It wasn't so much his views, predictable, trenchantly held and objectionable as they were. It was the vehemence with which he slammed the door in her face that took her aback when, at the age of twenty, she openly disagreed with him for the first time. The frenzy he'd worked himself into, the hatred in his eyes. In fairness, he apologized a couple of days later, she forgave him and that was that. They never spoke about the incident again.

Her thesis? Sandra was dead. The culprit? Dove Connolly, not that she spelled that out in the piece. Well, she might have, but the ageing hippies at *Howarya!* quashed anything that was too 'on-the-nose'. And looking back, they were right. But it was in there, all the same, *unsaid* for anyone paying attention. The why? A rejection too far. This is how she saw it at the time.

Sandra may have loved Dove, in a way. A schoolgirl way. Her diaries would suggest that she had a lot of affection for him, anyway, admiration for his artistic talent. She clearly took delight in his off-beat humour, his sense of mischief, not that Joanne noticed any of that particular quality in the self-pitying wreck with the long, ginger, pointy sideburns she interviewed in 1999. Who'd continue preening their face when they're supposed to be in despair?

In an ideal world, they might have been a proper couple. They might be married now, him selling fencing and bathroom fittings on the Main Street and Sandra a social worker, as per her diary, no longer the pixie of his puerile dreams. After all, they had a lot in common. They shared the same obscure musical tastes, liked the same books and films. They both loved *Twin Peaks*. But this was not an ideal world.

Dove was just a boy, seventeen, when Sandra was last seen. Although Sandra was younger than him, she was older in spirit, and her knowledge of the world was not derived solely from music and literature. A lot of this she learned from Sandra's diary.

Dove was variously described as *sweet*, and *innocent*, and *my adorable puppy. My brother*. But his grand romantic gestures were not always fully appreciated. When he had himself delivered to her house in a box on Valentine's Day she was not amused. She had other plans for the day. As well as being *gauche* and *trying too hard*, Dove – as inconsistent as everybody else in this world – could be *fierce jealous* and *possessive* and, after Fergal Coleman brought Sandra to an Aslan concert in Dundalk, *a big cry-baby*.

Sandra's mother had shown Joanne a photo of Sandra in a coquettish pose wearing a faux-fur bolero jacket she'd made herself from mopheads. A Jazz Age princess. A sixties starlet. A gangster's moll. A girl who got a lot of attention from older men. Or, you know what, just a child playing dress-up. It killed Joanne that so many people in the town inferred so much about Sandra from the way she dressed. After the rote expressions of concern, there'd be hints dropped about her character, her background, her 'promiscuous' ways, as if that was anything to do with anything.

'*Street angel, house devil?*' Joanne had asked Dove, trying to get a rise out of him.

'*Street devil, house devil,*' he'd replied, rising to the bait, tears in his eyes, before terminating the interview

On the night she disappeared, Sandra had spurned Dove's advances. He said so himself. And he – Joanne had no scientific or psychiatric evidence to back up this hunch – was at his most priapic, and him seventeen years old, at the apex of desire by any graph, aching for love and off his head. Any journalist worth her salt has a gift, a second sight, or what's the point, right? Why would you put yourself out there if you didn't believe that? Besides, you didn't need to be a genius to figure out he had a motive. He lashed out at Sandra, perhaps in response to a cutting remark, the latest of many verbal emasculations, felling her, not intentionally, but felling her all the same, with a single blow, or maybe two. That was the other thing people said. She had a 'fierce tongue' on her. It boiled down to this. Dove couldn't give Joanne a plausible explanation as to why he and his friend, Sharkey, had changed their clothes the night Sandra vanished. Why were their clothes dirty?

They claimed they were splashed with mud while pushing a car that wouldn't start, a local hoodlum's car. They'd been hitching a lift with Sandra to a nightclub outside the town when *bona fide* bad boy Fergal Coleman stopped to offer them a lift. The thing was, it wasn't true. Coleman didn't give Sandra a lift that night. He couldn't have. As Joanne discovered during her sabbatical in Tullyanna, in what was a pretty impressive scoop by any standards, Coleman had been else-where at the time, involved in the execution of a very different crime. Getting her hands on that information was probably the most thrilling moment of her career to date.

But what if she'd been wrong, Joanne thought, not for the first time in her life, a headache now poking away at her dormant insecurities. Perhaps the desire for justice for Sandra had blinded her to the truth. Perhaps the combination of ambition and inexperience, the *impetuosity* of youth, had clouded her judgement at the time.

She knocked on Carson's door, having decided she was going to drive the thirty miles to Tullyanna and attend the *funeral mass at 11.00 a.m. at Sacred Heart Church*. And while she was there, she'd ask the questions she didn't ask eight years ago and, if she had the time, she might atone for her own sins.

'Come the fuck in. Better be good news.'

'Stuart, I'm heading for Tullyanna.'

'Like fuck you are, Joanne. I have Rita coming in here any minute. And your tongue has an appointment in her arse.'

'Look, Stuart, this is important, do you think . . . would you mind doing the interview?'

'You taking the piss? I don't know shit about country music.'

'Isn't it time you found out? You've been here long enough.'

Stuart Carson had arrived from Armagh twenty years ago and was still regarded as a blow-in. Rita, one of the toughest old dames of Irish country music – one of that rare breed known throughout the land by her first name only, a single-name legend – had recently retired to her home county and had lots of stories to tell.

'Listen to me. When Rita gets here, make her a nice cup of tea, sit her down and let her rabbit on about shagging Johnny Cash or swinging on the chandeliers or whatever the fuck she was up to in Nashville, if you have any interest in continuing to write for this fucking paper!'

'Like it's the *Washington Post*.'

Carson was always threatening to sack people, practically every day.

'Well, Joanne, I have news for you, you're not Bob Bernstein.'

'Woodward.'

'We're a lot bigger than the *Washington Post*. Around here anyways. And they all love Rita. She's a god, to them, so she is. So, go out there and tickle her fanny and find out what the fuck is going on under all the sequins and the frilly fucking . frills.'

She didn't take it personally. Stuart screamed at everybody, partly as a result of the huge stress he was under, having been forced to sack half the staff due to cutbacks, and partly because he was a genuine prick. A harmless, sweaty fool, he had the quaint notion that this was how a newspaper editor was *supposed* to behave. He was a mess of contradictions, an Ulster puritan who overate and drank to excess and fucked his way indiscriminately around the north-east – mainly at dog shows – which was absolutely fine with her, except for the fact that he seemed to do it all without any relish whatsoever. What was the point of having that much fun and then hating yourself?

'There's any amount of hacks out there, a lot younger than you, and hungrier too, who'd bite my fucking arm off.'

'I know, sure they're queuing up outside. See you around, Stuart. Devlin can do it.'

'Joanne!'

When Joanne had one of her notions, there was no stopping her. Despite the priorities of her editor, she was way more curious about this 'abrupt' death in Tullyanna. If Dermot Connolly's death was a suicide and if Fergal Coleman, of all people, was going to be elected, as the polls would have it, there was a good story there. A potentially explosive story. Carson would be thanking her in the long run.

It was a story that genuinely gripped her heart. Sandra Mohan was more than a subject to her. She thought of her as a little sister. At school, Joanne had stayed behind a couple of days a week to help out at the homework club. Although Sandra was never less than secretive, they chatted away nicely, Joanne captivated by the little girl's designs and her curiosity about the world at large. Joanne ran out of chocolate buttons trying to catch Sandra out with the capital cities of the world and TV theme tunes. There wasn't a song she didn't know who sang it. When she asked her what she would like to be when she grew up, Sandra's answer, to this day, sent shivers up Joanne's spine.

'I want to be like you.'

Her mother, Carmel, had entrusted her with their daughter's diary for a spell after the guards were done with it. Did the guards even open it? Although it didn't yield anything in terms of evidence, the girl's melancholic reflections provided an indispensable insight into her mind. Through the diary, Joanne had gotten a sense of the light and shade in Sandra's life, a handle on people like Dove and Fergal Coleman. Whatever way you looked at it, Sandra had been in the latter's thrall.

Fergal listens. He understands.

But Joanne had ignored the implications of that. Coleman's compliments. The presents. The binges. The trips. The truth is, Joanne herself had been fascinated by Coleman. And as a result, it was just possible that she'd let her little sister down.

The father hen will call his chickens home

The baby started crying, giving Kevin the excuse to get up and play some Johnny Cash while holding him close. His grandson's tiny eyes were more alert than usual at this unearthly hour, and him comfortable in Kevin's arms, and him fed and changed, winded and serenaded by a doting grandfather in his underpants. Kevin pointed at things, *dah!*, the pair of them waltzing around the kitchen while he made coffee. The rain steady outside, they twirled through the house, not inelegantly, down the corridor and into the converted garage, now Kevin's office, where the temperature dropped.

'There she is. Your lovely mammy!' he said, showing wee Paul a photograph of Ciara. *Dah!* 'Give mammy a kiss!' They took turns kissing the photograph. He pressed play on the CD player to hear late-career Cash at his most evangelical, the baby nearly jumping out of his arms at the volume. Lest he wake Sheila, he turned it down again.

'And look, there's poor Sandra!' he went on, introducing, with a wave of his arm, a wall of photos of Sandra Mohan, as if her fate was hidden in some detail he had somehow not yet noticed. Indeed, there was a whole room-full of Sandra Mohan memorabilia, maps of the area and newspaper cuttings, and eyewitness testimonies piled high on the floor.

> 'There's a man going round taking names
> and he decides who to free and who to blame.'

Of course, the thing that kept Kevin awake more than anything else was the Sandra Mohan case. It had kept him awake for well over ten years now. It was time to share the load. It was time to confide in his grandson, Paul, whose warm body, sweet breath and pulsing heart gave him comfort. Not yet a year old, the boy was neither walking nor talking. Yet, early last Saturday morning, around about 7.00 a.m., when Ciara was still at work, on her second shift at Our Lady's, and Paul was asleep in his cot, a dodo on each finger, the doorbell rang. Kevin, who'd got up to prepare breakfast for himself and Sheila and was sitting on the toilet, straining in vain, as was his sorry lot, wondered aloud, 'Christymoore! Who the hell is that at this hour of a Saturday morning?'

To which Paul had replied, as clear as a newsreader on the nine o'clock news, the static on the baby monitor notwithstanding, 'it's a lady with a pram.'

Kevin leapt up off the toilet, all hope retreating, and ran down to Ciara's bedroom at the other end of the bungalow to find Paul in deep repose in his cot, the curtains closed to the outside world. He then ran to the front door. By the time he had unlocked all seven locks, the lady was on the road, a Traveller woman, the hair down, pushing what he would later swear to the Doc was an empty pram. She briefly stopped and turned to have a good look at him, shaking her magnificent chestnut mane in a gesture the tone of which he couldn't divine from where he was standing, before going on her mysterious way.

It's not that he thought Paul was clairvoyant. Or some sort of a sage. He was just a good listener. And, more importantly, he was available.

Look, Kevin had his theories. He had suspects. One of them was Councillor Fergal Coleman, no less, who had a whole filing cabinet to himself. Kevin knew more about the case – still officially a missing person's inquiry – than any man alive, for all the good it did him. Of course, he felt sorry for Dove and the Connolly family, but this was all about Sandra and no mistake. Dove wouldn't be where he was now if it wasn't for his intimate connection to Sandra Mohan.

'He was her boyfriend, do you see?'

The baby gurgled knowingly.

As usual, as they did every night, the house shaking like in a TV cartoon, Kevin and Paul time-travelled back to 1994. For the child's benefit he summarized what he knew, hoping, in the act of repetition, that he would somehow find new meaning. After all, every time a US president quoted Yeats, Kevin was newly enlightened. And sure, didn't his own son, Shane, tell him only the other day that the Oasis song 'Supersonic' – a song he had heard about a million times – was all about a dog, a Rottweiler called Elsa.

He had been on the desk, fighting sleep – at a time when sleep came easy – the night Sandra was reported missing. And in the weeks following her disappearance, as well as going house to house and searching where he was told to search by his superior officers, he was appointed to liaise with the poor girl's family. ('*I was chosen. For a reason.*') For all her troubles she was not, in his opinion, the type to just run away.

'Fearless she was, by all accounts, Paul, fearless.'

Despite repeated sightings of her months after the fact, Kevin always feared the worst. Frustrated with the slow-to-no progress being made and with the blasé attitude of his more experienced colleagues, hard-drinking men whose starting point, in fairness, was usually a dead body and perhaps a clue or two, he began to conduct his own interviews. Although this was not his job, at the time, and was frowned upon by his colleagues, he arranged these meetings discreetly with the relevant parties, some of whom played on his football team.

'They were just chats. Informal, you know. I'd buy them curry chips and we'd go for a wee spin. Say nothing.' He winked at the baby.

Periodically, after the initial interest in Sandra had died down, and after he himself had been promoted within the force, he'd have the case reopened, failing, time and time again, to find her, failing her and her family, failing young women everywhere, and failing to be the cop, the person he wanted to be. And in trying and failing, repeatedly, he'd found himself in a running battle of wits with the canny, feral Councillor Fergal Coleman.

Coleman, a master deflector, had mocked him for being obsessional and prurient, and for having an unhealthy fascination with young girls. A visitor to his 'den' might, Kevin conceded, feel the same way. Would he have devoted the same energy and commitment to the case if Sandra was a boy? He'd like to think that he would but couldn't be sure. Thankfully, no young boys had gone missing on his watch. And no other case that came his way had been so baffling or, in his opinion, had such far-reaching ramifications. God knows, he asked himself enough times if it was Sandra he was really looking for, or was it something else? Ego-gratification? Heroism? Fame?

On his way to school every day, when he was a young lad, he had regular Walter Mitty-like fantasies about saving people's lives. He imagined himself jumping into a river to save a flailing woman. Or getting an empty milk crate and placing it over the horns of a billy goat that was bucking wildly on the main street. Or, in a part of the world steeped in piety and political violence, he often envisioned a scenario in which some hirsute renegade threw a bomb into the church at Sunday mass. While the rest of the congregation panicked, young Kevin calmly left the pew and kicked the explosive device to safety through an open side door.

'Fortunately, Paul, the bomb was ball-shaped in that particular dream.'

He rubbed his grandson's belly with his head, eliciting a great big laugh that died on the breeze-block walls of the garage. He'd need egg-boxes.

'I'm such a fraud.'

His motivation in saving the imaginary faithful from maiming and death was not entirely selfless, he confessed. He wanted glory, praise for his footballing prowess, a medal for bravery and his picture in the local paper. In the glow of that scenario, as in every other scenario as he saw it, Sandra was definitely dead, her decomposing body a stage on which he was acting out some sort of redemption fantasy on behalf of humanity. In which case, it was all about him and neither he nor Sandra were real people, a thought that was profoundly disturbing. If that's what people wanted to think, there was nothing he could do about it.

Perhaps naively, he believed there was such a concept as the incontestable truth and that such a truth would prevail. Apart from anything else, he was convinced that Sandra's disappearance – and here he was probably open to charges of grandiosity – had implications not just for her immediate family and the local community of Tullyanna but for the country at large, no less. The State itself, he maintained, would be destined to remain in a sort of stasis, something of a para-democracy, until such time as Sandra was found, dead or alive. How could we move on with such a gaping hole in history? Which meant, of course, in that scenario, that Sandra was not just not a real girl, but a mythical figure, and you wouldn't wish that on anyone. Poor Sandra was the antithesis of your one, Cathleen ni Houlihan, Yeats's stand-in for Ireland. Sandra was the anti-Cathleen, her being youthful and liberal and, he had it on good authority, *opposed* to blood sacrifice, rather than an old keening crone craving blood. And that meant that he was not just an ordinary detective doing his job – with maybe a bit too much stubborn pride and would-be macho swagger – but a narcissistic nation-builder or, to be more accurate, a narcissistic *renovator* of the nation.

Paul was getting sleepy. Johnny Cash was singing away about trumpets and pipers and millions of angels singing. It seemed strangely appropriate.

Kevin consulted his notebooks. This much he knew.

Sandra was only sixteen when she was last seen but looked a fair bit older, if that meant anything. She was wearing a black pencil skirt at the time and a distinctive peach-coloured top she had made herself from a piece of satin. Neither was ever found. She was also wearing a Lee denim jacket, sporting a Pixies button badge. The jacket was lent to her on the night in question by young Dermot 'Dove' Connolly, to cover her slender shoulders, and was never found. Nor were found her high heels or her trademark beret. Was that prurience, knowing in excessive detail what she was wearing the night she disappeared? Was that obsessional? Berets were extremely rare in Tullyanna except, of course, at paramilitary funerals. A girl wearing a beret – more French Resistance in her case than graveside colour party – was daring. If nothing else, it was a clue to her character.

He rooted out a DVD copy of the crime-show reconstruction of the evening and played it for Paul. Sandra leaving her house. Sandra at JJ's. Sandra hitching to Shadows. Nothing titillating or salacious. In fact, it was surprisingly well-made for an RTÉ production. The whole town had turned out to watch the filming. It was quite remarkable the number of men who were on hand to help the actress get the walk right and the attitude. And that night in the pub, Dove, having had his earlier request to play himself in the film refused, tried to 'get off' with the actress, his persistent attentions finally thwarted by an intervention from the guards.

But he was getting ahead of himself. What *was* found was a pair of tights, sheer 12-denier tights, expensive beyond a schoolgirl's budget, stolen, as Kevin later discovered, from a department store on a school-trip to Dublin. They were found balled up in Dove Connolly's trouser pocket in a laundry basket at the Connolly home.

The tights were sticky with – no prizes for guessing – what transpired to be the boy's semen. The garment, Dove had insisted, was a souvenir presented to him by his mature-beyond-her-years girlfriend by way of a parting gift before she, in his words, *fucked off in Fergal Coleman's car.* The *jizz,* Dove's word, for want of a better, was discharged by him into the tights, disseminated in a solo effort, in a fit of loneliness and pain, and him concerned by then that the Sandra he pined for with every desolate cell of his being, with every pulse and every waking thought, had deserted him.

No wonder half the country believed he was guilty, not least the so-called journalist who wrote the reckless article, 'Small Town, Big Secret'. That cohort would be sleeping well now, seeing Dove's death as a closure of sorts, and the manner of his death as karma of sorts, and saying to themselves, serves him right and good riddance. For Kevin, it was anything but closure, it was the opposite of closure. Dove's apparent suicide was openers in a high-stakes game of hold 'em.

Curiously, a choker necklace – positively identified as being a 'typical-Sandra' accessory – belonging to the missing girl *was* found at a booth in the Crossroads café on the corner of Main Street and O'Connell Street, where witnesses swore she was seen, seated, eating a plate of egg and chips, *two days* after she was reported missing.

Detective Sergeant Healy showed baby Paul the timeline. It took up space on three of the four walls in his den.

Briefly, on 18 June 1994, at about 9.00 p.m., Dove and Philip Sharkey, the pair of them drenched in Blue Stratos, met Sandra in JJ's, where they played pool with a number of their friends. The town was abuzz. Not only had Ireland just beaten Italy at the World Cup, but an 'Arts' festival had been held earlier that day. According to the chairman of the town council, the festival had been an outstanding success. It consisted of a three-legged race on Main Street, which attracted a record number of entrants and a merciless baying crowd, and a Don McLean impersonator who stood on a trailer singing 'American Pie' over and over again, a song to which people jived as if their lives depended on it, jiving being the dance of choice in the area, no matter what type of music was on offer or what mood they were in. Bunty fellas, full to the gills, flung their equally bunty partners, tons of compacted meat in miniskirts hurtling through the air like comets in a disaster movie. Nobody cared about the consequences.

The dancing was lethal but tremendously exciting, was the consensus, only overshadowed by the star attraction, the crowning glory of the programme, namely a motorcyclist in a white sequinned jumpsuit. Somehow the festival committee had secured the talents of an Evel Knievel wannabe, all the way from Warrington, who rode his bike on a high-wire strung across the Main Street, a logic-defying novelty people were still talking about to this day. For many, this was the zenith of human achievement, up there with the moon landings and the discovery of milk – art, science and magic all rolled into one daredevil feat.

The barman at JJ's that night, Willy Ward, swore 'on my mother's grave' that he refused to serve Sandra any alcohol on account of her age. However, he conceded that one or more of the others – most of whom were also underage – *may* have purchased alcoholic beverages on her behalf, the poolroom being unobservable from his station at the bar. Kevin, based on numerous interviews with those present, estimated that she had in fact consumed 'a fierce amount'. Sandra drank at least two pint bottles of cider in JJ's and sipped regularly from a lemonade bottle that was full to the brim with vodka siphoned from her parents' stash at home. He further ascertained that young Philip Sharkey – a skilful centre half-forward on his minor team – had rolled a number of 'joints'. These Philip shared with Dove and Sandra out the back of the pub. This information was a particular disappointment to Kevin for whom Sharkey, an intelligent lad and the fulcrum of his football team, was something of a special project at the time.

At about midnight, after visiting a variety of pubs in the town, and drinking and smoking an impossible-to-say-for-sure amount, and mingling with various acquaintances, savoury and unsavoury, the trio headed for Shadows. Having missed the bus to Shadows, a nightclub about five miles from the town, they started walking in the direction of that legendary but frankly disreputable haunt. The girl was now cloaked in Dove's denim jacket.

A couple of miles from the venue, Sandra, according to her chaperones, announced that she needed to 'take a pee'. It was then she removed her tights and, in a flirtatious way apparently, handed them to Dove. He accepted them at the time as some sort of a promise and stuffed them into his pocket. A few minutes later, Sandra emerged from behind a tree, adjusting her skirt, when a car pulled up beside them. It was Fergal Coleman and his cronies.

These were lads in their early twenties, about four or five years older than the boys (and a good eight years older than Sandra). Sandra, it seems, got into the front of the car and sat on some fella's knee. She turned up the stereo full blast, only to hear Billy Ray Cyrus in his finest hour. Philip and the Dove, in the best of form, sang along in an ironic fashion, as was their wont, to the song 'Achy Breaky Heart'. It was all 'great craic'. They were about to get in themselves when the car stalled. At this point, Fergal asked them to give the car a push in order to kickstart her again. (Kevin interrupted his narrative at this point, not that baby Paul minded and he engrossed in the story, suddenly anxious about his thoughtless, throwaway gendering of the car. He wondered if referring to a car as *her* or *she* was being sexist or objectifying in some way, implying, albeit unintentionally, that a woman, like a car, could be *possessed* or, Jaysus, *driven*. But after examining the notes of his interviews with both Dove and Philip, he was able to relax. *They* had described Coleman's car in feminine terms.)

Anyway, in good humour, they pushed the car. ('*We pushed her, so we did.*') After a few yards, however, the car revved into life and *she* skidded away, splattering the unsuspecting Good Samaritans with a hail of stones and mud, 'destroying' their freshly laundered clothes. And so the boys, outfoxed by Coleman and his gang, turned on their heels and walked back towards town. At Dove's house, they ate burgers and changed their clothes. The ever-thoughtful Dove transferred the pair of tights into his spare jeans, in case Sandra needed them later. Irrepressible, for they were young and the night was young and they were pleasantly stoned, they went back out onto the road and hitched a lift to Shadows.

Kevin, of course, didn't need to refer to the timeline on the wall or the files on the floor for most of this information. This was all logged firmly in his mind, to the exclusion of almost everything else. If he could only transmit this accumulation of facts and suppositions and connections, telepathically, to the baby, then his work might not be in vain. In the event of his demise, if the case was still unsolved, Paul would be in a position to pick up the slack and make it his life's work until he, in turn, ran out of steam and passed the torch to some poor future sucker, and so on *ad infinitum*.

Kevin mostly believed Philip and Dove's testimony. Although, in fairness, there were anomalies. Retracing their movements, at the time, he could find no evidence of skid-marks on the side of the road. Dove's mother was also evasive about the boy's movements that night. But Kevin more or less believed them. What was far from clear, in Kevin's mind, was whether or not Sandra had ever arrived at Shadows.

By the time Dove and Philip Sharkey got there – let's say, an hour-and-a-half later – there was no sign of her. And although there was a crowd in attendance that night, a huge crowd of, some would say, five thousand souls, it being close to midsummer, one of the longer nights of the year, and the deep-rooted urge to revel was strong, nobody had seen her. That didn't mean she hadn't been there. Dark corners abounded on the premises, and the people of the area were cagey and unforthcoming by nature, by dint of history, recent and less recent, and there was a fog on the dance floor generated by record levels of body heat, dry ice and cigarette smoke. Just because Sandra had not been sighted by any of her friends, or by any of Dove and Sharkey's friends, didn't mean she hadn't been there.

Coleman denied that he'd picked up Sandra. And told the cops that Sharkey and Dove were liars. His evidence was backed up by his friends, Lonergan and Sheriff. They, in a puzzling twist, maintained that the car they supposedly travelled in that night had actually been stolen from the car park outside the celebrated nightspot later the same evening. This claim was corroborated by the journalist Joanne McCollum, who, in Kevin's view, was a meddler who had only managed to muddy more what were already, by any standards, fairly muddy waters. All three of them, Coleman, Lonergan and 'Omar' Sheriff, were very definitely at Shadows themselves, according to numerous wallflowers who saw them starting a fight. This was an altercation with an innocent-looking duck farmer from Emyvale, a teetotaller whom they accused of stealing drink. Moments later they became embroiled in a free-for-all with the security staff, who were some of the most forbidding bouncers in the entire north-east. Kevin himself saw, with his own eyes, the bloodied and bruised trio arriving at the station, escorted by no less than six of his garda colleagues. It struck him as strange at the time that there was no smell of drink off them, no signs of drunkenness, none of the roaring and shouting and need for sedation and possible confinement that he would have associated with this sort of incident. It was all very *convenient*.

In the early hours of the morning, at ten past six, young Dove Connolly arrived at the station in a highly agitated state. Distraught and sadly drug-deranged, he disturbed the fragile peace that had finally settled on the town that night, his incoherence matched only by his incapacity to stand up straight. Philip Sharkey's attempts to restrain him were futile. Dove vomited on the station floor in front of the hatch that Kevin's pleasant face filled, an action that was not guaranteed to ingratiate oneself with the law. Nevertheless, Kevin gave him his ear. The boy was slurring badly but, according to his notes, a copy of which Kevin showed the baby, he said: '*The bitch is gone, she's gone, Sandra's gone, the fucking bitch*.' Again, this was terminology not guaranteed to warm any officer's heart, even one as indulgent and even-tempered as Kevin, the doting father of a nine-year-old girl, and him knackered after a long shift.

And now, thirteen years later, Dove himself was dead. The coroner signed it off as a suicide. The guards dismissed Kevin's calls for an investigation, laughing at his suggestion that it might be a case of 'euthanasia'. Either way, Dove's sorry end had its beginnings in Sandra's disappearance. Until she was found, Dove would not not get justice, peace or eternal rest.

Kevin, his brain sore and sleepy now, unable to concentrate, and less able to trust his own memory than, say, a year ago, turned off the stereo. In his bare feet, he made his way through the house, nothing on the walls beyond his den, no paintings, no photos, no knick-knacks to call his own, as if he didn't live there, as if he was not alive. The house was only greyly lit, the sun not yet risen. He placed the sleeping baby in his cot before creeping back to his own bed, his beloved, indispensable Sheila snoring away without respite. Surely that was the sound of an unhappy woman, some sort of protest, he deduced, his final deduction on what was another fruitless day.

'*The father hen will call his chickens home.*'

PART TWO

Crossing the Mindfields

After the wake, Philip was above in his bedroom, doing what he did best, brooding. His father had been laid out in the same bed, his mother being squeamish about corpses in her boudoir.

'*You're the man of the house now,*' the elders had intoned gravely, investing him with a great responsibility, the nature of which escaped him. Did they think they were doing him a favour? It wasn't enough to lose a father. You had to all of a sudden become a man, whatever that was. Since then he tended to associate manhood with sorrow. The Algonquin people had an initiation rite in which the young men of the tribe were locked in a cage for twenty days. During this time they were forced to ingest a hefty dose of a hallucinogenic called wysoccan, which erased all memories of childhood. Drastic, but effective, he imagined. Definitely more practical than the Irish version – the twenty-first, a few pints and the bumps, and a lifetime of looking back in regret, trying to recall TV jingles and the players on the 1978 Dutch team. What he wouldn't do for some wysoccan now.

'Philip!'

Philip tilted his head back against the wall. Here we go again.

'Pippy, pet, is that you?'

Who the fuck did she think it was at this hour of the night?

'Yes, Ma.'

'There's a rhubarb tart in the oven.'

Of course, there was.

He sat on the bed and stuck his hand inside the plastic SuperValu bag handed to him at Connollys', not sure what he'd find within, what knick-knack or morbid jest from beyond the grave his old friend Dove had in store for him. If he was hoping for concrete information on Sandra Mohan's fate – like an address – he was disappointed.

What was in the bag was a padded envelope. He ripped that open to find a journal of some sort. On closer inspection, it turned out to be a thick, A4-sized sketchpad, bound in vellum, or whatever passes for vellum these days. A type of synthetic leather, he supposed, from an artificial calf perhaps. He opened the book slowly, afraid it might contain anthrax or some other spring-loaded tooth for a tooth. No such luck. It was just page after page of inky drawings, a graphic novel, was it, or some sort of a comic strip? What was Dove playing at? Was it the two fingers? Was it vanity? Did he expect Philip to ensure his work was published posthumously by way of compensation for leaving him frightened and alone?

The main character in the story was a superhero by the name of Brouhaha. This chiselled, scowling Übermensch was a cross between the ancient Celtic warrior Cú Chulainn – the so-called Hound of Ulster – and Judge Dredd. Philip had little enough tolerance for all that mythic bullshit – the stories of the Fianna and the Arthurian legends and Mega City One – that Dove was partial too, in his youth.

Mind you, even to a sceptic, it was good stuff if you liked violence and rain. The eponymous hero bish-bash-boshed his way through a post-apocalyptic landscape in a series of bloody adventures, in search of what, Philip couldn't say for sure at first. He lived in a hollow oak tree, big enough to house a banqueting table, a spiral staircase and a big flat-screen TV tuned to snow. All this was skilfully rendered, Celtic motifs – triquetras and triskelions and knots and squiggles – mercifully at a minimum. You could only tell it was supposed to be Tullyanna by the distinctive church spire protruding upwards through the ash and mud. It reminded Philip of the town of Plymouth, in Montserrat, buried under lava after a series of volcanic eruptions, a site he'd visited on a trip to the island while crewing on an Irish American investment banker's yacht.

Everywhere, there was desolation, suffering and death. The people – the ordinary, non-super-strength survivors of a nameless calamity – lived in holes in the ground covered by tarp or wood. Hollow-cheeked, they were covered in boils. It took Philip a few pages before he realized they were all tongueless, too.

Keeping the cowering populace in check were black-clad warriors, faceless beings who rode bareback on slobbering wild boars. A green man popped up from time to time, basically a box hedge in human form, a character 'good' or 'bad' or indeed indifferent to the plight of the forlorn people, Philip didn't know. It bore a likeness to a huge, life-like topiary sculpture that used to scare the shite out of Dove and Philip, as children, when they used to trespass on the old Wilson estate. The Wilsons, being outsiders, descendants of the original planters, were supposed to be pagan, orgy-loving occultists, initiates of the Hermetic Order of the Golden Dawn, who wouldn't think twice about sacrificing a mitching schoolboy on a pyre.

As Philip became engrossed in the book, it became clearer that Brouhaha's over-arching quest, for want of a better word, was to find something called the Middlemist Blue. However, each chapter, or story within a story, was self-contained, usually involving Brouhaha righting, with rough justice, some wrong on behalf of the community.

One of these phantasmagorical vignettes caught his attention. In it, Brouhaha was petitioned by a delegation of mute and toothless Biddies, dead children at their breasts, bearing pewter jugs of powder, mead and boars' teeth. Each of them, to his surprise, was clearly identifiable as a matriarch of Tullyanna. One of them, the hair-do intact, was, if he was not greatly mistaken, Philip's very own mother. The hairs stood up on his head.

They wordlessly beseeched the hero to, first of all, find a special oil, made from the rendered bones of the long-extinct Irish elk. To do this, he would have to cross the Mindfields, which no man or woman had managed to do successfully since the Fall. There were the usual threats to overcome. You had the boar-back Ramen, for instance, and the various insatiable multi-headed beasts with names too stupid, in Philip's opinion, to mention. You had the extreme weather conditions. And you also had the Effects – the obscene auditory, olfactory, gustatory and visual hallucinations that characterized the Mindfields – which literally blew even the most strong-minded warriors' heads off. If he survived all that, Brouhaha faced a whole new slew of equally challenging challenges in the Bog of the Damned, not least diving deep into the radioactive mire without a snorkel to find the skeleton of an ancient elk, taking it back to the surface and rendering it into fat. That achieved, he had to go back the way he came, now on his last legs, protecting the precious bone jelly at all costs from yet more stupid-named monstrosities roused from the unholy deep by its scent.

His destination was the Rocks, a pile of rocks under which a sort of resistance lived in an elaborate system of tunnels and caves. In one of the caves, Uncle Francie was cutting hair. Philip's own hair – no rest for the wicked – stood up again. In another cave, deeper and darker, the Biddies waited with a sick cow, the only cow left in that part of the world. So, it was fair to say, it was special. Doubly special. For while the ladies furiously rubbed their bony, withered hands together – like stridulating crickets – creating a sound hideous to Brouhaha's ears, he applied the ointment to the nethers of the ailing cow, reviving it and – more significantly – reviving the being gestating within it. The arrival of this child, for it was a child, or possibly a child–cow hybrid, a mini-minotaur, was prophesied by the prophets – who else?, says you – to do great things vis-à-vis hope, salvation and the like. Job done, Brouhaha returned to his oak tree, alone. He took out his syringe and injected into his arm some of the powder from the pewter jug. Then he lay down to dream of the Middlemist Blue, which turned out to be a very rare, most likely extinct flower, although try telling that to Brouhaha if you knew what was good for you.

All nonsense, you would think? And you'd be right . . . unless? Unless you knew Dove as well as Philip did. To him, it all made some sort of sense, on a level, it has to be said, a fair few leagues beneath the subconscious. He'd need to sleep on it.

On some of his adventures, Brouhaha was accompanied by his friend, Dearg Doom, and an armour-plated Wolfhound, a breed not prized for its intelligence, or its stamina, or indeed its longevity, but they were big dogs, and easy to draw. A terrier, like say a Kerry Blue, would have been more useful in righting wrongs than a needy, lumbering show-dog any day of the week, but you could never accuse Dove of being overly rigorous in his thinking.

The avenging warrior himself, Philip noted, as he flicked through the pages, specialized in saving damsels in distress. Most of these ladies – typical Dove – happened to be very well-endowed. In salvaging the ladies' honour, Brouhaha used the golden torc he wore around his neck as a lethal boomerang. He clearly took great pleasure in decapitating his many enemies. There were heads everywhere. Boggle-eyed heads, of man and boar, bouncing in all directions, the blood spurting from their necks, filling up whole panels on the page and luridly flowing beyond the lines of the panels.

For a frozen second, Philip had the notion that Dove had used real blood. And then, his eyes blurring, he saw Dove's accusatory face, or what was left of it, in the coffin – his ultimate work of art, a magnum opus that would, no doubt, fetch a high price at the likes of the Saatchi gallery.

Where were you, Philip?

It was heady stuff, the sort of style a boho hobo with tuberculosis and a taste for absinthe might have employed to illustrate a collection of late Victorian fairytales. Philip was tired, and tortured by what had happened to his friend, and torn between mourning him and getting on with his more immediate assignment. The reds were good. The blues were even more mesmerizing. *How the fuck did Dove produce colour of such depth and intensity in such a dreary, God-forsaken town?* Philip couldn't tell if it was ink, pencil, marker pen or even paint. Maybe Dove had his own private mine where he quarried lapis lazuli. If he did, you'd be asking the wrong man in Philip, who had taken Dove at his word when he told him all those years ago that he never wanted to see him again.

Brouhaha's cloak of midnight blue reminded Philip of the slightly subversive stained-glass windows in the local church that depicted the lives of the saints. St Brigid. St Dymphna. St Finbar. If he remembered correctly, they had a similar dreamy, decadent – would it be stretching things too far to say *erotic*? – aesthetic to Dove's drawings.

That said, every image of a woman – even that of an Art Nouveau-ish female saint painted in two dimensions on glass installed in a church wall – was erotic to a teenage boy, at mass, when all the girls of the town were on display, and the lads felt the need to kneel for longer than was strictly obligatory to hide their embarrassments, earning in the process, ironically, a reputation for piety.

Heady and grim. You didn't have to be a psychiatrist to see where Dove was coming from. Philip obviously didn't have the full insight into Dove's life and mental state over the last decade or so. But he imagined that knowing somebody, anybody, never mind a close friend and first love, was missing, presumed dead, and thinking about that every day, and fearing the worst, and not trusting anyone, would be enough to send any man into a nihilistic dead-end funk. It certainly wouldn't help. And if that wasn't bad enough, knowing that some people, friends and family included, continued to think you might have had something to do with her disappearance; and knowing that your best friend had betrayed you; and knowing whatever it was you recently found out that prompted you to reach out to your aforementioned treacherous best friend; all that would be more than enough to turn any man suicidal; and turn you to opiates and/or violent graphic art.

While it was all very fantastical and probably allegorical, it was boring the arse off Philip at this stage, and he not a fan of the genre.

Philip wasn't able to identify the dread feeling in the pit of his stomach. Was it fear for his own safety? Or guilt? Or just hunger? Frustrated at his own inability to decipher Dove's meaning and drawn to the comforting smell of his mother's home-baking, he set aside the book for the present and went downstairs.

The walls have ears

Philip hadn't eaten all day. A part of him had hoped that Sandra Mohan herself might have shown up at the wake. And she might have tapped a glass with a spoon and apologized to everyone for all the bother and confusion she'd caused. And then dropped the glass because what else would you do to top the drama you had just created? And explained, in that deeper voice she adopted sometimes when she had something important to say – the mock-serious voice that indicated to those who knew her that she was, in fact, being really serious – that she'd had some sort of a mental breakdown in her teens and wasn't able to cope at the time. She'd felt judged and used and had no choice but to run away and join a cult, some Bhagwan's commune in Germany, for the sake of argument, wearing shades of red, where, to her surprise, she'd been brainwashed but only mildly exploited, living on nothing but sauerkraut and willingly changing her name to Ruby.

In which scenario, Philip would have been able to relax and get on with his life, Dove's violent demise notwithstanding.

All was quiet on the ground floor. He was reaching into the oven for the rhubarb tart, salivating at this stage, all of the senses alert, it being the witching hours when all the toys come alive, when he heard a noise from out the back. He stopped in his tracks, keeping still and holding his breath, burning a finger on the wire rack. *Fuck*, says he softly. One of his good fingers. His trigger finger, not that he had ever handled a gun. There it was again. Unmistakably. It was a faint scraping sound, metal on cement. To his ears, it was the sound of a gas cylinder being shunted a fraction. And it was almost certainly the work of a person, a prowler, the wind being negligible that night and the cats in the area of regulation size and strength. *So this is it*, he thought, taking a deep breath. *This is how it starts.*

Calmly he trotted upstairs to his bedroom, two steps at a time, and removed his shoes. Reaching in behind the wardrobe, he took possession of an old fishing knife that belonged to his uncle Francie. His mother was listening to a meditation tape in her bedroom. (The usual. Whale sounds overlaid with a deep male voice, neither of which was in any way soothing. In his opinion, the whale sounded lonely and desolate in a vast ocean, crying out to a lifelong mate who'd recently been harpooned by an unreconstructed Japanese Ahab. And the guru himself sounded like a creep who preys on vulnerable women. '*You may wish to close your eyes now as you feel more and more relaxed*.')

In silence, in full ninja mode now, he climbed out the bathroom window, landing softly on the felt that covered the flat roof of the kitchen. Confident in his own stealthiness, Philip crawled to the edge of the roof and, under cover of darkness, looked down. A man was trying the handle on the so-called patio door that, strictly speaking, didn't lead to anything resembling a patio. There were no flagstones or garden umbrellas in that dismal space, no history of outdoor dining. There were no anecdotal records of excessive cocktail indulgence or echoes of salty chat. In fact, the door opened from the sitting room into nothing more salubrious than a dank concrete yard. Now, as always, it was coated in moss and green slime and fixed in Philip's mind as the place where he, aged fifteen, arriving home from school one day, found his father lying in a heap, dead from a heart attack.

Looking around and listening, he was satisfied there was only one snooper on the property. Without further hesitation Philip jumped from the roof, a distance of twelve feet. Well, six feet, if you factor in the initial lowering of himself off the roof, clinging full length onto the rusty guttering, until it gave way and he dropped to the ground. Although in considerable pain, it didn't stop him rolling forward in one admirable Chuck Norris-style movement and rugby-tackling the intruder before he knew what hit him. It was the smell – the sudden, nauseating stench of human waste – that suggested he was dealing with no greater a threat to mankind than Tommy Courtney, a turn of events that rendered his fishing knife redundant and the red alert over.

Unfortunately, Tommy's nose had been broken as Philip, rising again to his feet in another seamless action, propelled the intruder headfirst into the patio door.

'Who sent you?'

The junkie, no stranger to pain himself, in fairness, didn't reply and didn't complain.

Philip's mother, in her nightgown, and hair sensationally still in place, must have heard the commotion for she materialized to unlock the door. She ushered them both inside. And, without too much curiosity on her part, as if in a trance from all the meditation, she made a pot of tea for the lads before retreating upstairs. Typical. *I love you but I don't want to know what's going on.* After his father died, she'd gone through an intense period of grief – wailing loudly, foul temper, hunger strike – that lasted about a week. Then she got her hair done and busied herself substitute-teaching above at the convent and teaching immigrant children to read and write after school below in the house. He didn't know if she'd dated any men, but she certainly had her admirers. After Sandra went missing, the work dried up, and even the immigrants stopped calling, an association with the Sharkeys too high a price to pay for literacy. She had never asked him about Sandra, resorting to the old head-in-the-sand tactic that served generations of Irish men and women so well through centuries of British rule and religious oppression, screening all sorts of horror and abuse from their minds. Even during their monthly phone calls she shot the breeze as if nothing had ever happened, as if he was some globe-trotting humanitarian who'd be home for Christmas, instead of a haunted man in exile.

'I didn't want them to see me.' Tommy, frightened, sore, drunk and barely audible, tried to explain himself.

Whoever they were, and whether they were real or imagined, Philip didn't care to speculate. Not entirely trusting Tommy, he locked the back door and pulled the curtains. Searching the pockets of Tommy's greasy coat, he found a Stanley knife and a used syringe. These he duly confiscated. He didn't believe Tommy had designs to harm him, but he couldn't be sure. He also found a small silver candlestick and a supersize block of cheddar cheese. Booty, Philip assumed, pilfered at Dove Connolly's wake, cheese having a surprisingly high resale value in various barrios of the town since the Hardship hit, half of two-fifty being a not-to-be-sniffed-at one-twenty-five.

'I lied, so I did. I lied about the girl. I never seen her.'

Tommy, bloodied and snivelling and emaciated, turned his broken nose up at the rhubarb tart but seemed to appreciate the tea, despite spilling most of it on the floor.

'She was never on the bus. I lied. And that's the truth.'

A week after Sandra had gone missing in 1994, Tommy had sworn to him personally that he'd seen her on a bus above in Dublin. *'The number 15 to Rathmines and she was sitting upstairs in row 1. And, what's more, I was talking to her, so I was, and she was grand.'* He had told exactly the same story to Garda Healy and to anybody else who'd listen to him and had stuck to his story ever since. Until now.

'He gave me fifty quid, so he did. Coleman.'

Philip slapped him hard on the face. Tommy dropped the cup on the carpet but otherwise accepted his punishment with dignity. Philip hadn't come halfway round the world to give the likes of Tommy absolution.

'Why did you have to lie?'

'I don't know. Same reason you did.'

Philip grabbed the unfortunate's head and slammed it forcefully into the mantelpiece, a marble slab above the fireplace, an action that was long overdue but one he instantly regretted.

'Sorry, Tommy.'

A scattering of framed photographs crashed to the floor, among them one of Philip's favourites. In this particular snapshot of a better time, he, a blonde-y boy, was sitting proudly astraddle his father's shoulders outside Lansdowne Road. He'd been to his first ever rugby match in Dublin, a rare outing with the father he idolized. There was a crush after the game. The crowd was pressed up against the barrier to a railway line and he was frightened, until his father hoisted him up onto his shoulders to safety. The crowd cheered. Like a boy maharajah he waved benignly to his subjects. The photo was taken by a snapper from the *Irish Press* and featured on the front page of the paper, much to his father's embarrassment. Daddy was a taciturn man who had always kept his rugby passion a secret in a town besotted with the more native games.

Blood oozed from Tommy's head but, you could be sure, he was no stranger to blood any more than to pain.

'Everybody was blaming Coleman. And he was going up the walls, so he was, because he didn't do it.'

'Do what?'

'Nothing. He didn't do nothing. Tell them you seen her, he says, and he gave me fifty quid. That's what I'm telling you. What was I supposed to do?'

There had been two or three positive sightings of Sandra in Dublin around that time and one in Belfast. A few weeks later, a postcard arrived at her parents' house from London. From Greenwich, according to the postmark. It was from Sandra, saying she was fine, and not to worry, and that she had a job, and she'd be in touch. It was all very nonchalant, as if it was the most normal thing in the world for a sixteen-year-old girl to run away. Even more curiously to the majority of people who feared the worst, it was verified, the postcard, firstly, by her parents as being the sentiments of Sandra, no doubt about it, and, secondly, by a handwriting expert recruited by the gardaí. The postcards continued to arrive sporadically over the next few months, and then they stopped. By then, the powers-that-be had decided there was nothing to work with. No body, no case and, besides, they were at full stretch fighting a tetchy game of cat-and-mouse along the border with the rebels. Innocent men and women were being maimed and murdered left, right and centre. Armed robbery was rife. It was a desperate time. The army were drafted in to help man the border. It was a war zone. Gardaí themselves were being shot. Wasn't Healy himself shot? In the absence of hard evidence, the investigation ran out of steam.

'Where is she now? Sandra?'

'I don't know. I have to go. They're after me cuz I was hanging around with Dove.'

'Where is she?'

'Dove knows.'

'Dove's dead, Tommy.'

'He *knows*.'

Philip was frustrated. Tommy was bleeding and probably concussed and making less and less sense.

Tommy was adamant about one thing. He said he didn't know whether Sandra was alive or dead and refused to believe that Coleman or any of his old friends had anything to do with her disappearance. Philip could see that he just wanted to clear his conscience of the little he did know and clear the fuck out.

'What happened to Dove?'

'I swear to God. It was an accident!'

The gist of it, if you could rely on Tommy – big if – was this. About a week before he died, Dove had become very agitated and refused to leave his bedroom. Apart from his mother, the only visitor he was in the habit of receiving was Tommy himself, who was at pains to point out to Philip that he was not just Dove's dealer but the only friend he had left in the world.

'Somebody told him something. That's all I know.'

It was while staring down the barrels of the gun – purely to visualize what that looked like – research for a drawing he was doing at the time – that he must have touched the trigger.

'It was just a stupid feckin' accident. I was there. I seen it all.'

With Dove's parents at a novena in the church, Tommy cleaned himself up, or so he said, and slipped out of the Connolly house unnoticed.

Although his grief for his dead friend was not in any way lessened by this news, nor his resolve to find justice diminished, Philip was somewhat placated. If Tommy was telling the truth about the manner of Dove's death, at least that was one thing less he had to worry about. Mind you, Philip almost contorted himself with frustration at the report of Dove's clumsiness, his perennial incompetence. It reminded him of the time they were siphoning petrol from a car when Dove, fag still in hand, set himself on fire. Almost funny. The pit in his stomach deepening, he handed Tommy a tea towel and a twenty euro note.

'I'll run ya up to the doctor.'

'Fuck off! I'm grand. I'm off to Sligo, right. I've an uncle in Enniscrone. Say nothing.'

'Take care of yourself, Tommy.'

Tommy stood there, staring at Philip through haunted eyes. Philip had a good look at Tommy, too. After a minute or two, little was achieved by either of them in deepening their understanding of human nature, and this awkward stand-off came to an end.

'What about me stuff?'

Philip handed Tommy his syringe and his blade but, somewhat haughty, in Tommy's opinion, and no surprises there, Hot-shit Sharkey held onto the silver candlestick and the cheese, probably intending to return the plunder to its lawful owner.

'Look, Tommy. You can stay the night if you like.'

'He said you'd be back.'

'Did he?'

'You'd find out what happened to Sandra. If it was the last thing you ever did. That's what he said. Dove.'

'Did he now?'

'He said, *Philip'll be back*. And he was right. God rest him. You're back.'

'Good luck, Tommy.'

Tommy gathered himself, all four stone of himself, as best as he could and slipped out through the patio door. Philip picked up the photos, raising a concerned eyebrow when he couldn't find the prize-winning press shot of himself up on his father's shoulders. That day, he was master of all he surveyed. That day, he could see into a blissful future. Tommy, his penchant for silver undiminished by the battering he'd just received or the dark forces that had been awoken in recent days, must have pocketed the frame.

Philip, his appetite gone but with much to chew on, took the stairs two steps at a time, driven by an urgent need to reacquaint himself with Dove's Book of Revelations.

What the cat dragged in

Joanne was quite pleased with herself on the short hop to Tullyanna. The car, a second-hand Toyota, had been imported from Japan. All the little signs and instructions were still in Japanese. It was a right tip, butts in the ashtray, coppers in the little compartment for coins instead of silver, empty cigarette packets and plastic Coke bottles in the footwell. There were used tissues in the door pocket and used gum and hair slides and cans of deodorant, too. She often did her make-up in the car as she drove. Not this time, as a milk lorry tried to pass her out – bearing down on her for literally the whole journey – on a notorious single-lane stretch of road. The little shrines composed of flowers and crosses and faded photographs placed at intervals on the roadside testified to the danger. And the carnage.

The reason she was so pleased with herself was because she'd resisted a cigarette for the entire journey, having made a resolution not to smoke or drink for at least a full day. When she put her mind to it, Joanne could do anything. And today, she meant business. In good time for Dove's funeral, she arrived at the roundabout on the outskirts of town. There, she was greeted by a cheerful floral arrangement embedded in the grass.

Wellcome to Tullyanna

While the extra *l* in *Wellcome* was an affront to her sensibilities, she felt sorry for the illiterate horticulturalist involved. She knew only too well how the world worked. One little slip-up and you'd never be allowed to forget it. Mind you, there were worse crimes than misspelling a flowerbed.

She'd be lying if she told you she wasn't nervous. The roundabout was redundant, the industrial park to the left a building site, and the road to the right a dead end, ambitions for the town stalled for the present in the wake of the financial crash. Or, if you were to believe some people, the town was cursed, stuck in a spiritual stasis, destined to remain a purgatory until such time as Sandra was found. She drove straight on, past a huge hoarding featuring Fergal Coleman's huge face, his sincere expression advertising his suitability for public office.

His was an unlikely transformation, in her opinion. A hardman when she'd run into him eight years previously, he was, let's face it, a dealer and a thief, if not an actual out and out terrorist. He would appear to be – to outsiders at least – a bizarre choice of candidate for a party that was dedicated to rooting out corruption. But as well as being intelligent and smooth-talking he was, as they say, very well-got, which stood for a lot in the country. He couldn't do enough for you, even in his wilder days. Back then, he'd sort you out for hash, coke, speed, whatever you needed to get you through the week. Back then, if you wanted a cheap flat-screen TV or a pair of limited edition runners, Fergal Coleman was your man.

Now, he'd help to pull your wayward cow from a ditch with the tow-rope he always kept in the back of the jeep. You'd be surprised at the number of cows that ended up in ditches. Now, by all accounts, he'd sort out your planning permissions, no questions asked, your welfare entitlements and your social housing needs too. He made no secret of his colourful past and *styled* himself convincingly as a reformed character. His conversion was Augustinian. She knew this because she'd heard him with her own ears quoting St Augustine – the original hedonist turned theologian, the man who came up with the concept of Original Sin, no less, and, to cap it all, the patron saint of brewers – on the local radio station.

'*I stole fruit not because I was hungry but because it wasn't permitted. It was foul and I loved it. I loved my own error.*'

No wonder he was so well-got in the sticks. Well, Joanne, open-minded as she was, had her doubts.

The thing is, scrofulous backwaters like Tullyanna had a contrary habit of coughing up unlikely candidates – and *electing* them – out of badness, as much as anything, just to spite the holier-than-thou cosmo crowd above in Dublin. And, generally speaking, she couldn't blame them.

Coleman had a lot to thank Joanne for, in her mind, although he may not have always seen it that way himself. Were it not for her article of yore, he might not now be on the verge of election to the Dáil. He might not be a part of the historic breakthrough for his party in Irish politics that everyone was predicting. He might still be in jail.

It was her findings at the time, her first genuine investigative break-through, that had helped to shift the suspicion that he had something to do with Sandra's disappearance away from him. She, thanks to a source, had managed to place his car at the shooting of an RUC man across the border on the night Sandra went missing. How could he have done anything to a girl in Tullyanna when he was actively involved in a very different mission elsewhere?

That, as it happens, was a botched job that left the man, a Catholic, a leg short and his girlfriend, a Protestant, sightless, the pair of them sitting in his Daihatsu Charade on the north shore of Carlingford Lough planning an uncertain future together when they were attacked. The positive sighting of his car in the immediate vicinity didn't do Coleman's standing within the republican cause any harm at all. But, critically, nobody could put Coleman himself in charge of the gun or, for that matter, at the scene of the atrocity. For his part, he maintained that his car had been *stolen* earlier in the evening by persons unknown. The fact that it turned up a few days later, in one piece, jet-washed and steam-cleaned and parked neatly outside the community centre in town, did little to promote any of the various claims against him.

As for Coleman's drug-peddling, well, Joanne had witnessed this herself. In hindsight, she'd probably been a bit of an innocent, having been quite anti-drugs up to this juncture in her life, even in college, but two things. One, and she'd thought about this a lot, she must have been subconsciously waiting for the right moment, an opportunity to see what all the fuss was about, well away from the garda/big pharma marketing circles in which she moved in Mullinary town. And two, more to the point, she felt she *had* to get close to the Tullyanna *demi-monde*.

Anyway, having gained his confidence, she'd secretly recorded Coleman's underhand transactions. He was, it was true, arrested on her evidence, by Peter Keating, now a detective sergeant in the town and someone with whom she was still fairly tight. Coleman was charged and convicted, but only on the relatively risible count of possession with intent to supply. The amount being paltry, it resulted in a trivial twelve-month sentence. Most of this, by the way, was bowdlerized by *Howarya!*, which rocked her faith for a time in the magazine itself, journalism in general, and integrity as a concept.

Regarding him now up on that poster, more sombre, jowly, almost bald, and minus the smirk and the dimples she'd once found quite charming, it crossed her mind, not for the first time, that he'd played her. And she'd let him. Not just professionally, in terms of misdirection, but personally, in terms of being seduced.

She ran into Coleman after four days mooching around in Tullyanna. Of course, she knew him by sight. Who didn't? Like everyone else at the convent school, she was half-terrified of him. One lunchtime, he'd put a frog down her back. Avoided by a lot of the locals as a muck-raker, even by her old school friends, she welcomed his corny gambit by the pool table in JJ's bar.

'Look what the cat dragged in.'

'Maybe I am the cat.'

'If that's the case, I'll supply the cream.'

'It would have to be full-fat cream, if you have it. Any chance of a few words about Sandra Mohan?'

'Ask me anything, Joanne. I'm an open book, ha. The Book of Kells.'

She laughed loudly. As did his friends. Coleman was always surrounded by people, she noted. A pack. It was so unlike her, on so many levels, to walk into such a disreputable place alone, to trade in saucy small talk with a man like that. It was a leap into the unknown, a leap she felt she had to make if she was going to be the writer, the person she wanted to be.

He had an aura, a natural authority. Although he tucked his T-shirt into his trousers and wore his trousers high-waisted like an old man, and wore a baseball cap back to front, he was one of those rare people who seemed comfortable in his own skin. At the bar, twirling a cigarette through his fingers like a close-up magician, he described Sandra as a friend despite the seven-year age difference between them.

'A delightful wee girl. She couldn't do enough for you. Looked after the dog when I was away.'

Given Sandra's family circumstances, he'd been more than happy to help her in any way he could. *Obliged* to help her, having worked with her father, Tom, in the past.

'He was a troubled man, Tom. And Carmel, too. They were both troubled people.'

Joanne had been acquainted with Carmel through her volunteer work for the St Vincent de Paul. On Tuesday after school, instead of getting the bus home, she'd stay in town. Herself and Hector Burns would go to SuperValu, assigned to buy three or four bags worth of groceries and cigarettes and other household essentials with the VdeP donation money. Then, they'd visit the three or four families who'd requested help. It was awkward, mortifying, in fact, and, looking back, deeply patronizing and judgemental – why not just give them the money? – but that was how she got to know Carmel. On her doorstep. A frail chain-smoker with bruised arms. It was a good few weeks before she twigged that Sandra was her daughter.

'There's no mystery, Joanne. She's in England. Sure, even the dogs in the street know it. And who can blame her?'

They talked for hours that night, herself and Coleman, and not just about Sandra. They played darts. They downed shots of Redbreast whiskey. He wouldn't let her pay. Although a school dropout, and only born in 1970, he talked with confidence and seeming conviction about civil rights in Northern Ireland and further afield. He showed her the tattoo on his back of the Proclamation of the Republic. With a biro, he drew a tattoo on her back. The pack laughed. To this day she didn't know what it was he drew. They danced, wigging out to Primal Scream. He was a dancer. He had moves. At five foot ten inches she was taller than him. It was only when he started to pontificate about the Baader-Meinhof group that she realized he was, in fact, a chancer. (In the dissertation she wrote for her MA, Joanne contended that the Irish paramilitary organizations of the 1970s had more in common with the family of leftist terror outfits that sprang up in Europe at the time than with the family of rebel groups that were celebrated throughout Irish history.) But by then it was too late. She was coked-up for the first and only time in her life and knew with confidence and conviction that she was probably going to sleep with him. The single worst decision of her life. By far. St Augustine would have understood.

Joanne parked on the Main Street. Although the sky was anaemic, a davidsouldenim blue, she took the precaution of putting on sunglasses.

'Well, stranger!'

So much for the sunglasses.

'Geraldine! How are tricks?'

'Grand. Not a bother.'

'Still with Felix?'

'Och. Can't get rid of him. He's like a fecking carbuncle, so he is. What brings you to Tullyanna?'

'Ah, you know, just catching up with old friends. See the sights.'

'Shouldn't take long, says you.'

They smiled awkwardly at each other. Geraldine, still smiling through thinning lips, lowered her voice. 'You're not going to write another article about us, are ya? About how *terrible* we all are?'

'What, you mean, do my job?'

'I suppose. Well, look. A lot of people are still very sore. Just throwing it out there, ha? Be careful, is all I'm saying.'

'Thanks for the advice, Geraldine,' Joanne said, coolly.

'You're welcome. Making a show of us all, ha. A laughing stock.'

'I'm sorry you see it that way . . .'

'It was *low*, Joanne, fierce low altogether.'

'I'll tell you what's embarrassing, Geraldine. *Losing* somebody, a human being, and doing *nothing* about it. That's *low*. Nice to see you. And, here, say hi to the girls.'

More angry than shook, and with a few minutes to spare before the service, she took refuge from her old school friend in the shopping centre. Dermot Connolly's mural looked tired now, the colours drained of their vibrancy. She noted his satirical take on the floral arrangement outside the town.

Welllllcome to 53 N 6832 6 W 5336

A total of five zany *l*'s and GPS coordinates instead of the town name. What an odd man.

After a coffee – grey and barely drinkable, much to her annoyance, coffee being her chief pleasure now that she was newly abstemious – she walked towards the church with the intention of confronting Coleman. How can coffee be grey? It was only a couple of hundred yards to the church. The reformed Councillor Fergal Coleman looked down magnanimously from every pole, the posters of his rival candidates strewn on the footpath beneath her feet.

The elixir of Lethe

Kevin was licking a choc ice outside Kennedy's newsagent en route to Philip Sharkey's house when his old friend Doctor Collins pulled his car over and rolled down the window.

'Jump in, Kevin.'

'Doc!'

'How are things?'

'Couldn't be better, Doc. Where are we going?'

'Murder!'

Kevin didn't need a second invitation. They took a significant short cut to the scene of the crime, criss-crossing the border on two occasions, an option not open to the gardaí themselves who were a) forced to respect jurisdictional limits and b) right eejits. The Doc, an old friend of Kevin, was no slouch either in negotiating the trusty Saab over what was a seriously bumpy road. Where were the much-vaunted EU structural funds when you needed them? The ex-detective enjoyed the banter and the buffeting inside the car, an eight-mile journey that catapulted him back to a more fulfilling time in his life, when hurtling to and from crime scenes was part of the daily routine. He was grateful that the Doc, his occasional bridge partner, medic of choice and chief ally in fighting lost causes, had the decency to stop for him and he in haste to such an emergency.

'Fuck them, Kevin. It's their loss.'

'Ah now.'

'You're as good as ten of them . . . even with a screw loose.'

He burst out laughing at his own quip, the doctor, a great man for the slagging, his big beardy folksinger head bouncing off the ceiling of the car. There *was* a screw loose, it was true. Kevin couldn't deny it. There had been a worrying parallel between what was going on inside his head and his outward behaviour, and why wouldn't there be? He had earned quite a reputation for talking to himself in public spaces. He knew that. It didn't bother him anymore. The more he thought about it, the more normal it seemed to be, the whole talking-to-yourself thing. How else would you know what you were thinking? What was it the Austrian fella said? '*I prefer monologues when I'm in company and dialogues when I'm alone*' or words to that effect. A loose screw. One time, when was it?, he was staring out the back window of the house with a mug of milky Nescafé in his hand, admiring his son, Shane, tumbling away on the trampoline, a madman for the trampoline, and wasn't there a screw loose on the contraption, and the bouncing mat gave way, and didn't poor Shane plunge headfirst to the ground and break his collarbone – actually, it was a spring that came loose, now that he thought about it, a loose spring, not a loose screw.

The Doc's reckless driving was in vain for the guards arrived before them and were already in the process of cordoning off the scene. The scene was a drainage ditch at the side of the Annacorry Road, a straight single-lane road, about a mile-and-a-half from Derrykeen itself, flanked by fields high with unsaved hay.

'Look,' says the Doc, trying to humour Kevin, 'the pigs are at the trough.'

From his position behind the garda tape, roughly a hundred yards away, Kevin watched the doctor, a burly man, big hole in his jumper, as he was greeted by Detective Sergeant Peter Keating, 'Bad News Keating', as he was known, and the Doc approached the body, and Kevin wished he was walking between them.

Bad News had barely acknowledged him, as if he was just some idle gawker. As if they'd never been friends, ever since training college. As if they'd never been flatmates when they first set foot in the town. As if they'd never been rivals, in everything from table-tennis to love. It was Keating who started the ball rolling, the bell tolling for Kevin when he reported him to the chief super. He claimed that he felt *unsafe* with Kevin, that he felt his life was in danger, no less, as a result of his colleague's increasingly erratic behaviour. Keating, the turncoat who owed his life to Kevin. Keating loved all this, the hooha of it all, flares flapping in the breeze, bossing uniforms around, pointing for the sake of pointing. He didn't have a clue.

Knowing the Doc would be busy for a while, Kevin occupied himself by going for a walk. He went in the opposite direction, back towards town, inspecting, out of habit, the ditch, a hollow about two feet deep that fell away from the road. It contained maybe an inch or two of sludgy water. The flies were bothering him. The eyes were itchy. Spotting some blackberries, he threw one foot over the gully, steadied himself, now astride the stream, uncomfortably, and reached for a clump of the mushy, over-ripe fruit. A few feet away, a huge tractor lurched out through a gap in the hedge, driven by a slight boy of no more than twelve, incongruously wearing a New York Knicks basketball top. The boy shouted from the cab.

'Well.'

'Well, yourself.'

'There's a coat in the shed beyont.'

'Right.'

'It's not mine. Or me father's.'

'Oh.'

'Just, you know.'

'Right so. Thanks.'

'Good luck.'

'Good luck yourself.'

Civic duty done, the young fella roared off in his mighty machine.

Kevin wiped his hands on his trousers and, using an invisible rope, pulled himself back onto the road. He glanced over his shoulder, back towards the crime scene, now about three hundred yards away. No sign of it wrapping up for a while. He made a bold decision. His face smeared with the inky fruit, he stepped into the farmyard and marched straight over to the aforementioned shed. The sliding door was open and he slipped in.

To his surprise, it was spotless, swept clean, by the looks of it, to accommodate, weather permitting, an imminent hay bonanza. It was a fair few degrees colder inside the hangar than outside. And it smelled mouldy, mushroomy, like the cork from a corked bottle of wine. No stranger to hay-sheds, Kevin was afraid of ticks and buttoned up his jacket accordingly. He had a good nosey around the premises, lasered by sunbeams armed to the hilt with dust motes. It reminded him of the time he and Keating broke up a dog fight ten, fifteen years ago. It could have been the same shed. It reminded him of countless sheds in which he'd searched for Sandra.

Sure enough, there was a coat, a filthy anorak, hanging on a hook near the door. Kevin, feeling something resembling a thrill, although it was so long since his last thrill he couldn't be sure, searched the pockets of the coat. He found a used syringe, a Stanley knife and a photograph in a silver frame. It was a black-and-white picture of a boy on a man's shoulders on the way to or from a match. The man he did not recognize but the boy, watchful and intense, looked vaguely familiar. Reflexively he put the photo in the inside pocket of his jacket. He replaced the other items in the pocket of the coat. Suddenly the shed darkened as the door rolled to a resounding close. Clang! Disorientated momentarily and, truth be told, slightly afraid, Kevin felt his way along the wall towards the exit. To his relief the door opened easily and he made his way back towards the cordon, puzzled by what he had found and what connection, if any, it might have to the grim discovery down the road.

By now a small crowd had gathered.

'Bad news, I'm afraid. Tommy Courtney. Savage altogether.'

Detective Keating, removing a pair of rubber gloves, addressed the gathering, completely ignoring Kevin, who was shocked and saddened by his erstwhile colleague's revelation. Poor Tommy. He didn't like the relish with which Keating delivered the news, or the casual way he bandied about the dead man's name before the next-of-kin could have possibly been informed. Highly unprofessional in his opinion, but he kept his thoughts to himself, not wanting to give Bad News any satisfaction. A few of the onlookers blessed themselves. A few didn't. He didn't mention the shed or the coat to the serving detective. Cursing his own declining powers of deduction, he knew he should have recognized it as Tommy's, having seen him occupying it at the wake only the night before.

The gardaí would, in a matter of hours, widen the search and find the garment. They would assume, as he did now, that either Tommy had been sheltering in the shed or had been taken there by his killer or killers. Or his coat had been left there as a red herring. Giving Bad News the side eye, Kevin, hand in pocket, fondled the photo like a blind man using braille, trying to divine the identity of the boy. One thing was for sure, it definitely wasn't Tommy. In this world, the likes of Tommy Courtney never had any shoulders to sit on.

* * *

Sheila was reading a book in the so-called sunroom when Kevin returned to the house for his lunch, and he on somewhat of a high after the morbid events of the morning. He was surprised on a number of counts. First of all, Sheila was up. She was wearing a brand-new leisure suit he'd never seen before. It was in a style (shiny, possibly flammable) and colour (pinky-purple) that was unusual for her, the kind of thing a fitness instructor might wear on day-time television.

Furthermore, if he wasn't mistaken, there was a perkiness about her. Ciara's going away seemed, against the odds, to be giving her a new lease of life. The absence of bickering, he supposed, or of worry. Out of sight, out of mind. She was reading *The Woman in White*, a book he had tried to impress upon her on numerous occasions to no previous avail. And she was *lounging*, no less, feet tucked up under her backside.

The biggest surprise of all was that the sun itself was actually shining, streaming through the glass roof, warming the room and lighting, in the most flattering way, his lovely, clinically depressed wife. He loved his Sheila. They'd had their ups and downs, but they had always been compatible, in every way, right down to their respective late-onset ailments.

While he was making cheese and pickle sandwiches, heavy on the pickle, he relayed to her, with no embellishment, the doctor's news.

'Tommy drowned, love.'

Of course, the Doc wasn't a pathologist, nor was he tasked with ascertaining the exact cause of death. In fact, his only duty on the day was to say whether the man was alive or dead. And if, perchance, he was still alive, it was in his remit to provide the necessary medical attention until more specialized services arrived. That said, he was an experienced man, with a lively imagination, and, in his opinion, the man had drowned.

'Where?' asked Sheila.

'Annacorry Road,' said Kevin. '*In a shallow rivulet of unsanitary water*,' he added, quoting the Doc, an educated man and amateur poet and all too prone to flights of fancy.

Sheila didn't have much time for the Doc.

'Why there? Odd place to drown a man.'

'He was dumped there to die, Sheila. After a ferocious hiding elsewhere.'

'He was beaten?'

'Yeah, badly. As the Doc put it to me, *before Death took pity on him, before He kindly forced the unfortunate addict to imbibe the elixir of Lethe.*'

'Ponce.'

'Harsh. He's alright.'

'A man is dead and he's quoting . . . Dante or someone.'

'I honestly think he made it up himself.'

Tommy had been beaten and kicked, all over his head and body, with fists and boots.

'And a blunt object or objects, such as a golf club or tyre iron, or perhaps a poker,' Kevin speculated, acting out the various scenarios.

A cursory examination indicated that most of the victim's limbs had been broken, as well as many of his ribs, not to mention his skull, clavicle and pelvis.

'His head was like a beetroot, according to the Doc, purple, all the features erased, pounded into a mush, eyes smashed into the inside of his skull.'

Kevin knew Sheila would be annoyed if he left out any of the detail, no matter how shocking it was.

'How many people involved?' she asked, imagining the multiple injuries. 'In the attack?'

'Good question, love. Looks like there was a number of assailants, possibly as many as ten.'

'He tends to exaggerate, the Doc.'

'He does, but he said *at least* ten, given the sheer variety of weapons used and the type of wounds inflicted. The depths and so on. You'd know the terminology.'

Kevin teleported himself back to the shed, noting how clean it was, trying to see what Tommy saw, *who* Tommy saw before the blows rained down.

Bad News had only guessed the bloody mess was Tommy because of the distinctive earlobes, stretched, as they were, to encompass his unusual ear jewellery – discs of bog oak the size of old two-pence pieces.

'It's more than a coincidence, Kevin. First Dove, now Tommy.'

Kevin was heartened to hear Sheila taking such an interest. 'You're right, it's a *development*.'

It was a development, as tragic as it was inevitable, and the impetus Kevin had been waiting for to reopen the case – yet again – and, although he mightn't like to admit it, to rejuvenate himself. But would Tommy's slaying get the attention it deserved? Kevin wasn't so sure. Would the police properly investigate it in the febrile political climate? Would a junkie's death in a ditch even warrant a mention in the national press?

Sheila seemed, more so than usual, interested in his report. Well, she asked him questions. Questions about the incident itself and not like *what do you think you're playing at?* or *who do you think you are?* for a change. Kevin looked around the room for some wood to touch. The brilliant thing about the real, whole-of-her-health Sheila was that she never let him off the hook. Challenged by her endless questions, he had to explain and justify every thought, every opinion, every utterance. It was exhausting, sure, but, Jaze, he'd sorely missed it. The grilling. It kept him honest. No airs. She thanked him for the sandwich by way of a kiss on the forehead. He took his tablets and washed his plate and cup and left them draining beside the sink. And while she, after taking her tablets, attended to the baby, who'd just woken up, he went into his office and burned a CD, making a compilation of tracks he thought his old protégé Philip Sharkey might enjoy.

Deep Heat

Philip was in his bedroom, *Brouhaha* in hand, and he having been increasingly drawn into Dove's dystopian world, when Healy rang the doorbell. There was one thing he'd gleaned from his first pass. It was a subplot that left him discombobulated and rather sad. It only turned out that the main character – Brouhaha himself – had been betrayed by his sidekick and best friend in the whole pseudo-Celtic Pantheon, namely Dearg Doom. No prizes for guessing which real person Dearg Doom was based on. Philip winced. The skin in his cheekbones tightened. His stomach shrank. He deserved that. His shame, the secret shame that he lived with, was now immortalized in ink. In art. The book itself deserved a wider circulation.

The gist. The Ramen were consolidating their hold on the Plains, exacting loyalty and tribute from the hard-pressed people in the form of boars' teeth and the dried leaves of the hazel tree – a *fiat* currency as well as a cure for the haemorrhoids. It's exactly what Philip would have expected of the Ramen. When Brouhaha went to their rescue – as was his wont – he was, to his consternation, shunned. For he had been discredited by his erstwhile allies, a crowd called the Committee, one of whom looked very like the local mayor, Dinky Murtagh, depicted as a thief and a murderer. The Committee, for the record, wore animal furs and lived in a well-fortified compound around the ruins of the Tullyanna courthouse and, conveniently, near a well, the only source of clean water on the Plains.

As if being ostracized and hated by the People wasn't bad enough, there was a rumour doing the rounds that a bee had been spotted in the area, not so much spotted as *heard*. This was no ordinary bee, not that there were many of them left in the wild. This, the unmistakable buzz a giveaway, was the fairly big yellow-eyed bee (*megachile aurantius*), which was the only bee known to collect the nectar of the Middlemist Blue, the only bee, it should be said, that could actually withstand the toxic shock of the nectar of the Middlemist Blue. If the bee was in the area – Brouhaha put two and two together – there was a chance the flower itself, the one he sought, day and night, and fought for with all his heart and soul, might not be too far away after all.

But, and Philip, getting a handle on the method in Dove's madness, could see it coming, Dearg Doom, on his way back from a meeting with the Committee, saw the bee. Without telling Brouhaha – like, he could have blown his horn but *chose* not to – he followed the bee back to its hive. The hive was well-concealed in a culvert under a bridge – the bridge at Kilbride, to be precise, under which Dove and Philip had shared their first ever cigarette, a damp Consulate stolen from Dove's mother's bag. Dearg Doom, knowing it was wrong, reached into the hive and, eyes swirling in a manic, bewitched fashion, pulled out a honeycomb and ate it. Like a demented hyena, he gorged orgasmically on the honey, his face and hands sticky with the sweeter than sweet syrup of the Gods.

If the honey bestowed powers – wisdom, knowledge, the whereabouts of the Middlemist Blue – Dearg Doom didn't have time to find out. For he was suddenly ambushed by a number of screeching Ramen. One of them, armed with a flamethrower, incinerated the fuck out of the hive and all life and nourishment within. While Dearg Doom fought off his attackers with his sword, he couldn't escape the wrath of an incensed and broken-hearted Brouhaha. Although he spared his life, Dearg Doom was banished, shame-faced, from the Plains. Brouhaha retreated to his oak tree, which he near flooded with his tears.

Was that it? Was that all Dove wanted to tell him? That he was no mug. Or was there more?

Downstairs in the hall, Mrs Sharkey complimented Healy on his nice suit.

'I don't know about that,' Healy replied, coyly, before turning serious and lowering his voice for fear the devil would overhear him, ever alert to news of a fresh soul going a-begging. 'Did you hear about poor Tommy Courtney?'

He figured the whole world would know by now, but not, it seemed, Mrs Sharkey, and her not plugged in to the Tullyanna grapevine.

'Dead,' says he.

'No,' says she, blessing herself. 'Poor Tommy, and he was only here last night.'

'Sorry?'

'Tommy Courtney? He was here last night. Looked wretched, the poor creature.'

The shocking idea that Philip could have hurt Tommy trespassed Kevin's mind for a moment. If it was true, he would have to give up, not just cold case reopening and crime detecting generally, but life itself. His philosophy had always been simple, and it based on two premises. One, people were essentially good. And, two, a person, an individual such as he, or the likes of Philip, could make a difference, albeit marginal, to world happiness. If you didn't believe that, what was the point? If Philip wasn't a good lad, who the hell was? Had he wasted his life trying to make a difference to young men's lives, his philosophy now laid bare as pants? He spotted bloodstains on the mantelpiece.

Philip rounded the corner, wearing what looked like a pair of dungarees.

'Tommy's dead, Philip.'

Kevin watched as Philip slowly took a cigarette from a packet that was in the front pouch of his dungarees (the choice of garment bold, to say the least) and stuck it in his mouth, leaving it unlighted.

'I'll make the tea,' says Philip's mother, her face visibly blanching as she headed for the safety of the kitchen.

Whatever Philip was feeling, he kept it to himself. Kevin, at Philip's invitation, sat down. They looked at each other, nodding, nodding, and rocking too in Kevin's case, an awful man for the rocking lately. Always moving but going nowhere. Whatever about rocking, you couldn't do enough nodding in situations like these. It didn't help matters much, but it didn't do any harm either.

Studying him, Kevin was disarmed by the cool demeanour (as well as the acres of unfetching denim he sported, as if daring people not to like him) on the reception of such tragic news from the trenches. He wasn't to know of the chill wind blowing up and down Philip's spine or the tears flowing down the insides of his eyes.

His eyes wandering back to the mantelpiece, Kevin noticed the photographs and, putting two and two together like a real detective, he fished the photo from his pocket and handed it to his host. 'You haven't changed a bit.'

'Older and wiser, Mr Healy.'

'He was pulverized. Tommy. Hah? Pummelled. Face like a beetroot, they say. What can you tell me?'

'No blindfold this time?'

Kevin shook his head, smiling ruefully, not really in the mood for repartee. 'He was here? Tommy?' Kevin nodded towards the blood-stain. Philip nodded in return.

He had changed, and no mistake. There was a coldness to him that waylaid Kevin, a hardness that wouldn't have gone amiss in the county final against Cooksboro in the summer of 1993, when Kevin's purist, skill-based approach to football was exposed as jelly-bellied. That day, Philip, who'd played his heart out, who'd twisted and turned like a dervish, was, at the death, an inconsolable heap. Kevin had wrapped his arm around him, the smell of Deep Heat in the air, in the truck container that doubled as a changing room. They were still in a huddle an hour after everyone else had gone, the pair of them making plans for the following year. There and then they pledged to finish the job, the unfinished business of bringing home the cup, a promise that, due to unforeseen circum-stances – namely the disappearance and, let's face it, the likely murder of a young girl followed by the elopement, forced or other-wise, shortly thereafter of the team's star player –remained unfulfilled. They had had something. A what? A bond. Surely Philip remem-bered that?

'Look, we both want the same thing, me and you. It's high time you came clean. Thanks, Mrs Sharkey.'

Philip's mother placed a pot of tea and a rhubarb tart in front of him and, very alarmed, quickly left the room.

A geyser unplugged

Although he had a soft spot for Healy, Philip considered him to be, based on the two life-defining experiences they had shared to date, ineffectual. He was too nice to be a football coach, or indeed a cop. But his timing was good. He was sitting there right in front of him, all innocence and ears, and Philip had plenty to say. Plenty he needed to get off his chest.

'I was with Sandra.'

That was news to Healy. And he couldn't hide his disappointment, emitting the tiniest of yowls.

One line of enquiry the guards – not Healy, in fairness – followed at the beginning of the investigation back in 1994 was that Philip had been in a relationship with Sandra. And that he had personally facilitated Sandra's passage to Liverpool in order for her to procure an abortion. That was a very popular rumour at the time, placing Philip well above the likes of Charles Manson and Peter Sutcliffe in local hate-figure iconography. There were many people in the town – Dove's father, Gerry Senior, at the vanguard of this cohort – who far *preferred* the idea that the unfortunate girl might have been raped and strangled and dumped in a quarry than the idea she might have gone to Liverpool to terminate a pregnancy. At least she'd be in heaven now.

'It wasn't serious. Not even a fling. But Dove found out.'

'Right.'

'Your old mate, Keating, found out. He was always hassling me.'

News to Kevin, Boy George! But knowing Keating – ambitious and smart-assed – he would have mined that salacious detail for all it was worth.

'He only knew the half of it.'

Philip didn't know how to put it. In technical, teenage terms, it was only a hand-job, conducted strictly within the confines of his tight jeans, a hand-job and a quick reciprocal finger-of-fudge, a sticky exchange of favours he instantly regretted. Maybe she did too.

'There's no need to spell it out,' Healy whispered, the wind gone from his sails.

'I knew it was wrong. But . . .'

What he wanted to say but didn't think he could convey convincingly – because he didn't know if it was absolutely true – was that he loved Sandra. And that when the opportunity arose to be with her – in any way, but especially alone – he took it, without thinking of her state of mind at the time, or the effect such a thing would have on Dove, or, indeed, would have on Deirdre, his own girlfriend at the time. In hindsight, it seemed hideous, so much worse than it was – so opportunistic, so grotty – because of course she was never seen again. But at the time it seemed natural, inevitable, mutually satisfying and casually experimental in the normal, time-honoured, small-town way of things. He was hardly going to tell Healy about the insane pleasure he'd experienced – he couldn't speak for Sandra – like no other before or since, the rapture, the closeness, the awakening. He especially liked Sandra in those rare moments when they were alone together; when she was quiet and deep in thought because even though her thoughts weren't often shared out loud, he felt, rightly or wrongly, as a quiet man himself, invariably deep in thought, that they had an affinity, an understanding beyond the verbal. He may have been mistaken.

'She was Dove's girlfriend, no?'

'Nominally,' he snapped. 'It wasn't serious.'

She and Dove went to the cinema together. They held hands on walks. He hung out in her bedroom. They kissed. But, Philip had convinced himself, it wasn't serious.

Philip's head throbbed with remorse and – the old reliable – shame, now as it did then. In the sober light of day – and 1994 had been an unusually bright, hot summer – he had deliberated on the effect news of such treachery would have on his best friend.

'I decided not to tell him.'

'For the love of God, why?'

'I don't know. He annoyed me. The way only best friends do.'

Maybe Dove talked too much. He never knew when to shut his mouth. Or maybe he went overboard with some tedious Dove-like behaviour, pretending to be disabled for a cheap laugh, but that was no excuse. He knew that. He also knew that Dove was bound to find out. In a town like Tullyanna, that was a given. And in due course he did find out, told in confidence by blabbermouth Keating, who was clearly trying to sow division between them.

More unforgivable than his disloyalty to Dove – and to Deirdre – and him the worse for wear that night, was his failure to disclose to anyone when and where he last saw Sandra.

'It's called perverting the course of justice. You know that?'

Philip acknowledged the charge. To protect his own reputation, he had withheld damning evidence. Merely to conceal a tryst with his best friend's girl. At that divulgence, Healy sucked air in through his teeth, setting off the old neuralgia. This was serious.

'Why didn't you tell me?'

No answer. Not even a shrug. In fairness, there wasn't an answer to everything. Some things were too profound or too trivial to be expressed in mere words. *Ineffable*, as the Doc would have it.

'Did you ever hear tell of Johan Cruyff?'

'I heard of him. The manager.'

'The player. Before your time. The Cruyff turn, ha! Imagine having a turn called after you.'

'What are you on about?'

'I don't know.'

There was some point he wanted to make. But it was gone. Must be the medication. More silence. Then, fortuitously, the obvious question popped into his head 'Where? Where did this . . . encounter . . . take place?'

Philip didn't answer. Not immediately. Rather, he stared at Healy for a while, one hand on his stomach, the other rubbing his face. He then walked over to the table in the corner of the room, where some chess pieces were laid out on sheets of newspaper along with some paints and some glue. The pieces, many of them headless, belonged to a chess set with an American Civil War theme. He lit a cigarette, took a long drag and placed it in an ashtray. Then he proceeded calmly to glue the head of a pawn, a confederate infantryman, onto its body.

That explains the dungarees, thought Healy, with some relief.

Philip pointed at the chess pieces. 'Before you say anything, there's no significance to this. You needn't fucking . . . read anything . . . my mother asked me to fix them, so I'm fixing them. It was in Coleman's house.'

'What?'

'I met her in Coleman's.'

Healy lost his bearings for a moment. That night, 18 June 1994, Philip, in his own words, abandoned Dove outside the Garda station at whatever time it was in the morning. Behind him, his friend railed against the world, wailing, in concert with the birds squabbling and shrieking over the scraps of food on the ground beside the chip van.

'What the fuck were seagulls doing in Tullyanna, ha, a good fifteen miles from the sea? I made my way to Coleman's house alone.'

It was a council house in Fox's Demesne.

'I was looking for hash. Needed to come down.'

He'd been on a heady midsummer high.

'Coleman himself wasn't there. Sheriff was. Conked out on a couch.'

Stephen Sheriff, known to all as Omar, in honour of your man from *Dr Zhivago*. Omar Sheriff had been left in charge. Needless to say, being clean-shaven, weak-chested and deathly pale, Sheriff bore no resemblance to the debonair, backgammon-playing international playboy.

'It was Sandra opened the door.'

Listening to St Etienne, they shared a joint. 'Nothing can stop us.'

'I kept asking her what was wrong?'

And she'd smile, the mascara smeared, the little blue flower above her eye smudged, and he knew she was having deeper thoughts than he was. At some point, she put her hand down his trousers and he put his hand up her skirt. Curiosity. Boredom. High-jinks. A dream come true. A meeting of minds, a melding of souls. Call it what you will. Ecstasy. Transgression. Mortal dread. Human nature. And shortly after that, the memory indelible, and his heart racing faster than ever, he went home.

More air. More severe toothache. The beginnings of a migraine.

'You're saying Sandra was inside Coleman's house?'

'I am. She was.'

'This. This changes everything.'

Philip glued the head of the white king, Lincoln himself in his stovepipe hat, onto his body, keeping it in place with an elastic band.

Thus unburdened, Philip didn't feel any better. In fact, he felt worse. So much for the widespread faith in the therapeutic power of 'sharing'. There was a good reason Freud said the Irish can't be psychoanalysed, if, in fact, he said it at all. Wasn't it the last great frontier of medical science – the frozen wastes of the Irish mind? It's not that the Irish don't have problems. They do. And they're deep-rooted problems. They predate centuries of imperial oppression and Catholic occupation of the mind and the various invasions, Anglo-Norman and Viking, and all the interminable humiliations and disenfranchisements. Something terrible must have happened in ancient Celtic times and we never got over it. You'd have to feel sorry for psychotherapists in this country, Healy thought Philip was thinking. It must be fierce frustrating when the answer to every question is 'grand'.

How was your relationship with your father?

Grand.

Right. And how do you feel about being abandoned as a child?

Grand. Not a bother. Sure, you know yourself.

An expedition of neurologists and psychiatrists, in search of glory, could do worse than try to frack that impenetrable tundra.

Apart from rendering himself something of a disloyal liar, Philip hadn't done anything *wrong*. He was keen to impress this claim upon Kevin. He hadn't harmed Sandra. If anything, he had made her happy during her last hours on Earth.

Healy shuddered.

'You know what I mean, Healy. I really cared about Sandra.'

Healy didn't know what to think. If only Philip had told the guards at the time that Sandra had been in Coleman's house, Dove might still be alive. Tommy might still be alive. Sandra herself might still be alive. But Philip was adamant that his sins of omission and emission didn't make that much difference to the case itself. What was the big deal whether Sandra was last seen at 9.00 p.m. getting into Coleman's car or at six in the morning in Coleman's house? It's what happened afterwards that mattered, no?

If Kevin was sceptical, he didn't show it, and he let the man talk.

'What happened after that had nothing to do with me,' Philip maintained.

It should have been obvious that Coleman was the primary person of interest. The guards knew that everyone was afraid of him. Yet the guards, with the exception, in fairness, of the lugubrious character currently in his face, chose not to pursue that avenue with any great vigour.

'You can trust me. I'm not a guard anymore.'

By now, the whole tart was gone, some of it still churning around in Healy's mouth. The man was insatiable, like a labrador. Philip found some ginger snaps in a tin to keep the ex-guard going as he digested the latest information.

In truth, Kevin was disappointed to have his impression of Philip so sharply corrected. Another certainty dashed. You'd think you'd get used to people letting you down. But, not a man to give up easily, he took encouragement from the lad's late-in-the-day candour, his self-laceration.

'If I wanted you to understand, I would have explained it better.'

'What?'

'Cruyff. It's what he said to a journalist once.'

'Right.'

'I don't think it's that relevant after all. Go on.'

Kevin was hurt, in retrospect, deeply hurt, that none of them – his old colleague, Keating, or any of the suspects, Omar Sheriff, Dove or

Philip himself – had seen fit to tell him at the time about Philip's shenanigans with Sandra, not to mention the sighting of her in Coleman's house *after* she was reported missing by Dove. His ego somewhat bruised, he, who prided himself on knowing everything there was to know about the case, realized he knew practically nothing.

And Philip wasn't quite finished yet, by the looks of things, and him chewing the lip and cleaning his teeth with his tongue, limbering up the various muscles of the face for yet more guff. Inspired, perhaps, by Healy's description of Tommy's battered body, and the image of Dove's hideous visage so fresh in his mind, and Healy's imploring face so close to his own, and his own great need to finally, *finally*, says you, unbottle his thirteen-year-old memories, there was no stopping him.

The chess set was on the mend. He'd already described the *mano a mano* with Sandra, their illicit liaison chaperoned by a sleeping Sheriff. That weight already off his shoulders, Philip sat down beside Healy, looking at the photo of himself and his dad, and, prompted by a few of Healy's brain-dead questions, continued his sorry narrative, a geyser unplugged, years of pent-up pain gushing forth.

No pine cones left to kick

'Why didn't you tell the guards? Why did you leave the country?'

Although she was only sixteen years old when she went missing, it was days, weeks before most people began to take Sandra's disappearance seriously.

'No disrespect, but her parents were not the most reliable people in the town.'

To put it bluntly, they were fond of the drink and were either ignorant of or blithe to the regular absences of their somewhat secretive daughter. They were unconcerned when she didn't show up at home on the Sunday morning.

'It wouldn't have been the first Sunday morning she didn't come home.'

If the family were blasé, Philip himself wasn't. He was nervous, thinking she'd run away because of him. Maybe she felt guilty and wanted to avoid Dove? Isn't that how the solipsistic mind of a teenage boy works?

On the Monday, Dove, angry with her, asked Philip to help him find her. To Philip's consternation, he was displaying signs of jealousy, convinced she'd spent the night with someone else. He wanted his denim jacket back and he wanted to break it off once and for all. So, Dove and Philip, still tired and dehydrated, went looking for the girl. First, they called on Sandra's house. There was no reply, the parents catatonic. Then, they called on Coleman. He, bare-chested, was power-hosing the backyard. Another of Coleman's men, Lorcan Lonergan, was busy dismantling a wooden shed.

'Woodworm,' says he.

Coleman turned the hose on the boys and sprayed them for the craic.

'Youse need to cool down. Isn't that right, Lorcan?'

Lonergan chuckled.

Coleman assured them that Sandra wasn't there. Furthermore, he insisted, she hadn't been there for a good few days now, daring Philip to contradict him in front of Dove.

'By the way, thanks for giving the pigs the bum steer. I appreciate it. I was somewhere I wasn't supposed to be.'

He winked a lascivious wink.

'Keep the pigs on their toes, eh, Lorcan?'

'That's right, Fergal.'

He handed Philip and Dove a ten-pound note each, a tidy sum they pocketed with some reluctance.

'Cheer up, girls, that'll keep yiz in lollipops. If I see Sandra, I'll tell her you were asking for her.'

Philip explained to Healy that Coleman, via O'Dowd, had told them to say, if anyone asked, that they'd seen him on the road to Shadows that Saturday. Yes, he knew it was wrong. He even knew it was wrong back then. But it was before they knew anything had happened to Sandra.

Retreating from the house, Coleman's dog, Fuck, snarled at them.

'Shut up, Fuck!'

The boys spotted Sandra's beret on the table, the beret she'd been modelling cockeyed on Saturday night. Dove pointed this out to Coleman, whose face darkened a gnat's.

'So what, my friend? She's loads of them hats.'

'As far as I know,' Dove said, feeling particularly brave, 'she's only got the one.'

'Do you hear this?' says Coleman to his laconic batman before reeling on the Dove.

'I should know. I bought them for her. Three for the price of two in Belfast.'

'A bargain,' chips in Lonergan.

'A bargain is right. She left it here Tuesday, didn't she, Lorcan? Don't you worry about Sandra. Sandra is well able to look after herself.'

With that, he clicked his fingers. 'Fuck! Here, boy.'

Fuck was an Alsatian, not to be messed with, as Philip had learned to his cost when he offered him a bottle of beer, at one of Coleman's parties, and the animal, unimpressed and presumably teetotal, took a lump out of his back.

'Here, Fuck. Cheltenham Gold Cup!'

With that command, the dog ran the length of the house and hurdled a couch, the lads scrambling through the front door in the nick of time, departing to the sound of a barking dog as well as the hearty laughter of the men.

* * *

Was he always a fool, Healy asked himself? Not only was he sitting here, the hang-dog face being slapped repeatedly with new revelations, but he had to accept that he'd been hoodwinked all along by his star witnesses. And, more fundamentally, it was a glaring fact that he was forced to face for the first time in his life. He didn't know people at all. Someone as dull and gullible as him was never cut out to be a policeman. He should have been a writer.

So, if Philip was *now* telling the truth, the boys *didn't* meet Coleman on the road. And Coleman *didn't* give Sandra a lift to Shadows, although he paid Dove and Philip to tell the guards that he *did* give her a lift. Presumably this was to give him an alibi for whatever else he was up to that night. But Sandra *was* in his house *after* Shadows. Kevin's mind was addled. His blood was saturated with sugar. He was dizzy, at the height of the afternoon. He was unable to hold the story together, the various filaments floating from his grasp. But Philip had a lovely voice, a sort of alto-baritone-bass, to which Kevin surrendered.

* * *

All day they continued to search for her. Philip went along to keep Dove sweet but, he stressed to Healy, he wasn't particularly concerned about her welfare at this stage. They put out the APB amongst their friends, some of whom gave Philip the cold shoulder, miffed that he had missed a crucial match on the Sunday and it the height of the season. Kevin remembered all too well the shame of being beaten by Drumahair. Philip was sorry he'd missed it, too, the physicality of it all, if nothing else, the collisions, the oblivion you could find in some outer reach of the county. Being knocked out unconscious would have been a bonus, a common enough occurrence, too, the opposition more often than not being lunks fed on a diet of Angel Dust, huge farmers' sons who only answered to whistles.

At about seven o'clock that evening, the adventure now becoming tiresome and the tummies rumbling, Philip and Dove stopped for chips. In they went to the Crossroads café, where it would not have been unusual to find Sandra and her the centre of attention.

'You had all types in the Crossroads. But she gave as good as she got. Took no shit.'

She was not there. Charlie O'Dowd was there. He thought he'd seen her getting on the bus to Dublin, but he couldn't be sure.

The light faded. The town itself, embarrassed, perhaps, by the excesses of the weekend, blushed as the sun went down. Dove, by now very downcast, was drawn like a dog towards old haunts. He dragged Philip down the path through the convent land, where he and Sandra often canoodled, another fruitless detour, the pine wood deserted of human life. Dove became even more gloomy, going the full Joy Division, and started crying again. Philip, by contrast, was getting bored and giddy at this stage. There were no pine cones left to kick. He remembered bellowing at the swans in the convent lake.

'Dove was really sad,' Philip felt compelled to tell Healy. 'The swans, he feared, had let themselves go.'

They were not bedecked in their usual pristine white. This troubled Dove for some reason. It was a portent of some sort.

'Muted swans, he called them, bedecked in a slovenly grey.'

Coleman's behaviour, although obviously, in hindsight, highly suspicious, hadn't rung any alarm bells with Philip. Why should it have? Power-hosing was hardly a crime. The thing about Coleman, he was always up to something. And they, Philip and Dove, more often than not skint and mischievous and at a loose end, were sometimes on hand to enable him. Like any normal, sensible lads. Politics aside. Politics didn't really come into it, he insisted. Although there'd been a massacre that night that had made a big impression on even the most dedicated revellers. Lads watching the Italy match were gunned down just across the border. Healy remembered it well. The elation after the football turning to horror at the 'moral squalor' of it all as news filtered through of the slaughter.

Dove, in fairness, was the first to articulate the growing fear that Sandra might have met a sinister end. Over the following weeks, there was a gradual acknowledgement that something had to be done. People began to take her absence more seriously She became a talking point. Her picture appeared in shop windows and on trees. The *Northern Chronicle* issued an appeal. RTÉ sent a film crew. Philip and Dove joined search parties organized by the guards.

The family hired a diviner from Sligo. He was a monobrowed law-unto-himself whose hazel rod was five foot two. Exactly the same length as Sandra. He insisted on sleeping in her bed the night before his corpse-prospecting escapade, all the better to channel the missing schoolgirl's 'energy'. Despite this alarming pre-condition, he met with no success, the hazel rod being wonky, pointing, as everybody guessed it would, towards a lake. But there was no widespread panic, no clamour to lock up daughters, no pitchfork-toting marches on the police station. No great urgency at all.

Dove became more and more convinced that Coleman had some-thing to hide. Philip soon dove-tailed with this point of view and, being the less volatile of the two, and being the bigger and more practical-minded and assertive in type, he took command in calling Coleman to account. They initiated their own independent investiga-tion, parallel but at odds with that of the gardaí. If they were detectives on TV, they'd have been called Guilt and Loss.

Sadly, Guilt and Loss's joint efforts came to a juddering halt a while later when Dove was told of Philip's dalliance with Sandra. Loyalty was a big thing with Dove. He was the exception in an emotion-averse part of the world where professing undying love and loyalty to your friends was novel and not always well-received. But, Philip ruminated, loyalty works both ways. Dove was rarely to be found when, say, a fight broke out. Where was Dove when there was work to be done? When the strawberries were to be picked and the money was to be divided evenly? He often confused loyalty with histrionics. *I'd die for you, so I would.* Would he really?

Did he? Did he in fact die for him?

Shunned by Dove and ostracized by half the town as a suspect in the disappearance of Sandra Mohan, Philip felt compelled to clear his name. Thus, in that context, he squared up to Coleman one night in the pool room of JJ's bar. Present at the table were Coleman and O'Dowd. At the oche stood Sheriff and a fella called Macker, both of them wielding clumps of darts. Tommy Courtney was in the jacks while Lonergan, like a surveillance camera on legs, leaned against a wall, taking it all in. Philip, a fair few pints on board, after a restful day's fishing with his uncle Francie, announced his arrival by placing a 20p coin on the table. Then, in a loud voice, he asked the assemblage, 'Where's the body?'

A deathly silence descended on the establishment. Even the balls stopped dead on the baize.

It was O'Dowd who broke the spell. 'Which one?'

They all laughed, all except Lonergan, who went out to the bar and asked JJ himself for a cup of hot chocolate, a concoction he knew full well JJ did not stock. After wiping down his bald head with a tea towel, JJ scurried off to the shop, as fast as his old man's legs could carry him, while Lonergan locked the door behind him. Tommy Courtney emerged from the toilets, belting up the jeans. Adept from an early age at sensing trouble, he lowered his head like a bull and took a run at Philip, butting him in the stomach.

'He was a bunty wee fella in those days, Tommy.'

'Good man, Tommy,' trumpeted Sheriff, or maybe it was Charlie O'Dowd.

'Good man, me,' Tommy yahoo-ed in response.

The wind knocked out of him, Philip fell back against a table, spilling a pint of Guinness, a pint of Harp and a rum and Coke in the process. Sheriff and Macker held Tommy back as Philip got to his feet. O'Dowd stepped forward and pushed Philip to the ground.

'That's my drink,' he said.

'He's some cheek,' said another.

'Lick it up,' orders Coleman.

'Good idea,' agreed the chorus.

'Go, on! Lick it up, you cuntya!'

Coleman grabbed him by the hair and wiped his face in the slops.

'Jaysus, I think he likes it,' said Charlie.

'Did you like that, Sharkey?' said Coleman. 'Do you want some more?'

Philip turned his head and spat into Coleman's face.

'Murderer!'

With that, Fergal grabbed a clump of his hair and slammed his face onto the floor, breaking at least two of Philip's teeth as well as splitting his lip and dislocating his jaw. At this point, Tommy stopped struggling with the darts players and retired muttering to a corner of the room. This wasn't fun anymore. Philip was now on his knees, looking up at his adversaries.

O'Dowd, first in line, aimed a sneaky ju-jitsu kick at his solar plexus. His aim was surprisingly true. Fighting for breath and spitting blood, not an easy trick to pull off, Philip rolled over towards what he instinctively thought of as the safety of the wall. That was a miscalculation on his part. For O'Dowd, taking encouragement from Philip's inability to get to his feet, kicked him again, this time with considerably more force, in the small of the back. This blow struck his tailbone, wiring a high voltage of pain to every cell of his being, and clearly hurt O'Dowd's own foot in the act. O'Dowd sat down, holding his foot and howling curses at his victim. Philip, a strongish lad, conditioned by his football training, finally managed to get to his feet and stagger towards the door.

'Where are you going?' says Coleman. 'You're up.' His thumb pointed at the pool table.

Philip's coin was placed upright in the slot. The metal tray was pushed in with force and held, expertly, until the ominous rumbling began – the fiesta in the table's inner Pamplona – and a stampede of balls came clattering out of the pen.

'No hard feelings,' the ringleader continued, 'but if there's one thing I can't stand, it's people spreading lies about me.'

A cue was placed in Philip's hand, with which he tried to whack Coleman on the head. Coleman ducked and hit him a punch in the kidneys, the cue dropping to the ground. With his left hand, the crowd cheering him on, he then flung Philip, *World of Sport* on Saturday afternoon style, into the space previously occupied by Sheriff and Macker. His back smack against the dartboard, Coleman punched him four times in rapid succession. Once on the chin. Once on the nose, breaking what was one of his finest features. And twice more on the left ear. These two lacerating blows left him conscious of little but the sound of bells ringing and a receding image of his father dressed in swimming togs on the beach in Salthill. There was nothing Philip could do to defend himself, his limbs weak, his mind confused.

Coleman held him upright, while the weak-chested Sheriff delivered the next few blows, some to the head, some to the ribs, none of them with any great enthusiasm, but none, by the same token, aiding Philip's recovery in any way.

'Macker!' says Coleman, motioning the youth hither with a movement of the head. 'Your turn!'

'He's had enough,' opined Macker.

'Macker!'

'Go on, Macker!' urged the others, suddenly concerned for *his* welfare.

Macker, younger than the others, was the closest in age to Philip and a team-mate on the Tullyanna minors. He was duly jostled forward.

'Sorry, Philip,' says he, before giving his friend a few good digs, breaking a rib, the crack audible. This was followed by a kick in the balls for good measure, lest the gang thought he was soft.

'Tommy!' says Coleman.

'No.'

'You're up.'

'No way. Yiz can all fuck off.'

'Tommy!' Coleman commanded, his voice echoing around the room.

'He's only a young fella.'

Coleman, the blood up, head-butted the unwilling joker. Tommy, stung into action, bit Philip on the cheek.

'There now. Are ya satisfied?' says Tommy, a smidgen of blood on his lips.

'Good man, Tommy.'

'Right, lads, out the back,' says Lonergan, his clothes spotless, his moustache neatly trimmed.

As the boys scuttled away, Fergal unzipped his fly and did a farewell piss on Philip's face, while Lonergan produced a gun from somewhere and pointed it at the curled-up ball on the floor.

'You got off lightly this time, Sharkey,' says Coleman, one giant paw gripping the three constituent parts of Philip's manhood. 'My advice to you is to fuck off out of this town. Do you hear me?' he said, squeezing the ballsack with a weightlifter's steel.

'I swear to you, if I ever see your face again, I'll kill ya, stone dead, ha. And your mother too,' he added gravely. 'That's right, boy, I'll kill your mother,' he said. 'I'll rape her first.'

'He will.'

'I will, I'll rape her rightly,' he said, 'with your cock. I'll cut off your cock and ride your mother with it. And then I'll kill her. Do you get me? I'll shit in her mouth 'til she chokes.'

And he didn't seem to be joking. Philip had never forgotten that convoluted threat, the vivid imagery employed, or the implied dismemberment involved. He also remembered the tattoo on Coleman's neck, 53N792 6W239, the coordinates of the seaside resort of Clogherhead, apparently, where, he'd often boasted, he'd lost his virginity to a woman twice his age.

It was Lonergan who cleaned up the mess and Lonergan who dropped Philip off at the hospital. After a month or so of stitching and bone-setting, jaw-alignment and dental reconstruction, Philip said goodbye to his mother and set sail for London and the world. And there, without further distillation of the details, Philip's monologue ended. A silence enveloped the men.

'That's why I left Tullyanna.'

Healy, ashen-faced, wasn't a hundred per cent sure that he was not being sold a pup. Towards the end of Philip's story, he was reminded of Tommy's fate, the image he'd formed of Tommy's mangled body, courtesy of the Doc, hovering in his head. It would be perfectly understandable if Philip wanted revenge. Healy's body rearranged itself into the shape of a big question mark.

Philip placed the photo in its rightful position on the mantelpiece and somewhat indignantly addressed the more immediate elephant in the room.

'I didn't kill Tommy. I had every right to, but I didn't.'

He hoped he'd made himself clear and that no further elaboration was necessary. But that's not how the world worked. That's not how Healy worked. Healy wanted more than a mere denial. He wanted to know why Tommy was in Philip's house the night he died.

What could he tell him? Maybe about Dove's comic book, *Brouhaha*? Perhaps the one-time sleuth boasted subtextual analysis of the graphic novel amongst his legendary forensic skills? Maybe he'd better keep that to himself for now, Philip thought, for fear of undermining his own credibility, it being more than likely a wild goose chase, Dove having been a spoofer and all.

'We are where we are.'

Of more immediate interest to Kevin was Tommy's admission that he'd fabricated a sighting of Sandra in Dublin under orders from Fergal Coleman. Now we're getting somewhere, he thought. That was a bona fide breakthrough, although now that he was dead, there was no way of proving it.

'Poor Tommy,' says Philip.

'We'll nail the blackguards yet.'

The men tacitly agreed to cooperate, their respective eyebrows doing the heavy lifting in terms of the finer details of the negotiations. Allies now, in grief and common purpose, they shook hands. In the absence of a pen and paper or recording device, Kevin's mind was furiously filing away the conversation, the brain pulsing away. He was already projecting ahead, a visit to Sheriff on the cards. If what Philip said was true, that meant Sheriff was alone with Sandra that morning.

On his way out the door, Healy turned to his new accomplice. 'Oh, I almost forgot, I have a present for you.'

He handed Philip the recently burned CD. 'See you at Dove's funeral?'

Paying her respects

Joanne stood at the back of the church, an anthropologist, like Joan Didion or someone, surveying the sparse congregation, representatives of a 'tribe', as she saw it, frozen in time, a community that had stopped evolving thirteen years ago.

The crowd consisted of the few people who hadn't made the two-day wake, as well as the immediate family and friends of the deceased. And they were supplemented by the full-time funeral-goers. Golems. The word came to her from the trusty word hoard and she was pleased. If all else failed, she still had words to fall back on. And she believed in their *power*. A regiment of golems – deader than the deceased – had nothing better to do of a morning now that the economy was dead, and the community centre was closed for repairs, and the game of bridge was beyond their comprehension.

She tried to match current faces to faces she'd confronted with her blunt, unwelcome questions in 1999. One woman caught her eye. She watched her, a woman she knew to be only about fifty, yet shuffling, grey and wretched, into a seat as far away as possible from everybody else. It was Carmel Mohan, Sandra's mother, recently widowed, her prayers unceasing and, as of yet, unanswered.

In the pew directly behind the main Connolly contingent sat Lorcan Lonergan, Stephen Sheriff, Charlie O'Dowd, Macker and her old 'flame', the statesmanlike Fergal Coleman.

'Brothers and sisters in Christ, you are all very welcome on this very sad occasion when we remember Dermot who, while no longer with us

in body, will remain with us always in our hearts. Losing somebody we love is like losing a part of ourselves, a hand or a leg . . .'

Their romance, if you could call it that, was short-lived, lasting less than a night. Not her proudest moment by any means. She reddened, the embarrassment acute even now. The leg started jigging again. Her mind wandering, as it always did in churches, she wondered what *was* her proudest moment? Just a few months ago, in the taxi queue at Dublin Airport – a long, snaking, impatient queue – she experienced a quiet pride in herself when three business types blithely joined the *middle* of the queue, continuing a conversation about some *acquisition* they'd acquired in Warsaw. Although everybody was bristling at the boorish intrusion, nobody said a word. Nobody except Joanne.

'Hey, what the fuck do you think you're doing? There's a queue.'

'Oh sorry. I thought this was the end.'

'And what did you think we were all doing? We all want to get home.'

'Okay, you've made your point.'

'I haven't actually made my point. It's not just the queue-jumping. It's the *entitlement*. The whole country on its knees and you're wanking on about buying car parks in Poland. Pathetic.'

Nobody knew where to look. But she could tell they were impressed. There were plenty of proud moments to savour, but her mind kept going back to her least proud. After JJ's, they went back to Fergal's house, where all politics were local and all civil rights were violated and no one was complaining. The last thing Joanne remembered before she blacked out was the dog, an Alsatian, licking her face.

It was so unlike her, but at that time she was utterly convinced that Fergal was blameless when it came to Sandra. She hadn't, at that stage, heard about his foray over the border either. She was sure he was all bravado. Now, she wasn't so sure.

The last time she'd seen him was a few weeks later, *after* she'd heard about his foray across the border, when he invited her to go fishing for eels in Lough Dillon.

'*Wrap up. Fierce cold altogether.*'

She remembered there was a margarine tub teeming with live maggots in the back of his van. And there was a shotgun.

'*Are we going to shoot the eels?*'

'*You never know who you might meet out by Lough Dillon.*' He winked, lest she thought he was serious. '*No, it's for lamping rabbits. If we get bored.*'

He parked the vehicle in a lay-by. They walked for about a mile in their wellies through the pitch-black fields. It was so dark, Joanne had to hold on to his jacket for fear of getting lost. It was quiet by the lake. As well as the fishing gear and the Tequila, he had brought a sleeping bag. And an empty coal sack.

'*The ground is damp. We don't want you getting pneumonia, now, ha.*'

She remembered a conversation they had about men and women – three or four eels wriggling in a bucket beside her – as she swigged from the Tequila bottle.

'*You have depths, Joanne. I'm like a well, sure. I might be deep, but the water is clear. You, on the other hand, you are bottomless, do you know that?*'

'*What's that supposed to mean?*'

'*Did you ever hear tell of the Sargasso Sea? All currents and eddies beneath the surface, eels and weeds and the like – the eels reminded me of it. I saw a documentary, you know, shipwrecks and mysterious creatures in unexplored caves, seacows, the whole works, the Sargasso Sea, ha, where whole ships disappear, crew and all. I mean that as a compliment. You are unknowable. Like a female. I need to go for a piss.*'

She didn't know if it was the Tequila talking or what. What was he trying to tell her, that he was a deep thinker, or that she was in grave danger? It was a very long piss. Every sound – every hoot and rustle and snap – enlivened her senses. Should she run?

'*There was a wee deer. Its head was caught in a gate,*' he said by way of explanation when he returned, wiping his hands on his filthy wax jacket.

It had been an unnerving evening – the mercilessness of the natural world, the implicit threat, the soul-searching – but nothing *happened*. Apart from Coleman sneaking up on her and wrapping a live eel around her neck for the craic.

She jumped as a hand touched her shoulder.

'Joanne, isn't it?'

She couldn't quite place the face.

'Kevin Healy? Garda? Well, ex-garda.' He grimaced, chancing his arm by entering the church for the first time since he was firmly asked by the parish priest to stay away.

'*Lord, let us give thanks for the great joy Dermot brought to the world and let us now support as a community Gerry Senior, Deirdre and Gerry Junior and of course . . . ehhh . . .*' The priest looked down at the writing on the back of his hand. '*. . . little Marshall . . . and little Cliff in this, their time of great sorrow and, indeed, need. I didn't know Dermot personally . . .*'

'Here's the thing, Joanne.'

'Ssssshhhh,' hissed a mourner.

'Sorry.'

The last time she saw Healy was a year ago, directing traffic on the Main Street.

He lowered his voice. 'I think you should apologize to Dove's mother. There she is. Hah? Sandra was still alive at six in the morning in Coleman's house when Dove was wrapped up in bed. Fact! Dove couldn't have done it.'

Healy, *sotto voce*, spelled out each word, with his minty breath, barely able to hide his frustration with Joanne. It was a frustration that began when her article was published – effectively, in his opinion, helping to scupper the flimsy case against Coleman – and continued unabated to this day.

'If it looks like a duck . . .'

'The duck speech. Great. It doesn't look like a duck, Joanne. That's the thing, it never did. There are no ducks involved here whatsoever.'

'Sshhhhforfuckssake,' hissed what seemed like the entire congregation in unison.

'Let us all take a moment to reflect on the treasure that was Dove's life as we remember the good times we enjoyed with him before he was called by God . . .'

Healy beckoned her outside to continue the chat before the mass ended.

'I beseech you, Joanne, not casting anything, but if you can help in any way, now is the time. This is . . . Jaysus, Joanne, it's our last chance. Hah? Look at them, there, with the poker-faces and the pockets bulging with leaflets. A clear road between them and justice.'

Naturally, Kevin had read her feature in *Howarya!* He had enjoyed it himself. It was short and snappy. It read like a thriller. She'd painted a vivid and affecting portrait of the victim, fair play to her. That was something that was missing from the police reports, some of which he himself had penned, and, in so doing, suppressed his own literary inclinations. She'd managed to get inside a teenage girl's head, a feat, in all fairness, no man of his acquaintance had ever managed to do. She knew Sandra a lot better than he did. She could have been a great help. But, and this was really the thing, the only thing that actually mattered, she'd got it wrong. Badly wrong, like the best of people occasionally do when it comes to conclusions, and it behooved her now to try and set the record straight.

'Help me, Joanne!'

A flustered Healy stepped back as a trickle of people exited the church, the show rapidly winding down. Other people, unable or unwilling to endure the whole doleful rigmarole, were just arriving at the church. They were the clever ones, hoping to intercept the chief mourners at the door to pay their respects. They had it all worked out – they would get the same credit for their brief, belated appearance as the more dedicated mourners would get for enduring the whole service. It was an old tactic, but a risky one. God knows, Healy had done it himself often enough. Joanne had done it, too. There'd been a lot of funerals to attend in the border region. Kevin and Joanne were separated as the Connolly men loaded Dove onto the hearse under Duffy the undertaker's panicky supervision.

Joanne, regretting the duck speech, a line of argument she had long ago foregone, invited Healy to dinner later at the Old Forge.

'I'll try and help you, Kevin.'

She was just as surprised as he was when she heard herself issuing the invitation. Nobody knew how bad she felt for her part in discrediting Connolly's name. The anxiety was always there, in the pit of her stomach. Like a tumour. On the other hand, if he'd told her the truth, she mightn't have *slanted* the article the way she had. The only way she could make it up to Dove was to find out what really happened. And that's what she intended to do. In the meantime, she had other fish to fry. Other fishermen.

Excusing herself, she made her way towards Fergal Coleman, who was in a huddle with his men. Dove's father, Gerry Senior, stood in front of her.

'Are you happy now? Is this what you wanted?'

'I am so sorry for your loss.'

'My son was innocent.'

'I know that, Mr Connolly. And I know whatever I say won't mean anything to you. But I am sorry. I made a mistake. And I promise I will clear Dermot's name.'

It came out like a speech she'd gone over many times in her mind. That's because she had gone over it in the subconscious, in anticipation of a confrontation like this one. Joanne somehow maintained her composure as Gerry Junior held his father back. Somebody small, little Marshall or little Cliff, presumably, kicked her on the shins before he was scooped up by another relative.

Coleman, an unlikely knight in shining armour, grabbed her elbow and ushered her away from her pint-sized assailant. They went back inside, where they took refuge in a side chapel.

'Pick on someone your own size, Joanne,' said Coleman, highly amused at the situation. 'You okay? Just say the word, I could make him . . . disappear.' Fergal clicked his fingers. 'Like that.'

He grinned. His skin was better than she remembered.

'That was a joke, Joanne.'

'Good one, Fergal. The old murdering-a-child humour. Gets me every time. Can we talk?'

Coleman stood a bit too close for comfort, his left hand resting on the be-sandalled foot of the St Joseph statue. Looking her up and down with his husky-blue eyes, he feigned shock.

'I'm a married man, Joanne.'

'And Teresa's a very lucky woman, Fergal. I'd like an interview for the *Chronicle*.'

Coleman turned his back on her and put some coins in a box, the clash of the cash resounding around the chapel. Using an already lighted candle, he lit a fresh candle in one of the many red cups that were arranged on a brass rack. In the process, he spilled some of the hot wax on the back of his hand, not flinching, barely noticing, by the looks of things. He spilled some more of the molten liquid onto his hand until there was none left to spill. Then he turned around again to face Joanne. Not taking his eyes off her, he blessed himself and said a short, private prayer.

'For the deceased.'

'Sandra?'

'Dove, Joanne. Dove. A terrible shame. Big loss to the town. And the art world, what? Would you like to be cremated?'

'Not right now, Fergal. I'm kind of busy.'

'Buried or cremated, I mean? When you go?'

'I haven't given much thought to it, be honest with you.'

'You should.'

The flickering candles were reflected in his eyes. Was that a threat?

'I'd like to be buried, myself,' he continued. 'It's the way of it in these parts. The least we could do for the land that nourishes us, the land from which we sprang. My mother's people quarried stone. Did you know that? The McArdles, out by Donaghbane. Aye, generations. They lived in caves after the Famine. Would you credit that? Survived on weeds.'

He looked around him, a tear in his eye. 'They probably quarried this stone.' He ran his fingers down one of the fluted columns.

'Cremation is an abomination, Joanne. A pure disgrace. Sacrilege. We die. We are buried. The earth lives. I like you, Joanne. I'm an avid reader of the court reports. And I'd love to oblige. But two weeks to polling day. It's tricky. I'll tell you what. Speak to my director of elections. And we'll try our best to *squeeze* you in.'

'Mr Coleman!'

Lonergan appeared as if on cue.

'Speak of the devil. You remember Lorcan? Lorcan Lonergan. You know Joanne "Big Guns" McCollum.'

'Ah, yes. Hello,' says Lonergan, looking at his watch. 'Eh . . . the meeting with the nurses at twelve?'

'Aye, aye, be with you in a sec. You see, Joanne . . .'

'Call me Big Guns,' she said, bitterly.

'Sorry. I'm sorry. It was uncalled for. You're perfectly proportioned, in all fairness.' He smirked. 'How could I ever forget? Look. People are hurting out there. The nurses haven't had a pay rise in ten years.'

'The concern is touching. I'm tempted to vote for you myself. I've read her diary, Fergal. She was in love with you.'

Coleman smiled and sat down beside her in the pew. He picked at the wax scab on the back of his hand. Lonergan was lurking in the shadows behind them, with the Filofax.

'She loved you.'

'Infatuation, Joanne. Not the first one to fall for me,' he winked, 'or the last.'

'She was sixteen. You were planning to run away together. It's all in the diary.'

'Ah, Joanne. Come on, for fuck's sake. The ramblings of a teenage girl. Seriously.'

'Did you tell Teresa?'

'Look,' he reasoned, in his deep, cultivated twang, 'I have daughters myself. Very impressionable at that age. Sure, my eldest wants to run off with yerman, Timberland.'

'Timberlake.'

'What are you going to do? Have *him* arrested? You're barking up the wrong tree, Joanne. *Barking* full stop, if you ask me.'

'Your *eldest* hasn't disappeared off the face of the Earth.'

Fergal's eyes stopped twinkling. He leaned in, the big vein on his neck a string on a double-bass, throbbing Mingusly. He whistle-hissed in her ear.

'If you're trying to embarrass me or my party, you're wasting your time. For the record, and you can use this, I never had anything with her, the girl, Sandra, relations, nothing. Never. Okay? And for you to swan down here, on the eve, and . . . tell me something, Joanne, if you're so sure, why didn't you put any of this in your article?'

She looked at Coleman's hard, tense face, the eyes locking her into place.

'I'll tell you why you didn't put any of this in your article, Joanne. Because I have photographs of you in my house. You know what I'm talking about. And you know that if you ever publish allegations about me, scurrilous and *untrue*, by the way, every paper in the country will have those photographs. I've done my time.'

'Six months.'

'Twelve, reduced to six for good behaviour. I was a model prisoner. Did a course in comedy improvisation in the 'Joy. I was a wild boy, Joanne, I made mistakes, but I've changed. Have you? Ever wonder why you're still a nobody, working for that useless rag up in Mullinary town? I utterly reject and refute what you're implying. You've a sick mind.'

Coleman stood up. He dipped a finger in the wax and, before she could react, made the sign of the cross on Joanne's forehead.

'There now. You're cured.'

And then laughing, his shoulders shaking like Muttley, he walked away. Lonergan, hirsute and saturnine, emerged from the shadows and escorted his charge, unshaken, outside, where Coleman pressed the flesh of the stragglers at the tail-end of the somewhat ghoulish procession heading for the graveyard, before being whisked away in a Škoda to meet some disgruntled nurses.

Joanne, shaken, stayed in the church for about half an hour, deriving some comfort from the settling quiet, the light of the flickering candles and the lingering smell of incense filling the soaring spaces of the church. The statues were friendly in disposition, the stone consoling.

And the elaborate stained-glass windows told a touching story of the local people's devotion. The light shining through one of them – St Dymphna – warmed Joanne's face. She'd never paid much attention to the saints and was a bit surprised to be singled out by this one. Although an atheist herself, she often found solace in the faith of others. She often found herself defending God's honour against religious fanatics who depicted him as cruel and unforgiving, blaming every storm and misfortune on God's desire to punish us all for the error of our ways. Which is better – to believe in a horrible God or not to believe in a loving God? She might run that one by Carson for a feature at Easter.

Before she got too much solace, or became too exposed to the temptations of a void-filling faith, she removed herself from the house of God – such a fine building in such a no-horse town – and lit a cigarette. Oh well, she shrugged, one resolution down. She decided to call on Carmel Mohan, a woman of inexplicable faith, in Fox's Demesne, only a few doors down from Coleman's happy home.

She had no proof, of course, that Coleman had done anything wrong, but had faith in her own intuition and her own investigative powers and, despite her avowed Godlessness, in something akin to divine justice.

A shadow of his former self

Healy followed Sheriff home from the church. His quarry, for want of a better word, stopped off at the Spar to buy cigarettes and a sliced pan. Sheriff was a mechanic, currently unemployed and in the early stages of multiple sclerosis, a condition not helped, surely, by his somewhat meagre diet.

Kevin was pining for Ciara. He was sort of half-thinking to himself that if he ever managed to get to the bottom of this case, once and for all, himself and Sheila might just wander out to Australia for a while with Shane and the baby, Paul. How exactly this shadow-of-his-former-self Sheriff could help to expedite what was only an old pipe-dream anyway he was not at all sure.

'Stephen!'

The man twisted his body slowly, the key already in the door of his two-up, two-down.

'Do you mind if I . . .?'

Sheriff nodded, the skin drawn tightly over his face. The emaciated body, the jerky motion, gave him a somewhat robotic mien.

'Why should I talk to you?' says he, without hostility, and him putting on the kettle, his back to the ex-cop.

He produced a packet of chocolate digestives from a cupboard and placed them on the table.

'Ah, it's just with Dove gone and poor Tommy Courtney, I'm just . . .'

Healy tailed off, weary, hand rubbing his temples, suddenly sick of his tired old shtick, sick of himself, and he stuck in the past, moving neither forwards nor backwards, every bit as immobile as the recalcitrant stick insect in front of him who was supporting his weight with a hurley. Few people hurled in Tullyanna.

'Are ya alright, Mr Healy?'

'I give up, Stephen.'

'Ah sure . . .'

'Did you know my daughter, Ciara?'

'I did surely, nice girl. A good friend of my niece?'

'That's right. Orla.'

'Aye. They trained together.'

They sat in silence for a few minutes, sipping tea and dipping biscuits in the tea, before Healy got up. 'I'll go so. Nice wheels.'

A brand-new electric wheelchair sat unused, facing the wall like a bold boy.

'Coleman. The big shot. He got it for me.'

'Good old Fergal.'

'I didn't ask for it.'

Kevin's ears pricked up. Was there the tiniest hint of resentment in Sheriff's voice? Or was it just a note of denial from a man who hadn't yet come to terms with his medical fate?

Healy, standing up, scanned the room. He finished the cup of tea, watery old tea it was, squeezed, he twigged, from a used teabag.

'Springsteen, ha! The Boss.'

There was a poster on the wall, the only artwork as such in the man's sparsely furnished kitchen, and it commemorating the Bruce Springsteen concert at Wembley Arena. On closer inspection, Kevin noted, there was a ticket stub for the same gig, 10 July 1994, tucked under the plexiglass cover. A little bit of life flowed into Sheriff's face.

'Aye, deadly concert!'

'I've never seen him myself. Live! Ha.'

'Yeah, well, he's the best. No doubt about it.'

'So I believe. *This town rips the bones from your back, it's a death trap, it's a suicide rap.*'

'You a fan?'

'Well, I dunno, I always liked *Born to Run*. Listen, I'm sorry to bother you. Forget it.'

Healy was about to let himself out, the resolve waning, part of him not wanting to know anymore, afraid of what he might hear, when Sheriff suddenly made an announcement.

'I didn't kill her.'

Kevin didn't answer. He was actually one of the very few people in the whole of Ireland who, in social situations, was perfectly comfortable with silence. He'd always found that most people – the most taciturn, even the most hard-hearted of criminals – were inclined to fill a sonic vacuum, be it with drivel, or snatches of song, or, in extremely rare cases, a full confession. There seemed to be some obscure law of psychology that applied to Irish people which stated that if there were two or more people in the same room, at least one of them felt obliged to be gabbling away to beat the band. It was not an exact science, Kevin knew that, but in his experience the less he said, by process of elimination, the more others would have to say.

'I was in Coleman's house the night she died.'

He paused, waiting for a reaction. None came. Sheriff filled the silence.

'So I was.'

Kevin showed no surprise. He didn't betray any emotion of any sort at this startling declaration. Of course, he knew already from talking to Philip that Sheriff was in the house with Sandra that night. But this was the first time he heard any of Coleman's people acknowledge that Sandra was actually dead. Sheriff, it seemed, wasn't aware of his faux-pas and, a bit unnerved by Kevin's stillness, blathered on.

'He told me to keep an eye on her while he was out and about.'

Ciara used to tell him that he had the kind of face you didn't want to displease. And, as she pointed out more than once, that 'pissed her off no end'. She was a devil for the bad language, Ciara. In her teens, it infuriated her that she wasn't able to lie to him after a night out, say, drinking or courting. A little white lie about her whereabouts wouldn't have gone amiss. She'd be all set to spin him a yarn, but as soon as she looked into his kindly, inquisitive face she'd feel compelled to blurt out the truth, not that he was especially nosey or judgemental about that sort of thing. If he could do it all over again, she could lie all she wanted and he wouldn't love her any the less. Kevin's mind was wandering as Sheriff spoke. He had to focus. He knew that Coleman would have coached his men and that his men, if they'd been in any doubt as to their obligations before Tommy was murdered, would be well-primed now with their stories.

'I didn't shift her. I'll be honest, I tried, but she wasn't in the mood. Philip Sharkey was there.'

He hesitated for a moment to gauge Healy's reaction to this piece of information. Sheriff obviously thought it was a landmine. But his interrogator remained mute and unmoved, waiting for what – a deviation from the script, another little slip-een of the tongue, something he didn't already know?

'He shifted her alright, Sharkey, dirty bollox. And then he left, high as a kite. I always had my suspicions about that fella. Coleman came back around seven in the morning. I don't know why I'm telling you this. He'd kill me if he knew I was talking to you.'

Kevin often wondered who Paul's father was. That was something Ciara never told him. And he never asked. The mother and the baby were both healthy. That was the main thing. He was afraid if he found out the father's name, he might cherish the baby less. It pained him, daily, to think it might have been someone like Sheriff or O'Dowd, say, or, God forbid, Coleman himself. In which case he didn't know what he'd do. He fervently hoped it was somebody she met at college, somebody who was kind and gentle towards her, and not in any way complicit in the likely murder of a teenage girl.

'She took smack, Sandra. It was dodgy gear. And Coleman was worried about her. As true as God. That's why he asked me to mind her. That's why he lied to the cops. Your old friends, Mr Healy. You wouldn't think it, but Coleman has a heart of gold.'

Was that a hint of sarcasm? Something was nagging him, something Sheriff said, not the slip-up, if it was a slip-up, about the girl being dead, something else. His brain was pulsing away now, aroused by some tiny connection it had made, but straining didn't help the synapses clarify the info, as well he knew. And then the idea died, and the brain shut down, and he was left with the slip-up.

'You said the night she died.'

'What?'

'The night Ciara died.'

'Who?'

'Sorry, Sandra, the night Sandra died. Is she dead? How do you know she's dead, Stephen?'

'Disappeared. I meant disappeared or whatever, you know.'

'You know she's dead. I know she's dead. And you're going to tell me how it happened, why it happened and where she's buried.'

'Or what?'

'Or nothing. You'll feel better, son. It'll heal the soul.'

'I told you what I know. Coleman came back and let me go. I was fucked and went to bed. Sandra went home. That's the honest to God's truth.'

'So Coleman was alone with her in the house?'

'Only for a while. Then she went home.'

'He never mentioned that to the guards.'

'I don't know why you're asking me. Ask him yourself.'

'Maybe I will.'

'She's in England, so she is. That's all about it.'

'Maybe she is.'

Sheriff, exhausted, collapsed into the brand-new wheelchair and, fiddling absentmindedly with the joystick, lurched forward towards the wall. Kevin had learned something, but couldn't say what it was.

Of Mice and Men

Joanne was sitting alone in the 'good' room of the Mohan house as a whispered argument raged in the kitchen between Carmel and her well-preserved sister, Rose. At least, Joanne assumed it was her sister. She, although better turned out and more upright in stance, had the same narrow face and high hairline as Carmel. There were some other women in the kitchen, too, neighbours, by the looks of things, the tart and sandwich brigade, here to give Sandra's mother support on yet another painful day. Joanne was using the hiatus to try and stop time, no less, and look beyond what was in front of her, to catch a glimpse or a whiff or any sense of Sandra.

She had spent a night once with ghost-hunters, a mother and son unit equipped with headlamps and crude gizmos, in the old asylum in Sligo. It was a piece for a short-lived science magazine for which, she reminded herself, she still hadn't been paid. Yes, of course, she heard noises. Of course, she heard screaming and wailing. And indeed, she'd felt cold all of a sudden. And, as you would expect, the EMF scanner went ballistic. Yet she remained a sceptic. As one of her lecturers in DCU, a cultural theorist called Terry Gubbins, used to say, *Just because I don't believe in ghosts doesn't mean they aren't there.* Joanne was far more interested in the credulous ghost-hunters themselves than the ghosts of the mentally ill. What was missing in their lives? And why did they feel the need to fill those holes with such an outsider passion?

Even though it was a warm day, the room was chilly, little-used. Joanne sneezed. There were photos in frames on the sideboard. One of Sandra in her Holy Communion dress and little white handbag; one of Tom and Carmel on their wedding day, a handsome couple, he, naturally tanned, the spit of Vince Vaughan. She picked up a photo of the three of them eating ice-cream cones on a wall, Bundoran at a guess, judging by the big rollers in the background, but who took the photograph, wondered the ever-curious Joanne?

'They don't think I should be talking to you.'

Carmel, her hands a-tremor, placed two cups of coffee down on the coffee table and a plate of Nice biscuits. Joanne held up the photo.

'Who's the prom queen?'

'Ah stop, Joanne, you're a divil. He was a good man, you know, my Tom. He had his troubles, but he never laid a hand on her. His little angel, he used to call her. And the odd time he raised his voice to me, she'd stop him dead with a look. *Daddy, what the hell?* And he'd say, *Sorry, my little angel, I don't know what came over me,* and off he'd go up the town.'

Joanne wasn't here to reminisce about the good old days with Tom. She took a deep breath, hating herself for what she was doing to the poor woman.

'Tell me about Fergal Coleman, Carmel. I know this is hard for you, but do you think there was any chance at all they might have been in a relationship?'

'No. God forgive you.'

'I'm sorry, Carmel. It's just we have to look at every possibility.'

The hot coffee cups had left rings on the coffee table. Carmel belatedly heaved herself up from the green polyester couch and made her way over to the sideboard. From a drawer, she withdrew a few wooden coasters – with illustrations of clipper ships on the high seas – and put them under the cups.

'They're lovely.'

'Do you like them? Sandra got them for me. She musta been all of ten. Picked them out herself in Vinny Carroll's wee knick-knack shop – you know, beside the cobbler?'

'Oh yes, you'd never know what you'd find in there.'

'As right. Fergal was always very good to us. Especially after Tom, you know, after Tom got sick. He'd take us to our appointments in the Regional.'

Joanne's heart went out to Carmel, but she wasn't going to get anywhere by pussy-footing around the place.

'A real charmer. Look, tell me to get lost, and I know it's a long time ago, but is there a chance that Sandra could have been pregnant?'

Carmel closed her eyes and smiled tightly.

'Are you always this forward, Joanne? You actually remind me a bit of Sandra. There's no way my daughter was pregnant. No way. I empty the bins in this house. I'm her mother. Hundred per cent she wasn't pregnant. Look, I'll be honest, I didn't like her hanging around with Fergal. He was a good lad, but older, you know, and in with a bad crowd, Lonergan and them. But he looked after her. He protected her.'

'From who? Dermot Connolly?'

'Poor Dermot. You were very hard on wee Dermot in your col-yum. Very polite, so he was, Mrs Mohan this and Mrs Mohan that. The pair of them giggling away above in her bedroom. Dancing to beat the band. She was always very happy with Dermot. God rest his soul.'

Carmel insisted that Dermot didn't kill Sandra and that Fergal didn't kill her either. They couldn't have because, she emphasized, the eyes widening, Sandra was still alive. She eased herself off the couch again and left the room. Joanne heard her foostering about upstairs. Rose looked into the good room, her hand bunching her blouse, and gave Joanne a filthy look. Joanne gave Rose an equally filthy look. She nibbled on one of the thin rectangular biscuits, lightly dusted with sugar, the edges crenellated, a little flimsy castle of a biscuit, and the word NICE imprinted in big letters in the middle. For some reason, she found this effort in the design and manufacture of what was a plain, middle-of-the-road biscuit quite moving. The pointlessness of it all. Yet how serious a business it would be to all concerned. She dunked the remainder of the biscuit in the coffee where it quickly dissolved.

Carmel returned with a stack of home-made birthday cards all from Sandra to her mother. Joanne, having a brief wobble, held back the tears. She had never done anything like that for her mother. Her mother was a reader. And a gardener. A perfectly lovely mother, now that she thought of it, but not a talker, or a toucher. It was a few weeks since she'd spoken to her on the phone. Maybe they should go to a spa together, just the two of them, except they'd both hate spas. There were poems, drawings, lots of cutting and pasting heads, Carmel and Sandra's heads and celebrity heads juxtaposed in quirky collages. A picture of Carmel and Richard Gere on a motorbike.

'I always loved Richard.'

'I don't know, Carmel. There was something about him. Bit iffy, bit shifty, no? Always holding something back.'

'Maybe.' Carmel chuckled, resting her hand on Joanne's arm. 'But he was gorgeous.'

One of the birthday cards was mostly decorated with chocolate bar wrappers. *You are never a FLAKE . . . I love TWIRLing around the kitchen with you . . . when I'm down you give me a BOOST . . . don't listen to Auntie ROSES.* And so on, in shiny foil.

'This one arrived six years after she went away.'

Carmel handed one of the cards to Joanne. Curious. But it didn't prove anything, as Carmel, wilfully burrowing her head in the sand, surely knew. And it didn't look like the handiwork of a – Joanne did a quick calculation – twenty-two-year-old woman.

'She was just a lovely wee girl, Sandra. Cooked and cleaned when we were sick. Never complained, and God knows she had plenty to complain about. I wasn't a very good mother.'

With that, Carmel burst out crying, the tears getting no purchase on her waxy face. Joanne did her best to comfort her.

'I was a *terrible* mother.'

'No, Carmel. It's not true, Carmel. She loved you. As plain as day.'

To scowls and growls from the kitchen chorus, Joanne fetched a tea towel. After a few minutes the crying stopped. Carmel dried her eyes.

'She'd come in from school, taking off all the girls and the teachers. Doing the walks. And the voices.' Carmel tossed her head towards the kitchen. 'She did a great impression of yer one, me sister, Rose.'

'Did you show this to anyone?'

'Ach. What's the point?' The cuffs of her cardigan were frayed and damp. 'I showed it to Healy.'

'Healy!'

'Healy still calls to see me every year. More. Two, three times a year. He's had me down to his garage and all. Have you been to his garage?'

'No.'

'Healy's the only one who cares. He'll find her, so he will. Half-mad, but if you want to know anything about Sandra, he's the man. I don't know what to think anymore.'

Carmel stood up. Joanne stood up, and after an uncertain pause she reached out – uncharacteristically – and gave Carmel a hug. It was more for herself than for Carmel.

'I'll get out of your hair. I'm sure you have better things to be doing. Do you mind if I just have a quick look in Sandra's bedroom?'

'Go on ahead. Sure, what harm will it do?'

Joanne mounted the narrow staircase, a photo of Sandra face-painted as a Lion in the school play, all the other girls laughing at whatever it was she was doing. It was *The Lion King*. Joanne remembered it well. She'd been backstage in the Holy Family hall, making sure the younger girls had their props. She had zipped Sandra into her costume, after brushing her unkempt hair and wiping her runny nose. It was a small, three-windowed house in a council estate, semi-detached. There was nothing you could do in a house like that unnoticed.

She sat down on Sandra's bed, trying in some way to get in touch with Sandra. The old zebra-patterned rug was on the floor. There were a few cardboard boxes desultorily packed with some of Sandra's clothes, but otherwise the room was exactly as Joanne had found it eight years previously. Sandra had a decent collection of cuddly toys, the most worn and loved of which was a dog. Joanne forced her hand into a tiny tear in the stitching and internally examined the toy, its facial expression seeming to change at such an unexpected violation. Nothing could she find.

She looked through Sandra's drawers, not expecting to find anything evidential or incriminating but to reacquaint herself with the person, convinced that Sandra would reveal herself anew through her *things*. In the wardrobe, Joanne rifled through her school uniform, the dark blue jumper and grey skirt, and the orange-red-purple tops, and the kooky dresses, some of which she had made herself.

There were clumps of chewing gum stuck to the underside of the bed. Why were they still there? Should they not have been taken away and analysed? She cast her eye over the single bookshelf – a bridge between innocence and adulthood – bearing various titles from the *Chronicles of Narnia* to *Catcher in the Rye* to *Christiane F*. One book caught her attention. *Of Mice and Men*. By Steinbeck. A book on the Junior Cert in 1993. It was covered in dust. She sneezed again. Sandra had referenced the novel a few times in her diary. It had clearly made an impression on her. When Joanne opened the book, a few postcards fell to the floor.

'Oh!'

As she bent down to pick up the cards, the blood rushed to her head. Princess Diana. And? As her blood-enriched brain quickly pieced together the significance of the cards, Rose called to her from the doorway.

'Leave this family alone. God knows, Carmel has been through enough.'

In my hour of darkness

Philip put down the comic book. He'd already picked it up and put it down a few times that morning, becoming increasingly of the view that there was more to it than met the eye. He had smoked numerous cigarettes. He had done a hundred press-ups. Agitated, instead of going to Dove's funeral, he decided to go for a run to clear his head and his lungs. Dove would understand. Distracting memories from the night before were not helping his powers of concentration as he tried to find meaning in Dove's work.

Rummaging around in his old bedroom, he rooted out some sports-wear and limbered up for the run, his first such foray in over two weeks. His hams were still tight from his last run. Indeed, every muscle and sinew was still ginger after that epic event. At various stages during that race, he thought he might never walk again, never mind run.

Dove had artistic flair alright. Nobody would deny him that, not now that he was dead. But in terms of composition and narrative coherence, he was no da Vinci. He wasn't even the fella who drew the stuff about the Nazi mice. Spiegelman. That book had been recom-mended to him by a welder in Houston who shared Philip's interest in man's inhumanity to man. Philip was no connoisseur of the form – the graphic novel, dismissing it as juvenile – but like many a seeker before him he appreciated a good story well told.

The heartbeat quickened as he hit his stride at the town boundary where a sign reading *Please Come Again* sounded a little too desperate. It occurred to him, to his shame, that his old friend was still capable of irritating him, even now, from beyond the grave, which either said something unflattering about Dove or, more likely, about himself. A car was following him at a discreet distance. He might have been aware of it and he might not.

It was not always easy to tell who exactly was who in Dove's troubling saga. True, a lot of the characters *seemed* familiar, a facial feature here, a giveaway accoutrement there. Brouhaha – Dove's avatar – was the most consistent character on display, fluctuations in size notwithstanding. Every so often, he received visions and had to sit down. These vivid dreams were brought on by a special serum, conveyed to his bloodstream via syringe. Well, they do say you should write about what you know. The late Tommy had hinted that Dove knew what happened to Sandra. There was an outside possibility that through the medium of *Brouhaha*, Dove had chosen to communicate with him. If he did have information about Sandra, he was clearly too frightened and paranoid to trust that information to somebody else. Each of the stories he'd read contained numerous allusions to places and events that, while they didn't necessarily pertain to Sandra, had relevance to themselves, and themselves alone. If there were more specific messages, he thought they were most likely to be couched in Brouhaha's dream bubbles. Mind you, Philip, a sceptic by nature, after a couple of passes with and without a magnifying glass, was far from sure that there were any clues.

He couldn't help thinking that he could use his time better. The temptation to turn to violence was strong, fighting being a pastime in which he'd gained some degree of proficiency since the hiding that left him scarred and bitter above in JJ's bar. He wouldn't like to overstate his prowess, but as a bouncer in one of the rougher Irish bars in Westchester County he had learned to look after himself. A fly in his nose, he permitted himself a brief fantasy about cornering, say, the likes of Charlie O'Dowd. One slap on the face and that coward would surely talk. Without breaking his rhythm, he pressed one finger on his left nostril and blew the fly from his right nostril.

For the greater part of that morning, he had tried to focus on the scenes in the book in which Brouhaha's best friend, Dearg Doom, made an appearance. This character, aloof as well as disloyal, was no doubt modelled on Philip himself. (And towards the end of the book, it didn't go unnoticed, Doom died a gruesome and undignified death, flailing headless into a lake of fire.)

Philip's perseverance had finally been rewarded at about half past eleven when he had the first proper inkling that Dove was *actually* communicating with him. Brouhaha and Dearg Doom were resting by a dolmen. After routing a horde of Ramen – although, incidentally, the People were now siding with the Ramen against the Committee! – and yet another futile hunt for the Middlemist Blue, Brouhaha sat down, took out his 'works' and injected himself. He then had one of his mysterious visions.

In the capacious bubble above his head, a character by the name of Ingram Cecil Connor III, an oracle of sorts, with angel wings, appeared pointing towards the sky. (As well as wings, he had hands too, which helped no end with the pointing.) The unusual name brought a smile to Philip's face. As boys, he and Dove had shared many interests and party pieces. And one of them was knowing the real birth names of famous people in the entertainment world. Just as Archibald Alexander Leach was Cary Grant and Reginald Kenneth Dwight was Elton John, Ingram Cecil Connor III, as all music aficionados knew well, was none other than Gram Parsons.

But why Gram Parsons? What was Dove trying to say? He was *definitely* saying something. Did the influential country music star's pointing finger have any significance? It looked like he was giving directions, but directions to where? The location of the Middlemist Blue? There was nothing else in the background landscape, apart from the dolmen, perhaps. He made a mental note to compile a list of dolmens in the area. Looking more closely at the picture, he noticed that Gram's hand, the one pointing upwards, had seven fingers. He wondered whether this phenomenon was based on recorded biographical and physiological fact. Was the freakish hand a cause of the late singer's own addictions? Or was it a sign?

Upping his pace, now, in the early afternoon, his limbs warm and relaxed, his sludge-blood thinning nicely, his breathing regular, he ran wherever his legs took him. There was maybe a bit too much granola in the belly courtesy of his mother, who had wrongly assumed he was a granola man, and he a rasher and sausage man through and through. 'In My Hour of Darkness', the only Gram Parsons song he knew word for word, was stuck in a groove in his head.

He passed a building site, twenty-four houses in all, frozen in various stages of incompletion. There was a cement-mixer half-full of cement, agape – looking like it was crying out for help like the fella in *The Scream* – in the middle of the ghost estate. This folly, situated in a floodplain, a hollow in the middle of nowhere, was surrounded by a wooden fence, the faded poster on the hoarding still promising happiness to young families, it being a nice enough place to live, picturesque and all, as long as you could manage without shops nearby and didn't mind a spot of flooding in the spring. No harm, thought Philip, misery aside, and squandered fortunes aside, that the work had stopped. It had stopped suddenly, too, it would appear, like in Hiroshima or Herculaneum or one of them places, transformed utterly by disaster, be it manmade or natural.

No harm in taking stock, he thought, once in a generation, downing tools and stopping all activity bar introspection. It was important to, in no particular order, reappraise what was real and what was not, reflect on matters of the soul, separate the integral from the superfluous, draw lessons from the well of history and, of course, remember the dead. The irony that he, of all people, Philip Sharkey, a beneficiary of economic booms from Abu Dhabi to that Dutch city built from scratch in the Zuider Zee, his small fortune squirrelled away in the Allied Irish Bank in Shepherd's Bush, was pontificating, albeit to himself, about the desirability of economic busts was not lost on him. He continued to run, not slowing, not pausing for breath, not dwelling on pain, revelling indeed in his own athleticism and impressed even by his own powerful frame, as if running would get him to a better future faster.

Gram Parsons! He incanted the name over and over again, rolling the r's, as if the name itself was a spell that would magically unlock a compartment in his mind containing the answer. As if the answer lay within himself. He broke up the words, Gram and Parsons, to form anagrams just as he and Dove would have done in happier days, the pretentious wordplay invariably met with scorn from their more Philistine friends, a clear sign they were probably homosexual. Gramps Arson? Did Sandra's grandad burn her body? Did she have a grandad? Or what about Mrs Paragons? There was no shortage of virtuous matriarchs in the town – although few of them, in all honesty, could be classified as killers.

Endorphins doing their job, the brain was firing now, albeit in a scattershot way. He was dredging up everything he knew about the short-lived alt-country forebear, which wasn't much. It amounted to, in short, a vague recollection that he was buried beneath a Joshua tree in Death Valley. That fact would have been promising, in terms of leads, if there were Joshua trees in Ireland, or indeed deserts, at least of the geographical variety as opposed to the cultural, where he could start digging. He turned around one hundred and eighty degrees and jogged backwards, hoping the change in orientation would provide him with a fresh perspective. It did.

An image sprang to Philip's mind of something else he'd seen in Dove's book that morning. It was that of another mysterious pointing figure drawn in a bubble above Brouhaha's head. His memory was hazy, but the character in question was a military doctor who went by the name of General Practice. He was a grizzled, grey-haired US army archetype in full Gulf War camouflage, with a white armband on his sleeve sporting a red cross. A veteran of an apocalypse, and a seeker, like Gram Parsons, he appeared to be looking for a rare bloom in the desert. He had no wings, but was the possessor of modest powers nonetheless, being the dispenser of truth-telling pills. To underline this point, General Practice was holding a large box of pills, marked Truth, in his right hand. The general was pointing firmly to his right, the reader's left. Philip was pretty sure that Dearg Doom was also in the picture, a witness to Brouhaha's crazy dream. He reminded himself to have a closer look at the general when he got home, if he could find his way home.

Not quite sure where he was now, having lost sight of the town's spires (as did so many of his fellow parishioners in recent years), he finally stopped. The car, a green VW Jetta, stopped too. If he hadn't noticed it before, he probably did now.

Philip had a good ten miles under his belt, according to his internal tachometer, but, he estimated, he was no more than three miles from the town centre. He had tried his best to circumnavigate the metropolis, the narrow roads not much help and they not being part of a grid system designed for the smooth flow of traffic or the safe passage of law-abiding motorists. Law-abiding motorists were famously few in these parts. The roads around Tullyanna were not geared for traffic at all. They were not for going places but part of a maze to prevent your escape.

What did General Practice and Gram Parsons have in common, apart from their initials and a very definite sense of direction? Philip racked his brains, trying to recall anybody else he knew whose name began with the letters G.P. Apart from Gerry Peyton, a one-time goalie for the Irish football team, but not to his knowledge a murderer, he couldn't think of anyone. Perhaps there was somebody in the town that Dove was trying to implicate, a Gerry or a Gretel. Or a family doctor? Healy's mate, the Doc? Healy, a walking phonebook, might know.

He jogged back towards home, resolved to phone Healy, the sinister car speeding past him, spraying him with gravel.

Postcards from the edge

Kevin was the first to arrive at the Old Forge, and he a good ten minutes early. It was the best restaurant in town by a mile. It was the only restaurant really, apart from a bog-standard Chinese, the usual chippers and, of course, the hotel. Mind you, the Cunningham Arms was better known for its gargantuan portions than the quality of its fare. The last time he was there was for a neighbour's wedding and he was offered six different potato options with his main course. Six! Boiled, mashed, roast, chips, croquettes, and something the fat-armed waitress called *leenase*, from which liquid oniony mess he, a potato connoisseur, recoiled in horror. Most of the people, at his table anyway, conscious of all the jiving ahead of them, ordered all six. Serious eaters. Serious jivers. He, in defiance of the doctor's orders and his family's attempt to implement them, settled for chips on that occasion.

He was beginning to think that Joanne had stood him up.

The waitress at that wedding, he recalled, had employed a spectacularly useless technique to dole out the chips, using only a spoon and a fork as a makeshift tongs. Pure, unadulterated folly. In all his years at the carvery, he had never seen more than two chips at a time being transferred from a serving dish to a plate with that particular accessory. One chip at a time was the outside max, on a good day. Sometimes no chips at all completed the journey through space from tray to plate. He tried to take it up with the manager. Some sort of trowel would surely have been more productive, but the manager was busy, and the sweat pouring off him, there being over three hundred people at the wedding. You'd be better off picking them up with your hands. The

Irish were supposed to be an ingenious people, yet they weren't able to come up with a better way of distributing chips. *No wonder we are in the mess we're in.*

Kevin was in good enough form.

He'd never dined at the Old Forge and was literally salivating at the prospect, having heard nothing but good reports. Sheila wasn't one for restaurants and considered this *date* with Joanne an indulgence too far. No matter. This was no time for soft-soaping the missus. Wasn't there work to be done?

He asked the waiter to set an extra place. Philip had called him to ask about doctors in the area. He was a bit vague, but Kevin was flattered that he'd called nevertheless and took the opportunity to invite him along. He judged that there was merit to be had in putting their respective heads together, Joanne's head, Philip's head and his own head, a Trinity of like minds, father, son and whatever Joanne was, a flame-haired spirit of some sort, holy or unholy as the case may be. He was convinced, even if Philip mightn't be, that she had goodness within her and good intentions too. Better a Triad, full of fight and motivation and more likely to succeed, than a Monad (himself) or a Dyad (the likes of himself and Keating) that didn't get very far in the past.

He was in good form now, having been in bad form earlier in the day and for the last ten years or more, and not simply in anticipation of a good feed. He felt almost alive again having been as good as dead, fooling people with his impression of a human being. All too accustomed to false starts, he had to be careful, and him on the cusp of yet another new beginning, not to look back on all the time he'd wasted. The whole days and months and years spent staring at the walls. It could put you in bad form again thinking about that.

'Sorry I'm late,' says Joanne to Kevin, plonking herself down.

'You're grand.'

'Lively spot.'

'Yes indeed.'

There was but one other diner present in the entirely beige dining room. It was, now that he had a good look at him, the German angler, who, without the waders and the khaki-coloured, multi-pocketed gilet, he failed to recognize at first.

'Maybe we should go somewhere a bit quieter. A dry white wine,' says she to the waiter before Kevin could get a word in, another of her resolutions gone by the wayside. 'Actually,' says she, 'make that a bottle. It could be a long night.'

Without pausing for breath, the journalist launched straight into her post-funeral visit to Carmel Mohan. So much for the preliminary small talk. So much for the chance for Kevin to deliver the little galvanizing speech he'd prepared by way of welcome. Although he'd been close enough to the Mohans during the darkest of days, he'd never gained their trust in the way Joanne had. Anyway, the gist of it was that Carmel, her memory now blurred by the booze, and her useless husband dead in the ground, wasn't able to offer Joanne much in the way of sense or fresh perspective. But she did give her a free run of the house. And Joanne had a look in her eye.

'The postcards Sandra supposedly sent from London. I think she wrote them here, in Tullyanna,' says Joanne.

'Right?'

Okay, welcome aboard, says Kevin to himself, sipping tap water. Better late than never, he thought, hoping that that wasn't it, that that facile deduction wasn't going to be the sum total of Joanne's contribution to the party.

'I found another one. Another postcard. That was never sent.'

'Oh?'

Kevin straightened up, the napkin, tucked into his neck in the style of a country squire, falling to his lap. During the original search for Sandra, he'd spent a lot of time downstairs in the cold Mohan kitchen, red-faced and ill-at-ease, trying desperately to think of something to say to Carmel and her late husband, something consoling and anodyne. He could hear his more experienced colleagues upstairs ransacking Sandra's bedroom, fairly thoroughly if the racket was anything to go by. Once or twice, he'd taken the liberty of poking around in her room, when the parents, Carmel and Tom, covered in cigarette ash, were asleep below in the matching armchairs. Very flammable chairs now that he thought about it. It was strange and a bit annoying that an amateur like Joanne could just waltz into the house all these years later and find something of note.

Joanne placed the postcard on the table. The Mohan address was on it, and Sandra's mother's name, and that was it, nothing else, no content, no stamp, no postmark. Nothing. He flicked it over. Like all the others Carmel had received, the image featured Princess Diana, this time sitting tiny and pitiful in front of the Taj Mahal.

'That was some job you lads did, Kevin, you should be ashamed of yourselves.'

'I don't disagree.'

'The chewing gum, under her bed. It's still there. Why was that never taken away for analysis?'

'Well . . . I don't . . . it wouldn't . . . it would only prove . . .'

'Sandra herself could have been hiding under the bed and you lot wouldn't have found her?'

'I'm sorry, Joanne. Where did you find it, if you don't mind me asking?'

'It fell out of an old paperback,' Joanne said, enjoying the effect of her discovery on Healy, 'a bookmark, possibly. *Of Mice and Men.*'

'I've heard tell of it.'

The waiter turned up before he could impress her further with his erudition.

'She had mentioned in her diary it was her favourite novel. The guards would have known that. If they had bothered to read her diary. The goat's cheese, please, and the medallions of pork,' says she.

How had she decided so quickly, with barely a glance at the menu? He'd studied the menu for a good ten minutes, spectacles on and spectacles off, while he'd been waiting for her, eyeing up the rabbit and the hake and the pork medallions, but unable to come to a firm decision. The hand-reared sausages had given him pause for thought, and he partial to sausages.

'How would you hand-rear a sausage?'

'What?'

Joanne was looking at him strangely. They obviously meant sausages from a hand-reared *pig*, a point he would take up later with the management. He was beginning to think coming to the Old Forge was a mistake.

'The soup and the steak, please,' says he, panicking, 'very, very, *very* well done. No sauce.' And before the waiter, Polish at a guess, could get away in his too-tight shiny slacks, Kevin added, stealing a quick, guilty glance at Joanne, who didn't seem the slightest bit interested in what he ate, 'And chips. Plenty of chips.'

It was definitely something, the card, but what? Having no postmark, it didn't originate in England. That was for sure. Presumably, it never left the girl's bedroom. Stating the obvious, they agreed that Sandra had started working on that postcard at home. In her house. Or in somebody's else's house. But not in England. It wasn't a stretch to extrapolate that she'd written the other cards at home, too – the ones that did supposedly arrive from England. Perhaps she wrote them all together in a batch, one after another, in her careful schoolgirl handwriting, over the course of a wet evening.

A plate of fish fingers with ketchup and oven chips beside her. The radio on. The boy racers outside doing handbrake turns. She would have had fun writing the cards. The tone is light, right? Larky? Her imagining what somebody in England would write home to her mother to put her mind at ease. She was actually very close to her mother, despite what some people thought.

Perhaps Joanne's trump card was one the girl mislaid. She'd placed it absent-mindedly in the book and forgot about it. And nobody had found it, until now. Kevin was doubtful.

'You needn't be raising your eyebrows at me, Kevin. The investigation was a disgrace.'

'I suppose.'

'What goes on down in Templemore anyway? Ireland's answer to Langley. Is it all fucking handball? Sorry. I went out with a guard. He was a prick. I know *you* did your best, Kevin. And that's why I'm here.'

In retrospect, it was more than possible that his colleagues didn't go through every single page of every single book in Sandra's bedroom.

This new postcard's existence confirmed what he had long suspected. The cards were a ruse. But what else did it prove? That she had planned to run away. There was no law against writing postcards to your mother well in advance of sending them. Was there any way they could be tied to Coleman? That was the question. Or to anybody else? Or could it shed light on her current whereabouts, dead or alive?

'Did Carmel show you the birthday cards?'

'She did.'

He had expected Joanne to be stubborn and uncooperative, slow when it came to sharing confidences. He was fully prepared to break her down using all his old charm and powers of persuasion. But by now well-lubricated on her second bottle of Sauvignon Blanc, she surprised him by extemporizing, albeit wildly, on the subject at hand.

'Coleman,' she pronounced, 'was probably in a relationship with Sandra. Of sorts. You know all this. Or at least she thought she was in a relationship with Coleman. Clearly abusive, if that was the case but . . . you're crying, Kevin.'

'No, no, just . . . sensitive eyelids. Dust.'

She handed him her napkin. 'For some reason, for the sake of argument, she had become a hindrance to him, a millstone, a liability.'

Joanne had a great way with words. Kevin was enjoying her riff, moved by the very fact that she was engaging with him, and that little Sandra was being brought back to life, summoned to their little séance at the Old Forge. He joined his hands together, resting them on his midriff, his thumbs rubbing tiny circles on his tummy. He was not just rapt but rather envious, too. None of the policeman's dull precision for Joanne! None of his procedural obligations. She was a typical writer, in his opinion, impatient to get to the nub of the story, but with a lively imagination and a rich vocabulary that he could never emulate in a thousand years. It was unfair. The people with the stories to tell didn't have the tools to tell them and the people with the talent had no stories to tell. She could conjure up a story out of thin air. And she had a great appetite, too, he was glad to see – Ciara was always very picky – polishing off the goat's cheese while his soup went cold.

'Do you think she became pregnant?' Kevin asked, blushing. 'Maybe that's why she went to England?'

Joanne smiled at Kevin. 'Nice try. You don't think she went to England no more than I do. And I can tell you for a fact she wasn't pregnant. Carmel assured me. I'll spare you the details.'

Although Joanne didn't do coyness as rule, she didn't want Kevin fainting at the table.

'Whatever way you look at it, Coleman must have wanted to get rid of Sandra. The postcards – and the birthday card – tell you that he'd promised her they'd run away together, just the two of them.'

'Hold on, Joanne. Stall the digger. What are you on about? There's no mention of Coleman in the cards.'

'I knew you'd bring that up.'

'Thank you.'

'Bear with me. It'll be worth it. They'd leave this sordid small town behind them, Sandra and Coleman. They'd go to America and open a launderette, or something, a bar. And serve chicken wings.'

'Chicken wings?'

'I actually know somebody from Drumahair who opened a chain of chicken wing outlets in Chicago. Eithne Kirwan. She started off in a van at the festival in Slane.'

'Fair play to her.'

'Look. It's not important what or where. But, the key thing, Kevin, it was to be their secret. She wasn't to breathe a word of the plans to anybody, not to her mother, not to her friends. Certainly not to Dove. Coleman would have told her he'd already bought the tickets.'

'Is that . . . I mean . . . or is it just you . . . sorry?'

'It's just a scenario.'

'Right.'

'Now. What if somebody followed them, to, let's say, Chicago, to bring her home, to split them apart and throw him in jail, where he'd die of a broken heart? They'd need a ploy to misdirect the posse. It was then that he, Coleman, urged her to write the postcards to her mother. It was his idea. He was clever. He's so fucking devious he probably convinced her that it was *her* idea. They weren't the ordinary, generic postcards you'd get in the local newsagent's. Did you see the selection up in Kennedy's on the Main Street? A picture of a mill? And even that was out of focus. No. He'd gone to a lot of trouble, sourcing English postcards, ones of Diana, an iconic figure in Sandra's imagination. She had referred to Princess Di a lot in the diary.'

Healy nodded.

'How did Coleman procure them?' he asked.

'Ah. It doesn't really matter, Kevin. Why would that matter?'

'Sorry.' Kevin knew it was a pointless question, but he wanted to ask *something* to show he was still invested in her story. She could be a bit direct sometimes.

'The main thing is, he'd get someone, a friend, a trusted friend, to post the cards from London. Everyone would think she was in London. That's what matters, right?'

'Right.'

'Right. Would you like a medallion?'

She offered him a piece of pork, dripping in a cider sauce, on the end of a fork.

'You're grand.'

'One by one, at regular intervals over the coming weeks, the cards, more and more mundane, would be sent, throwing everybody off their trail. Naturally, Sandra thought all this was exciting, illicit, fun. Who wouldn't? It was Coleman's stratagem but *her* handwriting, her words. Now, and this is where it might get complicated, because Coleman was clever, a bit too clever. What would he do? What would you do?'

'Me? Jaze. I don't know.'

'He wrote some cards, too.'

'Do you think?'

'Of course, he did. It makes sense, doesn't it? He was in the room. In her presence. The same type of postcard or similar. Beefeaters, Scots Guards. Whatever.'

'I'm not sure about that, Joanne. You're speculating wildly there now. That's off the charts speculation. So it is.'

Kevin was getting lost. Was Joanne drunk? He was about to call off the meeting as a dead loss. The steak, for once, was *too* tough.

'He had to humour Sandra, reinforce the ruse. After all, she was convinced that he was going to be with her.'

'Ah okay, I see,' says he.

He didn't see at all. Kevin was very sceptical at this stage but let her carry on.

'Addressed to who, Lonergan, O'Dowd, one of the inner circle? It doesn't matter, somebody, anybody, just to show her how committed he was to the plan. There was no need for his postcards to be posted, obviously, because he wasn't going anywhere. So, when her back was turned, he disposed of the ones he'd written, burned them, I suppose, or tore them into little pieces . . .'

'That's all very well . . .'

'Ah-ah . . . Kevin . . . that is to say,' she corrected herself with a satisfied smile, 'disposed of them all . . . except for one.'

She fished out a postcard from her handbag and waved it triumphantly under his nose.

'This one here! I give you, Mr Healy, Exhibit B.'

Joanne tossed the card on the table in front of a taken-aback Healy. She'd been bluffing. He thought she had nothing, that she was wattling, but like the good cardsharp she clearly was, she threw in her hand with a cocksure flourish. Then she downed a long, celebratory gulp of wine.

'Holy God!'

'That is the correct response, Kevin.'

Coleman's postcard was addressed to Sheriff, sure enough, and it jocular in tone. In it, he asked him if he'd sold the 'jalopy' yet and reminded him to feed the dog. He told him that himself and Sandra were struggling financially in 'London Town', but otherwise doing just fine. Sandra was starting a job at a shoe shop while he was still on the 'scratcher'.

'Sandra would have read that card. She'd have been reassured.'

'And it's definitely Coleman's handwriting?'

'It shouldn't be too hard to find out.'

The card, Joanne explained, had fallen out of the same book as Sandra's.

'*Of Mice and Men*?'

To his shame, Kevin had never read it, one of about a million books on his must-read list. He too had read in Sandra's diary that it was one of her favourite books. And yet he didn't have the cop-on to read it. Maybe if he had they wouldn't be here now

'Steinbeck, hah? *The Pearl* was a very good book,' says he. 'I forget what it was about now, but I remember it made a huge impression on me at the time.'

Kevin was a reader, a reasonably discriminating one, who made it his business, dictionary at hand, to understand every word he ever read. To his immense frustration, however, he could rarely remember the stuff of fiction, the detail, the storyline, the characters' names. He was unable to quote a catchy sentence, or a bon mot. He admired people like his good friend the Doc who could pepper their conversation with literary allusions, bamboozling people with their learning. Although not in any way a show-off himself, Kevin's only ambition in life was to know everything. When reading books, he hoped, in some way, that the import, the writer's intention, his or her insight and wisdom, would somehow be absorbed and shape him for the better. He was half-thinking of writing a novel himself some day. Sure, who wasn't?

'He must have left it behind inadvertently. I mean, let's face it, it was possibly a drug-fuelled burst of creativity.'

The best laid plans indeed, thought Kevin. That wasn't Steinbeck.

'Robert Burns,' he said. 'Rabbie.'

'What?'

'*The best laid plans of mice and men gang aft a-gley.*'

'Right.'

'It means to go astray. In Scottish.'

That was one of the few lines of poetry he could recall. It was something of a mantra to him, the only sure thing he knew about criminal activity, as well as every other aspect of human endeavour.

'It's definitely something.'

'It is, Kevin.'

There was now, as far as Kevin was concerned, clear evidence that Coleman was either planning to run away with Sandra or pretending to plan to run away with Sandra. Either way, it required an explanation.

It was at that point that the pair of them, by now finished their main courses, and both of them flushed, one on wine, the other on a mixture of positive developments and vivacious company, were joined by Philip Sharkey. Any plans of getting carried away were put on hold as the dining room darkened and the temperature dropped a few degrees.

Philip has a chip

To say Philip was frosty towards Joanne would be an understatement. The eyebrows knitted, he was pre-livid. She was, as far as he was concerned, a two-bit journalist who'd destroyed Dove's reputation. And, although they'd never even met in person, she'd dragged his own name, for what that was worth, through the same indelible mud. He had plenty to be disgruntled about, in all fairness.

'Just to set the record straight, I don't like you.'

'I'll take that as a compliment,' Joanne said. 'There's plenty of free tables if you want to eat on your own. Or, here, go and sit with the German fella over there. Tell him why you ran away.'

'I didn't run away.'

'No? One of your good friends goes missing in very suspicious circumstances and instead of helping to find her, you leave the country? Do you think we're all fools? Now, either you had something to do with it, or she wasn't very important to you.'

Philip, the face on fire, an ad for coal, the only thing missing the red setters, looked as if he could have done anything. What he did – after giving a pair of daggers to Healy – was to turn around and walk away. As a rule, Philip didn't like confrontation. He didn't like to lose control.

'That's it. Run away again. Once a coward.'

Philip turned back to them. 'You must be very proud of yourself. Casually ruining people's lives. Is it the money? Fame? Or do you just get great pleasure from seeing people suffer? You killed Dove. You might as well have pulled the trigger yourself.'

All fired up, he poured himself a generous helping from what was now the third bottle of wine and knocked it straight back, the eyes boring holes in Joanne, who calmly replied, 'Well. It's a pity you weren't here to stop me.'

At which point Healy waded in with his hose.

'I think, we should all just take a breath . . .'

Joanne and Philip both roared back, 'Shut up!'

Joanne apologized to Kevin as Philip sulkily took his seat. Kevin carried on as if he wasn't in the slightest bit humiliated.

'Philip, meet Joanne. Joanne has some very interesting information for us. Joanne, this is Philip. He was just biding his time, weren't you? A finer man you couldn't meet.'

After Kevin filled him in on the postcards development, Philip nodded, a decision visibly forming in his head, and turned to Joanne.

'You were right about one thing, though. We lied, me and Dove.'

He poured another large measure for himself and, chivalry trumping resentment, took the opportunity to top up Joanne's glass. She, equal to his gaze, took the opportunity to order another full bottle from the waiter. Jaze! Kevin didn't know where to look, his carefully assembled team already showing cracks, not to mention a weakness for the drink.

'We didn't see Sandra getting into Fergal's car. That was a lie.'

'I knew it.'

'You know nothing. I don't know why I'm telling you this. He thinks you might be an asset. I'm not so sure.'

Kevin, a queasiness spreading in his very full stomach, was afraid of what Philip was going to say next. He half-wished that the young man would stop talking as soon as possible, before his faith in mankind was irrevocably erased, along with his abiding source of self-validation, in good times and in bad, namely his ability to judge a man's character.

'This is what happened. I didn't tell you this earlier, Healy. We started walking towards Shadows, Sandra, Dove and me, when Dove had one of his brainwaves. He wanted to show her something, something nobody was supposed to see. I guess he was trying to impress her. You know Dove. He was out of his box. Hyper. I said no. But he wouldn't listen. He was off like the clappers towards Macker's father's field. You know, Healy, beyond the Wilson estate, about a mile off the main road to Castlecock? I tried to stop him, but what could I do? Are you getting all this?'

Joanne was writing away in a pad.

'I don't remember reading any of this in *Howarya!* Oh, that's right. You weren't there.'

If Joanne was put out by his hostile tone, she didn't show it.

'Why didn't you tell Kevin this at the time? Would have saved us all a lot of bother.'

Philip ignored her. The silence in the dining room was overbearing. The German had slipped away unnoticed. They can be very highly strung, the Germans, thought Kevin. Even the James Last Orchestra had downed their wishy-washy instruments for an impromptu fag break.

'I was hammered. Pallatic. Balubas. Whatever. Running through the field, avoiding the cow dung, you know, falling about the place. It was a bit of craic. Sandra jumped up on my back. We had a piggy-back race. Dove was pretending he had Mrs Kennedy on his back, the newsagent, you know, Healy, the size of her.'

'I remember her,' said Joanne.

'His legs were buckling beneath him. Dove could be funny when he put his mind to it. I could feel Sandra's breath on my ear. She started humming the theme tune to *Black Beauty*. The most *spontaneous* person I ever met. Her breath in my ear was nice. Nearly unbearable. We shoulder-charged him to the ground. Sandra fell off. While we were wrestling in the mud, she was lying on her back, wriggling her arms and legs like an upturned beetle that couldn't right itself.'

Joanne, nervous about where the story was going, couldn't help but smile at the image.

'You had to be there. I remember punching Dove in the guts. Friendly fire, like, no malice. And I remember him puking all over my trousers. You wonder why we changed our clothes? Well, that's the why. Anyway, Dove had it in his head. He wanted to show her the fucking bunker. The bunker in Macker's father's field.'

'Barry McManus,' mansplained Kevin, for Joanne's benefit, '*the* Barry McManus.'

The name rang a bell, as it should have. A very loud bell.

'Thank you, Kevin. I do read the papers from time to time.'

'Sorry.'

She wrinkled her nose. Macker, of course, was one of Coleman's acolytes. 'So Macker is Barry McManus's son?'

Kevin and Philip exchanged a knowing smirk.

'Do you mind?' Philip asked Joanne, not waiting for an answer as he drained the third bottle into his glass.

'My pleasure,' she replied, 'anything to help you calm down.'

She liked his laconic delivery. His control.

'Macker had shown it to us about six months earlier. On St Stephen's Day. We found it handy enough using an old oak tree and a shed as points of reference. He had a good sense of direction, Dove, a good sense of spatial awareness. As did I. With his bare hands, he pulled away at the sods that concealed the entrance to the bunker. You're talking a manhole, basically. And he lifted up the metal hatch. I said I'd keep nix. This was not my idea of fun, knowing Macker's dad. Not my circus, not my monkeys. Anyway, Dove leading the way, they both climbed into the hole, himself and Sandra, down the steel ladder. I'd been in it before, the last time with Macker, and was sworn to secrecy. I didn't need to see it again. There was a tunnel about ten foot long that led to two rooms, one on either side of the tunnel, both of the rooms fairly solid by way of construction: concrete walls, concrete floors, electric light, ventilation, the whole works. It was fairly elaborate by any standards. Dry enough, too. One room had bunkbeds and a stock of canned goods, a camping stove, Scrabble. Darts.'

'Scrabble? Holy God!' whistled Healy through his bushy moustache.

Philip stared at the table for a few seconds. He picked up a cold chip from Kevin's plate and sucked the salt off it before putting it down.

'And the other one? The other room?'

'The other room? Well, I don't have to tell you. Guns.'

'Guns?' gasped the hitherto unflappable Joanne.

'That's right, guns. You seem surprised. I thought you knew the whole fucking story.'

She knew of Barry McManus. And she knew never to enter his field. There were all sorts of rumours associated with the property, ranging from fairy forts to gun ranges, but nobody knew anything about a bunker. Apart from Philip obviously.

'I thought all the bunkers in the area had been decommissioned?'

'This one wasn't,' he snapped, correcting himself, more civilly. 'Well, not at the time, no. It was stuffed, so it was, floor to ceiling with weapons, all sorts of weapons, Kalashnikovs, Uzis, I don't know the brand names, the whatdoyoucallit, the calibre. There was any amount of ammunition. A rocket launcher. There was even a flamethrower, for fuck's sake. What they needed with a flamethrower I don't know. They didn't stay long below, the pair of them, a couple of minutes at most, before Sandra screamed. It wasn't a giddy scream. She was spooked, seriously spooked. And next thing she scrambled back up the ladder. And ran. Suffice to say, Dove's plan failed.'

'The best laid plans . . .'

Philip gave Healy a withering look.

'She ran back across the fields, high heels in her hands. We sprinted after her, not especially alarmed by whatever it was triggered her dramatic flight. To us, in our state, it was all a laugh, a comical situation, surreal, the whole thing, us, filthy, running across the fields, and conscious of the danger we'd be in if we were caught. Could you imagine, Healy? If Barry McManus had caught us?'

'I could.'

'We went back into town, the three of us. She wanted to go home and change. Likewise, Dove and me. We said we'd we see her later at Shadows and that was that, we went our separate ways. As you know, she didn't show up there.'

'Why do you think she was spooked?'

Philip studied Joanne for a full minute before he answered her, somehow keeping his eyes from abseiling down her body. He impressed himself with his self-control. His distaste for her was real and justifiable, although somewhat honeyed by meeting her in the flesh. Face to face, she was clever and loquacious, and down to earth, and that was before she even opened her mouth, a disarming smile not far from her lips. That was a bit of a head-wreck. He had braced himself for a showdown with a po-faced, self-righteous, uptight, narrow-minded, set-in-her-ways hypocrite. And, in fairness, had got one. What he wasn't braced for was *humour*. Nor *mellowness*. Nevermind *sexiness*. Of course, this was no time for such distractions. Besides, she might be putting on an act.

'I don't know.'

'But you have an idea?'

'Maybe I do.'

Healy was looking at Philip imploringly, like a dog who hadn't been walked for two days. He was willing Philip to put his differences with Joanne aside and, for the love of God, get on with the story.

'I got the impression, not at the time, mind you, later, much later, that maybe, maybe she'd been there before. In the bunker. She had some sort of a flashback.'

Kevin made a mental note to check out the field, Macker's father's field, and the bunker beneath it, if such a thing still existed. Most of the bunkers in the area, and by all accounts there had been loads of them, had been destroyed, as Joanne suggested, and their lethal contents decommissioned under the watchful eye of the Canadian peacemaker, the General de Chastelain. Not being in possession of thermal imaging equipment himself, or diggers and sniffer dogs, he knew he was going to have to approach the guards sooner rather than later. He'd have to appeal to his old back-stabbing friend Detective Sergeant Peter Keating's better nature, with a view to searching the place on the off-chance Sandra's remains were there. Philip's impression that Sandra had a connection to the place wasn't an awful lot to go on, but at the same time it mightn't be nothing.

The problem, as Kevin saw it, was that Barry McManus, a farmer and, formerly, if you were to believe everything you hear, a maker of bombs, a master bomber, no less, the brains behind the blowing-to-bits of a building in Manchester in which two men were killed, was now a fuel smuggler. And, apparently, his farm was off-limits to civil servants of every grade and department, for reasons too convoluted to detail, bound up with the Peace Process. His past was forgotten, for the sake of the Peace, his current illicit trade tolerated, his lorries, hogging the road, allowed to come and go as they pleased, his millions untaxed, his slate clean. All in the name of Peace. Peace didn't come cheap in these parts.

'It was Coleman who asked us to lie about his car. Well, O'Dowd did, on Coleman's behalf, out on the dance floor. I remember him screaming in my ear, "*You're to say Coleman gave her a lift, in his car, do you hear me? Coleman gave her a lift.*" They were trying to muddy the waters. Telling us one thing and other people something else. Create confusion left, right and centre. That's why we told the guards what we told them, not knowing what we know now. You see, you know this, Healy, we hung around Coleman's. We did little jobs for him, Dove and me. Everybody did. He looked after us, you know what I mean. We weren't *involved*. We weren't trusted. Not that we wanted to be involved or trusted.'

'How do we know you're not lying now?' says Joanne to Philip.

'You don't,' says he, 'but we are where we are.'

Joanne excused herself and, impressively steady on her feet, went outside for a smoke. She had warmed to Philip as he told his story. She liked his seriousness. But, and there was no getting away from it, she was a bit *rocked* by what she'd heard. Why had he kept all this to himself? Why hadn't he gone to the guards with this information at any time in the last thirteen years? Why was the bunker still there? Sandra could be in that bunker. There might be evidence in the bunker, fingerprints, clues. Was that all he knew? Likeable as he was, he was very irresponsible. And seemed to be simmering away with a potentially destructive rage. And she wasn't a hundred per cent sure that she trusted him.

Inside, Healy tried to make sense of the recent findings.

'You're some boy, hah.'

'Sorry?'

'Sorry, says you, is that all you can say? Jaze, you're full of surprises. What else are you going to tell us? You know what happened to Shergar? You could be arrested.'

Philip sighed. He was having second thoughts about this whole strategy of Healy's. Talking. Sharing. All that over-rated gibberish. You could get yourself in trouble talking. More trouble than not talking, and that was trouble enough. You could be misunderstood. In fact, the main outcome of most conversations was catastrophic misunderstanding. No matter how articulate you were, and he was aware that he wasn't in the highest percentile in that regard, no two people spoke the same language. That was the root of the human tragedy.

A man of few words, his policy had always been to keep his thoughts to himself. It was a policy that had served him well. He was fine with grunts and whistles, the perfectly intelligible lingo of the building trade and expat GAA clubs. But he knew from his occasional lapses in concentration that you could get intoxicated on your own guff, saying something you'd later regret. One of his big failings as a human being was that he used to give people too much credit. He credited them with emotional intelligence, an ability to understand what you were thinking and feeling, without you having to spell everything out, slowly, in capital letters, as if you were dealing with a child. Singing, of course, was a different matter entirely. Singing, in his experience, could get you out of the trouble you'd talked yourself into.

Philip, furrowing his brows, asked a question he'd been meaning to ask.

'Why do you bother?'

'Give her a chance. She's grand.'

'No, *you*?'

'Ah.'

'Why do *you* bother?'

'Me? You have to do something.'

'Why this? I don't get it. Why the obsession with Sandra?'

'It's not an obsession, Philip. More a hobby. I'm just curious to find out what happened. That's all.'

What he should have said was, *I want to get my life back. I want to rewind the clock, undo all the damage I've done to my family. I want all that time staring at the walls to count for something. I want purpose and meaning in my life.* But he didn't want to scare him away, so he smiled instead, as if he was the happiest man in the world.

Another appalling idea crossed Kevin's mind that he also thought wasn't worth mentioning. That his obsession, there was no two ways about it, with Sandra Mohan was the *excuse* for his paralysis rather than the cause. If he had solved the case in 1994, as he should have, would he really be any different now? Would he be high-flying in a permanent state of bliss? If he solved the case now, would that really change anything? As long as the case lasted, he wouldn't have to answer that question.

'Curiosity? Is that it?'

'Well.'

'Me, I want to clear my name. I want Dove to be exonerated. What's in it for you?'

'To tell you the truth, Philip, I don't know what's in it for me. It could be very little. Or it could be an awful lot. That's another thing I want to find out. What it all means for me.'

The last sentence came out in a whisper. The man's face deflated. The bags under his eyes, bulging, Philip noticed, with nought but sorrow.

'Sorry for asking.'

'No, no. I ask myself the same question every day.'

While they waited for Joanne to return, there was a very long pause in the conversation during which tectonic plates shifted and volcanoes smouldered. Healy eventually spoke.

'C'mere, Philip, can I ask you something?'

'Sure.'

'Do you think I should pay for this?'

'What?'

'She invited me to dinner. But I invited you. What do you think? The etiquette? I mean, as the convenor, let's say, of this quango, I feel I should stand you two the meal.'

'I didn't eat.'

'Well, yes, but you did have some wine, if you don't mind me saying so.'

'A glass.'

'Two or three glasses, in fairness, Philip, not that I was counting. And a chip.'

'A chip? I licked the salt off a chip.'

'It's just, she might be on expenses. And it *was* her idea to meet here. What do you think? I mean, I don't mind paying.'

'It's up to you.'

'Or maybe we should split it? Hah?'

Joanne returned to the table.

'Ah Joanne, good woman, you're back, I was just saying, I should be hitting the road. The wife!'

Kevin winced. Why did he have to say that to Joanne? She'll think I'm very old-fashioned, he thought, Healy the hen-pecked husband! A country bumpkin! A dinosaur! A sexist prig!

Joanne sat down and ordered another bottle of wine and, without consulting Philip, a couple of double Hennessys. Kevin asked her if he could take the two postcards, Sandra's unfinished one and the one Coleman allegedly wrote, and make copies of them. It was a request she politely refused. Although nonplussed and slightly hurt, he apologized for asking, remembering that she was a journalist, first and foremost, and probably had her reasons. She apologized, too, justifying her stance on the basis that she didn't know him well enough, not, she added, that she didn't trust him. What had she heard about him, he wondered, trying not to appear hurt? By way of conciliation, she photographed the postcards on her phone and said she'd send them to his email.

A number of ideas floating in his head in need of mooring pronto, he got up. A sudden bore of pain barrelled through his innards. Between the pain, and the serious mulling he had to do, information processing that was better done alone, he had decided to go home. Despite the new findings, the unlikely trio were all of one mind not to involve the guards, at least not yet.

Kevin stood awkwardly beside the table. Over-hot in his coat and not knowing what else to do, he bowed. He clicked his heels and bowed, something he had never done before, in any situation, not even when he socialized with the General de Chastelain when he was in town that time to decommission the arms.

'Will I get the bill?'

'That would be great, Kevin,' says Joanne, her eyes locked on Philip. 'I'll owe you.'

Brilliant, thought Kevin, at the till, his credit card in his hand, his pension stretched in all directions and Sheila's legacy, at this stage, practically zilch. God knows where they'll get the money for Shane to go to college – that's, of course, if the lad knuckles down and gets the points for college! Holding his breath in an attempt to starve the writhing creature in his stomach of oxygen, he was sorry to be leaving the party.

But between the three of them, they were getting somewhere. No doubt about it in his mind. Sandra was calling out to him. Her plaintive voice was getting clearer. In every murder case he was ever involved in or ever read about somebody knew something. That goes without saying. And if the time was right (months later or even years), and if the circumstances were right (the inciting incident that was Dove's suicide), that somebody might just spill the beans. Or at least a bean or two. All you needed was patience. Endless patience. And a bucket to catch the falling beans. Already, Philip had provided new evidence, too much, says you, and Joanne herself, in all fairness, had produced the goods, too. All he had to do was listen, tune in to the right frequencies and let Old Bessie do her business. He tapped his head.

He was confident that it was the right time, and that he had the right team, and that all the pieces were finally falling into place.

Joanne on fire

'Does anyone really know anyone?' Philip asked, licking the last drop of Cognac from the rim of the glass.

Was he having a dig or what?

'What are you driving at?'

'You don't know the first thing about me. I don't know the first thing about you.'

'No argument there.'

'You definitely didn't know Dove.'

'No, Philip, you're absolutely right. I didn't. Nobody really knows anyone, but that doesn't mean we should all stop trying to figure each other out?'

'Mmm.'

'By using our *imaginations*, Philip, on the evidence of our eyes and our ears and our basic cop-on, we can create a picture of someone.'

'A wrong picture.'

'Well, you have to start somewhere. Christ.'

Philip caught the waiter's attention. He pointed at the two rapidly drained brandy glasses. 'When you're ready, boss.'

'You give your impression,' Joanne pressed home her point, 'I give mine. And somebody else gives theirs. And we might get somewhere. You have a *composite*. A fuller picture of the person.'

'Sure.'

'You get a *sense* of the person. You look fierce sceptical.'

'A wrong sense.'

'Jesus. You're some craic. I'm glad I stayed.'

Joanne, well used to arguing, and bolder with drink on board, leaned across the table and pointed at him.

'You are who you *appear* to be. Not who you are in your own *head*. Or who you *want* to be. You are who you are to *others*. *You,* for example – based purely on my recent observations – are a gloomy fucker.'

'Ha. You got that right.'

Philip laughed for the first time that evening. That month. It sounded to his ears like one of those go-to arguments, a notion that hardens as fact the more times you say it. It's not that he disagreed with her. They stayed in the dining room drinking for hours, long after Gregory the waiter had gone home. They moved into the kitchen. A seriously peckish Philip lit up a gas ring. He opened the fridge. 'You hungry?'

Philip made bacon sandwiches, scraping the white stuff off the fried rashers. Joanne found some Marsala wine.

As honestly and accurately as he could, Philip collated his recollections of his brief time on Earth with Sandra Mohan. Two years at most. He recalled how they first met.

'It would have been the teenage disco at the Holy Family hall. She would have been all of fourteen when she *gravitated* towards us.'

Joanne could visualize the scene.

'There was a guy, you might remember him, David Salmon? Davey. He won a disco-dancing thing in Dublin, a competition, thought he was great.'

'Vaguely.'

'We used to call him Bojangles, Mr Bojangles.'

'Yeah. With the headband?'

'Exactly. Such a dick. Moved over from England. So obviously he was *cool*.'

Joanne smiled. That's right. Anything remotely English *was* cool.

'His father was a wrestler. Nobody believed it until he turned up on *World of Sport* one Saturday afternoon.'

Joanne, to her surprise, found Philip's delivery quite diverting.

'Anyway, he was doing his thing on the floor, with the serious head on him, all his little fans around him, swooning. And Dove made a headband for himself, out of a T-shirt, and started copying Davey's moves. At which point Sandra came over to join us. She'd been hanging out the other side of the hall with some of the chief arseholes of the town, all pushing and shoving, the usual, trying to cause trouble. At first, we thought they were putting her up to it, you know, taking the piss out of us innocent dry-shites. But no, she stayed the whole night. She thought Dove was hilarious. He was. And that was that. Part of the furniture.'

Joanne put herself in Sandra's shoes. The deliberate decision on Sandra's part, as she unsteadily embarked on that momentous journey across the dance floor, to seek a better life in a new world. *Christ, this Marsala is rough!* Joanne was slightly annoyed that Philip didn't seem to know the Sandra she knew in glimpses – the poverty, the *judginess* she would have endured, the condescension, the *strain*.

'You're right. I don't think I really knew her at all. At that age, girls are a mystery. A curiosity.'

'Don't get me fucking started.'

'What?'

'That's exactly it, Philip. Do you have any idea what it's like to be a mere *curiosity*? A girl growing up in a small town like Tullyanna or Drumalair? Stared at. Inspected. Like meat. Every time you walk up the street.'

'Fuck me. Who's the misery guts now? You know I fancied you?'

'Sorry?'

'You used to come to our school for the honours maths, on Thursdays, you and two other girls.'

'I remember.'

'It was the highlight of the week. I'd be waiting for you all morning, looking out the window. I used to dream about you.'

'There you go.'

'I used to put wax in my hair on the off-chance you'd spot me in the yard.'

'Fuck me. I rest my case.'

There were some coy looks. Some adjusting of body positions on the stainless-steel units. Some meaningful stares. Some lulls in the conversation as they mulled over the advisability of giving in to their fleeting wants and needs. The pragmatics of it all. The contradictions between their *politics* and their *natures*. Philip had left the gas ring on after frying the bacon. The back of Joanne's blouse had caught fire and she unawares. Philip, not wanting to cause any alarm, approached her cautiously with a damp chef's apron in his hand. She was slightly alarmed, not knowing of his honourable intentions, as he, enveloping her, expertly doused the flames. Apart from that, as far as he was concerned, *nothing* happened. The last thing Philip remembered was embracing Joanne outside the Old Forge and heading for home.

PART THREE

Thunder Road

Healy, after the excitement of the evening, and after filling himself up with coffee and analgesics, was in no fit state for bed. After kissing his sleeping wife, and kissing his sleeping grandson, he tiptoed into Shane's room and tried to kiss his only son, who gently brushed him off.

'Dad, I'm still awake.'

'Sorry.'

Had he been a good father? Well, he was *there* all the time, in body at least, if not in mind, if that meant anything, a familiar and fairly benign feature of the house. Like a bit of old coving. He feigned interest in all their activities. That's not exactly right. He was interested. Very. It's just that enthusiasm had been hard to come by, ever since he was shot. So he had to fake it, as he had to fake all the other emotions too. Hopefully, it amounted to the same thing, the real and the fake, and had the same desired effect. Hopefully, the love he had for them but couldn't express registered with them in some way. Ah well.

Kevin retired quietly to his office, closing the door behind him. There, he shuffled through his vast collection of vinyl before selecting an album. It was Bruce Springsteen's *Born to Run*. He hadn't played it in years, not being overly enamoured with the man's penchant for cut-off sleeves, wasteful, in his view, of good plaid. He wasn't too sure about the old draft-dodging either – *alleged* draft-dodging, to be fair – not that draft-dodging was a bad thing in itself. If Springsteen, for the sake of argument, had been a delicate lad, with dainty heels and some sort of affliction, like Sever's disease, that would be one thing. If he was the son of a retail king, you wouldn't be surprised to hear he'd cried off the war. You'd think, *Typical, Daddy, the Mattress King of New Jersey, pulled a few strings*. If he just held his hands up and admitted, fair cop, that he was scared, a scaredy cat, his decision to avoid the war would have been under- standable. And acceptable. And forgivable. Being shot at is no fun. Being shot just once, one bullet, by one man. No fun at all. Kevin wouldn't wish that on anyone. Never mind being riddled with bullets for years on end, day and night, by any number of men, and women too by all accounts, who were every bit as hostile as the men if the historical record was anything to go by. But, the thing is, and there was no getting away from it, Springsteen was supposed to be a tough guy, tender but tough, an uncomplicated American everyman, an average dancer, a man of the people and not just any old cute hoor from an influential family. Dodging the draft was, surely, whatever way you looked at it, at odds with the image. It flew in the face of the whole fist-pumping patriotic routine. No offence to the Boss.

And although the sound was great, and the songs undeniably catchy, Kevin didn't care much for blue-collar escapist fantasies either as a genre. Hollow promises, lies, in fact, as far as he was concerned, peddled to the young and impressionable. Like everything would be grand if you just ran away. Totally irresponsible.

And while he was on the subject – aware he was procrastinating before getting down to the more urgent business of the night – Kevin loathed the term 'blue collar'. He'd heard Springsteen fans bandying about the expression and it entirely irrelevant to most Irish people – the industrial revolution having bypassed the country, and Spinning Jenny being a 'medicine woman' from Clare who danced to save the harvest and was accused of witchcraft – farmers and shopkeepers and the like, the majority of whom never held a blowtorch or wore a visor in their lives. In fact, many of them avoided the city at all costs, except to see Bruce Springsteen on the rare occasions he came to town. And then, and only then, they threw on the new jeans and went into a jiving blue-collar frenzy. Some of them even wore bandanas. Jaze!

The guards whose ranks he'd once distinguished were *literally* blue collar. They *wore* blue collars. *They* were the rightful heirs to that title but got little or no recognition for it. He himself grew up in what a sociologist might call a working-class home, his father a farmer and mother a nurse, but such crass distinctions didn't tell the full story. They didn't tell any story at all.

Kevin didn't dodge the draft. Not that he was in any way drafted. He wasn't *forced* to join the guards. He volunteered. Proudly. Against his parents' wishes. Mind you, he was *forced* to leave the guards. *Drafted* into civilian life, you could say, against *his* wishes, and he a conscientious objector at the time to being a civilian.

Still, he was supposed to be good live. Bruce. His was a great show, by all accounts, although at three hours a bit long, a bit eager to please, in Kevin's opinion, the result of guilt, probably, guilt about his blue-collar buddies spilling their guts in Vietnam while he was dreaming up tortured torch songs in his bedroom. There was a reason he stuck on Bruce Springsteen. What the hell was it?

Right, the postcards. He'd been over this about a thousand times. It was definitely Sandra's handwriting on the postcards. According to the handwriting expert, who, Kevin recalled, had passed himself off as a bit of a genius, he could tell the difference between a forced hand and a free hand and those postcards she sent to her mother were undoubtedly written of her own volition.

Kevin found himself humming along to 'Thunder Road', drumming his desk with his fingers, the reservations about Springsteen disappearing in the rear-view mirror as he mentally hit the road, his mind mercifully escaping from his body. And then a miracle happened – well, a connection. Two distinct facts fused. Elated, he felt like a physicist must feel on discovering a new equation, the music, expanding and slowing the mind, something of a catalyst.

The poster! The feckin' poster! Wasn't Stephen Sheriff at the Springsteen concert in London on 10 July 1994? He said so himself. *A deadly concert!* Kevin opened his laptop and double-checked the date. Bingo! And unless his memory failed him, one of Sandra's postcards had a postmark showing the exact same date: 10 July 1994. A coincidence?

Kevin, the mind quickly reuniting with the body, moved towards a battered filing cabinet and extracted a folder. Hands shaking, he flicked through the photocopies he had kept of the original six post-cards Sandra 'sent' and found the one he was looking for. It was postmarked Greenwich, 10 July 1994. The image on the front was a picture of Princess Diana, wistful as usual, and all dressed in white at the Pyramids of Giza. There were no two ways about it, Sheriff must have posted the card.

Unless.

Abruptly, he stopped the music by lifting the needle with a shaky index finger, scratching the LP in the process. No matter. He wouldn't be listening to that shite again. Unless it was, say, Philip who posted the card. Philip, after all, had moved to London around that time. As had half the country. It could have been anybody. He was annoyed at himself, the joy in his tiny triumph stillborn. Doubt and the enormity of what he'd taken on threatened to overcome him again. The familiar hamster of panic scuttled around inside his chest. No. Stop it! It had to be Sheriff.

But he needed to be absolutely certain. He knew well, no matter how many scraps of evidence you could assemble, lovingly and with patience over many years, solving a case like this one was next to impossible without some sort of a miraculous intercession. You were, generally speaking, looking for a *deus ex machina* in the form of a tip-off from a member of the public. Or, better still, a dead body. But a tip-off would do. Most police success, in his experience, and he was embarrassed to admit it, was as a direct result of a phone call. In fact, he couldn't remember a single crime he himself or any of his colleagues had so-called 'solved' without the tip-off, without some timely intervention by a bored and lonely busybody, or some half-cut but highly observant insomniac, or some turncoat accomplice who'd recently found God. The talent, if there was any talent involved, was perhaps to be found in selecting the right person to lean on, or in recognizing a genuine lead when it was dangled in front of your face. A phone call wouldn't go amiss now, Kevin thought, or, failing that, some sort of a landslide that would unearth Sandra's corpse. While waiting for an earth-shattering intervention from the gods, Kevin would, of course, continue his painstaking, one loping foot in front of the other, approach to the job.

Sheriff had a sister in London with a strong stomach, by his reckoning, and her working for Lewisham council. Her latest contribution to that august body, if a cursory internet search was to be trusted, was a policy paper she'd co-authored on 'cohesion' within the community, called *The 2007 Cohesion Review*. He didn't have time to read the whole thing but found it fascinating. The sister, if she was as compassionate as her work suggested she was, might be able to tell him if her brother was indeed the man who posted the cards.

The room suddenly felt cold. He froze on the spot for a second, the sweat on his back now cold, the hands clammy. He felt the breath on his neck as his own breathing became short but was afraid to turn around. Kevin had secured all the doors and windows religiously, as he did every night. And the night was still and no wind was stirring. Falling forward in slow motion, the blood pressure dropping dramatically, the consciousness receding, he thought he saw a face at the window.

The phone rang. Kevin leapt to his feet to answer it before immediately fainting again thanks to the old hypotension. He struggled to his feet more slowly this time and pounced on the phone, not wanting to wake the family and it four in the morning. It was his daughter, Ciara, calling from Sydney, at, he did a quick calculation, doing his timezone arithmetic on his fingers, about lunchtime Down Under. She was calling from a police station in a place called Kings Cross and she was crying, missing her baby. Knowing Ciara, she'd probably skipped lunch, too, a divil for the low blood sugars. Runs in the family. The police didn't hold out much hope of finding her handbag, which contained, needless to say, her phone and her baby photos, as well as her passport. Although she didn't say it, he knew she'd lost the walnut too. Of that he was sure. That was why she was calling him in the middle of the night. Not to tell him that. The gudgeon pin keeping the whole show on the road. The keystone holding the world in place. No more than himself, she couldn't rely on luck alone from now on.

He was ashamed of himself for thinking of the walnut at a time like this and his only daughter at her wits' end, and it only a walnut. But the charm's value was incalculable, either worth nothing or priceless. It had been pressed into his hand by an old man, an apparition on a lonely stretch of the Camino near Ventas de Narón. It was a ghostly figure that emerged from a blizzard of snow, it being February in the north of Spain. A poor man, trousers held up with string, he had a premonition that he was going to die and exhorted Kevin to pray for him in a language he didn't understand. He begged him, in fact, in the most urgent way, to kneel down and pray for his soul in the famed cathedral of St James in the city of Santiago when Kevin reached the end of his pilgrimage. The man even showed the *peregrino* how to kneel, lest he was an unbeliever – as if Kevin was on a mere hike – and traced with his hand in the air the twin towers of the church, a destination the dying peasant had never reached himself, despite living his whole life not fifty miles from there. All this Kevin divined, his Spanish being non-existent, the old man's great need surmounting the trivial language barrier between them. Walnut firmly in hand, Kevin looked around for his travelling companion but the Doc had gone on ahead. When he looked back, the old man was gone.

Three days later, jubilant and fulfilled on his arrival in Santiago de Compostela, having completed the one hundred kilometre walk and raised 1,370 old punts for the Simon Community and gorged himself on no end of octopuses, he knelt and prayed in the imposing Gothic edifice, the resting place of St James, by far and away his favourite saint, after St Dymphna, and prayed for a good hour or more, for everyone he knew, and he a religious man, at the time, for his family and friends, of course, and for Sandra, too. But didn't he forget, in all his fervour, to pray for the soul of the walnut man, by now deceased, although Kevin wasn't to know it. Although he prayed for the stranger every day since, he could never forgive himself for that tiny lapse in concentration. He mustn't let his mind wander. Lose sight of the grail.

'Are you still in touch with Orla?'

'What?'

'Orla, you know? What's her name? A niece of Stephen Sheriff. Nice girl with the gap in her teeth.'

'Daddy, my bag was stolen.'

'Sorry, love. I'm sorry.'

'Orla O'Reilly? She's in Portlaoise. What about her? Is she in trouble?'

'God, no, I was just wondering if you were still friends.'

'Well, yeah. Daddy, are you okay?'

'Grand, love.'

He told her a little of the comings and goings in town over the couple of days since she'd left. Dove's suicide got a mention, as did his funeral. Philip Sharkey's return and Tommy's untimely departure from this Earth got a look-in as well, as did Joanne McCollum's arrival on the scene. It was a bulletin that didn't make Ciara any more homesick than she already was. The report succeeded, if anything, in taking her mind off her own little setback. It encouraged her, in fact, to count her blessings. She was also heartened to hear that her adorable father was in better form than she'd left him.

'Do you have her number? Orla's?'

'Eh, my phone was in the bag?'

'Sorry. Of course.'

'I'll get it for you.'

'Thanks, love. It's actually her aunt's number I was looking for, her aunt in London.'

'I didn't know she had an aunt in London.'

'She does. Noeleen. That's her name. Noeleen.'

'Okay. I'll see what I can do.'

'Good woman.'

Forty minutes later, he persuaded her to put him on to a policeman, who, tickled by Kevin's diplomatic niceties, collegial manner and canny appraisal of the Australian cricket team – cricket being another of Kevin's off-kilter interests – promised him he'd find Ciara's bag. Luckily, the Aussie cops were paying for the call.

He hung up and stared defiantly into the garden. He didn't care who was there – the hooded men, the Galician peasant, Sandra Mohan herself, or any of the other people, alive or dead, who might have a grievance with him.

* * *

After he was shot in his car outside the front door of the Blackhill post office, Kevin found it hard to look people in the eye. Keating, his then partner, had been nosey-ing around at the back of the premises, trying to figure out why the post office was closed at half-ten on a Tuesday morning. To this day, Keating could never forgive Kevin for being shot. Even though it wasn't in any way Keating's fault, it didn't reflect well on him. Your partner being hit and you doing nothing to stop it was not a good look in anybody's book. That was something Keating was going to have to live with, and no amount of wise-cracking and throwing his weight around would erase it from the record. So they stopped looking at each other in the eye.

For months after the event, Kevin was wary of every man he met, friend or stranger alike. He sized them up, wondering if he might be the triggerman. For years. No matter who he was talking to or how well he knew them, he wondered, was this the man behind the mask, the man who watched him bleed? The man who inexplicably let him live? Or, if he wasn't the shooter himself, did he know who the shooter was?

After the initial wave of euphoria passed, the elation at still being alive, the confidence began to drain from him day by day. He became suspicious. Despite the hours of counselling, it got to the stage where he thought that everybody, except himself, knew the identity of the armed robbers. And that they were either actual accomplices of the attackers or approved, in some tacit way, of the attackers' actions. That was the beginning of the Saul Bass tumble into the void for cardboard Kevin. It wasn't long before he became a bit reclusive, with a penchant some people regarded as excessive for home security.

He went about fortifying the house with extra locks and bolts, burglar alarms, iron grilles on the windows, CCTV cameras and an inordinate number of crucifixes to protect the family home. For a time, he became convinced that he was being followed, spied on. In his paranoid state, his convictions hardened. He stopped going to the shops, sure that he would be targeted again. Apart from his immediate family, he couldn't trust anybody. But hiding away didn't help his mood. Because he loved them so much, he began to feel his presence at home was actually putting them in danger.

By now, his paranoia was such that he got it into his head that he was the insurrectionists' number one target. As far as he was concerned, their main objective in life was to eliminate Kevin Healy. And they would stop at nothing to get him. They'd bulldoze the house. And he began to understand why.

He, personally, was a threat to them, the men of violence, a threat greater than any they had faced before. You see, they had found out somehow that he was the Second Coming. Kevin could smile now at how ludicrous it all was then. But at the time, it seemed very rational. He started to leave the house more often during the day, daring them to do anything about it.

Throwing caution to the wind, he went around pubs, determined to unite all men in peace and love, rendering such trivialities as national borders and notions of statehood irrelevant in the process. And, most gallingly to his antagonists, he picketed their homes, praying for their souls loudly and in public. They didn't like that, the implication being that they needed praying for, that their souls were in some sort of jeopardy. They were, of course, in many cases avowed Catholics, it being a sectarian conflict after all, at least in part. You could see how His presence on Earth – in Tullyanna – would have posed a bit of a dilemma for them. Doing away with the Second Coming mightn't go down well with some of their more religious supporters.

It goes without saying that he was experiencing delusions – well, according to the medics anyway. Sure, who wasn't? What normal person could function without a decent set of delusions? At times he felt invincible and all-powerful as anybody might after surviving a gun attack. It begins with the notion that you were spared. Why? Why you? Why were you singled out to be shot in the first place? And then to be spared? It gnaws away at you. He didn't specifically remember ever thinking that he was a Messiah or anyone of the ilk. In fact, he believed that the medics themselves were part of a conspiracy trying to plant those ideas in his head.

He could laugh about it now, now that he was well. Mind you, it was possible, he was prepared to admit, that during the worst throes of his illness, having been undoubtedly traumatized, he might have said a few things. He might have uttered a few biblical-style pronouncements, issued a few Christ-like warnings. There was the time, he recollected, when he had to be physically removed from the church for disrupting the service, being told in no uncertain terms not to darken the door again.

He might, in hindsight, have encouraged certain people to suspect that he did in fact think of himself as a Redeemer-type, if not the actual son of God himself, at least some near relation of the Supreme Being. It was an act. Sort of. He couldn't say for sure himself whether he was *pretending* to think he was the Messiah, *did* think he was the Messiah, or *was* actually the Messiah. Ultimately, it amounted to a similar thing. He was deemed mentally ill and put on medication. It didn't help matters that some people thought that he *was* actually an incarnation of Jesus Christ. Or at least he thought that that's what they were thinking. It was the reverend way they looked at him, the surreptitious way they blessed themselves as they passed him on the street. The jokes.

'*Heal me!*'

Although nobody had ever been arrested for the attack, suspicion naturally fell on elements of the republican movement. They had been responsible for a number of robberies in the area at the time. In fact, upright citizens that they were, they strongly disapproved of anybody else conducting armed robberies.

Kevin kept staring out the window until dawn. Until the creatures of the night had retreated to their lairs. When the mist cleared, he couldn't help noticing a freshly dug grave in the middle of his back garden.

The art of deception

Philip, figuring he'd need to be in the whole of his health in the coming days, went for another run. No amount of shaking his head or stretching his limbs could rid his mind of Joanne's image. Joanne! Of all people. She had a presence, right enough, as unignorable in the imagination as it was in the flesh the previous evening. Was that an invitation to her room – albeit unvoiced – as they shared a last cigarette? A come-on conveyed via the medium of exhaled smoke, her lassooing him with the smoke rings, his foot resting on the decorative plough by the restaurant door? Or was it just the vanity that was getting the better of him?

Philip was no expert in such delicate negotiations, no rogue. In fact, he freely admitted he'd never had a clue. He'd passed many's an open door before. And, by the same token, knocked himself out on portals firmly closed. He wasn't sure where he was in relation to her. He didn't know whether she liked him. Or whether he liked her. Was the desire he felt for her even benign? All he knew for certain was that he wanted to touch her, hold her, handle her. Hurt her?

Feeling pathetic as well as confused, a semi-aroused Philip, pathologically wary in such matters, tried to resist her intrusion on his heart. Since Sally in Hanoi, his heart was a no-go zone. Since Sandra, really, if he thought about it. Which he didn't, if he could help it at all. He was inclined to dismiss such feelings as nothing more than a boyish crush. The crush could have been triggered by any number of factors. A combination of age and loneliness, but mostly loneliness. He was physically in his prime but didn't have a friend in the world, male or female. Or maybe it was boredom. Boredom and its bedfellow, a self-destructive appetite he'd always had for something to happen. Anything. He craved adventure, the more visceral the better, anything, big or small, legal or not, that would make him feel alive. That would make him forget. A stupid crush like this would fit the bill, something vitalizing that could only come to no good.

Although they were never a couple, Sandra was the only girl he'd ever felt comfortable with. Maybe *because* they weren't a couple, and his heart wasn't always racing when she was around, he could be himself in her presence. Until he went and ruined it all. For Christmas the year they met she surprised him with a terrier pup, a Kerry Blue. How did she know? He might have mentioned it once in passing, weeks previously. Where did she even get it? By the middle of January, the pup, Johnson, had been blinded by a cat, and his mother, despite his objections, handed it over to the rescue. He could never get close to anyone since Sandra. For fear they'd die, too. And he'd be to blame.

Like the cat with a dead bird outside the patio door, he wanted to present Joanne with a gift. A piece of the puzzle he could paw proudly at the next meeting with her and Healy. If only could he crack Dove's code. His reward, a saucer of cream, an elixir that would erase the memory of the night Sandra Mohan disappeared.

A car, its engine silent, rolled to a halt beside him, the sunlight bouncing off the bonnet, rendering him temporarily blind.

'Get in, hi!'

There were four men in the car, a green VW Jetta with tinted windows, the driver and chief spokesman for the quartet being Mr Charlie O'Dowd. Beside him sat his old friend, Macker, and in the back were two outsized goons he did not recognize. They looked like nightclub bouncers in black bomber jackets, one of them pointing a gun in the direction of his face.

'Well, lads, out canvassing?' says Philip, nonchalant, leaning in the driver's window. 'You're wasting your time with me. I don't think I'm on the register of electors in this particular jurisdiction.'

'Get in the fucking car, Sharkey.'

O'Dowd spat out the words and him twitching, two hands on the steering wheel, the shades failing to conceal the fear in his eyes, the quiff unusually flat.

'There's no room,' says Philip, still unperturbed, daring anybody to make a move. 'Come back for me when you've dropped these fat bastards off to Weight Watchers.'

'Shut your fucking mouth.'

It was a Northern accent, from the back seat, whip-crack, Belfast.

'We just want a chat,' says the bould Macker, in a more reasonable tone.

'Is that what you said to Tommy, Macker? A chat? Is this how it all works now? *Que pasa, mi amigo? Pensé que eras un botánico ahora?*'

Philip, his Spanish passable, having spent a season working in an adventure resort in Costa Rica, in charge of the climbing wall, no less, was surprised and somewhat disappointed with Macker. He had always expected better things from him. A decent footballer in his day, he once made the panel for the county team and at school vied with Philip to be 'the best in the class' despite stiff opposition from the vet's son, who went on to be an international pianist. Among his many talents, Philip recalled fondly, Macker could draw a map of the world freehand. And, as it turned out, he could speak Spanish fluently This accomplishment only came to light when he was arrested in Peru, of all places, a few years previously, where he was charged with training clueless second-generation Shining Path guerillas in the art of rocket launching and in urban terrorism techniques generally, a push on Lima long overdue, jungle living having become a pain in the hole.

Although travelling on a false passport at the time, Macker pleaded innocence, claiming he was a mere botanist, *un botánico*, studying rare flora, despite, as everyone knew, suffering from hay-fever. Philip was above all disappointed in Macker because he didn't fight his destiny. He didn't escape from the maze. Despite his talent and wit, he dutifully became his short-arse father's son, the scion of a war-hero, feted at *feis ceoils* and pawed at playfully by gunmen on the run, groomed to be a foot-soldier in a cause he did not fully believe in. To this Philip could swear, his memory of their drunken nights out as teenagers clear.

At the very least, Macker didn't believe in the cause passionately enough to become as involved as he did, his precocious abilities squandered, his sense of humour exorcised, his revered insurrectionary father now a peddler of laundered diesel, destroying car engines, not to mention the rivers and lakes of the border region, and its economic survival depending on tourism, water-skiing, and fishing and the like. Macker was as much a botanist as his father, Barry McManus, was a businessman, as much as Coleman was a politician, and as much, he acknowledged ruefully, as he himself was a detective. All of them were liars. Their whole lives were founded on lies.

Philip weighed up the risks of getting into the car. They might kill him, which wouldn't be ideal, and him so close to a breakthrough. Although with Tommy Courtney not even in the ground, and with the general election a mere two weeks away, and they riding high in the polls, that was, on balance, unlikely, wasn't it? On the plus side, any quality time spent with Charlie and Macker might yield some minute particle of information useful to him, not that you could believe a word that came out of their mouths.

Philip, self-taught as he was and reasonably well-read, was no current affairs buff. He hadn't paid much heed from afar to his own country's ongoing metamorphosis as it struggled to emerge, sticky-winged, from what was a particularly tight-fitting chrysalis.

Philip was not partisan, but he was biased. Listening to the radio over the last week, it was clear to him that Coleman's party had much to hide, as does every side in every war. In the lurch from romantic nationalism, now with O'Leary in the grave, as every Irish schoolboy knew, to socialist utopianism, a long tiring old march, in fairness, the occasional denial was understandable. In the transmogrification from guerilla army to populist political party, the odd obfuscation, the odd lapse in memory, was surely forgivable even to the most implacable of foes? Mistakes happen in all wars. That goes without saying. You'd expect errors of judgement, here and there, sporadic unsanctioned outrages, from time to time, excessive self-policing in the community, and the like, especially in wars that were conducted almost wholly in the dark. In his youth, Philip, to his shame, cheered when soldiers died.

In the interests of peace and reconciliation and bringing men like Macker's dad in from the cold, you could argue that the childish questions about who was who in the leadership were superfluous. Political codology. As were the never-ending questions about who ordered which kidnapping and which torture session and which execution and so on, and under which beach the so-called 'disappeared' were buried. There were no easy answers. Memories were hazy. Beaches change character over time subject to the tides. Sure, some of the beaches themselves had disappeared. Philip, if he was in any way an objective man, could probably have seen some merit in the judicious use of dissembling, in drawing a line in the sand.

But Philip, at this moment in time, was in no way an objective man. Dove was dead. Tommy was dead. And Sandra was still missing, presumably dead. It stuck in his craw that some of these fine people, some of them possibly sitting in the VW Jetta before him, were prepared to kill for Ireland, and some of them were even prepared to die for Ireland but, perversely, few of them were prepared to tell the truth for Ireland. To put the bereaved families' minds at rest? To put Sandra Mohan's family and friends' minds at rest if, of course, they had anything to do with it? What the fuck was wrong with people? Killing and dying was fine but telling the truth was somehow taboo?

Lying was handy, as he well knew, no mean practitioner himself in the art of deception, and him a man. He once went by the name of Adrian O'Hara during a stint on a building site in New York and for no good reason too. Just to see if he could pull it off. (He could.) And for how long he could get away with it. (A month. Before he was rumbled by a doorman in a Yonkers bar, a Finegan from Drumduff, wouldn't you know, one of the Shifty Finegans with the fizzy orange hair, who it transpired, ironically, had been styling himself in gay chat rooms as Keyser Söze. Small world.)

The biggest lie was the oldest one, i.e. that the Cause is greater than the Organization and the Organization is greater than the Leadership. This time-honoured, fundamental principle of every political and religious outfit, of every sporting club and charitable society, of every gathering of men and women ever, was upended by the first sniff of electoral success. Especially now that the original cause was more or less forgotten in the mists of time.

Macker held up the only known copy of *Brouhaha*, the graphic novel that had been exercising Philip's mind all morning, the very same memento bequeathed to him by their mutual friend, Dove.

'Look what I found,' says he.

'I'm more of a *Beano* man myself,' says Philip.

'Desperate Dan, ha?'

'That was *The Dandy*.'

Endless misunderstandings. Tommy might have blabbed about the book as he was bludgeoned to death, and why wouldn't he? Was Macker himself present at the ceremony? There were no marks on his face that Philip could discern, no scratches made by Tommy's feral hand, the dying scrapes of a desperate man. And he couldn't imagine Tommy, feeble and all as he was, going down without a fight. 'What happened Tommy?'

'It was criminality, man, pure and simple,' says Macker. 'Some spat over a drug debt. These people are animal, pure animal. Poor Tommy.'

The story doing the rounds, circulated by the likes of Macker and other activists, was that Tommy was nothing but a petty criminal who fell foul of a criminal gang. And people believed it. It was a paltry amount he owed, to be sure, the line went.

'No regard for human life,' chimed in O'Dowd, 'a scourge on the community.'

It made sense to people in the town. And by the way, the eradication of the said scourge was an absolute priority for the party. It was a fable that sat well with the guards, and sections of the media, and even with the mainstream parties, not to mention the electorate. One prominent member of the government, when asked about it on the radio, said while of course he condemned the violence, sadly, it did appear the deceased was involved in 'criminality'.

'I hope you didn't mind me going up to your room, Philip,' says Macker.

'You were always welcome in my house, Mac,' he replied, meaning every word. 'You were a good friend.'

'Charlie there kept your mother amused,' Macker added, not for a moment moved by Philip's sincerity.

'Did he?'

'Good-looking woman,' affirmed Charlie, the chutzpah returning.

Philip had enough. 'Move over.'

The blood rushing to his head, he grabbed the handle of the back door, thinking, come what may, he might get closer to the truth. The larger man, without saying anything, dragged Philip into the middle of the back seat, Philip taking the opportunity to knee the other man, the man he was dragged over, in the balls.

'Fuck,' moaned the thinner man.

Firmly wedged between the two men, he was not in a position to do further damage.

'Well, Macker. Where are we for?'

'We're just going for a little spin, Philip.'

The man to his left pulled out a hood from under the seat in front of him. Philip's innate confidence and feeling of invincibility immediately diminished. The thin man then pulled the hood down over his own head. Philip was confused. And even more unnerved

'He's very shy,' explained the driver, O'Dowd, glancing at Philip in the rear-view mirror. 'We heard you were looking for Sandra, said we'd give you a hand.'

The big man, a scar on his right hand, was busy texting on his phone, occasionally snorting at a message he received.

'You alright, big man?' says Philip. 'Chicken wing stuck up your nose?'

Philip received an elbow in the ribs for his impertinence.

'Leave him,' instructed Macker firmly, turning to face Philip.

'Tommy didn't say anything?'

'About what?'

'Anything Dove said?'

'I'm not following you, Mac?'

'Look, man, I'm on your side.'

189

'Really? Then buy some deodorant for this fat cunt!'

Another dig in the ribs. They were heading east, towards the coast.

'We going for a swim?'

'The thing is, Philip. Dove might have known something about Sandra. He was acting a bit funny lately. Her mother deserves to know.'

'If I knew anything, do you think I'd be sitting here with you?'

O'Dowd, gripping the steering wheel, hit the hammer hard and the car lurched forward.

'Fucking hell,' said the man in the hood in a gentle Northern accent, his head hitting the headrest in front of him.

A couple of miles north of Blackrock, on a back road, the smell of the sea in the air, O'Dowd swerved into an entrance. It was an agri-business premises of some sort, a poultry farm, by the looks of things. And the smell of things. He turned off the ignition. There was a fierce shrieking from inside the plant. The chickens at this stage were not the only ones in distress.

'I might stretch the legs,' says Macker.

'I'll keep you company,' says O'Dowd.

They walked off together towards a wooded area. Two men in blue boiler suits, both wearing balaclavas, emerged from behind a shed. One of them was carrying an oven-ready chicken. The big man pulled Philip roughly from the car while the hooded man stayed put. Philip didn't resist. He did, however, resist as best as he could when the two men in the boiler suits grabbed an arm each and held him down. Once they'd wrestled him to the ground, the big man pulled off Philip's shorts.

'Fucking perverts,' he roared, panicking now. Then, despite Philip's best bucking jennet impression, the big man managed to pull off his jocks. Not much Philip could do to stop him. He was a very big man. Philip could feel the gravel tearing into his buttocks. Over in the coop, the broilers by now were hysterical.

'Hurry up,' said one of the men in the boiler suits.

'I want him to enjoy this,' said the big man, the oven-ready chicken in his hand.

Philip, although he was in a right state of terror, didn't say much, as the man placed the dead bird's cavity – for want of a better word – over his – for want of a better word – penis. It fell off once or twice before the very big man, now sitting on Philip's tiring legs, manoeuvred it into a satisfactory position. Once in place, he took out his phone and photographed the arrangement from a few different angles.

'Now, chicken-fucker,' said he, 'this is your last chance. Tell us where she is. Or I'm sending this to your mother. And everyone you know.'

'I don't know anything,' pleaded an exhausted Philip, not sure what was going to happen next. 'I don't know what you're on about.'

Macker and O'Dowd returned. The men in the boiler suits dematerialized while the big man helped Philip to his feet and bundled him into the Jetta.

'Don't forget your lunch,' growled a grievously wounded and very angry Philip. If they thought they were going to humiliate him or intimidate him or even embarrass him, they could think again.

The mood in the car was subdued. They drove back towards Tullyanna in silence. The big man, unlike Philip, seemed to be ashamed, struggling to remember, perhaps, where sexually assaulting people with dead chickens fitted in with the ideology. Eventually the car stopped. They were roughly back where they started, Philip another warning of sorts under his belt.

'Sorry, Philip,' says Macker, 'for any inconvenience.'

With that, another car pulled up some twenty yards behind them. Philip got out. O'Dowd, after a quick glance in the side mirror, switched on the ignition and sped off, not before Philip, with very little room to manoeuvre, managed to rabbit-punch him on the back of the head through the open window.

A tall, thin man got out of the other car, hitched up his trousers, and loped over towards Philip.

'Detective Sergeant Peter Keating,' said he.

Philip nodded, preferring not to accept the man's outstretched hand.

'Long time no see. That's my partner, Bill Higgins, there. Bill!' he shouted. 'He's pretending he can't hear me. I keep telling him not to drink coffee in the car.'

Philip looked back towards the unmarked car where a bald man with a bulldog face was trying to wipe clean his chinos with some man-size tissues.

'Friends of yours?'

'Nah. Just some guys looking for directions.'

'We were following them. Well, until we ran out of petrol. They called to your house earlier.'

'Did they?'

'They did. They went inside. Spoke to your mother. They were there for a good ten minutes.'

'Is she okay?'

'Is there anything you'd like to tell us?'

'Why didn't you arrest them?'

'No law against social calls. Not a police state. Not yet anyway, says you.' Keating smirked at his own tremendous witticism.

'No.'

'That's right.'

What sort of a state was it, though? Philip wondered as Keating, the small blackish eyes darting about in the narrow head, and it in turn revolving on the scrawny neck, surveyed the scene.

'Nice weather,' says he.

'Lovely.'

'We've had a complaint, Philip.'

'And there was me thinking nothing ever happens in this town.'

What was it? Tommy? Did Healy tell him about Tommy's blood on the mantelpiece? Did his mother shop him?

'Joanne McCollum.'

'I'm not surprised, officer.' He was surprised. Very. 'A lot of people complaining about Joanne around here. She's trouble, so she is. Who was complaining about her this time?'

'Smart. You were always a smart boy. *She* made a complaint about *you*.'

'Me?'

He was startled but he tried not to show it.

'A complaint?'

'Bad news, I'm afraid, Philip. Seems to me, you just can't behave.'

Wrong-footed, he furiously rewound last night's events in his head, working the muscles in his face hard to maintain his deadpan façade. What had she said?

His mind was reeling. Had he made a lunge? He was drunk, sure, and couldn't remember going home, but he would have remembered a lunge, a drop of the hand, an over-eager pass. He had probably kissed her on the cheek. That was about the size of it. That's what people do these days, isn't it, the world over? By way of greeting and farewell? Personally, being a wary man, he favoured a bit of awkward shuffling or a barely perceptible nod. But not wanting to be accused of being square or stand-offish, he might have leaned in. Perhaps he lingered a little too long in the embrace, inhaling her perfume, her soft neck exposed, her breasts beckoning, his loneliness overwhelming? He would have remembered. Perhaps his finger, gently twisting a curl of hers, sticky with hairspray, got stuck for a moment, pulling her head sharply backwards. Perhaps she was over-sensitive. Or maybe she was just playing games.

'What sort of a complaint?'

'She said you've been interfering in a missing person's case.'

'Me?'

Detective Keating, the narrow head now still, let this allegation settle for a second before he carried on.

'I think you should come with us, Philip. Give us your side of the story.'

He almost laughed at her – what would you call it? – audacity, as he followed Keating to his car. What was Joanne's game? Either way, he liked her even more.

A spanner in the works

Joanne's bedroom was one of five hastily added to the Old Forge restaurant in a fit of hubris after one good review in a national newspaper. '*Unfussy food . . . well-prepared . . . the smoked Lough Neagh eel was a revelation.*' This country did her head in sometimes. In the heyday of the boom, at a time when anything seemed possible, it seemed that couples might come down from Dublin and, after a decent feed, stay the night in Tullyanna. Of all places. No beaches. No mountains. No museum. Not even a bookshop. Or locals, fat on the proceeds of selling land to expanding supermarket chains, might crash there either, too lazy and full of chicken supreme and smoked eel to walk the few yards home.

There was only one other guest staying, as far as she could make out – the German fisherman who Joanne had seen leaving the premises with a pair of binoculars and some kind of whistle at four in the morning as she stumbled up to her room. She had a vague recollection of *lambasting* him in the corridor about Germany bullying Ireland into an unnecessary bailout, and an even vaguer memory of the pair of them singing the chorus to '99 Red Balloons'.

Her room was called, rather grandly, the Patrick Kavanagh Suite, in honour of the vagrant poet whose bitter way with words she quite liked at school, although there was nothing inside the room to underline the association, not as much as a pen. She was annoyed by such a lack of rigour. Such cynicism. The plumbing was no great shakes either. She'd blocked up the plugholes in the sink and shower with damp cotton pads to no avail. The stench seemed to be coming through the walls. And although not an *aesthete* by any means – the very word ungainly – and architectural injustices not being her foremost passion in life, Joanne was actually quite affronted by the extension to the old blacksmith's forge. A huge concrete cube, still unpainted, just slapped on to it, like, looming incongruously above the original thatched cottage with the nice nougat-y walls.

It wasn't 'til the following morning, her tongue furry, that she decided to speak to her old friend Keating. Having missed breakfast at the Old Forge, she was already in a bad mood. She opened the lid of the kettle to find it was already half-full, although it was obvious to her that nobody had stayed in the room for months. The water in the kettle was mouldy. Mouldy water was a new one on her, and she had stayed in some grotty rooms in her time. There was the B&B in Tralee, the time she was doing the story on the county councillors' expenses – four of the fuckers sharing a car to a conference below in Kerry and all of them claiming the mileage! Even Carson was impressed that she managed to get the lads on tape bragging about their latest *stroke*. The mouldy water combined with the smell of sewage in the room made her gag. It was as if the whole town's waste was trapped with nowhere to go, the sludge endlessly circulating beneath Tullyanna. There was a blockage in the pipes, and it was up to her to release it. She was in danger of going all Travis Bickle – as Welly would call her when she was on a mission – she was well aware of that – but, Jesus, someone had to take control of the situation. This was not a game.

Local poet Patrick Kavanagh was a pariah in his lifetime because he drank too much and told the truth and dared to rise above his station. And now he's on the English syllabus. And feted at an annual festival down the road. And has a suite called after him in a jumped-up guest-house. A fucking *suite*? And a seat by the canal in Dublin. The double standards appalled her. It was one of those mornings, when every little thing annoyed her. And everyone mightily pissed her off, including herself. Mostly herself. She was all too familiar with the symptoms. The empty feeling. The frontal lobe shrivelling defensively – she could literally feel it – empathy and humour taking the day off.

The receptionist, long dark hair in a ponytail, tortoiseshell glasses on the tip of her nose, was about the same age as Sandra. Not really a receptionist, more of an owner's daughter, she was making a little man out of pipe cleaners.

'Not a bad morning now.'

Joanne wasn't going to stop but she did.

'Sorry, if you don't mind me saying. There's a smell in the room.'

Like most Irish people, she started far too many sentences with the word, *sorry*.

'A smell? That's a dread,' the girl replied, not in the least put out. 'I'll get Gintaras to have a look at it. Apart from that, are you enjoying your stay?'

'It's great.'

There were leaflets on a stand. Some were for renting a boat. Some for Coleman's Taxi Service.

'These are for you. It doesn't say who they're from.'

The girl produced, from behind the desk, a ballotin of Diane's Divine Chocolates. Joanne smiled curiously but the thought of chocolate, at that hour, made her sick.

'You can have them!'

'Are ya serious? Thanks a million.'

Joanne pointed at her artwork. 'Did you, by any chance, know Sandra Mohan?'

'Sandra? I did surely.' She adjusted her glasses. 'It's a holy dread.'

'What do you think happened?'

The glasses ever so briefly fogged over.

'Lemme call Gintaras for ya.' She picked up her mobile. 'Any plans for the day yourself?'

She did have a plan. And hoped her plan would not be misunderstood. Walking towards the Main Street, Joanne was struck by how many people were out and about, shoppers chatting and laughing, a group of boys with a ball, a traffic jam, tractors hauling trailer-loads of hay with boys and girls perched precariously on top of the bales, the boys with the ball shouting obscenities at their only marginally more rural counterparts on the bales. What was wrong with them all? Why was the sun shining? Why weren't they all out looking for their friend and neighbour? Why wasn't there a missing poster at the Old Forge reception? She felt like shaking them. It's only been thirteen years.

* * *

At the garda station, she was greeted warmly by Keating. She liked Keating although he could be a bit awkward, stabbing her in the face with his big nose. Ever since she'd implicated Coleman on the drugs charge, they'd stayed in touch. She'd bump into him from time to time in and around the courts, where they'd share information. On the odd occasion, they might have lunch together. A lanky detective, he had an oval face and longish, fine hair. He clicked his fingers, loudly, at some junior outside the door.

'Coffee. The good stuff. And Hobnobs. Make it quick!'

Then he turned towards Joanne, running his hand through his longish, fine hair.

'Sit down, Jo.' He waved his hand, expansively, as if there was an endless choice of chairs. 'Hit me! With your rhythm stick, ha!'

He was one of those guys who sat on the table, as opposed to a chair, in a manner that was meant to be casual and cool but merely looked uncomfortable. His uncool socks – beige and diamond-patterned – were showing beneath his too-short trouser legs.

For Joanne, it has to be said in her defence, the story came before all other considerations. The story came first. She genuinely felt that she was a dispassionate person, a cool head, the only sane, objective one in the whole area who had a fighting chance of solving the mystery once and for all. If Philip was so concerned about Sandra's fate, he wouldn't have run away. He wouldn't have withheld evidence that might have even saved her life. With a very heavy heart, she made her complaint.

'Peter, it's Philip Sharkey.'

'I fucking knew it.'

'No, Peter, you need to keep an eye on him. He's . . . volatile.'

'I know what you mean. A loose cannon.'

'Exactly.'

It was best to let people like Keating think they came up with the idea. Although she had hugely enjoyed the evening with Philip and had spent all morning agonizing about what she was going to do, she strongly felt that it was in Philip's best interest that he take a breather. He was lucky, in fact, that she'd developed a soft spot for him and chose not to tell the man known as Bad News all she knew.

'I just feel he's going to get himself in trouble, rampaging around like a bull. You saw what happened to Tommy.'

'I'll have a word. Look, between myself and yourself, we were going to have a word with him anyway. We have a lot of questions.'

As long as Sandra was still missing, nobody could afford to have a vengeful, temperamental Philip getting in the way. By drawing the attentions of the gardaí towards him, he would be stymied, at least for a while, and mightn't be inclined to do something stupid. Like get himself killed. There were no hard feelings. Far from it. In her mind, she was doing him a massive favour. With Keating on his back now, he'd have to cool the jets.

While she was at the Garda station, having raised her concern about Philip, there was something else – something more important – she felt she had to say.

'Come on, Joanne. Out with it. I can tell when you've something on your mind.'

'Jesus, Peter, you're a mindreader. I always said that about you. Look, I've a tip for you.'

The minion with the coffee knocked on the door.

'Not now, for fuck's sake,' Keating roared at him. 'I don't know where we get them these days. Go on!'

'I don't know if there's any truth in this now. It's just something I picked up on my travels.'

'Jesus, Joanne, you're getting me all excited.'

'Apparently, there's a *bunker* in Barry McManus's field.'

'No.'

'It's a reliable source.'

'We can't go in there. Bunker or not. No way. You know the craic with McManus.'

'Hear me out. There's a chance, only a chance, mind you, Sandra Mohan is there.'

Keating got up and paced the room, running both hands through his longish, fine hair, pondering the possibilities, positive and negative, for his career. For his life, says you.

'Jesus, Joanne. Do you know what you're saying?'

'It's just a rumour. Something somebody heard, that's all. If you're not interested, I'll talk to the boys in Ardee.'

'Joanne, I know for a fact that bunker was destroyed. Sure, wasn't I there myself?'

'Maybe there's another one somewhere in the field. Or she's in the rubble of that one. Look. All I'm saying is, it's a strong tip. I've never let you down, Peter.'

'True forya. Leave it with me.'

Joanne put her hand up as if to say halt.

'It's urgent. With all that's going on, I'd say it's a priority.'

'Jesus, Jo. You can be a right pain in the hole sometimes. I'll see what I can do.'

Keating strode out of the room, leaving the door open. A gentle, pimply guard left the coffee and the biscuits on the table. Joanne, adamant that she was doing the only responsible thing, would have a bit of explaining to do to Kevin and Philip. While she waited for Keating to return, she tried to call them. No luck. After about half an hour and many phone calls later, an excited Keating was pleased to announce he'd been given the go-ahead to search the site.

'Helicopter and all,' he declared, rubbing his hands.

First thing in the morning, no expense spared, he informed her he had a full team at the ready and, furthermore, that she had permission – from the very top – to go along for the ride.

Scraping the barrel

'You had visitors.'

'Oh.'

'Charlie O'Dowd. And Mickey. Mickey McManus. He's a nice lad, Mickey. Very mannerly.'

'Yeah.'

'It's great that you stayed pally with all your old friends.'

Philip closed the bedroom door behind him. Tears lurked in his eyes. He willed them back inside. *It was just a fucking chicken.* A pathetic attempt to scare him off. Macker had done a fairly thorough number on the room. Apart from the comic book, he quickly noted the absence of other belongings, not having much to his name to begin with. He was missing a few items of clothing – underpants, socks, a T-shirt – and his toothbrush, nothing to which he was overly attached. Mind you, nothing good could come from their misappropriation either.

He had worn those pants for two whole days, on the convoluted three-flight journey home, and him sweating copiously all the way. If it was his DNA they were after, they were in luck. Up to half his DNA could have leaked out of him during that journey, absorbed by his cotton jocks. They could probably clone him using only that undergarment together with some sort of an electrical impulse.

There was nothing he'd put past them, resource-wise, or in terms of ingenuity and bare-faced cheek. Although he had an inkling that it was less of him they wanted, not more. Multiple Philips hampering their masterplan to take over the world! Less immediately replaceable, and of more personal significance, were his passport and his fishing knife. They were gone too.

When his mother had called to tell him that Dove was dead, he had only packed the barest of essentials. To that haul, he'd added, at Schipol airport, a bottle of Canadian Club, a gift for himself that was waiting patiently beside his bed, the seal intact, and, for his mother, a bottle of lime and basil body lotion, an aged Gouda cheese, and the obligatory Toblerone.

Remarkably, the whiskey was still in situ. Fair play to Macker. There was hope for him yet. He opened it and drank straight from the bottle. What was Joanne up to at all? Was she warning him off or reeling him in, inviting him to play some sort of a game? If so, what was the game and what were the rules? Either way, he'd promised Keating that he'd keep to himself for the foreseeable future, as best as he could in a small town like Tullyanna. He'd assured him that he had no intention of sticking his nose into the Sandra Mohan case, remembering only too well how far it got him thirteen years ago. He had only come home to pay his respects to Dove and was spending some time with his mother while considering his options. He didn't think Keating was buying it.

Luckily, his mother's laptop was spared by the recent interlopers. Bottle of whiskey close to hand, he flipped it open, in the little-used dining room of the house, the musty smell now enlivened by rye. After his brush with the big man and the chicken, he was determined to redouble his efforts. There and then he googled Gram Parsons. There was no mention anywhere of him having seven fingers on either hand. By all accounts, even on the Gram-is-still-alive sites, his hands were perfectly normal, probably the most normal thing about him, sporting, as they did, the ideal number of fingers for the guitar fretwork in which he excelled.

There was no way he was going to let Joanne's strange decision hamstring his efforts to find Sandra. After hours of researching the life and work of the wayward genius and listening, with pleasure, to his songs – balm for the sorriest of souls – songs he wished he'd discovered sooner, he felt he knew the man, alright, inside and out.

But he couldn't relate his life or his legacy to the Sandra Mohan story. He was never sure if he was hallucinating or not at the best of times, but one thing was certain in his mind. Tommy Courtney had told him that Dove knew where she was. And putting two and two together, he was of the opinion that the solution to the puzzle was to be found in Dove's book, *Brouhaha*, now, of course, in the possession of Coleman's people.

It must have been about five in the morning when he had an epiphany of sorts. Exhausted though he was, the eyes swollen and raw, he began seeing the world whiskey-clear and hyper-real.

It was while scraping the barrel that he lazily keyed in the letters GP on his mother's computer, expecting nothing but further disappointment. A little menu dropped down from the search box advertising a list of results. These, presumably, were the most popular or pertinent results, according to the arcane algorithms – the Torah of Code – that governs what Googlers see. Anyway, the first suggestion offered up was 'GPA'. Upon further examination, GPA turned out to stand for grade point average, the scoring system used widely in education. That was hardly a true measure of any man, he thought, his own current GPA, according to a quick calculation, no more than a modest one point two for his work to date on the case.

It was another entry in the list of search results that proved to be the bolt of lightning that jolted the fast-fading and usually unflappable Philip into life again. He sat upright, lest he choked on the whiskey reflux that rose in his gullet, when the term 'GPS coordinates' appeared nonchalantly on the screen.

GPS. Global Positioning System.

Although bitter experience suggested that the horses be held, his mind unbridled raced ahead. It could only mean one thing. Dove, the tragic and much-maligned Dove, could be trying to provide him with the exact location of Sandra's body. Gram Parsons and General Practice were the GPs. That was surely plausible? Or was it the stupidest idea he ever had in his life? And God knows he'd had a lot of stupid ideas. It made a sort of sense. Himself and Dove used to laugh at the coordinates tattooed on Coleman's neck, speculating humorously on what it might represent. Granted, that was a tenuous connection. But then, there were the coordinates in place of the town's name on his mural. Maybe he was reading too much into it.

Dove was nothing if not vexing. Their whole relationship had been based on verbal jousting and witty one-upmanship. But if – and it was a big if – Dove was sharing the coordinates of a specific location relevant to the case, why did he have to make it so difficult? So puzzling? Was Dove so far gone that he thought his enemies could read his mind? And if he'd tried to pass on the information in a conventional way, they'd somehow find out and simply move Sandra's body? Hence the extravagant level of encryption?

He wanted to be right. Obviously, number one, he wanted to find Sandra. But also, if he was right, this coded message would be a vindication of sorts, proof that his friendship with Dove had been real, founded on something, a unique understanding between them. In the absence of religion or ideology or any sort of anchor in his life, a connection like that, a friendship – however fleeting and obsolete and *abused* – was not to be sniffed at.

He warned himself, his father's sensible voice in his head, not to get too carried away, but having recently downed a bottle of whiskey, that wasn't a runner. For such a taciturn man, he wasn't able to stifle a tiny whoop of joy. Gram Parsons. General Practice. GPS. He felt like Scott of the Antarctic closing in on the South Pole, until he suddenly remembered that Amundsen got there first. And Scott himself died. Frozen in the ice along with the rest of his expedition.

Expectations revised, he was tempted to call Kevin, or even Joanne, but momentum got the better of him and, twitching all over with anticipation, he continued his bareback exploration of cyberspace.

He familiarized himself online with the whole GPS concept, learning about the various notations used in finding a location. To get his bearings, he first put his own address in Tullyanna, the house he was currently in, into the search box on a random GPS website. Seconds later, he was informed that he was currently residing at 53°N 53' 49.113" 6°W 28' 1.549", which in layman's language, he soon learned, meant a latitude of 53 degrees north and 53 minutes and 49.113 seconds and a longitude of 6 degrees west and 28 minutes and 1.549 seconds. The result also indicated that his mother's house was 244 feet above sea level. Jesus, no wonder he felt dizzy.

There was, of course, one glaringly massive and seemingly insurmountable problem that soon brought a halt to Philip's giddy march. Without the book, he was in no position to test out his theory. The Lord giveth and the Lord taketh away! What sort of a Lord would do a thing like that? Philip cursed the heavens. He searched his bedroom, looking for the graphic novel that he knew wasn't there, the futility of this gesture enraging him even more. Perhaps there was another copy of the book in existence?

He collapsed on the bed, still in his sweaty running gear, the whiskey vapours seeping from his pores rendering him, in all likelihood, flammable, and slept for two hours. At 9.00 a.m., he ate a banana and ran the few hundred yards to Dove's house, not that he was in a hurry, but so as he'd look like a man out running instead of a hungover bum.

Philip waited for Gerry Senior, the head held high, and he clad impeccably as ever in shirt and tie – a sombre-coloured suit, instead of the usual houndstooth, the only clue to his recent tragedy – to leave the house. Dove's father duly emerged and walked briskly towards the town – with his ridiculously short steps, a boon to local mimics – to open his hardware shop. Then Philip knocked on the door.

Dove's mother, Dee, wrapped in a dressing gown, red-eyed, her grieving for the day well underway, let him in. She was grateful, it appeared to Philip, for the distraction. Dee asked after his mother and clicked on the kettle. They settled at the kitchen table. A smell of stew on the range, left by good neighbours, uneaten, pervaded the room.

Philip listened as Dee talked fondly of her son, the life returning to her as the morning wore on, her laughter alternating with her tears. They swapped stories. The photos came out, some of them featuring Philip himself. Nothing in those early snaps suggested trouble ahead, never mind the scale of the calamity that befell them all. Whoever said the camera never lies was full of shit. A charlatan. Dee nodded in assent when Philip asked her if he could spend some time in Dove's room.

On entering the room, he briefly lay down on Dove's bed, a hang-over taking hold, looking at the ceiling, trying to see what Dove saw, trying to figure out what Dove knew. He didn't know what, precisely, he was looking for. A copy of the book would do for a start or, failing that, some preliminary sketches. Or, better still, a map of the area with a big X on it. But after a sweep of the room, not exactly to FBI standards, nothing of consequence could he find. Well, apart from Dove's newfangled phone which, without compunction, he duly pocketed.

Dove's guitars stood upright against the wall, bizarrely parked alongside the shotgun that had shortened his life. His records and CDs and – bringing a smile to Philip's face – his cassette tapes were neatly boxed and catalogued. Surprisingly for a junkie, Dove had accumulated, and held onto, quite a lot of kit over the years, speakers and amps and all sorts of sleek machines with knobs and dials and premium brand names, hooked up to each other in a spaghetti of wires. Where did he get the money, Philip wondered?

He pressed play on an innocuous-looking tape-deck, clutching at straws now, hoping for a musical clue, or maybe to hear Dove's voice itself with important news. Instead, he heard the Stone Roses playing 'I Wanna be Adored', as did half the town if the deafening sound that almost knocked him to the ground was anything to go by. Although he greatly approved of the song to which Dove died, he switched off the music, no more enlightened, and continued to root around the room.

While they'd always been on similar wavelengths when it came to music, he and Dove diverged radically in matters of taste when it came to books. The dead man's shelves held reams of paperbacks, mostly in the fantasy genre, from Tolkien to Pratchett, and back again through loops in time. Most of the authors' names were unfamiliar to Philip. Some of the books were at the more lurid, soft-porn end of the spectrum. Philip had no time for hobbits. God knows, he had little enough time for the human race. The novels were complemented, non-fiction wise, by tomes on conspiracy theories, urban myths, and other unsolved mysteries. Included among them was the copy of *Howarya!* containing Joanne McCollum's infamous Dove-incriminating article, entitled 'Small Town, Big Secret'.

There was a sickly-sweet stench in the room. At first, he thought it might be the lingering smell of the embalming fluid blending nicely with the decaying scent of the lilies, lifeless in a vase on Dove's desk. Sniffing the air more intently, he discovered that he himself was in fact the source of the smell. Great.

He flicked through the lengthy piece, pausing at the photos of Sandra. In each of the photographs, she looked lost, her future a done deal, her fate sealed the day she was born. There was nothing he could have done to save her. There was nothing anybody could have done. For some people, it was true, the cliché somewhat redeemed, the camera never lies.

Sandra, herself, the person, with the small mouth, hardly mattered anymore in the big scheme of things. But it still mattered that she was found, that he found her, or that somebody found her, preferably him, because, leaving justice aside, and noble but nebulous quests for the truth aside, and personal interest and the cosmic desire for order aside, the perpetrator or perpetrators had to be stopped. And their enablers and apologists had to be confronted head-on and held to account.

He couldn't bear to see them getting away with it. Just as the chemicals used by the diesel launderers had leached into the ground – literally contaminating the water supply in the whole border region, there was talk the swans in Muckno were dying – a poison was released the day Sandra disappeared. A noxious gas had been spreading over the town ever since, clouding minds and debilitating bodies, and in recent days claiming the lives of Dove and Tommy, too. It was an existential threat that, somehow, by someone, had to be stopped.

In securing peace, no mean achievement, Philip could appreciate why the powers-that-be might turn a blind eye to the racketeering of the former commandos. But ignoring murder, post the ceasefire, and tolerating the casual sanction-free beatings of lads like Tommy who merely stepped on the wrong toes was an appeasement too far. A compromise possibly fatal to the State. To civilization itself. As their bloated trucks ferried their cargo far and wide, the enterprise, cash-rich and tax-averse, grew, as did the notion of impunity, as did, coincidentally or not, the fortunes of the political party, the party to which Coleman belonged, the party of protest, the party of the poor, a juggernaut that was in serious danger of careering out of control.

He felt a bit paralyzed, as usual, powerless and hardly equipped for the trials that lay ahead.

She did matter. Sandra. Despite what the big scheme of things decreed. That summer, every time he saw her, she had handed him a packet of Panini World Cup stickers. He didn't especially care about the football but had collected them when he was younger. It was their little joke. They'd stick the players in unlikely places. On lampposts and on people's backs. When he mentioned that he liked Nirvana, she presented him with a CD a few days later. Sandra was nothing if not a very thoughtful shoplifter. The reason she made her own clothes was because she had no money. She stole books from the library because there were no books at home. The reason she was so bony – oh how he would have loved to gnaw on that bony shoulder – was because of neglect. He knew that now. He probably knew it then but had ignored the signs, the small-town classism in his very marrow. He didn't know about the horror show at home because he never asked her. He never wondered why she didn't invite people back to her house. He never wondered why she stayed out all night and disappeared for days on end. Would he have been more concerned about her welfare if she'd been from a more 'respectable' part of town? Would he have even made a move?

He closed the magazine. The heroine of 'Small Town, Big Secret' bore little resemblance to the Sandra he knew. Mind you, it dawned on him, reading between the lines, that he could find out all he needed to know about the author, Joanne McCollum, if he was of a mind. He wasn't.

Hanging in Dove's wardrobe were eight denim jackets, all the same size. Seven of them were Levi's. Some of them were identical. One was a wool-lined folly, rarely worn, and one was fairly well-worn, although by the looks of things freshly laundered. It was a Lee jacket with a Pixies button badge on the lapel. Philip had to sit down.

Either this was some sort of sick joke, or it was the very same jacket Sandra had borrowed from Dove on the night everything went awry.

Fondling the garment, Philip's head began to spin, a pain, in stereo, throbbing from temple to temple, nausea rising from the core of his being. There were no incriminating stains on the jacket. There was no souvenir of Sandra's in the pockets, no house-keys, for the sake of argument, no lip-sticked smeared tissue, nothing that might prove it was the jacket in which she was last seen. That jacket, to the best of his knowledge, had never been found.

The guards had searched Dove's house, on more than one occasion, sending Gerry Senior into a class of apoplexy rarely encountered this side of nineteenth-century English novels. His was a rage that never truly relented. His wife, Dee, who'd been observing Philip for some minutes from the door of the bedroom, moved towards him, wraith-like, her gown a-flap, and wrapped him in her arms. She stroked his hair and kissed his forehead, possibly confusing his alcohol-induced anguish with her own.

'A parcel arrived a few weeks ago. For Dermot. That was in it, the jacket.'

'Who was it from, Dee?'

She shook her head. 'No idea. No note or nothing.'

'Did you tell the guards?'

'God no, Philip. Dermot wouldn't hear of it. He begged me not to breathe a word to a soul. He was very down, Philip, the last few months, my poor little baby.'

Dee, sobbing, sat down on the bed. Philip sat down beside her and, not sure of the etiquette in this sort of situation, rubbed her back.

'To be honest, I wouldn't have gone to the guards anyway. Do you know,' she whispered, 'it was years, *years* before people came back to the shop, our best customers, after the business with the Mohan girl.'

What the locals did for nails and picture frames in the meantime, who knew? They probably went to Dundalk or Drogheda. Philip could understand perfectly why the Connollys would want to avoid the guards, given Dove's delicate mind and all, not wishing to invite that sort of intrusion into their lives ever again.

'Poor Gerry went in every day – you know Gerry, he can be very headstrong. God forgive me, I don't know what Dermot ever saw in her. Sandra.'

Philip stopped rubbing her back. The old assumptions. If something bad happens to you, you must have invited it in some way. If you don't have much, you don't have much to give.

'Dee. I don't know what he saw in her either. I don't know what I saw in her myself. I could sit here telling you about how beautiful she was, and clever, and kind. Special. The effect she had on stupid boys like us. But you know what, Dee? She was just a girl, an ordinary girl in a small town. Carmel's daughter, Sandra. Doing her best with what she had. And maybe Dove loved her. And maybe he didn't. Maybe he was just besotted with her, like we all were. But I'll tell you this. She didn't deserve to die.'

Philip bit his lip, but it didn't do much to stop the tears. Dee rubbed his back. It was shortly after the package arrived, she told him, that Dermot shut himself away up in his room.

'In a rapture, he was. Making the book for you.'

Philip pictured him, labouring day and night at his desk, by candle-light, like a monk of old in Mellifont.

'*It's for Philip*, he kept saying it, over and over again, *it's for Philip, he'll know what to do*.'

What he meant by that, she didn't know. It was more of Dermot's delirium, she thought at the time. Philip was in no fit state to be jumping to conclusions, but one or two possibilities immediately occurred to him as Dee prattled on. One. Sandra was alive and in a burst of nostalgia and/or pity, she decided to return the jacket to her would-be beau. Two. It was yet another case of misdirection years after the event and Dove was meant to think she was still alive. Three. There was a third possibility. Perhaps there'd been somebody out there, in the locality, trying to help Dove, somebody with a conscience who knew what really happened. This insider was trying to steer him towards his, and now of course Philip's, holy grail. He preferred the third option, hoping the mole, or whistleblower, would continue his good work and in so doing transfer his allegiance to him.

Dee's monologue and Philip's mulling over, for the time being, the silence was interrupted by the sound of a phone ringing. The ringtone was conventional but shrill. The double surprise in Dee's eyes alerted Philip to the fact that the phone was Dove's and that it was ringing in the pocket of Philip's shorts. Philip, without feeling the need to apologize or explain himself, calmly extricated the device. He looked at the screen. Who'd be calling Dove a week after he died? He was disappointed to note that the contact name read No Caller ID. He answered the phone. Nobody spoke on the other end of the line. Rather, it was just the sound of somebody tramping through mulch, three words, he thought wryly, that might be a good name for his own autobiography. *Tramping through Mulch*. It was just a squelching noise that revealed nothing of the caller's identity, his or her location, or the reason for the call. He hung up, not ruling out the likelihood that somebody had dialled Dove's number by mistake.

'The only thing I'll say,' Dee levelled with him. 'If anybody else calls on my son's phone, you'll tell me, won't you? And you'll tell me if you find the poor Mohan girl.'

The destroyer of worlds

By the time Philip woke up, in a pool of sweat, it was early evening. The smell of freshly stewed rhubarb was in the air. Otherwise, he was well on the mend, the headache now a soft tremolo coda to the earlier cacophony. He quietly ate his tea. It was an old favourite, mushrooms on toast, his mother, in fairness, quiet herself and not overly judgemental or in his face, and on the money with her timely refills.

He switched on the six o'clock news, the newsreaders inexplicably, in his opinion, standing up while relaying the news and wandering around the studio as if they were looking for teabags. Was there a clamour for change as regards news presentation when he was out of the country? Was there one person who grumbled that the news wasn't sinking in? Either way, it was an unnecessary distraction, detracting, if anything, from the import of the headlines, one of which caused an immediate cessation of the savouring of the tasty fungal supper.

Following a tip-off, apparently, a search had gotten underway this very morning for one of the so-called 'disappeared' near Tullyanna. After delivering this alarming headline, the newscaster, with an unpronounceable Irish language name, and her dressed to the nines in zips and chains as if she was going clubbing, walked from one side of the studio to the other. With a little wave of her hand, an image appeared behind her, as if by magic.

It was a landscape all too familiar to Philip, it being Macker's father's field. And it was swarming with men and women in white jumpsuits. Like something out of a sci-fi film. He was half-expecting a giant ant to appear on the scene and chase them all away.

211

The people were all busy wandering in and out of a big white tent with important-looking equipment, guns, sonar, or possibly radar at the ready. They were juggling their instruments and styrofoam cups of coffee and trying to avoid being mangled by one of the two diggers clawing manically away at the earth.

The men and women at the helm were enjoying their day in the sun when a helicopter descended from the sky, spewing out the unmistakably lean figure of Detective Keating, his hair unravelling, and behind him, in what was surely a breach of the protocol, the current bane of Philip's life, Joanne McCollum herself. A shard of longing stabbed him in the heart.

Sandra, whose name was not mentioned in the bulletin, was never categorized, even during the brief period when her cause was championed, as one of the 'disappeared', the term eerie and alien, borrowed from conflicts elsewhere, most notably South America.

The gardaí, to placate the families of those unfortunates who'd upset the paramilitaries so much that their burial sites were never disclosed, conducted these searches from time to time. They were exercises in optics as often as not. Unlike Sandra, that ghostly horde, lumped together as 'the disappeared', were more obvious victims of the Troubles. They were *squealers,* apparently, in most cases, a slur vigorously disputed by their families. It's not as if their captors, and their interrogators, and their torturers, and their murderers just forgot what they did with the bodies. After all, they had famously long memories. They had eight hundred years of grievances stored away in their heads. Surely, they'd remember digging a grave?

Somebody, a senior figure on the army council presumably, must have made a decision at one time or another to import the tactic. *That's what we need now, the very thing to further the cause of Irish unity, the exotic act of 'disappearing' people.* They would have read, with fascination, of its growing popularity in Buenos Aires and Rosario and the Chilean capital, Santiago, and murky Medellín. They must have sat around with mugs of tea and crunchy Goldgrain biscuits and calmly discussed the idea of making people vanish – housewives, small-time hoods, whoever – to send out a strong message to the communities they served and protected. It must have been quite exciting doing it for the first time. A thrill, taking somebody from their home, a woman, say, her children screaming, holding on to her leg. It lent a bit of gaucho glamour to a campaign going stale on car-bombs and mortar attacks.

By the end of the news, nothing, no body or body part, had been found, to nobody's great surprise. Not as much as a freckle, although the search would continue on the following day, according to the newsreader, now laughing as she swatted away a fly. Philip, although there was nothing he would have liked more than to hear that Sandra had been found, didn't hold out much hope for the search team. The McManus clan were smarter than that.

Out of curiosity, he typed in the address of the McManus family farm, to see if the coordinates tallied with anything he could remember from Dove's comic book. That initiative, needless to say, went unrewarded. With a weary heart, he took out Dove's phone. It was an expensive-looking gadget, a prototype. Strange, he thought, that his old friend hadn't needed to sell it in order to feed his habit.

Philip scrolled through Dove's old text messages on the off-chance that he'd sent the comic to somebody else as well. Most of the recent text exchanges were between himself and his partner, Claire, and they were fraught. Heart-breaking arguments over childcare, for the most part. Philip tried his best to resist reading them in any sort of detail.

Philip was getting impatient, looking for shortcuts. Not that he was in competition with her, but Joanne had Keating's ear while he was stuck with Healy. There was little charge left in the battery of Dove's phone, less than 10 per cent and dwindling rapidly, and he didn't have a suitable charger in his possession. If the phone did die, he didn't know Dove's passcode to get it going again. He looked through the emails. There was nothing encouraging there either. Getting desperate now, he opened Dove's photos, and it was lucky he did. To his delight and relief, he realized immediately that Dove had had the good sense to photograph each page of the comic book. Good man, Dove.

His mother tiptoed into the dining room and placed a slice of rhubarb crumble and yet another cup of tea beside him.

'Jaysus. Not now, Mammy.'

'Suit yourself.'

'Sorry.'

He put down the phone, not wanting to disappoint her further and her at her wits' end, although she tried not to show it, with his behaviour since his return. He knew it was not working out at all as she'd hoped, not one game of Scrabble having been played between them. The son jumped up from his chair and kissed the mother on the cheek, an extravagant and wholly unexpected gesture that seemed to do the trick in containing the disappointment for now. There'd be plenty of time for ostentatious displays of mother–son affection after he found Sandra.

'I'll explain later.'

With haste, the battery draining before his eyes, he flicked through the photos, searching frantically for the images of Gram Parsons and General Practice, in particular.

General Practice made his appearance on page six. His house, he instantly recalled, consulting his notes to make sure he wasn't fooling himself, was situated at six degrees west. Could the page number be relevant? This was promising. Philip hardly able to contain his excitement now was practically riding the chair. The general was pointing, unarguably, towards the west. Six degrees west? It was not implausible, his theory. It was still a runner, if not a dead cert.

He thumbed rapidly through the album to the photograph of page fifty-three. Fifty-three was the other coordinate of his own house, the northerly co-efficient. Fifty-three degrees north. The page numbers were obscured on the tiny screen but he soon found it, half-expecting, half-dreading to see Gram Parsons there. Luckily, he wasn't. At least, Sandra wasn't buried under his own patio. That was something.

The battery icon now indicated that there was only 4 per cent of power left to play with. To his immense satisfaction, Gram did appear on the next photo, a replica of page fifty-four. He was pointing upwards in what was undeniably a northerly direction. Fifty-four degrees north. This suggested to Philip that he was indeed on the right track. And that Dove, who was going up in his estimation, was definitely trying to tell him that Sandra was to be found not a million miles away.

Hangover almost gone, the headache a mere pulse, he studied the image again and again. He zoomed in and out by pinching the screen with his fingers. The seven fingers on Gram's hand surely had to be significant. Nothing else on the page was quite as anomalous. Perhaps, he tentatively surmised, in full boffin mode now, the number seven also belonged to the GPS coordinates. In which case, he deducted empirically, it would represent seven minutes. That would make one of the coordinates a more specific 54°N 7'. He was enjoying himself now, the bit between the teeth. If he was correct, and it was beginning to make a lot of sense, or at least he willed it to make sense, it followed that the drawing on page six might well cough up another relevant number.

Scrolling backwards, time against him, he found the angry-looking army doctor. Despite his military background, the general had all his fingers intact. He scrutinized the picture, squinting in search of an incongruity, some Dove-like prank. Philip couldn't help noticing that the character wielded a box of pills in his pointing hand. And that this box contained the unlikely total of 44 pills. A box of 12 pills or 24 or, at a push, 48 would be considered normal in pharmaceutical circles and might not attract a second glance. But the number 44, in the absence of any other anomaly on the page, was clearly an invitation, as far as Philip was concerned, an exhortation from the grave, to make further inquiries. And so Philip, flat out, burning calories at an unsustainable rate, deduced that 44 was the number of minutes west of the 6th degree longitude. That gave him a rough overall locus of 54°N 7' 6°W 44'. This was some craic, he thought.

It actually suited him, this type of work, scientific calculations and the like, although part of him wished it didn't. He had always suspected he was left-brained and tried to deny it, tried to resist that preordination over the years. Willing himself to be right-brained, he sang and dabbled in poetry and samsheparded his way around groovy bars and boudoirs. A complete waste of time. He could see that now. He'd been fighting his own practical nature, confusing the two sides of his brain. No wonder he had a permanent headache. He could see a future opening up before him in teaching. Not as a teacher of maths or science but a teacher of basic cop-on, going around schools quashing the boys' fancy notions. But first he must use his rediscovered talent to pinpoint the exact place he was looking for and find the girl.

Typing at the speed of light, he quickly determined that the GPS coordinates corresponded to a location just outside the town of Castleblayney, towards the Armagh border. It was a distance of about 25 kilometres away from where he was currently directing operations. He leaned back on his seat and exhaled deeply. This must be how Oppenheimer felt in Los Alamos, the vital statistics of Little Boy finally clicking into place. 'Now I am death, the destroyer of worlds,' he whispered to himself, Oppenheimer's quote – lifted from the *Bhagavad Gita* – emerging from the not-entirely-redundant right side of his brain. Well, the destroyer of Coleman's world anyway, with the help of God.

He thought he better download the photos onto his mother's laptop before the phone lost power. He actually congratulated himself for his quick thinking.

'Mammy,' he shouted.

'Yes, love.'

'Have you got a fucking . . . lead?'

'No need to curse.'

'Do you have a lead, a connection, where do you keep the wires?'

'I don't know what you're talking about, Pip. What wires?'

And then Dove's phone died.

'Ah for fuck's sake!'

And he flipped closed the laptop, its fan in overdrive. And then he drank his cold tea, in silence, and ate his dessert, content, to an extent, with the evening's work.

Without the seconds – the third part of the formula – added on to the degrees and the minutes, he didn't have the complete picture yet. He wouldn't be able to isolate, so to speak, the U-235 isotope. According to his sums, Sandra's grave, if that is where Dove was sending him, could be anywhere within a square mile area. That wasn't necessarily the end of the road, but it was no walk in the park either.

The problem, now that the phone had died, was that there were no more clues available directing him to a more precise site. What those clues might be, he had no idea. He could only speculate blindly. Were we talking about the dimensions in millimetres of the individual panels? The number of blades of grass under Gram Parsons' feet? He was convinced, his faith in Dove firm, that given just a few more minutes, he would have found the answer.

The day of the dig

When Kevin first heard about the kerfuffle on McManus's farm, his curiosity aroused by the chopper flying low, he and Sheila drove out there, along with half the town, to see for themselves what was going on. A helicopter was a novelty in that part of the world, boding either very good news or very bad news.

There was all sorts of speculation. A sheikh, some said, in the mood to acquire a stud farm. Or an American tycoon visiting the ancestral home. Or the rockstar, Sting, who apparently had a family connection to the area. A chance to sneer at Sting was not to be sniffed at in a small town.

Flashing his old badge, he managed to get past the rookie, an out-of-towner, manning the first cordon below on the road. Healy still looked like a cop and carried himself like a cop and, ignored by the Dublin-based technicians going up and down the lane, felt like a real cop, too.

Bad News was relishing his role as chief archaeologist, already mentally polishing the medals that would surely be his should any trace of the girl be found.

Before his old pal shooed him away, he spotted Joanne.

Joanne!

'Sorry, Kevin,' she mouthed at him from the other side of the tape. He quickly worked out that she had gone on something of a solo run. No sooner had they joined forces than she had stolen a march on himself and Philip and secured herself a ringside seat at the circus. So much for his managerial skills. Mind you, he couldn't really blame her. Look how far his *dithering* had got him in the past.

There were a couple of other reasons why he wasn't overly peeved with Joanne. One. He was fairly buoyant after a totally unexpected yet wholly successful sexual engagement earlier that morning with Sheila. And the main reason? In his opinion, there was no way McManus would tolerate such an incursion if he actually *had* anything to hide. Knowing him personally, a thorough man if ever there was one, that bunker would have been well and truly destroyed. Whatever secrets it might have contained in the past would have been lost forever after it was fumigated and sterilized and blown to bits, as agreed with the decommissioning commission. Overseen by them, no trace of life, animal or vegetable, would have been left behind.

Of course, there was always a teensy chance something else might materialize. And that's why Kevin was there. Something might have been overlooked by the scheming bandit. Something might have been dropped or mislaid during all the subversive comings and goings on the property over the years. Something might have been planted by a former comrade – disgruntled, and God knows there were plenty of them, the terms of the Peace not having been universally accepted – or by a rival within the fuel trade. Some shred of clothing, perhaps, one of Sandra's shoes, a buckle, a fibre that linked the girl to the place, something might have landed on a tree when it, the bunker, was blown up, a finding that would compel the gardaí to investigate further.

As he and the other onlookers were pushed back, he could see Joanne turning her back on the dig and walking towards a group of serious-looking men, their arms folded. A phalanx of defiant feckers, they were standing in a defensive formation by an oak tree a couple of hundred yards away from the epicentre of activity.

Even now – now that he was well – Kevin couldn't help wondering if the man who shot him was among the men Joanne brazenly approached in McManus's field.

* * *

Kevin went back to his car, where Sheila was sitting happily, listening to the radio and knitting a pair of bootees for Paul. It had been an

219

eventful morning. There was a picnic in the boot of the car. Earlier, he'd managed to make contact with Sheriff's sister, Noeleen, in London, having been provided with a contact number by his daughter, Ciara. The success of that call to Noeleen did no harm to the early-bird conjugal high-jinks.

He didn't tell Noeleen he *wasn't* a cop, which was probably a bit cheeky of him. He didn't tell her he *wasn't* the Risen Lord either. You mightn't know yourself if you were the filler of those mighty sandals until some showdown 'twixt good and evil revealed your true nature to yourself and the world at large. Rather, he presented himself as a friend of Stephen's, which wasn't necessarily a lie. Kevin was thinking he might yet be the best friend Stephen Sheriff ever had. The woman turned out to be a pleasant, sensible person. She had a very croaky voice, but no ideological baggage whatsoever or, glory be, misguided loyalty towards her brother.

'Is this about Sandra Mohan?'

They were her first words. Kevin was speechless. She talked freely, telling him that she had attended the Springsteen concert in Wembley on 10 July 1994 with Stephen. She had bought the tickets herself for his birthday, and she confirmed that the show was indeed *deadly*.

'Is this about the postcards?'

Noeleen, terribly willing to oblige, as if Kevin was a researcher for *This Is Your Life*, was also in a position to recall, with certainty, that Stephen had stayed with her on each occasion that one of Sandra's postcards was dispatched. Unprovoked by Kevin, who had mentioned the dates alright but not the cards, she volunteered the news that she saw her brother, with her own eyes, in possession of a Princess Diana postcard on two separate dates. Knowing that he was republican-minded, unlike herself, she challenged him on this incongruity.

'Why would he be celebrating members of the royal family? Both times, he passed it off as a joke, although I could tell the handwriting wasn't his.'

She had come to the conclusion that he was up to no good.

'What took you so long?' says she to Kevin.

'What took *you* so long, if you don't me asking?'

'He's my brother. But I always said, as soon as anyone bothered to ask me, I'd tell them what I know.'

Kevin was stumped. The woman had plenty to say, more than he dared to hope for. Obviously accustomed to speaking her mind, she spelled it all out it in a deliberate way, clearly welcoming the opportunity to discharge some sort of a burden she'd been carrying.

'It must feel great cutting loose the old sandbags.'

'I don't know what you mean by sandbags,' says she.

Noeleen had agreed to go on the record. That was a clincher. It would prove that Sandra was never in London. And Sheriff and Coleman would have a lot of explaining to do. But he had to tread carefully. Towards the end of the phone call, she became a bit irritated by his amateur psychology.

Of course, he dug a bigger hole for himself by opting to elaborate on the sandbags metaphor instead of shutting his stupid mouth. He probably shouldn't have compared her to a hot-air balloon. He meant it as a compliment. Now that she was free of the sandbags, she'd be able to soar as a person and a public servant. Like a balloon. Objectively, you would think, it was an inoffensive remark. But in fairness to her, she must have been distracted by this call out of the blue, a call she'd been waiting for for many years, and she must have been agitated at having made such a profound commitment to give up her brother. She probably misinterpreted what he was saying, thinking he called her full of 'hot air' and a 'balloon', two insults guaranteed to raise the hackles of anyone, especially a woman as assertive as Noeleen, and her most likely on the frontline of the gender wars in London. She also seemed very disappointed when she learned that he wasn't a real policeman.

The interview over, neither party entirely satisfied with the finale after such a promising start, he went back to bed. His frustration at his own cack-handedness was quickly forgotten, however, when Sheila, in a pair of new polka-dot pyjamas, emerged from the ensuite with massage oils and a scented candle. Surprised at first, a bit wary and certainly not aroused at this stage, being the unassuming man he was, he watched her position the candle on the bedside locker, dim the lights, remove her new spotty pjs, swallow her pills and mount the bed.

She then removed his pyjama bottoms, leaving his top on, neatly buttoned, and motioned for him to flip over onto his belly whereupon, to his utter amazement, she began to massage oil into his well-padded buttocks. This was a turn-up for the books. All thoughts of Noeleen Sheriff were put to one side as his wife delved un-squeamishly deep into the crack of his behind. Just as he was coming to terms with that violation, she then hoisted him into a crouching position, backside in the air like a Muslim at prayer, and started to tickle the back of his testicles. By this time, he was more or less in a state of shock. He held his breath, hoping the moment would never end, fearing one false move, one badly timed exhalation, might break the spell and scupper everything.

The most surprising thing of all was that he thought she wasn't talking to him. He could tell when she went out into the garden that morning to do her tai-chi in her bare feet that she wasn't best-pleased to see a six-foot-by-two-foot rectangular hole in the ground. And him lying in it. He was alive, and only trying it out for size, but still, it must have alarmed her. It occurred to him, as she turned on her heels and floated back inside without a word, that this might have been the last straw. Either the grave itself, or him lying in the grave, might have been the granite block on which his bone-china marriage finally cracked. Gratifyingly, for whatever reason, it had the exact opposite effect. He didn't think about his son Shane in the next room. He hardly thought about the case at all.

* * *

The day of the dig was a hot one. There was talk that it was the hottest day of the year. They stood at the back of the car, the boot open. Sheila was eating a curly sandwich.

'They're having a press conference in the Cunningham Arms tomorrow,' said Sheila, in her understated way, as if this day couldn't get any better. 'It's all over the news.'

'Who's this now?'

'The Party.'

'Ho-ho,' said he, ploughing straight for the home-made cupcakes.

The lovebirds didn't stay long. Not that Kevin wasn't still curious, but it looked like the search team was just going through the motions. It was a performance for the cameras. But, crucially, it had the effect of sending Coleman and his party into a bit of a tailspin. Maybe Joanne's tactics were right. You could see people, their faces darkening, as they muttered into their phones, hurrying back to their cars. He noticed the fixer, Lorcan Lonergan, breaking off from a one-on-one with – of all people – Joanne. What was that all about, he wondered? Without having to say a word to each other, himself and Sheila abandoned the picnic and went home for yet another go in the bedroom.

Kevin was actually a bit concerned by this turn of events. For a start, he didn't think he had the stamina. At this rate, he genuinely thought he might die of a heart attack or do himself a serious injury. He was worried about Sheila, too. After he'd emerged from the grave – the resurrection, says you – he got the spade and calmly filled in the hole. For this own amusement, he made a little cross with two twigs and stuck it in the clay. *Good riddance to old Kevin*. When he went inside to wash his hands, Sheila had a cup of coffee waiting for him in the Hermès mug that, as far as he could recall, had never been used. That was how it all started.

Between the dig and the impending press conference, there was fierce excitement in the town. Joanne rang him.

'Did you hear about the press conference?'

'I did. That was some stunt you pulled, Joanne.'

'I know, I should have warned you. But it's having the desired effect.'

'Maybe. I just feel we should be going about this *quietly*.'

'That's where we differ, Kevin. We need to make a *splash*. The Leader himself is going to be there. And the other *grandees*. We have them by the balls. Will I see you there?'

'You will, indeed.'

He hung up wondering what other surprises Joanne had up her sleeve. Well, it was something to look forward to anyway. Apparently, they were going to address rumours that were swirling around on the internet about the disappearance of Sandra Mohan. It would be very interesting to see how – even with all the PR savvy the Organization had accumulated over the years – they'd manage that.

Jumping the gun

Next morning, the garda operation was wound down. The TV crews packed up. Nothing was uncovered. Keating will look like some eejit, thought Kevin, mildly amused. Outside the pharmacy, he sat in the car and watched a caravan of shiny buses, bespattered in slogans and Party colours and the Leader's clean-shaven face, sweep into town. Uplifting dance music emanated from speakers attached to the vehicles, a far cry from the bloodcurdling ballads that rallied their electoral cavalcades of yore. He rubbed some balm on his swollen lips, sorry to have left Sheila at home in a hot flush. She was resolved to do a bit of weeding in the garden, having dropped the baby off at the crèche. Where was she getting the energy from at all?

'I have my own weeding to do,' he said, and winked at his wife, when she asked him where he was going. Sheila threw her eyes up to heaven. Thankfully, she seemed to have resigned herself to his old tropes, and to what she considered to be his dangerous obsession with certain people, and they with roots in the town, deeper roots than his.

'They're *real* people, Kevin,' she stressed, 'with good and bad in them like the rest of us, not *weeds*.'

He tiptoed out of the garden.

'Tiptoeing doesn't make it any better, Kev. Not when I'm actually talking to you.'

'Sorry, love.'

'Like a thief. Or a coward. Walk like a man!'

Was that a half-smile?

'*My hour for tea is half past five and my buttered toast waits for nobody.*'

He grinned broadly, scrunching up his face, the joyous tingling beginning behind his eyes and spreading through his body down to his feet. She was back. If she was quoting *The Woman in White* – implied threat notwithstanding – they were going to be okay. A thousand possibilities crossed his mind, by way of retort, all jumbled references from that most quotable of novels, but he couldn't remember any of them word for word. *Something about not engaging unprepared with a woman in a fencing match of words.* But he didn't say it out loud.

He settled for 'I love you' and kissed her on the lips, like a man going off to war.

He knew he should probably take the day off and do the garden with her. A day like this was rare, in terms of weather and warm feelings between them, and them on a new plane altogether, lending itself to all sorts of connubial bliss. The image of the pair of them, on their knees, passing the secateurs over and back, serenaded by their own private hedgerow orchestra was foremost in his mind. It had a strong appeal, but other appeals, this day, were stronger.

In his head he had planned an extravagance, namely to eat in the Cunningham Arms amongst the great and the good of the town, the solicitors and the estate agents, ruddy-faced connoisseurs all of the carvery lunch. He wanted a break from the sex and the new-found marital happiness and to rub shoulders with the visitors who had descended upon the town for the press conference. He wanted to eat steak and chips while absorbing the pre-event babble. It would be nice to see Fergal Coleman squirm for a change. Would he have the confidence to speak up from the back of the room? Ask him about the postcards?

It's true that Coleman and his family belonged to the town in a way that Kevin, a blow-in from Wicklow, never could. He was surrounded by all sorts of kin, blood relations, relations through marriage and legions of friends, this network providing him with a legitimacy denied to interlopers the likes of Kevin. (You'd think Kevin's contribution to the Gaelic football club and the am-dram society and the chess club and the Tidy Towns committee – until he fell out with

Kitty Carroll – and countless other voluntary activities would count for something, but no.)

Together, the Coleman clan had seen whole industries come and go, fortunes rise and fall, and people live and die. There was an ownership there, a claim to the place not based on land or property rights, or money or job title, but one bestowed on Coleman through his very DNA and in the shape of his face, a claim backed up by every elongated vowel that slow-drawled from his mouth. Ciara and Shane both had the accent, right enough, bereft of all intonation and colour. They possessed the requisite deadpan demeanour, too. You never knew what they were thinking or feeling, if they were thinking or feeling anything. But even they were in no way a hundred per cent embraced by the Brahmins of the town. That was probably down to him and his interfering ways.

No sooner had Kevin parked his car than his grand plan for the day was thwarted. His phone, the old Nokia, snug in its old leather case, called him to his senses. It was Philip Sharkey on the other end of the line.

'I need to see you immediately.' He expressed himself urgently.

'Feckit anyway,' Kevin muttered under his breath.

'The old electrical sub-station on the Corrabawn Road. Twenty minutes.'

'Obscure. I'll see you there.'

There goes the big lunch and the press conference, thought Kevin grumpily, the day more or less ruined. He eased out of his space, in the Renault Megane, the car held together by Sellotape. It had better be important. One didn't need to be a genius, or an orienteer, never mind a know-all with his exile's in-depth knowledge of the area, to figure out that Philip did not want to leave his house by the front door. Obviously not wanting to be seen, he was planning on leaving by the back door and walking across the fields, skirting around McGeough's piggery, to reach the Corrabawn Road.

Kevin arrived at the power plant, on schedule, the transformers humming ominously, and picked up Philip, whose shoes were smelling of manure. He had a good look around before getting into the car.

'That's a hot one.'

'Did anybody follow you?'

'I don't know, Philip. To be honest with you, I wasn't my normal careful self. I'm hungry.'

'Drive around or something.'

'We'll be grand,' said Healy, the innards gurgling. 'They're all at the hotel. Coleman's crowd. *And* the guards. What's on your mind?'

'I think I know where she is.' Philip informed Kevin of his findings.

'Japers!'

'Is that all you can say? Japers! This is a fucking game-changer.'

'Are you going to tell me where?'

'Near 'Blayney. We'll need maps. Big fuck-off ones. Ordnance Survey.'

It was a game-changing disclosure by any standards, namely the potential whereabouts of Sandra's grave. Philip briefly filled him in on his sources and his methodology, as Kevin raced home to pick up the maps. If nothing else, at least Kevin could provide some quality maps.

A potentially huge development was the last thing he was expecting to hear at this point in time. In fact, he was a bit alarmed at the sudden surge in the pace of the investigation, being more of a slow and steady man himself, but, at the same time, he didn't need to be told twice to put the boot down.

This was what he missed most about his old job. The cut and thrust. The not knowing what was going to happen next. The blind alleys and the open roads. The camaraderie. Having somebody to talk to – or not talk to, as the case may be when you were sitting in a car with the likes of Philip Sharkey. Keeping off the main roads, the duo soon made their way to the imprecise address Philip had earmarked. He knew Philip was a practical sort, but didn't have him down as a man of science.

When they reached the town of Castleblayney, they got out of the car, beside the GAA pitch. Kevin carefully unfolded the relevant OS map on the bonnet. Philip gave him the GPS coordinates: 54 degrees 7 minutes North and 6 degrees 44 minutes West.

'What are we going to do now?' asked Philip, at a loss.

Kevin grinned smugly and took out his notebook. 'I'm not just a pretty face, you know. Right. I'll need to project the geodetic ellipsoidal coordinates onto the grid.'

'What the fuck are you on about?'

'The latitude and the longitude to the eastings and northings. Using the old Transverse Mercator Projection in conjunction with Old Bessie,' he pointed to his head, 'which won't be easy on account of the hunger pains.'

Healy closed his eyes and went into a little trance, Philip watching him in disbelief. Then he sucked the top of his pencil before jotting down some calculations using the following equations.

$$X1 = (v+h)\cos\varphi1 \; \cos\lambda1$$
$$Y1 = (v+h)\cos\varphi1 \; \sin\lambda1$$
$$Z1 = (v(1-e2)+h) \; \sin\varphi1$$

'Right, I have it.'

Philip looked at him not so much in admiration as shock. They studied the map, Kevin running his fingers up and down the boxes.

'We're talking about . . . Lough Oughter.'

'A fucking lake. Brilliant.'

'Not necessarily. There's a park there, a recreational area. Look. Lough Oughter Forest Park.'

Philip, in a hurry, scrunched up the map.

'No,' Kevin screamed. 'Don't crease it. Fecksake.'

Furious with Philip, he folded the map properly, stuck it in the glove compartment, and headed for the park. It was a place Kevin was familiar with, having been there once at a regatta, not that he had any interest in boats.

But he had been friends with an enthusiast of all things aquatic, a fella called Garda Benny Kiernan, a European match-fishing champion in his day, and an environmentalist to boot, and, as you would expect, given that deadly combination, a bit of a bore around the station. Whatever happened to Benny?

It was a heavily wooded facility, a headache inherited by the state from the ever-generous landed gentry, about a thousand acres in total of deciduous and coniferous trees, oak and sycamore, Scots pine and larch, all rubbing along together, although who knows what arboreal chicanery goes on on the forest floor, in the eternal scrap for survival.

The estate, in a state of neglect, had been for sale for many years and never sold before the government reluctantly stepped in. It upset the locals that tax-payers' money was spent on bailing out a run-of-the-mill Anglo-Irish dynasty, the current baronet a clown best known for his extensive stamp collection.

The house itself was unremarkable, long cleared of any knick-knacks of note picked up in India or on a Grand Tour. The family were no great shakes either. They weren't even remembered for their cruelty during the Famine. Somehow, they had managed to lie low for centuries, throughout the War of Independence and the more recent Troubles. But they couldn't survive the dot-com bubble, the baronet, Edward Giles Lowman, having invested heavily in a pet supplies company. Now they were gone. And the family seat was a tourist amenity, the council having put to good use a surfeit of duckboards and little pointy wooden arrows.

The woods surrounded a sizeable lake, another thousand acres, at a guess, full to the brim with bream, roach, hybrids and tench, and, on special occasions, if you were lucky, Mr Pike himself. That's if Benny hadn't caught them all.

At the park, Philip and Kevin stood there scanning the noticeboard advertising the park's attractions, which included various types of duck, a children's playground, and, more to the point, two smallish islands on the lake, known as Black Island and White Island. They were both readily accessible and used year-round by a few of the less sociable local anglers. Whether that made it more or less likely that either of the tiny islands hosted a dead girl's body, Kevin and Philip couldn't say.

Philip was a bit disillusioned. After his brainwave and Kevin's excellent cartographical work, it was obviously crushing to find a big lake in the way.

'If I was disposing of a body myself,' he said aloud, 'I'd have picked a lake, too.'

In trying to console his ally, Kevin pointed out that it wasn't an especially reliable tactic.

'Dead bodies, no matter how well weighted, or how long sunk, have an inconvenient habit of slipping their binds and rising to the surface.'

'I see.'

'Besides,' he added, ever the optimist, 'lakes are just as dangerous for the wicked as they are for the righteous.'

Although Lough Oughter wasn't exactly the Atlantic Ocean, the weather still had to be taken into consideration. Sudden squalls and poor visibility were the dread of many's a sailor, even on such an obscure and innocuous-looking body of water. And while dumping a corpse, even one as light as Sandra's, there was always a chance that the boat would capsize. Or that the nefarious deed would be witnessed by a fisherman, embedded for the night on a nearby bank with his bar of dark chocolate and his even darker thoughts.

Philip remained pissed off but agreed – what choice had he? – to start searching the park, his only *aides-de-camp* on this ambitious caper his intuition and his untrained eye. There were few people around, and it late August and, by common consent, a scorcher.

Anyway, the quietness suited their purposes. Not wanting to take any chances, they decided to keep a low profile all the same, electing not to engage anybody in conversation. To save time, they decided to split up, Philip taking the red path, Kevin, the blue.

In advance of this effort, the latter, feeling quite faint by now, opted to pop back into the nearby town of Castleblayney for a quick sandwich. Obviously, it could take two men months, or maybe even years, to scour the whole park. If, by the end of play today, the search proved fruitless, they would come back again the next day and the next, *ad infinitum*. And at the end of time, if they were still unsuccessful, they would pass themselves off as fishermen, hire a boat, and check out the islands. After that – after the end of time – if they were still standing, well, they'd have to consider their options. None of the options was appealing. All Kevin could see ahead of him were endless searches of the woods, and perhaps a few diving lessons. Most likely they'd have to give up altogether and hand the job over to the police, with all the hassle and hindrances to justice that might entail.

At one o'clock on the dot, as Philip zig-zagged his way along the red path, Kevin found himself at a nearby service station. The RTÉ news announced itself on the radio with the usual hysterical fanfare, as if they were about to reveal the meaning of life itself, as Kevin, served by a young man from Nepal, forked out over the odds for a chicken and stuffing sandwich and a bottle of Coke. They did, to their credit, reference the press conference that was about to start in Tullyanna.

Everything changes, nothing dies

Joanne took her place at the back of a busy function room in the Cunningham Arms Hotel. She had the jitters. Her intention was straightforward enough. She was going to ask, pointedly and publicly, as the well-brought up person she was, a few awkward questions. She wasn't exactly expecting a *mea culpa*. But by keeping the story alive in this way, she hoped the Party, under pressure, with the national media present, would be forced to cooperate and eventually cough up some useful information. It might be in their interest to do so. After all, they had assisted some families of 'the disappeared' in the recent past without significant damage to the *brand*. As long as Joanne stayed cool, she thought, what could possibly go wrong?

She spotted some familiar faces in the crowd, girls she knew at school, traders in the town. Most of them studiously ignored her. Welly O'Boyle, however, to her surprise, turned up for moral support. One of his hands was in a plaster cast. Typical Welly, an accident waiting to happen. She nodded at him in gratitude, needing all the self-belief she could muster on this occasion. Near him stood a stooped McEntee, a savvy-suave political correspondent with republican leanings who doubled up as a sports presenter on Saturday afternoons. As if the news wasn't enough. He had been one of her tutors at DCU, one of those lecturers who liked hanging out with the students. Mind you, she liked him, straggly eyebrows and nose hair notwithstanding. Like a good claret, he gave off notes of tobacco and leather and maybe a bit of tar. He sidled over to her, sidling being his primary mode of transport, now as it was when she was at college.

'Pity about the dig.'

He also knew things. He was connected. Although a journalist, and a good one, he mostly operated in the spaces between words. There wasn't a notable occasion in recent memory where he wasn't to be seen sidling in the background and whispering in people's ears. Ghost-writing the history books, they say.

'Where is she then?'

His face, craggy and unknowable as the Burren, gave little away.

'*Omnia mutantur, nihil interit*. Ovid.'

'Spare me, Ted, I didn't go to private school.'

'Everything changes, nothing dies.'

'Except Latin,' she retorted, quite pleased with herself.

McEntee smiled, indulging her in an affectionate way. 'You were always a clever girl, Joanne. But you don't listen.'

She didn't mean to disrespect McEntee. His writing was one of the reasons she got into journalism in the first place. As a mentor in DCU, he couldn't help being enigmatic. Latin was probably his first language. He probably knew Ovid personally back in the day. But it was never less than infuriating when men – it was usually men – spoke to her in riddles. Especially men she admired. It was condescending, but what *did* he mean? Nothing dies. Was he trying to tell her that Sandra wasn't dead? Would he know? If he did, would he tell her? You could spend weeks trying to work out what he meant.

'Everything must change so that everything can stay the same.'

He pointed at the crowd. There he goes again, Joanne thought, furiously trying to place the quotation and its meaning in this context. Or at the very least come up with a witty comeback.

'*The Leopard*. Di Lampedusa. Look, love, we're all characters in a shadow play.'

Before he had a chance to elaborate, the meeting was called to order. Was he wilfully misdirecting her or, ever the shadow puppeteer, directing her? Towards what? The only thing she learned for sure was that McEntee, with his latest literary allusion, had outed himself as just another conservative masquerading as a radical. She'd seen the film.

'Let it go, Joanne. For your own good.'

It was the concerned, paternal way he said it that alarmed her. Dropping the scholarly mien for a moment, he took her hand and said, 'There's still time.' And then he sidled away again.

It was a room more used to wedding parties, in a hotel that was once a stately home. How time changes. Its shabby grandeur still intact, the hotel – like McEntee himself, like the watchful drumlin hills beyond the window – had seen it all before. Phlegmatic, that was the word, if hotels and hills could be such.

On the podium sat the Leader, silver hair like a helmet, visage benign as ever, flanked on his right by a harassed-looking Councillor Fergal Coleman, who'd just been harassed by the Leader himself. The Leader had excoriated him, telling him in no uncertain terms, according to a lipreader present, to '*get your fucking house in order*'. Further to his right sat other cowed local representatives, one of them still a schoolboy, who looked like he'd been crying. On his left, the Deputy Leader pursed his lips while other officials of the Party shuffled papers and conferred on matters of vital importance out of the corners of their mouths.

Literally talking through the tiniest aperture in the corner of your mouth through otherwise zip-locked lips was an ability, or possibly a genetic adaptation, unique to the border region. Joanne had often marvelled at this local form of ventriloquism like a racist Victorian anthropologist might have marvelled at a Hottentot's pronounced buttocks. Mind you, she'd used the technique often enough herself. It was a useful mutation to have in a world where you had to be very careful about what you said.

Lorcan Lonergan, the most composed man in the room, called the meeting to order, bilingually, slipping seamlessly between Irish and English. Lonergan was one of the men she had spoken to in Macker's field the previous day. He had slipped away from his company and headed her off.

'This your idea?'

Although curt to begin with, he was courteous thereafter, even going so far as to buy her a not-bad crêpe from the back of an old

2CV van, there being a mobile crêperie parked opportunistically on the lane.

'There's a good chance Fergal won't win,' he'd said, wiping a smidge of Nutella from his chin. 'And you know what? That wouldn't be the end of the world.'

There had been a festive atmosphere in the field. It reminded Joanne of the summer fair in Drumahair, the highlight of which was the Guess the Age of the Hen competition. The joke was that it was easier to win the next year because they used the same hen. The main attraction, yesterday, on what was a midge-infested day, was a state-of-the-art search for a missing girl, an exercise that in no way seemed to miff Lonergan.

'Certain things could come to light, so to speak, that could, for the sake of argument, affect his chances,' he'd said from the corner of his mouth. 'We're realistic people.'

She hadn't noticed Lonergan's lisp before. It was slightly surreal, sitting on a tree stump, shooting the breeze with one of the suspects in Sandra's murder. But was he actually offering to sacrifice Coleman, or was she reading too much into what he – no less cryptic than McEntee – was saying? And if he was, what did he want in return? Rightly or wrongly, she felt encouraged, empowered by Lonergan, to confront Coleman at the press conference.

After a short, visionary address by the Leader, rapturously received by the crowd, her new friend Lorcan introduced Fergal Coleman. He read out a prepared statement denying any involvement, in the light of recent innuendo, in the disappearance of Sandra Mohan or, he sneered, going off-script, Lord Lucan for that matter, his attempt at levity eliciting a wince from the Deputy Leader.

'But seriously, on a more serious note, all joking aside, this has taken a big toll on me personally and my family. I can accept any criticism that comes my way, it's part of the job, but it's not right my children should be subjected to such hate.'

'Hear, hear!' chanted the crowd.

He went on to say, a firm hold on his words, that there wasn't a day went by when he, personally, didn't think of Sandra and what might have happened to her.

'Hear, hear!'

'I appeal to anybody out there who has any information whatsoever to come forward to me, in strictest confidentiality, or to the gardaí themselves. I know I'm not perfect.'

'Hear, hear!'

'Everybody in this room knows me. I toil day and night, no stone unturned, to make the world a better, fairer, juster place for everybody.'

For that, he received a gentle pat on the back from the Leader, and more murmured words of encouragement in his ear, *'one more mis-step and you're fucked'*, or words to that effect.

Lonergan then fielded questions from the floor. There followed the usual back and forth as one or two of the hacks, their contrarian roles well-rehearsed, asked the Leader the standard vexed questions about his past. In response to a question about the killing of Tommy Courtney, the Leader was unequivocal.

'I personally asked senior members of the now completely defunct military wing of the organization if they, or anybody they knew, had any involvement whatsoever and they told me, on their word of honour, and that meant a lot, that no, no, they had not. And that assurance was good enough for me. And it should be good enough for everybody else.'

'Hear, hear.'

'Councillor Coleman, Joanne McCollum. *Northern Chronicle.*'

All heads turned towards the back of the room. Joanne, wearing a cream-coloured blouse with a floral print, was somewhat camouflaged by the wallpaper. Suddenly feeling self-conscious, Joanne walked down the central aisle towards the platform at the front of the room. It reminded her of the momentous night she'd crossed the Rubicon into JJ's eight years ago, and also the night Sandra crossed the dance floor in the Holy Family hall.

'Yes, Joanne.'

'Hi. I have here a postcard. I don't know, you might be interested in it.'

She held the missive aloft and waved it around in a theatrical fashion, its significance lost to all but Coleman. He was seated at a table, draped in white linen, like the top table at a wedding or, she thought, the Last Supper. The carpet was sticky beneath her feet. That would be the residual juices of the previous night's twenty-first. The Cunninghams would be turning in their graves.

Her mouth was dry, tongue thick, lips sticking together. It reminded her of the first ever press conference she'd attended, at the opening of the new slaughterhouse in Ballyhaise, Midland Meats. Larry Midland, the controversial beef baron himself, was there in person. She'd failed to ask him a single question, despite the numerous allegations against him.

What was she so afraid of? That people would think she was stupid? Or not articulate enough? Or too clever? She remembered McEntee sidling up to her, at the bar in DCU, and paraphrasing an old Chinese proverb, '*he who asks a question is a fool for five minutes, he who does not ask is a fool forever*'.

Standing in front of Coleman now, she could hear his deep, controlled breathing, in through the mouth and out through the nose, as she handed him the postcard. Feeling lightheaded, she rested her hands on the table, getting as close to Coleman's mic as she dared to make sure her words were heard.

'That postcard,' she paused dramatically, 'was written by . . . you. I found it in Sandra Mohan's bedroom. And it proves beyond doubt that you were planning to *elope* with her.'

A murmur rose and fell around the room as people tried to parse the import of her claim. Coleman, his heart audibly thumping, put on a pair of glasses. She could feel a wave of energy coming from the table, as if somebody had just turned on a hot fan. Her left leg began to jig uncontrollably.

The Leader leaned forward and, smiling a wolfish smile, whispered, 'This is not the time or the place.'

Coleman, stumped for words, looked down at his notes. The answers weren't there.

'I'm sure there's a simple explanation,' he waffled.

'Would you like to share it with us, the explanation? Were you in a relationship with Sandra Mohan?'

Joanne felt more in control now. She was beginning to enjoy the experience, like a barrister in court might enjoy toying with a witness.

'It could be a forgery. You might have put it there for all I know. There are any number of reasons.'

'Is it not time to tell the truth, Councillor Coleman, once and for all?'

Joanne did not have a barrister's patience. And unlike a barrister, she had a tendency to ask questions to which she didn't already know the answer. And the censor in her head, in this pressure cooker, had suddenly gone AWOL.

'Where is she buried?'

The room erupted in an explosion of outrage. Many of Coleman's supporters leapt to their feet and reeled on Joanne. One woman, she'd swear, took the opportunity to spit at her. But she was uncowed. This is what she'd half-hoped would happen, that they would drop the pretence and reveal their true colours in front of the media delegation.

'Why did she have to die?'

Her inquiry was drowned out.

'Shame on you!' they cried. 'Fucking disgrace!'

When the noise eventually subsided, it was Coleman who called for decorum, in the absence of MC Lonergan, who, it was later noted, had briefly stepped out of the room.

'Give the lady some space.'

'You're honestly saying that you can't explain how a postcard in your handwriting was found in Sandra's bedroom. You can remember every little *tiff* in history going back to the arrival of Strongbow, but you can't remember writing a postcard? A postcard suggesting you were in London, but one that you never actually posted . . .'

She sensed that she was losing the audience. Coleman immediately capitalized on her creeping self-doubt.

'Sorry, Joanne, I'm not following you.'

A few people tittered at Fergal's sarky interruption.

'If you don't mind me saying so, you're no Miss Marple,' he added to guffaws from the gallery. The Leader filled his pipe. The Deputy Leader remained stony-faced.

239

Getting a bit flustered now, Joanne was unable to articulate herself fully. Granted, it was a complicated story she was trying to sell to an audience that didn't want to listen. It was summertime and attention spans were short, hers as well as theirs. The faithful were infected with election fever and were impatient to get back to the hustings and the doorsteps to tell their rather more uplifting story.

She had to be careful here. She knew that. There was a danger she might be written off as a loony or, worse, a bore. In which case she'd be ignored. And the story she was trying to revive would lose what little traction it had gained in the past few days. Every story has a shelf life, as does every storyteller. She didn't need a *savant* like McEntee to tell her that. But she couldn't and wouldn't accept that the fate of Sandra Mohan was old news.

The thing that flustered her the most was that nobody, apart from Welly, backed her up. Obviously, she didn't expect the average rank-and-filer of the Party to have his conscience pricked and publicly express misgivings. It was not that sort of party – one that brooked dissent or internal debate or independent thought or any deviation whatsoever from the *message*. Your average aficionado and assorted hangers-on were, understandably, in their element at this point in time, carried away by the momentum, by the showing in the polls, by the intoxicating message of hope, of salvation, of a better world. They were carried away by the novelty of it all, and the youthful character of it, the sophistication of the Party machine, and, yes, perhaps the fetching whiff of sulphur was part of the attraction, too. Nobody was denying it. But what was most appealing to people – people who were so often dismissed as losers – was the genuinely serious chance of being part of a winning team. Joanne herself would have voted for them if only they'd come clean.

She didn't expect any of them to back her up. But surely, she thought, a local person, conscientious and uncompromised, would step forward in solidarity? She was about to leave the room at that point, in disgust, and furious with herself for her amateur attempt to catch anybody out, when Coleman started waving a red rag in her face.

'I hate to say it. Everyone knows poor Sandra was a *troubled* young lady. From a very difficult background. Quite *promiscuous* in ways. A lot of people, let's say, took advantage of her. So . . .'

Troubled. Promiscuous. Joanne, the hackles raised like a hoary Elizabethan ruff around her neck, lashed out at the assembly.

'Are you going to take this? You all going to stand back and let him do this? *Malign* Sandra's character? In the same way Tommy Courtney's name was maligned after he was beaten to death? There must be someone here who knows something. No? *One* person with a conscience? With a backbone? Someone who's *curious* at least? Sandra Mohan could have been your daughter. Your sister. She was just a child, who sang along to songs on the radio.'

To many of those present, the floor itself, the sticky carpet, became, all of a sudden, riveting. Joanne was back at DCU in the Debating Society chamber. This time she had no notes, none of her customary preparation, no witty asides. This time she went off-script, meaning every word she said.

'Tullyanna is a great town. I love it. Is this how you want to be remembered? A byword for infamy. Up there with Darkley and Greysteel? The place where a little girl disappeared? Councillor Coleman talked about a "juster, fairer" world. It's easy to say. But Carmel Mohan doesn't know what happened to her daughter. How is that *just*? Or *fair*? Going home every day to an empty house. You have no right to talk about justice and fairness as long as Sandra's missing. How can you be *trusted*? If you're all so afraid of a little girl, how will you cope with the rigours of high office? We're all dying for change.'

'Hear, hear.'

'The other crowd, they're supposed to be the corrupt ones, right?'

'Hear, hear.'

'They're the liars, aren't they? The thing is, you're supposed to be *better* than them, *fairer* and more just. You're the ones who tell it like it is. Well, now's your chance to prove you mean it. Are you for real? Are you fucking mice or are you men?'

Leaving the function room, to the sound of her own footsteps, she decided to do what she did best and write a piece about the postcards and – with Philip's permission – *his* damning story of the night Sandra disappeared. In the lobby, Welly, with his remaining good hand, touched her arm.

'Fair play, Joanne. You did her proud.'

'Thanks, Welly.'

She wasn't so sure. It had not been her intention to get emotional.

On a fast ferry, standing still

Philip set off, at a briskish pace, on the red path, looking for a sign, some sort of marker. Hood up, covering his head lest anybody recognize him, he knew in his bones and in his blood that he was close, but that without the full GPS address it was a futile quest. After a couple of hundred yards he stopped and let out a roar. This is madness, he thought. A quick visit to a phone repair shop would save a lot of time and effort. A child would have had the cop-on to do that. Some unscrupulous tradesman would surely be able to unlock Dove's phone, allowing him to study in more depth his old friend's instructions and, fingers crossed, refine the search for Sandra.

He turned on his heels and cantered back to the entrance to await Healy, the oracle himself. The walking encyclopaedia, they used to call him behind his back at football training when he'd draw on quantum physics or the Irish regiments at Gallipoli or the behaviour of ants to illustrate a point about defending a free kick. Healy was a man whose knowledge was as broad as it was shallow, more suited to the table quiz than the Academy, but he'd have a good idea where to go for the technical services required.

If it wasn't for Joanne raising the stakes with her mystifying complaint against him, he probably wouldn't have been so foolhardy in jumping the gun. Her treachery aroused in him a competitiveness, to go with the other forces driving him on, compelling him not just to find Sandra but to find her before Joanne found her. Rejecting for the moment everything he knew and hitherto believed about good sportsmanship, he wanted to win the race and then rub her nose in it, preferably in public, and then, if she was on for it, to continue what they had started in the kitchen of the Old Forge.

Somewhat sated on his return to Lough Oughter, although now complaining of heartburn, Healy was surprised to see Philip sitting at a picnic table smoking a cigarette. In truth, both men, on reflection, were a bit embarrassed by their impetuosity in dropping everything and rushing over to the park. What were they expecting, some sort of an epiphany? Because they deserved it? Did they think there'd be a headstone awaiting them in plain view? The older man suggested that they drive over the border as far as Armagh City, where they could, with relative anonymity, recruit a dodgy phonegeek to their cause.

* * *

In Armagh, Kevin, feeling unwanted, explored on foot the historic city. It was a holy place, known throughout Christendom as being the ancestral home of St Patrick himself, the nation's patron saint. Actually, he discovered, after passing two cathedrals, that it was the home of the *two* St Patricks, the Protestant one and the Catholic one, neither of them a patch, in his opinion, on his own favourite saint, St Dymphna. She – the patron saint of lost causes, of the mentally afflicted, of nervous wrecks, of runaways, of self-harm, of survivors of incest and sexual assault – died at the age of fifteen, decapitated by her own father. He was annoyed with her because she refused to marry him. Nothing much had changed since the seventh century. If anybody could help him to find Sandra, it would be St Dymphna.

* * *

Meanwhile, Philip plonked himself down in a coffeeshop named Scones. Dove's phone was looking up at him, having been unlocked and fully charged by a man from Brazil who was fifty euros the richer for his trouble.

He opened Dove's photographs. Flicking between the photo of page six of the comic book and the one of page fifty-four, he looked for patterns that might yield the missing numbers. According to his research on GPS, the number representing the seconds should contain five digits, two of those to the left of a decimal point and three to the right.

To think, this time only two weeks ago he was lying in a motel room in New Mexico, Tucumcari to be precise, on historic Route 66, rehydrating in an ant-ridden bed he hadn't left for three days except to get ice. He had been near enough death, not for the first time, and seriously addressing the meaning of life – the meaning of his life, in particular.

He'd been in a fever state after finishing an extreme running event, the Badass Race, one hundred miles of pure punishment, mostly uphill, in searing desert heat near the Mexican border. There were few other entrants in the race, the Badass having had a particularly bad rap thanks to three fatalities the previous year, one from exhaustion, one from snakebite, and one knocked down by a pick-up truck driven by Brandon, the organizer of the event, an hour before the race began. This man, Brandon, a charge of reckless endangerment hanging over him, and clearly no stranger to crystal meth, took Philip's money, gave him a map, and wished him well.

He had nobody with whom to share the joys or the sorrows of the ordeal, the pleasures or the pains. No one to gauge the attendant toll on his health, his organs having been slow-cooked in that giant earthen oven known as the Chihuahuan. A snakebite would have been a mercy, he felt, as he slow-turned on the bed, a playful tickle compared to the fully comprehensive pain he'd earned on completing the course, the venom but a mild anti-inflammatory.

His mother rang with the news. *Guess who's dead? You'll never guess. I'll give you three guesses.* The old quiz show. A family favourite. At first he thought, in his delirium, that she was informing him about his own death. When she mentioned Dermot's name he sat up in the bed. His aches and pains disappeared. He leapt out of bed, the sheets soaked in his sweat and blood, thinking he'd be a happier man and him with new meaning in his life. Indefatigable and undeterrable, he started for home.

The trouble, of course, with having too much meaning in your life was that it could fool you into thinking you were unstoppable. There you were on a fast ferry, that went by the name of Destiny, its speed masking the fact that you were on deck, all the while standing still.

A mere two cups of coffee later, he cracked the code. Dove, in fairness, was obviously feeling generous and more or less spelled it out for him. He should have spotted it earlier. On page fifty-four, having emerged from his dream state, Brouhaha was removing his trusty wolfhound's helmet to clean it of Ramen remains. Solemnly, he turned to Dearg Doom and said gnomically, '**A D**og **C**an't **G**o **B**ackwards.'

That sounded true. On the surface, it sounded like wisdom. A moral lesson of some sort. But when you thought about it for even a second, it wasn't true. Simple canine observation would prove otherwise. Dogs were always blundering into trouble and reversing out again. If he'd said, 'a shark can't swim backwards', that would be true and it wouldn't jar. If you pulled a shark by its tail, it would die, advice that mostly went unheeded by foolhardy surfers. If the character had said, 'a bird can't fly backwards', that would be almost true – the exception being the hummingbird, more of an insect than a bird – and wouldn't attract a second glance.

But, no, he said, '**A D**og **C**an't **G**o **B**ackwards.'

Dove would know that Philip would know that that wasn't factually correct. Lest there be any doubt about the writer's intentions, the first letter of each word was capitalized and in bold type. Philip remembered a similar device they'd employed at school when passing notes to and fro under the teacher's nose. Each number represented a letter of the alphabet and vice versa. It was not the most unbreakable of codes. In fact, it was your basic, entry-level cryptography. But it was as effective now as it was back then.

If he was right, **ADCGB** represented 14372, or in GPS terms 14.372 seconds.

He scrolled backwards to the photograph of page six. Underneath the panel of the pointing General Practice, there was a scene in which Brouhaha and Dearg Doom, although both of them injured and bleeding, enjoyed a rare moment of levity. Brouhaha had climbed to the top of his oak tree, where a laying dove had its nest. He grabbed two of the eggs, their antiseptic and blood-clotting properties indispensable to a man with his lifestyle. While climbing down again he was distracted by the sighting of an ominous dust cloud approaching from the north and dropped the eggs on Dearg Doom's head.

'Brouhaha Can't Juggle Eggs, Doom!' he grinned, as he gathered his weapons – his torc, his sword, and his sling – in readiness for their next trial.

Philip had to laugh. Dove, he recalled fondly, *could* juggle eggs, and juggle them well. One of his many party pieces was juggling eggs, up to five at a time, until he saw fit to let them fall. **BCJED** could mean, according to their foolproof childhood system, 23054, or 23.054 seconds. Not in any way triumphant, he finished his coffee and waited for Healy.

The spoils of victory

Healy filled his notebook full of little observations on the history, politics and architecture of what he deemed to be a charming market town. His friend, the Doc, had encouraged him to write everything down as he would have done by rote at the height of his powers.

From time to time, they'd go through his notebooks together, the Doc and he, and analyse the contents. A grounding exercise, the Doc called it, although many's a time there were no contents to discuss, the pages being blank. Although he knew that he was the Doc's special project – his professional bit on the side – he would be forever grateful for those sessions.

The current notebook, a little Moleskine number with squared paper given to him by Ciara for his birthday, was full of drawings too, although he would have preferred lined paper. He had just sketched the town's unfathomable one-way system, for example, guaranteed to keep all but the most determined of visitors at bay. He drew a reasonable likeness of the famous observatory and an outline of a pre-Christian enclosure in a field outside the town.

Its purpose was anybody's guess even now, thousands of years later. Was it a burial chamber or a place of sacrifice, a temple or a royal court? Nobody had a clue. To boost the appeal of the fort – was it a fort? – as a tourist attraction, the local authority rounded up some of the long-term unemployed, dressed them in period rags, and persuaded them to sit around a turf fire that was burning dangerously, in Kevin's view, on the floor of a wooden hut or roundhouse, with no outlet whatsoever for the smoke, a bird's nest obstructing the hole in the centre of the thatched roof.

When Kevin, by his reckoning the only visitor to the re-enactment that day, surprised the actors by entering the hut, two of them were in the process of getting off with each other, the lady's rough woollen smock no protection against the man's hands. Another layabout was drinking from a can of Fanta orange, and yet another man was urinating against the wall outside, which, all in all, was probably an accurate enough representation of life for most people in prehistoric Armagh barring, of course, the incongruous can of fizzy orange.

Healy, although well-acquainted with Celtic mythology, and a dreamer and a wishful thinker himself, wasn't really a one for glorifying the past or projecting nobility on the ancients, a sentimental habit of historians, in his opinion, the implication being that we in the present were a bit 'shit' by comparison, a bit *ignoble*. A simple man, he preferred simple explanations to archaeological mystifications, man's base nature and over-reverence for the seasons usually, in his estimations, the relevant factors in why people did what they did and still do what they do. The corral, for want of a better word, was probably nothing more than a whorehouse, he thought, with a sudden and, it has to be said, uncharacteristic cynicism. Some sort of harem. Or a bunker. An arms dump. The men would come back from warring with some upstart clan with their captive women and their booty and their rudimentary weapons. He coughed, the smoke burning his throat.

'Greetings, stranger!' said one of the lads, discarding his fizzy drink and scrambling to his feet, and in so doing interrupting a thought that was developing in Kevin's head, something he was at pains to keep hold of, a Healyesque association of sorts, of words or images, but of what import he couldn't yet put a finger on.

'Good man, yourself,' he replied.

'Is it far you have come?' enquired the girl, her shift covering her thighs again, her face a flaming red, warmed by the fire, the frenzy of kisses, or the embarrassment, he couldn't tell from where he was standing.

'It's fierce smoky altogether.'

'Och, you get used to it. Is it a drink you'll be having? Tea or coffee?'

'Look, there's no need to talk like that.'

'Like what?'

'Is it far you have come? Is it a drink you'll be having? It's a bit weird.'

'Fair enough. It's just . . . we thought you might be a spy.'

'A spy?'

'Aye, an "independent consultant". He did the thing with the fingers that represented inverted commas. 'Sent by the council, you know.'

'They do be checking up on us, you see.'

'Right. I'll say nothing.'

There was a fairly long pause while the fire crackled and Kevin nodded beatifically and the actors, in what was a fairly awkward tableau, made search-me faces at each other.

'The spoils of victory.' Kevin broke the silence.

'The what?'

'What?' said Kevin, unaware that he'd in fact spoken.

'You said, "the spoils of victory".'

'Did I? Sorry.'

There was another interminable pause before the horny lad piped up helpfully, his still-erect penis peeping out over the top of his waistband to see what was going on.

'They found a monkey's head.'

'What?'

'He means a skull. A monkey's skull.'

'Aye.'

'A macaque,' the woman elaborated. 'It was a macaque.'

'Aye, that's right, a macaque.'

'That was the main thing they found here, when they were digging. A macaque's skull, if that's any use. It's in the museum below in the town.'

'Fascinating.'

It occurred to Kevin that the world had ended and this motley troupe and himself were the last people standing and, furthermore, that the post-apocalypse situation was not dissimilar to the pre-civilization state of affairs, the survivors dressed in rags and burning turf fires and, he sniffed the air like a bear, using cowpats as fuel.

'It'll be off I'll be going,' Kevin said, backing out of the doorway, trying desperately to catch the tail of an earlier thought.

He walked passed a huge mound of earth about forty-foot long – a mass grave full of dead macaques or dead girls? – and, for some reason, St Dymphna came back into his head. Her father, Damon, had been a minor chieftain in these parts. Perhaps he'd attended a ceremony here where, grief-stricken for his dead wife, he was given the go-ahead by the powers-that-be to pursue his own daughter's hand in marriage. By all accounts, the innocent Dymphna looked the spitting image of Damon's wife, and her a beauty, and no other woman would do him.

One Sunday in June, at a low point, and Kevin not responding to medical treatment or the more gentle ministrations of his doctor friend, Sheila had taken him to St Dymphna's Well in the north of the county they call Monaghan. There, on her feast day, surrounded by all sorts of half-wits like himself, he tied a rag – an old pair of his underpants – to a tree, and he supped water from the well and instantly felt better. He didn't really believe in God (his father?) anymore, but he believed fully in the powers of the diminutive saint. Her lust-demented father eventually caught up with her in the town of Geel in the country of Belgium, and when she resisted his advances, he chopped off her beautiful head. By then she was already in business, although still a wisp of a lass, caring for the mentally challenged, a vocation possibly informed by an earlier intuition that all was not right in the head with her father.

Naturally, Sandra's father, Tom, was a suspect. No minor chieftain, he. A handsome man in his prime, he made furniture. There was talk at the time of her disappearance that Tom had an interest in Sandra other than paternal. People assumed, as they do, that her rebelliousness must have been rooted in some unnatural relationship with her father. But there was no evidence – no medical reports, no record of any intervention by social services, no confession – to prove it. Nothing in Sandra's diary that would indicate he was that way inclined.

At any rate, his long-suffering wife, Carmel, provided her husband with a great alibi. On the Bible, she swore he'd never left the armchair, never mind the house, the day Sandra vanished, worn out by all the jiving at the 'Arts' festival. Nor did he move in the days after she vanished, not even for fags, her Tom being on a bender and the flat season in full swing.

Where was he? There was something irritating Kevin as he made his way back into town, some little dingleberry of a thought chafing away at the arse end of his mind.

Never rains

When Joanne got back to the Old Forge, the young receptionist was being stretchered into the back of an ambulance.

'Severe food poisoning,' according to one of the attending paramedics.

Joanne noticed the empty box of Diane's Divine Chocolates on the floor, not wishing to think too much about their provenance. Or the intended target.

She had a number of missed calls from Carson. Having gathered her bits and pieces, she paid for her upkeep, which included the bacon sandwiches Philip had unlawfully made in the kitchen, no flies on the management. A silent, hostile woman behind the desk wouldn't even lend her a pen to sign the chit.

Joanne hesitated before opening her car door, a slight panic momentarily coming over her. She did a quick tour of the car, inspecting the tires for damage and looking underneath the chassis for any untoward modifications, chastising herself for being ridiculous.

Back in Mullinary town, at the offices of the *Chronicle*, Welly was already at his desk.

'You were quick.'

'I just love my job. You okay?'

She nodded. She wasn't. She felt *exposed*.

'Carson wants a word.'

'Great. What happened the hand?'

'You won't believe me, Joanne. Bitten by a dying swan in Muckno.'

'Fuck off.'

'Just my luck. I was interviewing the County Wildlife Officer. Near tore the hand off me.'

'You're like Kate Adie. And what did the Wildlife Officer do?'

'Laughed his hole off. That's what he did. The bollox. He said he felt sorry for me alright, but that it was literally the funniest thing he ever saw in his life. Didn't even put the swan down.'

Joanne went into the editor's office. Carson was unusually quiet.

'How was Rita?'

'Devlin did the honours.'

'I'm sorry, Stuart. It won't happen again. I have a story for you.'

Carson put his head in his hands.

'What's the matter?'

He lit two cigarettes. Handed one to Joanne.

'Joanne. You *are* the fucking story.'

He turned his computer around. There was a photograph of Joanne snorting cocaine in JJ's bar. It didn't look great.

'I'm going to have to let you go,' he said, the eyes wet. 'You know what people are like round here, Joanne, this breaks my fucking heart. You're my star reporter.'

Joanne let the news sink in. It wasn't so much losing her job that was her primary concern. Or how she'd pay her mortgage now. It was her parents. Their faces. How disappointed they'd be when they saw the pictures.

'I was going to retire next year. This seat had your fucking name on it. Why the fuck, Joanne?'

There were numerous photographs of dogs on the wall. They all had the same dignified – bordering on snooty – bearing. She couldn't look at them. For some reason, she didn't think they'd do it. At least not that quickly. She'd convinced herself – foolishly, as it happens – that by releasing the photographs they'd be compromising *themselves* in some way.

'You fucked me good. I look like some gobshite now, ha. Think of the biggest arsehole you know. And build a fucking bowling alley in it. That's me. Thanks to you.'

Joanne was struggling to get her head around Carson's baroque imagery.

'Forgive me, Stuart. But this is not about you. I'm writing the piece anyway. You can have it if you want.'

'Joanne. I hate to break it to you. *Nobody* is going to touch you. Just . . . clear your desk. I can't look at you.'

'I don't have anything on my desk. I'm not a child.'

'This is a fucking disaster. Go.'

Thus dismissed by Carson, she left his office and looked out over the Diamond, at the odd octagonal memorial to some ascendancy buck who died in a hunting accident in Victorian times. Somebody was trying to drink from the fountain that hadn't worked for decades.

'People have come back from worse.' Welly handed her a coffee. 'I was listening at the door,' he said by way of explanation. 'Look on the bright side. You're making waves.'

He showed her a news item online. *Candidate has questions to answer in missing girl puzzle.*

Small comfort.

Her phone pinged. It was a message from one of her housemates, saying she'd finally gotten the transfer back to England and was giving Joanne a month's notice.

'What's Northampton got that we haven't?'

'Not the wee Indian one? Anjali,' said Welly, mock anxiously, and he in mock-love since she kissed him once at a party. 'Is she having a going-away?'

'Never rains but it fucking pours.'

'Mind you, Aisling will be on her own now. Might need someone to cheer her up.'

'Welly. You're a dog.'

Welly barked.

'Keep the head up, Joanne. Carson'll cool down. *You're too big to fail*, as they say.'

'Thanks, Welly.' She smiled – crushed to her core – appreciative of his attempt to humour her. 'I have to go home.'

White Island

The full address now read 54°N 7' 14.372, 6°W 44' 23.054. Healy opened up the map, and did his incredible *Rain Man* routine again, his finger finally resting on one of the islands in the Lough Oughter Forest Park. White Island, to be precise. Philip grunted his appreciation.

With his little diagrams on his knees, he was able to navigate his way out of the city with ease, and it rush hour, a fairly subdued Philip hulking by his side. When they reached the forest park, they threw caution to the wind. With no attendant present on the jetty, and nobody else around, they appropriated the first seaworthy vessel they could find, a skiff called *Nina*, and rowed out to White Island. Nice name, Nina. Nina Simone. The *Nina*, the *Pinta* and the *Santa Maria*.

'What are you on about?'

'What?'

'What are you mumbling about?'

Philip was getting a bit ratty. Young fellas think they can go all day without food. Or a shit. He's probably holding it all in, Kevin decided, chuckling away to himself.

'You remind me of my granny. Muttering away about nothing,' groused his companion.

Lovely. Just lovely. Great company. Granted his lifelong habit of saying the first thing that came into his head *was* annoying. Making little associations. It annoyed himself. But he couldn't help it, could he, if he indulged himself in a little flight of fancy, and him on the *Nina*, holding onto the sides for dear life, his fear of water profound, the light breeze from the lake tickling his neck, making him shiver, if he did feel a bit like Columbus himself, Columbus Molumbus with the eyeglass above on the bridge, on the verge of discovering America and plundering the land of its riches. The spoils of victory. Obviously, Columbus didn't 'discover' America, no more than Kevin was going to 'discover' White Island.

Kevin, taking his turn with the oars, was seriously short of breath. Sheila would be raging with him if she ever found out he was on a boat, never mind not wearing a life-jacket. St Brendan got there before him. To the Americas. A thousand years before Columbus. In a boat made out of leather. A leather boat? Jaysus.

'Who?'

'Nothing.'

One of the stupider saints, in Kevin's opinion, he didn't have the cop-on to take home the gold, leaving Paddy in the doldrums right up to the 1990s. And ten thousand years before St Brendan, didn't the Asiatic peoples 'discover' America when they walked across the Bering land bridge with the woolly mammoth in tow and the mastodon and the scimitar cat and the Arctic camel and the moose and the muskox and even, to give them their full dues, the horse.

What natural wonders did Columbus introduce to the natives? He recited them all, in no particular order.

'Smallpox, measles, influenza, bubonic plague, diphtheria, typhus, cholera, scarlet fever, chicken pox, yellow fever, malaria, lyme disease, q-fever, leishmania, whooping cough, African sleeping sickness, filaria, dengue, septicaemic plague, schistosomiasis, try saying that after eating a few cream crackers, Philip, anthrax, botulism, tetanus, toxoplasmosis, tape-worms, I have a terrible fear of tape-worms, did I ever tell you that, staphylococci, streptococci, mycotic diseases, legionnaires' and of course syphilis, not that I'm suggesting for a moment Columbus personally suffered from all thirty ailments.'

Funny how he couldn't remember poems or songs but had no problem reeling off a list of infectious diseases.

'What is wrong with you, Healy? That's just mental. This is literally my worst nightmare. Trapped on a boat with you and not being able to swim.'

Although records of St Brendan's voyage were scant, Kevin was satisfied that *his* gifts to the new world – and him being a Kerryman – were most likely limited to verbal diarrhoea and chronic melancholia. Anyway, whatever about America, Kevin and Philip would not be the first people ever to step foot on White Island.

'Fuck it. No signal,' said Philip.

Nearing the island, they could see that it was a manageable enough size, ten acres at most. And although dense with trees, it was readily penetrable by men as intrepid as they were, men with right on their side. Kevin's shoulders were sore. The island was further from the mainland than it looked. As soon as they arrived – the boat noisily scraping the bottom of the shallows – the navigators clumsily disembarked. Their shoes and socks were soaked, as well as their trouser legs. They left the *Nina* on the tiny pebble beach and immediately started looking for Sandra's remains. There were plenty of signs of life close to the cove where they had coasted to a stop, crisp bags and such, cigarette packets, the colours washed out, bottles both plastic and glass, and a used condom that Kevin somewhat optimistically lifted up with a twig and placed in a freezer bag.

'You never know,' says he, in response to a disdainful look from his unnervingly quiet partner.

A patch of blackened earth suggested a fairly recent campfire. It was hardly the work of fishermen, better known for leaving no trace of themselves whatsoever. Rather, the charred remnants of school textbooks and copies suggested to Kevin evidence of an end-of-term conflagration back in June. No student he, until later in life, he could certainly see the attraction in that. A catharsis after the Leaving Cert, consigning maths and Macbeth to the flames, and getting drunk on Bulmer's and maybe getting a sneaky ride into the bargain. He was twenty-five, fresh out of Templemore, before he and Sheila took the plunge in a caravan in Courtown one Hallowe'en.

The lake was now still and quiet, the sole water-skier long gone, the stillness broken now and again by the explosive call of a coot, or maybe a moorhen. Either way it startled Kevin, who didn't know one bird from another. There was an uneasiness gnawing away now at his neck, and not just because he'd been reminded of yet another gap in his education. Mind you, he knew that White Island was so-named because it was home to white birds exclusively. Well, grey birds, to be exact, grey herons, which probably looked white through the mist the day the island was named, presumably by monks, myopic from all the late-night illustrating of manuscripts by candlelight. Likewise, the neighbouring Black Island was called after its habitat of black birds. Coots. It was quite a curiosity – the old avian apartheid in Lough Oughter.

'Maybe we should leave Keating out of it altogether, what, and go over his head and have a word with the Chief Super, or maybe the Assistant Commissioner herself above in Dublin?' Healy said.

He was getting anxious. On squelchy ground that near sucked the shoes off his feet, he was uncertain now that they were, in fact, following the correct course of action. What with laws being routinely flouted – the stealing of Dove Connolly's phone and the theft of a rowing boat, for starters, and law-breaking being anathema to him – they could be leaving themselves terribly exposed. All their efforts would be wasted, their credibility – what was left of it, says you – shot to bits. Besides, what would Sheila think if he was caught? Hadn't he put her through enough?

They continued to push through the vegetation. Sweat was pouring from his head although the evening was cooling considerably. He shouldn't have worn the mac. Or the tie. Feeling woozy, he sat on a fallen trunk, one of many arboreal casualties who'd lost their footing on that boggy ground.

'Healy!'

He heard his name being called. He knew the voice. Japers, he must have dozed off.

'Healy! Come here!'

It was young Sharkey, a good wee player, but a hothead. He probably needs somebody to tie his laces.

'Philip!'

Was he a good coach? Sometimes, when it rained, he'd sit in his car, with the radio on, a *Time* magazine and a Dime bar on his lap, and watch the boys training from there.

'Philip!'

He tried to speak, but no sound emerged from his throat. All was dark in the tree graveyard, the carnage, the fallout from some macro-cosmic war that was beyond human comprehension, or even knowledge. He had the briefest notion that he didn't exist at all, that he too was a hollow trunk, being slowly reclaimed by the bog, the light wind whistling through him. He was a natural flute, native to White Island, playing a gentle lament. Either way, he'd swear that his spirit, the irritating entity that was constantly chattering and cackling away in his head and making word associations and always drawing *significance* from his surroundings and from every little thing that happened to him, had become detached from his body and was in serious danger of becoming lost in the void. Sure, there's worse things that could happen, he thought, before his thoughts stopped completely.

He was a divil for finding meaning in the mundane, and not just during his illness either. Always on the look-out for patterns. Once, while sunbathing in Clogherhead, he was stung by a hive of wasps. The face, the neck, and the arms came off worst in an attack that left him with seventy-two stings in total. It was not the number that was significant – although, as most people knew, seventy-two was not an unimportant number. After all, Noah's ark spawned seventy-two races. There were seventy-two steps to heaven. And didn't the jihadi martyr enjoy the company of seventy-two virgins in the afterlife? No, it was the *arrangement* of the stings that counted. The map. The constellation of bumps. He spent days, in a fit of apiarian astrology, trying to work out what the wasps were trying to tell him, while Sheila soothed the wounds with bits of cucumber and apple cider vinegar and gentle kisses. Not long after that he asked her to marry him.

Just as quickly, his spirit, for want of a better word, returned, reuniting itself with his body at warp speed. He bolted upright, fighting for breath, the nausea rising in his gullet. The undigested chicken and stuffing sandwich he had eaten earlier was clogging up his guts. He thought he was going to burst. The pain in his shoulders had spread to his arms and his chest. The smell of mud filled his nostrils.

'Healy, over here.'

Lying on the ground, he could just about make out Philip, a fine, strapping man, standing about thirty yards away, looking at a tree.

* * *

Philip, for his part, unaware that Healy was slipping into unconsciousness, was staring straight ahead at a beret, in fairly good nick, nailed to a tree trunk at about head height. Beneath the hat a rectangle of bark had been neatly removed. There, the initials M.B., in loving script, were carved above the all too familiar letters RIP, and beneath an etching of a flower and an epitaph, *Oft hope is born when all is forlorn.* The memorial, intricately carved, no shortage of flourishes, curlicues, and the like, was clearly the handiwork of an artist. It was a memorial of sorts, but was it a grave? And if it was a grave, whose grave was it? Had Philip come this far only to find the resting place of some fucking randomer? M.B.? Who the fuck was M.B.? He studied the memorial again, his brain scrambling for traction. The flower! Could it be the elusive Middlemist Blue, the object of Brouhaha's quest? He'd had more than an inkling that the Middlemist Blue was some sort of a metaphor for Sandra.

While rooting around in the gloomy undergrowth behind the tree, in what was a sheltered spot on the quieter north-facing side of the island, Philip stumbled in a hollow, almost turning his ankle. After clearing away, with his bare hands, some branches and some stones, he discovered that the dip was about the size and shape of a bath. By the looks of things, the topsoil had been disturbed, in the not-too-distant past, whether by animal or man, he could not say. A piece of plastic protruded from the earth, the ear of a thick plastic bag that he immediately recognized as a coal sack. It was a hundredweight bag, the likes of which he and Dove had used as a sleigh in his youth on the hill behind his house. The adrenalin that propelled him down that hill in the snow was surging through his body now as he tore into the task before him. He could hardly see what he was doing through the tears brought on by that poignant memory, or the prospect of what he would find now. On all fours, ferally scrabbling in the dirt around him, he found a bone. In his estimation, it was a femur or a humerus, one of the bigger ones anyway, from an arm or a leg. Moments later, watched by a heron, he disinterred part of a ribcage, too. He gathered these solemn treasures and placed them with reverence in a pile.

'Healy', he shouted again, asphyxiating on the emotion of it all. 'Healy!'

Not waiting for a response, he continued his manic dig, the exhilaration of 'success' quickly giving way to the disappointment/anti-climax known as 'closure', which just as quickly gave way to the numbing reality that Sandra was dead. He was never a man to dwell for long on either joy or sorrow, being barely able to distinguish between the two of them at the best of times.

A few yards from where he found the bag of bones, he found a human skull and held it aloft, as if it would talk to him and tell him what it knew. It felt sacrilegious. A violation post-mortem to stroke a person's head without permission, just as it would be if she were alive. If only she were alive. In the absence of a heart, or a brain, the skull seemed like the most essential part of the dead person, the most alive part of the remains, the most significant. The heron had seen enough. It squawked and flew away to spread the news. Philip hurried, stumbling, disorientated, skull in hand, over to where Healy lay. It was dark now and spluttering rain.

'Healy! Healy!'

Despite vigorously shaking the man, there was no response.

'Kevin!'

He sat him up and slapped his face. Healy's eyes opened, momentarily, a look of terror in them, perhaps a reflection of the terror in Philip's own eyes.

'I found her.'

Excalibur

Clarity returned to Philip, as did focus. And it was just as well. There was a lot to process. He wiped the tears from his face with the back of a muddy arm, his own. Healy was in a bad way. He'd found Sandra's remains. Dove, he was sure, had visited the grave. Judging from the decent condition of the beret and the unweathered etching on the tree, he had been there as recently as last week. Not long before he killed himself. The death notice was his doing. Of that Philip had no doubt. The calligraphy was Dove's. And the quotation, now that he thought about it, was not Yeats or Keats. It was from *Lord of the Rings*. And it was sentimental. Or possibly ironic. Both hallmarks of Dove.

Philip was trying to think straight. He was sick of the whole business. The immediate concern was getting Healy to a hospital. Then, in order of priority, he had to hand Sandra over to the gardaí, wash his hands of the affair, go to college, and settle down. He had no specific time frame in mind.

He searched his pockets for a cigarette. Nothing. Although he took no great satisfaction from his accomplishment, he had done what he had set out to do. Well, partly. He still needed to find out who had left Sandra rotting on White Island. And why.

Before he handed Sandra over, he needed to get his story straight, to avoid incriminating himself. Where had the beret come from? Perhaps Dove had received it in the post? From his mysterious benefactor? Along with his long-lost denim jacket? It wouldn't be enough to give them Sandra. It should be, but it wouldn't. He had to give them a theory. Maybe Dove had the beret in his possession all along, ever since the night Sandra went missing? You wouldn't know with Dove. All sorts of disquieting ideas crowded Philip's mind. It even occurred to him, in that moment, sitting on a tree trunk, without a cigarette, that Dove might be still alive.

Maybe that body he saw in the coffin in the Connolly house minus the face was not Dermot's but that of one of his junkie friends who agreed to the switch in exchange for a fix. Stranger things have happened. There was that cannibal in Germany. Didn't he eat a man who volunteered to be eaten? Perhaps Dove *had* killed Sandra after all, furious at Philip's betrayal. Perhaps he'd faked his own death and lured him here to White Island?

The midges found him. Thousands of them in his hair, his nostrils, his eyes. He'd had enough. Healy was still breathing, but he had to act fast. He stood up, only to discover his *drive* was gone. Clarity and focus were all very well but without drive he was fucked. He couldn't do this alone. To help him clarify what exactly he was going to do and how exactly he was going to do it he decided to ring, in the absence of anyone else he could turn to, Joanne. No signal. A twig snapped.

'Fuck!'

It was a voice that was vaguely familiar. He turned around sharply, only to be walloped on the side of the head with a shovel by a rotund man wearing a hooped football shirt. The hoops were unflattering. The man he recognized as one of the Nordies in O'Dowd's car. The man who tried to abuse him with dead meat. Another man, slender in shape, possibly the other one from O'Dowd's car, although he couldn't be sure in the gloaming, was on his knees, checking Kevin's pulse. Philip was pretty sure he wasn't a doctor. In a somewhat delayed reaction, Philip keeled over in slow motion, like one of the White Island trees, uprooted in a storm.

'Not so smart now, boy, ha!'

His assailant, the eyes almost entirely concealed by rolls of flab to the north and south of them, raised the shovel above his head. With great accuracy and, by the looks of it, no little experience in these matters, he brought it crashing down on the exact spot where Philip's now bloody head had been resting just a fraction of a second earlier. As the shovel came towards him again, Philip discerned that the man's right hand was badly scarred. Such was the force of the blow that the blade of the shovel got stuck in the ground.

Fortunately, Philip had managed to roll away in the nick of time, his *drive* mercifully returning. In the same life-preserving manoeuvre he upended the man by kicking him full-force in the back of the legs. As his bulky, good-for-nothing, no-neck adversary wobbled, Philip jumped to his feet athletically and eased the shovel from the earth, like King Arthur removing Excalibur, proving beyond doubt that he was the rightful sovereign of White Island.

The fat man pulled a gun from the pocket of his voluminous track-suit pants. Philip swung the implement, knocking the weapon from the man's hand before he could do any more damage. Before the fat fuck could react, Philip literally dug him in the stomach, the blade horizontal like a very wide bayonet. Then, as the chubby menace doubled over, he hit him upwards full in the face, pleased to hear the crunch of breaking bone. A most satisfying crunch. He wanted to hear it again. As he was winding up for another go, the man's partner, who'd been enjoying the show, stepped forward, pointing his gun at Philip.

'Alright, alright, that's enough. Hands up, as they say!'

Philip, deafened by the earlier blow from the shovel, the pain in his head noisy, couldn't hear him and was understandably slow to respond.

'I said, put your hands up!'

Philip did as he was told, not taking his eyes off the man, a slight enough fellow in his mid-fifties with a head of tight grey curls. He looked familiar. To make matters worse, he had a kind face, which only heightened Philip's wariness.

'Now, first of all. Hello. I'm Ian! Secondly, sorry about that. Paolo,' he said, indicating his partner, 'he gets a bit carried away. You alright, big man?'

Paolo, holding his injured mouth with his deformed paw, didn't answer. Ian, dressed for the day in a denim shirt, nicely tucked into a pair of denim jeans, no arse to speak of, laughed softly to himself.

'So, Philip. It is Philip? You found the wee girl. Well done. Now, as you can probably tell, we have a bit of a problem here. So,' he sighed, 'we can do this the easy way or the hard way, as they say.'

Philip wished he'd stop saying, *as they say*. If they were prepared to bandy about their real names, Paolo and Ian – if they were indeed their real names – then that didn't augur well for people with real names like Philip or Kevin.

Paolo, still winded and unable to join in the conversation, collapsed to his knees and started feeling around in the clay and the weeds for his piece, as they say. They won't want to use their guns, Philip suddenly realized, a glow-worm of hope pulsing in his breast. At least not yet. The silencers were not yet fitted.

Assuming they were professionals – albeit a bit rusty since the peace agreement – Philip convinced himself they wouldn't really risk shooting people on an island in the middle of a lake. Unless they had a speedboat standing by, or a helicopter, the getaway would be amongst the slowest in history. By the time they reached the shore, every Garda unit within a forty-mile radius of the amenity, alerted by the gunshots, would be waiting for them. And so too would every curiosity-seeker and cop coat-tailer in the area – a sizeable majority of the local population. On high doh, not able to believe their luck, they'd film the unfolding farce on their phones. The escapade would be uploaded onto every epic-fail website in the world before the lads were even frogmarched off to jail.

Grim humour aside and hope notwithstanding, Philip's life flashed before his eyes. His mother and father, Healy, Dove, and Sandra all figured prominently in the highlights reel. While reflecting on the rights and wrongs and what-might-have-beens of his life, his reverie was rudely interrupted by the sight of Ian falling forward. The stranger, the spit of that seventies singer Leo Sayer, now that he'd had a good look at him in the LCD that only impending death could bring about, was out cold. He'd been clubbed on the back of the head by the miraculously risen Healy, who immediately fell down again, barely conscious, on top of his unconscious victim. But not before the latter had reflexively pulled the trigger on his gun, the resulting shot shattering Philip's shoulder and the silence of the park.

Philip, without pausing to congratulate Healy on his unlikely resurrection, or dwelling too deeply on the indignity of being shot, took a step forward and kicked the dumbstruck Paolo in the head. Paolo jelly-rolled onto his back whereupon Philip jumped into the air and landed two-footed on his face. He then kicked him in the stomach, a poor option, his foot being immediately engulfed by the man's limitless paunch, leaving the kicker ominously unbalanced on the one leg, it being his less steady left leg.

Paolo, or rather the former champion boxer inside Paolo, managed to grab two-handed Philip's right foot and push him away. Respect to the deceptively agile ogre. Unable to use his injured right arm to break his fall, Philip hit the ground heavily, cushioned only by his bullet-mangled shoulder and his shovel-damaged head. Although the pain was excruciating, he managed to get to his feet ahead of his cumbersome foe and quickly resorted to stamping on the man's bald head again and again. In the process, remembering vividly their last ignominious meeting at the chicken farm, he rearranged his multiple chins and relieved him of many of his teeth.

'That's for Dove,' he said, not knowing if the man was alive or dead, and not caring either, 'and that's for Tommy, you fat useless cunt, and that's for Sandra,' he added for good measure, picking up a rock with his good hand and smashing it down in a frenzy on Paolo's face.

Satisfied that both attackers were now immobilized, he tried to help Kevin to his feet.

'Jaze. You can't even have a heart attack in peace!' Kevin said, smiling before going limp in Philip's arms.

His arms he no longer recognized as his own, and with no power to command them, he let Kevin slip to the ground. Philip, all the feeling gone from his legs too, staggered for a few steps until he fell in a heap beside the beloved man – would it be appropriate to call him a father figure, and if so, would it be too late? – who saved his life. With his considerable injuries and, you would think, in a state of shock, he blacked out amongst the various bodies strewn around him, their mortal status unknown, beside the holy relic he had recently retrieved, Sandra Mohan's skull.

Clay and wattles

*Arise and go now, arise and go, and go where, Inishmean, or Inisheer,
raise the bar and go now and go to Inisheer, I want to break free-ee,
Queen, free, I will arise and go now and go to Inisfree,* did he ever live
the dream, the poet, as they say, on the reality shows, it's been a great
journey, I've made some lifelong friends, I learned so much about
myself, and he, by all accounts, wheezing, a weak chest and little enough
get up and go, being of a melancholy disposition, weighed down with
affairs of State, and the state of the world generally, and of the other-
worlds, the senses being all too easily stimulated, by nature and the
sublime, whatever that is, and tortured by love unrequited, and he on
the chaise longue half the day, languorously with the blanket, the blanky,
where's my blanky, Ciara, languishing languorously on the chaise longue,
he'll like that, the Doc, longing for love, surrounded by ghosts, serves
him right for tricking around with the paranormal, and trying to build
wee cabins out of wattles, like an eejit, it's all coming back now, the
wattles, whatever wattles are when they're at home.

* * *

Kevin was a great admirer of the mystic poet, but he couldn't imagine
Mr Yeats or Senator Yeats, to give him his full title, building as much
as a sandcastle by himself, never mind a whole cabin, in the linen suit
and the slip-ons, with those delicate creamy hands, one suitable for
human habitation anyway, and him hellbent on using such flimsy
materials, the likes of clay and wattles, Jaze, the story of the three little

pigs and the big bad wolf springing to mind, probably looked a lot easier on paper, drawing up the plans, in the bed, with a hot-water bottle, *a hockey wocky bockey*, Ciara, brandy on the bedside table and a Borzoi hound at the foot of the bed, one eye open, various ladies of a certain age fussing about, matronly, enabling him, the *artiste*, soaping him down once a week in the free-standing bath, you would think, a certain expertise, a basic grounding in architecture, a practicality of some sort would be required in the construction of even the most primitive dwelling, not casting any aspersions on the willingness to work, or the good intentions, or his ambitions for the redevelopment of White Island, rows of beans and what have you, nine or ten, for Jaysus' sake, not to mention a beehive, on a roll now, rolling off the tongue, at this rate, it might all come back, every line of every poem, and every sentence ever read and every word of every conversation ever had or overheard, released, drip-drip, from the database deep within the old cerebrum, as infinite as the ocean floor, free of all distractions, temporal, the advantage of having a heart attack, says you, the temporal lobe, the seat of hearing, a hive for the honey bee, ha, *I will arise and go now and go to Inisfree*, Thoreau, it's all coming back, the inspiration, sounds French, a Yank begod, practically invented America, the poet's father read it to him when he was a child, some bedtime story, not exactly Lemony Snicket, Shane had him demented, the Baudelaires, ha, Kevin's own father was more of a whistler, God rest his soul, a type of cruelty, reading Thoreau to a child, Henry, *Horrid Henry*, Shane or was it Ciara, hilarious altogether, tried to read it, *Walden*, no real story, no murder mystery to speak of, no dead bodies, dreamers they were, believers in something better, island Utopias, continental, nay planetary Utopias, not to mention ideal love, did that include or exclude intercourse, the Doc would know, wouldn't have survived a day on White Island, an hour, Yeats, or the other lad, Thoreau, an unforgiving place, a dreadful place, herons, Sandra Mohan's very own Inisfree, *sans* hives, French, and *sans* the bean rows, *ní raibh aon* bean rows *ar an tOileán Bán*, Irish, all flooding back now, no bean rows, no hives, no cabins, only condoms full of teenage jick, dead trees, and a cold, cold grave.

PART FOUR

Ying and fucking yang

While the political parties were still haggling over the formation of a government – the country getting on fine without one – Joanne visited Philip in prison. She was wearing her sunglasses. They had a fair bit of catching up to do.

'Happy Christmas, Philip. How are you?'

'Great. Here to have a look at the murderer?'

They sat down at a formica table in a visitors' room that smelled of sad families, Joanne tapping away nervously on the table-top with her fingers. Amongst other things, she'd been playing the piano for six weeks non-stop at her parents' house in Drumahair.

'*The Well-Tempered Clavier*. By Bach.'

'I didn't have you down as a Bach-head.'

'My mother had a book with the sheet music and some encouraging *maxims*. It was written by a banker turned concert pianist.'

'There's hope for us all.'

'She thought it would be good for me. And it was.'

Philip not being in a talkative mood, Joanne found herself trying to cheer him up, figuring that his predicament was significantly worse than her own. She'd found the endless repetition – five or six hours a day at the piano, playing Bach's preludes and fugues – consoling, if not actually *a lifesaver*.

'Bit dramatic, no?'

'That's why I said it in such a lighthearted way, Philip. But listen, enough about me.'

Although she was familiar with the story, she encouraged Philip to open up. He had been charged with the manslaughter of Paolo Sweeney. This affront to mankind did not go unnoticed. Philip's victim was a valued former member of one of the leading paramilitary outfits of the era.

'And I'm a nobody.'

'True.'

'Thanks.'

'I can make you a somebody.'

In the days and weeks after his arrest, from his hospital bed Philip had read Paolo's obituaries, and all the supplementary 'think-pieces', in an increasing state of agitation.

'You'd be forgiven for thinking the world has been deprived of one of its great characters.'

Reading between the lines, the man who took Paolo's life must have been, by contrast, some sort of heartless monster.

Many of the articles stressed that Paolo was the father of three children, with little mention of the countless lives he destroyed. More notably, he belonged to that mythical body of men, the Burn escapees. As such, not only did he gain his literal freedom from the Burn, one of the most notorious and secure prisons in the world. But as a reward for such daring, for reflecting such glory on the Organization, he was granted the metaphorical freedom of his home city, and the freedom of the future Utopian all-island republic, and the immediate freedom to do more or less as he pleased. How such a corpulent figure managed to squeeze through the Semtex-blown hole in the prison wall and remain hidden from view for so long only added to his mystique.

Prior to his demise, Paolo was the owner of a fleet of ice-cream vans. As such, he was a big loss to the sweet-toothed children of West Belfast. As Sweeney's legend grew in death, Philip's chances of a fair hearing in this life diminished.

'Ying and fucking Yang.'

'The eternal jesters.'

'I don't want to talk about it, Joanne. When did you start playing the piano anyway?'

'When I was fourteen.'

Joanne remembered with a shudder the lessons she'd had with Sister Wendy in the convent in Tullyanna.

'She was a tiny woman, ancient, terrifying, a bundle of pure evil, a wee Brazil nut of a woman.'

'I know the type.'

'She used to dribble on my hand.'

'No. Stop.'

Philip smiled. Having pleaded with his mother to stay away, Joanne was his first visitor in weeks.

'You could see the dribble forming at the corner of her mouth, getting bigger and bigger, and you knew it was going to drop any second, and you couldn't concentrate on the scales, and as soon as you made a mistake, she'd slam the lid shut on your knuckles.'

Philip smiled some more.

'I still have nightmares. A huge drop of nun drool landing on my hand.'

Joanne was different. Although listening attentively, she seemed more at ease within herself.

There were other charges pending, one of them relating to the dese-cration of human remains and one to perverting the course of justice. If the arresting officer, Detective Keating, had his way, Philip might yet be charged with conspiracy to murder Tommy Courtney, too, traces of Tommy's blood having been found on the fireplace in Philip's home.

And furthermore, it was not beyond reason that he might yet be charged as an accessory in the murder of Sandra Mohan, the suspicion hardening in some circles that Dove was primarily responsible for that deed. All of this fact and speculation were regurgitated endlessly in the papers and on the radio. Although a *cause célèbre*, he had nobody of consequence in his corner, Healy's credibility, not to mention his health, being at an all-time low. He wasn't even in his own corner, having declined to contract a lawyer and decided to say nothing. Joanne let him talk, although he had a suspicion that she knew something he didn't.

He was tired. And felt misunderstood.

'Tell your story.'

'To who? You?'

'Yes. Who else would listen to you?'

Maybe some day, he told her, when his story was fully formed, after the subconscious had done its quiet, monumental work behind the scenes, he'd spill all.

'Like Robert Emmet in the dock.'

'Yeah.'

With perfect diction and dazzling verbals, he'd set the record straight, exonerating himself and indicting his various antagonists in the process.

It was a surprise to see Joanne. A pleasant surprise although, as ever, he was watchful. Since he'd been transferred to prison, apart from State officials – gardaí, prison officers, State-appointed solicitors – he'd had little company. He hadn't mixed well with the other prisoners. By the time Joanne came to see him, he could barely speak.

'You're going to get out of here.'

'Joanne, you've been watching too much *Midnight Express*.'

He laughed-coughed. When he was seventeen, he saw *Midnight Express* at the cinema in Tullyanna. He was on a double-date at the time with Deirdre Callan, and Dove and Sandra. It was the least romantic film of all time, set, as it was, in a sadistic Turkish prison. Every time you looked up at the screen, some poor fucker was being tortured, scenes not in any way conducive to romance.

'To be honest, I spent most of the film watching Dove and Sandra necking.'

Philip bore no malice towards Joanne. The weeks in confinement after years, too many years, of wandering had cleansed his mind to an extent and calmed his soul.

'This suits me down to the ground.'

'Sure. I can see that.'

There was definitely something to be said for inertia, he maintained, embracing powerlessness for a change. Saying and doing nothing. Not trying to be powerful for once, or to force your will on the world. Such folly.

Joanne reached across the table, took his jaw – now well on the mend, having been broken in several places by Paolo's shovel – in her hand and kissed him gently on the mouth. His desire for her had cooled considerably in the interim, his needs both material and carnal now at an all-time minimum. Nevertheless, although she tasted of cigarettes, a habit the newly ascetic Philip had well and truly kicked since his incarceration, he did not resist her kiss.

'It's more than I got from Deirdre Callan that night at the Cameo.'

'I'm sorry about Keating,' she said, removing the sunglasses so as he could have a good look at her sincerity. 'I genuinely thought you were going to get hurt. And I was right.'

'It's okay.'

'I've been speaking to him again. Keating. We have an understanding.'

'God love you! And God love *him*!'

He looked at her curiously. She had aged in the few months since he'd seen her. She had bags under her eyes. She had put on weight. She was an attractive lady. The desire flickering in his loins he quickly extinguished, mastery over the emotions a newly acquired skill of his, mental strength and conditioning being his pastime of choice in whiling away the long days in prison. He didn't blame her for his troubles. There were others, if he was a man inclined towards bitterness, who were well ahead of her in that particular queue.

Paolo, the man he'd killed with his bare hands, the man who visited him nightly in his cell and sat on the end of his bed in his bloodied football shirt, with his jowly head in his hands, had caused him considerable trouble. There was no doubt about that. However, he didn't hate him anymore. He didn't really feel anything towards him. Described in the tributes as a family man and a community activist – whatever that is – and eulogized in a packed church, his presence on White Island had been glossed over.

Philip was, naturally enough, bewildered and distressed at the time of his arrest for all sorts of reasons. He wasn't expecting a medal or even credit for leading the police to Sandra's grave. But he wasn't expecting to become an outcast either. A scapegoat. Paolo's penchant for extreme violence warranted scarcely a mention in dispatches.

Maybe a respected representative of the commentariat needed to actually receive a blow on the side of the head with a shovel and experience the recurring headaches and the hallucinations and the attendant memory loss to gain a fuller appreciation of people like Paolo in all their complexity.

'I couldn't agree more,' Joanne said, nodding her head vigorously.

For the first few weeks after the incident, Philip was a little bit frightened by how much he'd enjoyed the sound of crunching bone and by how much he'd relished the smell of blood. For a while there, he was forced to examine his conscience. Prompted by all sorts of inquiries from Keating and his kind, and his mother too on the phone, not to mention the voices in his head, he questioned the amount of force he had used and deliberated on the rights and wrongs of taking a person's life. And he was forced to suffer the less sensible voices, too, the most shrill being the little jockey on his back, there from the day he was born, little Willy Mince himself, in his silks, straddling his neck, and holding onto his hair, and whispering caution in his ear, whipping him on the back, warning him of impending damnation.

Now, with Christmas around the corner, he felt next to nothing. As his old friends in the Scientology movement in Munich – the misguided people who briefly sheltered him, fed him with sausage and plied him with beer, but crucially failed to foist their far-fetched philosophy upon him – would have it, he was now Clear. Clear as a bell. He had shaved his head. If he had access to a drill, he would have trepanned his own skull in the interests of further purification. In doing so, he'd be able to release any smidge of negative energy that may still be trapped within and let in more light and more air. But deemed by the experts to be a risk to himself, and possibly to others, he was kept away from the workshops and from the other prisoners, too, and given a cell to himself, where he spent up to four hours a day standing on his head.

The other man, the man who shot him, had certainly caused him trouble, too. No end of trouble. Although the shoulder reconstruction had gone as well as possible, he wouldn't be going bowling any time soon or, indeed, battering people to death. Ian, the Leo Sayer lookalike, the soft-spoken one, the apparent leader of the murderous double act, turned out to be a former *loyalist* paramilitary!

Philip, like the rest of the country, was amazed at this revelation. His would-be executioner was none other than Ian 'Licky' Stewart, *the* Licky Stewart, the renegade, founder member, and ruthless boss of a ruthless UVF offshoot, the RVF. The Royalist Volunteer Force was best known for the indiscriminate killing of Catholics and the ingenious use of torture, before and *after* death, on their victims. Released from prison under the terms of the Good Friday Agreement, he was a born-again Christian, a renowned speaker of tongues, a lay preacher, and a community activist.

'Aren't they all?' said Joanne, drily.

Since his release, he had not come to the attention of the police, north or south, until the gardaí were called to Lough Oughter Forest Park at summer's end. While investigating a missing skiff, they heard a shot and called for back-up. An hour later, a small army comprising uniformed officers, the Special Branch, and the sub-aqua unit descended on the island. There, they found three men in various states of disrepair: one dead, one in the throes of a massive heart attack, and one severely concussed. A fourth man, Licky himself, they found hiding in a tree. His story, that he and his rotund friend had been on an inter-faith fishing trip promoting peace and reconciliation when they were set upon, was hard to square with the presence of his fingerprints on the gun that fired the shot. Nor could he convincingly explain the presence on their boat of a toolbox containing various instruments, some, such as hammers and pliers and saws, that would be familiar to tradesmen everywhere and some that wouldn't be so familiar. This latter set of tools looked as if they'd been improvised by a welder with a vivid Heath Robinson/Marquis de Sade style imagination and motives, apart from an interest in gouging, unclear.

'You're lucky to be alive.'

'Am I?'

Philip could, and did, consider himself quite lucky that he was still in possession of all his organs, external and internal. Despite his status as a man of God, and his rock-solid references from eminences in the highest echelons of Ulster Unionism and the British establishment, Licky was arrested and charged with attempted murder.

'How is the shoulder?'

'Grand.'

'It's not over, Philip.'

'I honestly don't care.'

In reporting the case, many journalists, in fairness, asked the obvious question. Why would two people such as Paolo and Licky – polar opposites in many respects – be in cahoots in such a murky affair. They were sworn enemies, surely. One of them was Protestant Unionist, the other a Catholic Nationalist. One was self-denying and teetotal, the other piggish and alcoholic. Apart from a mutual passion for inflicting pain on others, they had nothing obvious in common.

All sorts of theories were leaked and spun and inspected from every angle and lapped up by the unsuspecting public. The ludicrous fishing-trip idea was given credence by at least one respectable Belfast newspaper. According to that innocent wrong-place-at-the-wrong-time narrative, the unlikely couple must have bumped into another pair of anglers while resting on White Island. An altercation ensued, perhaps over territorial fishing rights – as if Lough Oughter was the North Sea and full of cod – and Paolo was unfortunately killed. But why were they carrying guns? To shoot the fish?

Other full-time students of the human condition, summoning up all their knowledge of the post-conflict and the post-crash fallouts, respectively, declared that the debacle was the result of a drug deal gone wrong. These assumptions incensed Philip in the days after his arrest, when he was still at the mercy of his emotions. How could people not see that they were hired hands? Selling 99s and sharing the Gospel of Christ, while almost certainly thrilling and fulfilling at times, were no substitute for their true calling. Fidgety, adrift on the still waters of peace, the likes of Licky and Paolo – who, incidentally, was the great-grandson of an Italian craftsman who'd installed mosaics and terrazzo flooring in Belfast's up-and-coming Catholic churches in the Victorian era – must have been bored. They must have missed the old rough and tumble and the validation – the cover – that 'war' provided for their more primal inclinations. It was also plain as day that somebody must have hired them to bump off himself and Kevin. Come to think of it, Philip wondered, what was his life worth in monetary terms?

Paolo – also apparently the grandson of an organ-grinder whose monkey had famously disfigured a boy outside City Hall in 1924 – was mourned as a hero, a martyr, his coffin wrapped in the Irish flag. How could it be otherwise? Getting killed was probably the best thing that ever happened him. Just as the undertaker tidied up his face, the Party's peerless PR machine tidied up his life story. To have a living Paolo up and about and open to charges of hypocrisy or corruption or worse would have been embarrassing. It would undermine the mythology the Party worked so hard to create and preserve, the lore about the nature of the participants and the justification of the cause. When people ask why a good God would allow famine and war, they are told that God works in mysterious ways. And that, better than no explanation at all, is usually enough for the faithful. Likewise, sympathizers of the cause who might be inclined to question their faith in light of a troubling turn of events such as this were assured that this was *mysterious*. The fatal alliance between one of their own highly regarded foot-soldiers – the son, no less, of Paschal Sweeney, a man equally renowned for running a fine chippy in West Belfast and his ferocious temper who, in a fit of the said temper, forced Paolo's hand into the deep fat fryer as punishment one time for stealing a can of Lilt – and a rabid loyalist, one of the most feared and blood-thirsty participants of the Troubles era, and that was saying something, was a *mysterious way*, the Party being known to work from time to time in mysterious ways.

But none of this bothered Philip anymore. He was powerless. Behind bars, he never felt so free. He refused to get exercised any more about the things he couldn't control. He had found Sandra, hadn't he, for all the good it did him. Or her. Let others take the glory. Let others finish the job, or not.

'You seem serene.'

'What do you want from me, Joanne?'

'You can't give up now.'

'That's good. He topped the poll. What more do you need to know? Nobody gives a shit anymore.'

'I do. Kevin does. And I know you do, too.'

'That's great. I'm in prison. Kevin's in a mental home and you, you're a pariah. Seriously, Joanne. I like you. I do. But you're fooling yourself. Or, worse, fooling me.'

'It's a good act. I like it. I'm impressed,' she said. 'Very Zen, very Kung Fu. But you can't keep it up forever.'

He had never seen her so serious.

'Try me.'

What did she know? What did it matter? He didn't care.

'Tell your story. You're a big enigma out there. People are curious.'

'You going to write a book about me?'

'I'd have to get to know you first.' Joanne winked. But there was no flirty fun in it. No promise. It was just an old reflex. On reflection, it mightn't have been a wink at all. Merely a twitchy eye. Something clicked in her pocket. She placed an old dictaphone on the table.

'Jesus, Joanne. Do you ever fucking stop?'

'I've run out of tape.'

'That's illegal.'

'The case is alive, Philip. You found her.'

'Nobody cares.'

'I care. And there's the cards. We're close.'

'The cards? Really? Seriously? Still banging on about the cards?'

'We can tie them to Coleman.'

'It's a dead end.'

'You can have the tape, if you want. Take it! Or you can let me use it?'

'You're an outcast.'

'I know you didn't do it. I know Dove didn't do it.' She took a breath. 'I think I know who did do it.'

Joanne put on her sunglasses and stood up.

'I have it on good authority. They're dropping the charges. You'll be out in the next few days.'

The end of the cycle

Kevin, since his heart attack, had been declared dead on three separate occasions. Apparently, that was an Irish record. He defied science by bouncing back to life – *bouncing* perhaps being something of an overstatement – a phenomenon, all in all, that did little, according to certain retrograde wits in An Garda, to diminish his old Messiah complex.

After suffering a fairly massive cardiac arrest on White Island, he died, in the arms of a paramedic called Nuala, and was dead for a good three minutes before she managed to turn his fortunes around, with the timely arrival of the defibrillator.

Later in the hospital, after yet another fairly massive heart attack, he briefly died again, only to be revived this time by Karel, a nurse from the Czech Republic, who shared a mutual appreciation for Velvet Underground and chocolate digestives. To stabilize him during surgery, a coma was induced, from which he did not emerge for four-and-a-half weeks. As such, he missed Sandra Mohan's Christian burial.

When he came to, he found Sheila, Shane, and Ciara in his room, the walls a salmony pink. Ciara had aborted her Australian adventure to be by his side. They were all saying the rosary, continuous multiple rosaries, having given him up for dead. After a short and happy convalescence at home, the old ticker scaffolded by stents, and the mood uplifted by love for his family, and their love for him, he disappeared for a while behind the curtains of a particularly grim, Ibsen-esque play.

As a consequence, he spent a week or two above in St Dymphna's hospital before returning home again, where he remained, contrary to Philip's information, in his bedroom mostly, comatose, catatonic, physically safe from harm, but in retreat from the real world, a whale adrift in the depths of the subconscious sea, in a sort of dreamscape, sifting through a lifetime's flotsam and jetsam, more asleep than awake, and no harm, his waking hours on Earth having been largely disappointing of late, and them synonymous with grief and misery in the relentless pursuit of some clue that would nail Sandra Mohan's killers.

What good can come of any day that begins by getting out of bed? A good question. An aphorism by a *fin de siècle* Austrian wit – there's a paradox if ever there was one – although, in fairness, he'd only ever met one Austrian person in his life, a police dog-trainer, on second-ment to the north-east division, but she was easily the most humourless person he'd ever met, managing to knock the craic out of the entire garda dog unit, man and beast alike.

If he admitted to Sheila, or to his doctors, or to anybody else that he was still on the Mohan case, they'd have him committed again, or, worse, they might actually let him die. And he wouldn't blame them. He'd have to be careful. He wouldn't go back to the island, or up the town, or even down to his office. They wouldn't suspect a thing.

He'd lie in the bed, like the metaphysical poets and the aphorists of the ages, with the *blanky* around him, relying exclusively on the contents, extant, of his own mind, the sum of all human knowledge contained therein, give or take a gigabyte, alone, uncorrupted by chat or by civic interaction.

Fin de siècle. It was French for 'end of the century'. He never really knew what it meant but liked the sound of it, liked saying it aloud when he stumbled across it in books. For ages he assumed it meant the 'end of the cycle'. All he knew for sure was that it suggested loss and regret, and that was good enough for him.

Once Sandra's remains were found, Kevin foolishly believed that a thorough investigation would follow, and a trail would surely lead to Coleman's door. It didn't. Instead, they were back at square one on the snakes-and-ladders board, at the tail-end of a snake. Dove Connolly once again was the main suspect, positive sightings of him at Lough Oughter Forest Park in the weeks before he died the clincher.

Bonfires were lit on the approach roads to the town the night Coleman returned, shoulder-high, from the count. He was wearing a white Stetson hat, honouring a wager of some sort. He'd come to regret the choosing of such an accoutrement. The voters of the constituency were fickle and, although favourable to cowboy *mores* generally, were often violently opposed to any sort of sartorial flourish. Wasn't the young fella who won the disco-dancing competition run out of town for wearing a headband?

Mere hours after his election, the backlash was already beginning. There was a party in the Cunningham Arms to celebrate his victory. It was the same night Carmel Mohan took possession of her daughter's bones and there was little or no fanfare to mark her homecoming. At Coleman's reception, Lonergan made the introductions. In bigging-up Coleman, he set tongues wagging when he described the '*atrojious*' job his protégé had done. Nobody could work out for sure what he meant by 'atrojious' – a cross between 'Trojan', as in hard-working, and 'atrocious', as in very poor quality. Was it a slip of the tongue or a coded message?

The death of Paolo Sweeney, on that little island of all islands, was an inconvenience, to be sure, for the Party 'mid all the election hoopla. In and around the subsequent negotiations, it was not easily dismissed as a coincidence, but people were hedging their bets for now. The pillars of the community – the police, the press, the politicians – were keeping their powder dry, as they say, sitting on their hands, keeping schtum, using only the most uncontroversial of clichés until they could see which way the wind was blowing and which side of their bread was buttered.

'Daddy! You have visitors.' Ciara's lovely voice.

There was talk of a place in the cabinet for Coleman, a junior ministry, at the very least, in forestry and fisheries, the irony not lost on Kevin, who so nearly perished in a forest park that might soon be part of Coleman's political domain.

'We can come back another time.'

Who was that? Husky.

'No, no. He can hear us rightly,' says Ciara. 'Daddy, don't be so rude. It's Noeleen.'

Ciara was the only one wise to him. Smart girl. Noeleen. He knew a Noeleen. He opened an eye. No, he didn't recognize her, a stout lady, dyed curly hair, a reddish tint, looked the image of the actress Brenda Fricker.

'Daddy, cop yourself on! There's nothing the matter with him. He's just feeling sorry for himself. Daddy!'

Ciara herself had brought him back from the dead on the third occasion he died. It was she who found him crumpled on the floor of his bedroom, his heart stopped again. She'd had a feeling, she told him later, that something wasn't right, and ran upstairs fearing the worst. After a few good thumps on the chest and a bit of awkward mouth-to-mouth, he regained life, impressed beyond words by his daughter's presence of mind and all-round enfermological ability. He could have died happily knowing she was competent, dutiful, and of a pleasant disposition, perfect in every way and probably, as an added bonus, possessed of a sixth sense, a catch for any man lucky to have her and, thanks to his third death, likely to be regarded forever-more with a certain reverence as a lifesaver. What he didn't tell her or anybody else was that, on this occasion, he had actually stopped his own heart.

He opened a second eye.

'Hello, Noeleen,' says he.

'I'll leave you to it,' said Ciara, looking at her father suspiciously. 'Paul is acting up.'

The woman leaned towards him, a forward curl tickling his forehead and a powerful reek of the fags forcing him to turn away.

'You're a very brave man, Mr Healy,' says she. 'I'm prepared to testify.'

Kevin sat up in the bed, fully dressed, shirt and tie, shoes and all, but he was far from fully awake.

'Who are you?'

'Noeleen Sheriff. Stephen's sister. We spoke on the phone.'

'Ah, Noeleen. The end of the cycle.'

'The what? Mr Healy . . .'

'The *fin de siècle*.'

He knew he had to apologize for something.

'Sorry about the sandbags.'

'Are you okay?'

Kevin tried and failed at first to stand up, dizzy, the senses all fuzzy. He was aware that he was blathering but unable at present to do anything to stop himself.

'Stephen's downstairs in the wheelchair. He'll testify too.'

'Will he?'

'He will when I'm finished with him.'

That was good. That was a development. Testify about what, though?

A no-nonsense woman, he appreciated the way she got straight to the point. He wished to impress her with his command of his own faculties, his general competence and, time-permitting, his erudition, but knew that he wasn't in any danger of succeeding with those ambitions in the immediate future. Little did they know, the visitors, that he had actually summoned them to him, to his bedside, via extra-sensory means, the extra senses, in contrast to his regular senses, being razor sharp.

'Is it a drink you'll be having?'

'What?'

'Nothing. Sorry. I'm . . . Noeleen, isn't it?'

He woke up. They went downstairs and into the sitting room, where Stephen was parked in the middle of the room. Baby Paul was crying in the kitchen next door.

'It was me sent the cards.'

'Good man, Stephen.'

Here we go, he thought, wearily, the cards! Omar was thinner, if that was possible, than he was the last time Kevin interviewed him. He was basically just an alimentary canal at this stage in a cheap cotton jumper. You could hardly take him seriously with his wee shrunken head, until he opened his mouth and said what he had come to say.

'She wants me to tell Keating. I told her I don't talk to cops.'

'Can't blame you,' said Kevin.

'I wanted you to be the first to know.'

'Fair play!'

'I was over and back to London for work. He told me to send the cards, Coleman. I knew Sandra was dead, but I swear, I swear to God, I had nothing to do with it. I don't know who killed her. But . . .'

Noeleen held a glass to his lips and he took a sip of water that, in Kevin's estimation, must have doubled his bodyweight.

'. . . I do know why. I know why she was kilt.'

Kevin sat forward, very alert now, straining to hear the confessor's every word, the sickly man's mouth now dry, his breath shallow.

'You see. She went bananas the night, you know, the night . . . she had a kind of flashback, some bad experience she had with one of the on-the-runs. The thing is, Sandra was a hoor.'

'For God's sake, Stephen. She was sixteen years old,' says his big-haired sister in her smoker's broken voice.

'I'm only saying.'

'She was a child.'

'Coleman would get the call from . . .'

At this point, he beckoned Kevin to come even closer and whispered a name into his ear. It was a name that was familiar to Kevin, as it would have been to any keen student of the conflict.

'He'd call Coleman and tell him to send the girl.'

'To the bunker?'

'Aye. The Hole. The bunker. We called it The Hole. People have the wrong idea of Coleman. He wasn't, like, a dirtbird or anything like that. He never rode her himself. Sandra. Well, at least, not after the first time anyway. After he broke her in.'

'Jesus Christ, Stephen!' his sister cried. 'Don't speak like that. Do you hear yourself? Do you hear him? That's no way to speak about another human being.'

'Sorry. I'm just, I'm trying to tell you something here. If you don't want to hear . . . he was only doing what he was told. Mr . . . shall we say, X, Mr X liked them young. Coleman had no choice.'

'The spoils of victory,' muttered Kevin bitterly.

'The what?'

'Go on.'

'In fairness, he'd get her out of her box so as she'd forget, so as she'd have no memory, you know, of whatever went on. That was the kind of him, he could be very decent like that, so he could. We'd bring her to The Hole, Coleman, meself, Lonergan sometimes. She'd be nearly passed out but we'd blindfold her all the same, so as, you know, she wouldn't know where she was. Yer man was living there for a few months after the . . .'

Again, Sheriff leaned into Kevin's face and this time mouthed the name of a place, a town synonymous with death.

'She was on for it, she agreed to go along, but she'd be upset after, you know the way. I doubt it was pleasant. And she'd have the odd bruise too, the odd scratch, but he paid her well, Coleman, money, clothes, drink, drugs, the whole works. They were the best of friends. He'd tell her he was saving himself for her until the wedding night, that's what he'd say, and she'd swallow it, and he'd tell her he was dying to have another go at her himself, and all this kind of craic.

'Anyway, she arrives at his place that night, you know, in a right state, shouting and screaming, and raising all sorts of hell. "I thought you were at Shadows," says he, "with your little boyfriends." And she starts hitting him, and biting him, and roaring and shouting, going on about the bunker and this, the bunker in McManus's field, the one that was in the news there, and mentioning people by name, names she shouldn't even know, never mind be mentioning out loud, and all the things he did to her, you know, threatening to go the guards if Coleman didn't do something about it. It wasn't the first time she'd kicked up a fuss, she'd been out of control for a fair while by then, a few weeks anyway, and Fergal was mighty pissed off, so he was. So anyway, after a few spliffs she calms down, Coleman was rubbing her hair and filling her full of all kinds of shite. I was sent out for the chips and a few battered sausages and when I came back she was grand again, the best of form. Anyway, that's the why. That's why she had to go.'

Noeleen was sniffling away to herself while Kevin assessed the man's sorry claim.

'But she was still alive at six in the morning. When Philip was there.'

'Look, Mr Healy, I don't know exactly what happened before or after. I wasn't keeping an eye on the clock – I was elephants meself that night. Lonergan came around and the lads, himself and Fergal disappeared for a few hours. I stayed with Sandra. That's when they went over the border, you know . . .'

'The RUC man?'

'Correct. The job had been on the cards for a few weeks, he had a bit of a routine, the pig, no offence, he was always there of a Saturday night, getting the ride, but Lonergan decided to bring it forward with all that was going on. They came back later and that's when we went out to Shadows and started a fight. I don't know what else I can tell you. Only . . .'

At this point in his story, he turned to Noeleen, a pained expression on his face, a death rattle in his chest. He was running out of time. That was one handy thing about Catholicism in this country. It was directly responsible, in conjunction with bossy older sisters, for many's a deathbed confession.

'I'm sorry, Noeleen. I never told you this bit.'

'That's okay, pet.'

'I was in charge of getting rid of the clothes, so I was. That was my big job. It was the next day, Sunday, around three o'clock. They gave me a bag, a refuse sack, all wrapped up in Sellotape, and told me to get rid of it, burn it, they said, absolutely incinerate the shite out of it and don't ask any stupid questions, the usual. As you can imagine, curiosity got the better of me. I looked in the bag and there were the clothes, skirt, top, Dove's jacket, the beret and the shoes. No bra, no knickers. She wasn't wearing any as far as I know. That was the kind of her. I didn't know what to do. I didn't actually want to believe that she was dead, so I kept them myself, you know, in case she turned up looking for them. I hid the bag in my uncle's loft, Robert.'

'Robert Daly?'

'Correct. Out by Lisnaglack. We used to hide stuff there from time to time. Guns and so on, you know yourself. Youse never thought of looking beyond in Bob's house, did you? No. It was a good hiding place, so it was. You'd never know what you might find out there.'

Kevin vaguely knew the man referred to. Robert Daly was an old man, reclusive, blind, and half-mad, living in a house bereft of electricity and water, who wheeled his bike without tyres in and out of town on a Thursday.

'I don't know why I kept her clothes, in all honesty. I certainly meant no harm. That's for sure. It was me sent the jacket to Dove. And the beret. I don't know why I did that either. It was out of goodness or badness, I suppose, I don't know which. But I didn't know where she was buried, honest to God, or how she got there, or who did the dirty deed. God rest the girl's soul.'

He tried to bless himself, but his arms – mere reeds – failed him. With her thumb, Noeleen made the sign of the cross on his forehead and gave him another drink of water, wiping his mouth with a towel. She then whispered something in his ear. He whispered something back into her ear whereupon she reached into a bag that was hanging on the back of the wheelchair and handed Healy a crumpled envelope.

'I don't know if that's any use. It was in the jacket pocket. I put it in the envelope myself.'

Healy opened it. At first, he thought it was empty and looked to Sheriff for an explanation. Noeleen grabbed the envelope and shook the contents out onto the nearest table. Kevin nodded, his body a-tingling, a delicate web of ice spreading across the back of his head.

'Yes.'

'You see.'

'I see.'

What he saw were a few strands of hair on the table.

'It might be of some use. It might not. You can do what you like with it.'

Baby Paul started to scream the house down.

'We'll go,' says Noeleen.

'You're grand.'

'I don't know why he won't give it to the guards. He insisted you have it.'

'Don't worry, I'll pass it on to the relevant persons. Stephen! Thank you. I appreciate the effort. But I think you should go to the guards,' he said, and it almost made him sick to say it. 'I think you should talk to Keating.'

'That's what I said,' says the sister.

'My conscience is clear.'

As the Sheriffs turned to go, Kevin, in turmoil, brushed away his tears, moved that someone like Stephen chose to confide in him, but sickened beyond the reach of medical science by what he'd heard. If only Ciara had let him die.

The long and the short of it

After the visit of the Sheriffs, Kevin was soon back to his old self. Not his old, *old* self. He wasn't the naive young man who'd graduated top of his class, or the athlete who'd played football for his home town, or the selfless cop who'd taken a bullet for his country. But he was back to something resembling his pre-White Island heart-attack self.

The Doc was a regular visitor to the house. During one of their endless chats, long after everybody else had gone to bed, Kevin confided in his friend a thought that had plagued him for some time.

'Part of me never wants the case to end. If it's all tied up nicely, what have I got to live for?'

Kevin was all too aware of the innumerable blessings he had to draw on – his supportive family, the books, and the rare friendship he enjoyed with the portly, refined man who sat with him of an evening surrounded by empty cans of Dutch Gold, the Doc's weakness for cheap lager at odds with his refinement, a consequence of unfortunate investments in property he'd made during the boom.

'I know what you mean, Kev. Somehow I can't see you in a men's shed with the other down-in-the-dumps.' The Doc slapped his leg.

'Woodwork, ha! It's not really my scene,' agreed Kevin. 'Making little birdhouses.'

'The avian property market is saturated at present. Birds can be every bit as picky as human beings when it comes to their accommodation. When it comes to anything, says you.'

Kevin laughed. The Doc could be a right comedian sometimes. Naturally, he wanted justice for Sandra and wouldn't do anything to slow down or hinder the investigation. But, of course, it was completely out of his hands now, his recent audience with Stephen Sheriff notwithstanding. He was feeling at a loss. His work was done and for the first time in his life he felt truly redundant.

* * *

Then, one Monday in December, two events came to pass, both of which served to invigorate him and prevent any further slippage into the hot springs of self-pity. By arrangement, he visited the Garda station at 11.00 a.m. It was a cold morning, wet and whitey-grey. Kevin stamped his feet in the *vestibule* – the Doc's vocabulary rubbing off on him – to shake off the rain. Young O'Loinsigh was at the desk. He not only buzzed Kevin in without any questions but stood up and saluted him, too. A promising start to the day, by any standards, and there wasn't a hint of irony in the gesture as far as Kevin could tell.

Kevin pushed open the door, a barrier closed to him for such a long time, and entered the dayroom. Once inside, the seven or eight gardaí present spontaneously burst into applause. Kevin was stunned. They continued to clap and cheer for a good minute or two, the sound, to Kevin's watery ears – otitis being another of his ailments – like chips being lowered into a deep fat fryer. Even Keating came out of his office and joined in the celebration. Kevin was chuffed to bits. In fact, he was so overcome with emotion that he momentarily went deaf and blind. Lovely.

Keating, only a bit peeved at somebody else getting the attention, hurriedly ushered Kevin into his office, shutting the door behind him with his heel. A typically inelegant Keating *arabesque*. Still a prick. He sat on his desk, facing Kevin, and folded his arms and got straight to the point.

'Bad news, I'm afraid. No match for the hair.'

'Ah well.'

The conveyor of the hair sample, Stephen Sheriff, had passed away the day after his visit to Kevin's house. Kevin had feared for the spindly creature's safety. However, to his surprise, he died of 'natural' causes.

Well, the bleach he swallowed made light work of his already ravaged organs. A cup of tea or a sneeze could just as easily have tipped him over the edge and sent him spinning to his eternal restlessness, light as a sycamore seed. He was lucky he died the way he did. If the likes of Fergal Coleman thought for a moment that Sheriff was a squealer, he would have saved him the bother of committing such a mortal sin.

After paying his respects to the Sheriff family, Kevin had decided to swallow his pride and share with Keating all that he'd learned. That done, he'd presented Keating with a few strands of the hair Sheriff had given him, to have it tested. True to form, Kevin had kept some of the hair samples for his own records, not entirely trusting his old colleague. Noeleen had backed up his evidence in an interview with the detective and was subsequently taken into protective custody. Her current whereabouts was unknown to Kevin.

'It's not Coleman's.'

'Oh?'

'No. Afraid not. And it's not Lonergan's neither.'

'Stephen Sheriff?'

'Nope. Nobody in the database. Nobody with any sort of a record. Kevin, there's something I've been meaning to say.'

Was this it, Healy wondered? The apology? Keating, the big galoot, had never really forgiven him for winning Sheila's favour, not that he did anything in particular to win it. True, they'd both been smitten by the lady at exactly the same moment. It was the day they went to the travel agency to book a week in Tenerife, and them a pair of young bucks, pacing the room, fit and strong and full of beans, in advance of a first holiday abroad. Sheila, behind the desk, was pretty and distant, a bit like a Canary Island herself.

'I appreciate all your help,' said Keating. 'I do and I'm . . . frustrated, fierce frustrated. Every bit as frustrated as you are, believe me, but without a match I just don't know, I don't think we have enough to go on.'

Maybe Keating had nothing to apologize for. Maybe he, Kevin, *had* been a bit of a liability after being shot, although he genuinely couldn't remember any of the incidents Keating had reported to their superior officers. He had read the reports alright, internal Garda enquiries as well as press accounts, of a bizarre high-speed chase involving a maverick republican known as the Badger who operated both sides of the border but only at the dead of night. This man had stolen a fire engine and gone on a rampage, ramming numerous cars along the Main Street of Tullyanna. He had reversed into shop windows and tried to mow down a member of the force. He was a man, in other words, bent on destruction with no thought for his own safety.

The chase went on through the night through nearby towns until the man was finally stopped on the new road between Aughnaboy and Drumahair. A squad car, in a game of high-stakes chicken, was driven, as per the reports, at 125 mph, in a straight line towards the fire engine's headlights. At the very last second, the Badger, of all people, lost his nerve, swerved off the road, and crashed into a ditch. When he was finally cut from the wreckage – no easy job given that most of the necessary cutting equipment was actually on board the stolen vehicle – he was apprehended by an extremely shaken Detective Keating. Keating had been a passenger in the squad car, convinced that he was going to die. Healy had no memory of driving the car that night. He refused to accept the testimony of Keating and the other occupants that he – a conservative cop, a careful driver, as slow and steady a man as ever there was – would be capable of such a reckless act. Maybe he'd been wrong. Maybe he'd done Keating a disservice.

'I'm sorry,' said Kevin.

'So am I,' his old friend replied.

Keating whipped out his handkerchief and honked into it. What either of them was sorry about was not specified and life moved on. Since White Island, Keating at least was taking him seriously again. But hidebound by the political impasse, his own caution and careerism, and the lack of cast-iron evidence, he wasn't in a position to make arrests.

Despite examining Sandra's remains, with the combined expertise of the technical bureau and the forensic science laboratory, not to mention specialist state-of-the-art assistance from Europe and the United States, the gardaí could not establish a cause of death. It was definitely Sandra. That much *was* ascertained. All they could say for sure was that she was dead. They were no mugs. She was dead but hadn't been shot, or, to be more accurate, none of her bones had been damaged by a bullet. Small comfort to those who loved her. No bones were broken apart from a few small ones in the fingers of her right hand. Although the picture vis-à-vis the fate of Sandra was clearer, it was impossible to say who had killed her.

'That's the long and the short of it.'

They shook hands.

'Good luck.'

'Good luck now. Say hello to Sheila.'

Lonergan is the key

Later that day, Kevin's heart skipped a beat for a second time when Ciara's voice woke him from a nap.

'Daddy! It's Philip.'

Although he'd heard that Philip had been released from jail, he hadn't actually seen him in the flesh since their altercation with the boys in the forest park, very little of which he could remember. In fact, nobody had seen Philip Sharkey around town, not even his own mother, the assumption being, in a town not slow to come forward with the assumptions, that he'd skipped the country again. Reputations were easy to come by and hard to shrug off in a town where people prided themselves on knowing their onions.

Philip explained to Kevin that he'd been to Mount Athos, a men-only enclave of Greek orthodox monasteries near Thessaloniki, for a week. Advised to lie low, he had travelled on a temporary passport speedily arranged by his new sponsor, Bad News Keating. There, he'd lived on honey and yoghurt and wildflowers, the names of which he couldn't remember.

'I'm not a bee,' he declared wryly, in response to Kevin's interminable questions. 'I thought I'd find peace.'

The peace he'd sought was not forthcoming, Philip told him, in so many words. Nor were the revelations he sought about himself and the world around him.

'That's the thing about revelations,' said Kevin, not wanting to disabuse his friend of any idealistic notions he might have adopted. 'Revelations are never revealed when you need them the most.'

The sort of peace he sought was not available to man, full stop, Philip concluded, without a trace of bitterness, and him wiser now after his latest adventure. They were on the same wavelength finally. In Kevin's opinion, Philip looked all the better for coming to that conclusion. The stress was gone from his forehead. A worldly smile decorated his handsome face. The blindingly obvious secret to happiness (which, surprisingly, only Kevin seemed to know) was to seek nothing.

'The secret is, Philip, eliminate your wants entirely, do you get me? Not by *satisfying* them, but by not *having* them at all in the first place. Basic fecking common sense.'

While residing among the holy celibates of that fabled Greek peninsula, Philip, in the absence of the other sex, thought about nothing but women.

'Or, should I say, one woman in particular, no prizes for guessing the name. What do you make of that?'

'Her heart is in the right place.'

The small talk was out of the way sooner than Kevin would have liked, the reunion of the dream team not having been uppermost in his plans for the day. Kevin was eager to compare their respective post-traumatic experiences, but Philip was having none of it. He produced a keyring. The key was still attached.

'I found this.'

'In Greece?'

'At home. In an envelope waiting for me on the hall stand. I wasn't going to open it, but I did.'

Philip was as surprised as anyone that the DPP had dropped the charges against him due to, of all things, lack of evidence. Laughing incredulously, he'd tried to explain to the DPP that he had repeatedly stamped on a man's head and, what's more, greatly enjoyed it. But the DPP wasn't having any of it and explained to Philip that, in their considered view, he'd clearly being acting in self-defence. And with that, the DPP, metaphorically winking, on behalf of the State, at the behest of History herself, showed him the door.

Among the many vows that he had made on Mount Athos, Philip had vowed not to involve himself further in a murder investigation that had caused him no end of pain. But he had always been an impulsive lad, deeply wedded to the philosophy *du jour* – be it martial arts, Marxism, pro-life or pro-choice – until he wasn't. *Love is eternal for as long as it lasts,* as the fella says. He couldn't remember where he'd read that, but for some reason it had stayed with him – a romantic sentiment on a greeting card, or a cynical truth on a barrio wall, possibly in Cartagena?

'Gabriel García Márquez.'

'How in the name of fuck do you know that?'

'No idea. I just know.'

'Anyway, I opened the envelope.'

Upon close inspection, the keyring looked to Kevin like a cheap souvenir sporting a coat of arms.

'It's a fairly shite coat of arms,' said Philip.

'Not exactly eye-catching, no.'

The emblem, for want of a better word, comprised a blue chevron on a white background and criss-crossed above that a couple of red arrows symbolizing, most likely, the family's utter lack of imagination. It could have been his own Sharkey coat of arms for all he knew about heraldry.

Of more significance, in Philip's opinion, was that a key was attached to the keyring.

'I'm no genius, but I presume it opens something.'

'You might be right.'

What it opened, Philip couldn't say. A padlock, he guessed, given its size, or a locker of some sort, or maybe, at a stretch, a suitcase?'

'A *valise*?' Healy offered, channelling the Doc.

'I don't care, to be frank. That's why I'm handing it over to you.'

Whatever sort of a repository it was, Kevin helpfully explained, it most likely contained something that would shed light on the case.

'Well, personally, I'm not interested anymore.'

'If I'm not greatly mistaken,' says Kevin, 'that would be the Lonergan coat of arms.'

And how the fuck do you know that as well, you old know-all wizard? That's what Philip wanted to say in response.

'Like I said, it's a bit shite.' That's what he did say.

'Well, Philip, that's a ridiculous thing to say about a family crest. What would you prefer? Like, a rat or something on top of a . . . kettle. There are rules. Conventions and so on.'

'They could have done better, the Lonergans.'

'The chevron there, you see, that signifies protection,' Kevin went on, the brain – Old Bessie – awake, the eyes ablaze, excited to share his knowledge with his amanuensis, and his vocabulary too, a bit like the way a novelist might want to display his extensive research at the expense of the narrative. There'll be no stopping him now, thought Philip.

'The arrows . . .'

'Let me guess,' Philip interjected. 'Military readiness.'

'Good man, yourself.'

'What about the starfish?'

'They're estoiles, you clown, the yellow colour represents generosity. Two questions immediately spring to mind,' said Kevin, interrupting himself, oblivious to his friend's growing impatience. 'Who sent you this? And what does it open?'

'Joanne sent it.'

'Joanne! I thought she'd gone to ground.'

'You must be joking. She's like a cockroach.' Philip flexed his injured arm in a Pete Townsend style arc. 'Look. I don't know what's going on. I found Sandra. Sorry, *we* found Sandra. We did our best. But I'm afraid I don't have your patience. It's all yours.'

'Okay, leave it with me,' Healy said.

Philip took this as his cue to go, whereas it was in fact the cue for Healy to begin a little Shamanic performance designed to get Philip to stay. Philip, half-turned towards the door and a new life for himself, watched rapt as Healy closed his eyes for a minute or two, humming to himself, the gears in his mind audibly grinding.

'Lonergan is the key,' pronounced Kevin, the eyes still closed.

'What?'

'Maybe.' One eye open.

'You're saying it's just a fucking message?'

'Could be. The key itself is not important. *Lonergan is the key*. Do you see? Mere conjecture on my part.'

'I have to say,' said Sharkey, slowly, 'that's disappointing. If the key itself is of no consequence, that's very disappointing indeed.'

'I thought you said you weren't interested.'

'I'm not. But I imagine it would be very disappointing for the likes of yourself or anybody who *was* stupid enough to be still interested.'

'All I'm saying, maybe he *is* the key.'

'All *I'm* saying is maybe he's not. Even if Lonergan *is* the key, what's the big deal? Talk about stating the obvious. We all know he's up to his fucking neck.'

Healy sucked on that egg for a minute or two, his faith in crime detection long diminished, his head holding myriad thoughts simultaneously, some of them related to the case, some to literature, some to what he might do for the rest of his life. Birdhouses were a waste of time. But he might, on mature reflection, make little wooden toys for children. He'd buy himself a lathe and some wood. Such a pastime surely couldn't do any harm to anybody? Although, he'd have to be careful about the paint. Didn't the Chinese get in trouble over some sort of toxin in the paint? And sure, children nowadays wouldn't be interested in little wooden monkeys anyway – with or without drums. Unless there was a screen to finger on the monkey's face. Maybe he'd give the old carpentry a miss after all, he thought, suddenly conscious again that he was in the middle of a conversation with Philip, who was clearly not as at peace with himself as he was maintaining.

'Mmm. Of course, it might be a *real* key after all.'

'Do you think?'

'Well, you never know.'

'See, that's what I thought.'

'Yes, well. You might be right.'

There was a brief hiatus in the negotiations before, tears forming in his eyes, Philip cried out, 'I killed a man.'

* * *

They had a body. They had a motive, courtesy of the sclerotic corpse that was formerly Stephen Sheriff. They were together again, reluctantly, it must be said, the playthings of Fate. It was a partnership indivisible, soldered in blood and common purpose. They were in search of a killer, or killers, the only clue now a key of somewhat dubious provenance. Kevin invited Philip to join him in his man-cave where, accompanied by a medley of carefully selected tunes, they reviewed what they had.

Healy, at this point, relayed the details of Sheriff's sordid tale to Philip. As gently as he could, he outlined the abuse Sandra was subjected to at the hands of Coleman and the on-the-run. Philip didn't take it well. It was shocking to see a man visibly shrinking before his eyes, hollowing out, to actually see the churn of emotions – the sorrow and the anger – contorting his features, to hear the howls of anguish coming from his soul. After half an hour and a few valium, he calmed down.

'Sheriff's dead. It's all hearsay.'

'I heard him say it.'

Kevin told him about Omar's non-disposal of Sandra's clothes in defiance of Coleman and Lonergan's explicit orders, and his conveyancing, via the post, of the beret and the jacket to Dove.

'Noeleen was there. She heard him too.'

There were still lots of things they didn't know, the main one being *how did Dove know where Sandra was buried?* But Philip kept that thought to himself, not wanting to spoil the positive mood in the room.

'Oh, I almost forgot, poor Stephen gave me this.'

Healy opened a small cellophane bag. With a tweezers, he carefully extracted a few strands of hair, which he then, with the appropriate ceremonial reverence, laid out on the table. He explained that the locks were found in the pocket of the jacket that Sandra was wearing on the night she went missing. They were most likely pulled, in some sort of tussle, from the head of one of the last people to see her alive.

'That's convenient,' said Philip, the cynicism returning, 'probably framing some innocent cocksucker.'

'I hadn't thought of that.'

Either way, he said, they weren't able to find a match above at the park. It was nothing to do with the age or the condition of the samples. The samples were fine, apparently. But the upshot was that the clump didn't belong to Coleman, or Sheriff, or Tommy, or, to Philip's great relief, the Dove.

'What about me?' Philip asked, remembering all too well Sandra with his head in her hands.

'You're not on the database. We never actually arrested you. Not at the time, no.'

Philip's antennae suddenly stiffened.

'What?'

'Nothing.'

It was embarrassing. Hardly worth mentioning. But a thing nonetheless. He had a childish hobby once upon a time, collecting locks of hair from Uncle Francie's barbershop floor. There was a scrapbook somewhere. He used to keep it under the bed, although he was fairly certain it wasn't there now. Perhaps it had been nicked by Macker. In which case, fuckit. All the young men of the town had been patrons of Uncle Francie's salon at one time or another. In his heyday, they were attracted by the dirty jokes and the cool music and his ability to 'spike' even the most lifeless hair of the aspiring neo-punk clientele. It was a long shot, but there was nothing to lose. Crazy as it might sound, if the scrapbook could be located, Healy's sample of hair might match one of the entries in his own private collection.

* * *

The hair directory wasn't in Philip's bedroom. His bedroom, of course, was clean. Mammy, ha! The posters had been taken down. The sheets were new. In advance of his return home from prison, his mother, in the interests of her troubled son having a 'fresh start', had done a thorough makeover on his room. Philip shook his head.

'That old thing. It's in the attic,' his mother shouted up from downstairs.

He scrambled up to the attic. It was stupid. The whole thing. Macker could have stolen the precious scrapbook. His mother could have thrown it away. It was probably of no use anyway. In fact, the embarrassment of even acknowledging that he'd compiled such a record in his late teens was so great, it almost outweighed its potential as evidence in catching a murderer.

If nothing else, he'd take down his guitar and strum 'The Tea Song' to console himself. His voice had deepened since he'd played it last and no doubt he'd be able to sustain the sorry 'Ohhhhh' notes all too well.

In among the jumble of suitcases that were full of his father's clothes and the boxes of photographs and the old sewing machine, Philip found a plastic storage box. It was labelled 'Pip'. *The name was Philip.* He opened the box. There were a few school essays and a project he'd done about a local piggery. There was nothing he didn't know about pigs. Very clean animals that rolled around in their own shit.

He shuffled through his birth cert, and his provisional driving licence, and his Leaving Cert results, which he'd never actually seen before, and other souvenirs of his youth that left him equally unmoved. His Judo books, as good as new, were housed in a similar container along with his cassette tapes (the Top Twenty taped from the radio on a Sunday afternoon) and other keepsakes curated by his mother. They would be of no use to anybody unless he became *famoso* – for reasons good or bad – and fell into the hands of a biographer. Would the fact that he got an A in honours maths or that he loved the Stone Roses shed any light on his later homicidal instincts? What could anybody know of another man's trials?

Being a man who valued his privacy, he was briefly tempted to set the attic on fire. A few years previously his laptop, containing five years of photographs and emails and contacts and snatches of song lyrics and endless clumsy attempts at writing the same old story, crashed on a plane from Seattle to Anchorage. In doing so it noisily destroyed the hard disk and everything on it, erasing him digitally from the Earth. He was upset. He had a mini-crisis that lasted just a few hours, during which time he cursed the Apple corporation and cursed his rotten luck. But after that a calmness descended. Anxiety turned to relief, an anagram of re-life. He was strangely happy, happier than he'd been for a while. Rebooting himself, he felt a lightness that must have lasted a whole week. Without the sentimentality and the nostalgia and the accumulation of incriminating evidence of who he was, he felt leaner and freer. On the front foot for a change. There was definitely something to be said for dumping your laptop and burning your attic. On his way out of the attic, he found the dossier with the hair samples. It was behind the door.

Looking through it, he couldn't help laughing at his old naivety, not to mention his appalling handwriting. The subjects were in alphabetical order. There were about fifty entries in total, a whole page dedicated to each man. Francie's was a man's salon. If Healy's hair sample belonged to a woman, they were fucked.

Coleman, now of course bald, had been a customer. His hair, stuck crudely onto the page with Sellotape, was fair and the comments favourable. *Good craic. 8/10. Wouldn't like to cross him*. Although Philip was pessimistic about the value of his document, he admired Healy's perseverance.

First thing the next morning, after a rasher sandwich with lashings of ketchup, he passed it on to his indefatigable maharishi.

Between thought and expression

Kevin, after a quick call to an old friend in Forensics, decided to personally courier the tonsorial cache, and the possible identity of Sandra's killer, to her office in the Phoenix Park. There, after an interminable pause during which she seemed to smoke a whole cigarette, reminding Kevin of the Lou Reed line '*between thought and expression lies a lifetime*', she said, 'I'm very busy, Kevin.'

Very busy smoking cigarettes! Somewhat perversely, he'd decided to bring his grandson Paul along for the spin. It was partly for the company. The baby was now a good sixteen months old and better company than most people. And it was partly to satisfy a long-smouldering curiosity of his own – the identity of Paul's father. As well as Philip's scrapbook, he slipped his friend, Karen, a little freezer bag. It contained a few hairs he'd clipped from the boy's head for DNA testing, on the off-chance that Paul's father numbered amongst the late barber's customers. Kevin's faith in technology was infinite for a man of his age.

Karen laughed and lit up again, her interest aroused. This was more like it. Karen had her own pet ambition – to undertake mass DNA testing in small towns. She was concerned that too many children didn't know who their fathers were and, more to the point, that it was the same few studs fathering *all* the children, the consequences for the gene pool and the future health of the nation – and the midlands in particular – be damned. Kevin thought he'd never get out of there.

He could, of course, have just taken the boy's hair to Dublin and not the whole boy, but he knew that Ciara and Sheila would be delighted with the break. It would please Ciara no end to see to her father enjoying life's simple pleasures again, inter-generational excursions and the like. What he would do with the information – the name of Paul's dad – if Karen gave her lungs a break for a few minutes and got her act together was anybody's guess.

Before he left, Karen warned him that it might be a few days before they'd have any results. Kevin felt disappointed. Usually such a realist, he had convinced himself en route that he'd only have to wait an hour or two at most, given the importance of the mission. That would have given him enough time to visit the nearby zoological gardens with Paul and treat themselves to an ice cream and maybe an illicit plate of chips, his dietary regime, of late, being the least of his worries. But, as Karen pointed out, due to the sheer number of murders in the capital – an average of one a day at this stage – he'd have to be patient. A bag containing bits and pieces of a bodybuilder found crushed in the back of a bin lorry arrived at that very moment, as if to underline her point.

Paul enjoyed the zoo, although a lot of the animals seemed to be absent. Dead, Kevin mused, possibly murdered, knowing Dublin.

With temperatures plummeting to record lows, and the roads in danger of freezing over, he set out for home. He drove slowly, taking the M1 for safety. He had gotten as far as the airport when his phone rang. It was Karen, who'd skipped lunch and tea because she was sufficiently amused by the novelty of Philip's scrapbook. The gist of it was that she'd run a few tests. A laconic lady, at the best of times, Karen paused for effect. Kevin pulled into the hard shoulder, a passing council lorry spraying his car with grit.

'I think we might have a result.'

On hearing those few words, he closed his eyes and did something he hadn't done for a long time. He thanked God. Without elaborating further, for reasons of strict confidentiality, Karen suggested that if it was convenient for him to do so, he should drive straight over to the Park. There, she would deliver the news face to face. He told her that it was convenient to do so. Mind you, he wasn't a hundred per cent sure if the result in question referred to Sandra's killer or Paul's father.

On his way to the Park, a journey that took him ages, and it rush hour, and it slippy underfoot, and he extra careful, he called Ciara. He told her that Paul was fine, which was the truth, and that they'd be home in a few hours, which wasn't strictly speaking true. He then phoned Philip, who was with Joanne at the time. Next on his list was Peter Keating, upon whom he also impressed the urgency of the situation. He invited them all to join him at the lab at Garda HQ to share the news.

Philip's new hat

While Kevin was making his way towards Dublin – ostensibly, as far as his family was concerned, to buy himself a new coat, a Kraftwerk CD impelling him beyond the comfort of the speed limit – Philip was meeting Joanne for a coffee in the lobby of the Cunningham Arms.

'What's the story, Joanne?' he whispered, the reverence for hush in small-town hotel lobbies non-negotiable, the four or five tables spaced well apart, the various huddles and confabs more than likely concerning matters that skirted legality at best.

'Dreck,' she complained, pushing her cup to one side, her coat and voluminous grey cardigan softening her on what was an icy-cold morning in Tullyanna.

'You look like a woman who sells pottery.'

There was a German-style Christmas market in full swing outside, taking up half the street and the one small car park in the town, on the Market Square, at a time of the year when extra parking spaces were needed, if anything – a clear example of globalization gone too far, in his opinion, and him being what's known as a grinch, the attraction of shopping in temporary wooden huts with fake snow on top of them being a mystery to him, tat surely being tat whether purchased indoors or out, and fondue, as the whole of Europe had learned to their cost in the seventies, being a shocking waste of good cheese.

'I got you this.'

Joanne – her apparent transitioning to Earth mother a slight concern – presented him with a knitted hat, Faroese by the looks of things, and it complete with bobble and earflaps and garish wintry motifs.

'In case you're mistaken for a neo-Nazi,' she explained, pointing at his shaven head.

The key belonged to a sturdy ABUS lock. He had worked that much out himself – the word ABUS was engraved on the key.

'No flies on me.'

The lock possibly belonged to Lonergan as per the coat of arms. The key, Joanne told him, had been sent anonymously to her at the *Chronicle*, obviously by someone who wasn't aware of her current job status. Her old colleague, Welly, had dropped it out to her, at her parents' house in Drumahair.

Joanne paid the bill. They wrapped up and headed for the grave-yard.

'I don't understand. Who gave you the key?'

'I don't know, Philip. I actually think it might even be Coleman.'

'Coleman? Are ya mad?'

'He has the most to lose. If Lonergan is the killer, for the sake of argument, then it makes sense. Coleman would know that and give him up to save his own skin.'

'Do they not come as a package?'

'Yeah, but even so, even if Coleman *is* responsible for Sandra's death, he'd still want to *pin* it on somebody else. Lonergan.'

'You've it all worked out.'

'I had a lot of time to myself.'

They walked up the Main Street, neither of them hiding. Gerry Connolly, Dove's father, was hacking ice from the footpath in front of his shop. He put down the spade and made a point of shaking Philip's hand.

'Thank you, Philip, for all you've done.'

And then he turned to Joanne.

'And as for you Miss McCollum, I underestimated you. Both Dee and I were very moved by the article in *Howarya!*'

And with that, Gerry shook her hand and went back to his business.

'You *moved* Gerry. There's a first!'

Defying Carson's dire prediction about the end of her career, the old reliable *Howarya!*, the voice of the dispossessed, had just published an extended piece about the case. Using a lot of Philip's account, with his blessing, together with her own and Kevin's findings, she had substantially revised the story she'd written eight years earlier. In it, she'd painted sympathetic portraits of Sandra and Dove. She'd rehabilitated Tommy Courtney's reputation. And left a lot of open questions relating to Lonergan, Coleman, *et al.*

'It might have been somebody who read *Howarya!*,' Philip suggested, 'if it wasn't Coleman. Or somebody who was at the press conference?'

'The main thing. We have the key.'

They turned into Church Street. There was a lengthy queue outside the butcher's. Macker was crossing the road, a turkey in one hand, a ham in the other.

'Well, Macker.'

'Philip. Joanne.'

'Congratulations on the result.'

'Thanks.'

'I'm sure Fergal will do a great job.'

'We'll see. Nice to get the mention in *Howarya!*, Joanne.'

'My pleasure. Wouldn't want you to feel left out.'

'My father was very happy. Anyway, delighted you found Sandra. Hope you find who killed her. If there's anything I can do to help, let me know. I mean that. Happy Christmas.'

Philip watched his old friend get into an Audi, two toddlers on their iPads in the back of the car. He turned to Joanne.

'It could have been Macker. He was always an operator. By the way, why did you give the key to me? And not to Keating?'

'I did give it to Keating! You don't think I gave it to you by choice?'

She explained. Keating agreed with Joanne that the source of the evidence was somebody close to Lonergan, somebody within the movement, a snitch, presumably, with an itch to scratch. The Organization, growing at pace, was obviously a victim of its own success. The compromises it had made – even if it was just window dressing – in achieving respectability were seen as a betrayal in some quarters.

Lorcan Lonergan, according to Keating, had been under constant surveillance for the past ten years or more. But being a meticulous man – in all matters bar personal hygiene – he gave little away. Not wishing to alarm the suspect – and him a player – the gardaí had kept their distance. In the past few days, however, now that he was spending a lot of time in Dublin as a member of the Party's negotiating team, Keating had, thanks to Joanne's production of the key, searched Lonergan's home.

'Daring for him.'

'And illegal. He didn't have warrants.'

'Fair play to Keating.'

'They even went to Lonergan's place of work. A refrigeration plant near Louth village.'

'What was he? The ice?'

'They didn't find anything. The all-important ABUS contraption.'

The thinking was, based on the garda profile of Lonergan built up over many years, that he was something of an enforcer within the Organization. Not only that, he was something of an *archivist*. He had 'the goods' on everybody and, as such, was uniquely able to maintain discipline among the ranks. That was the thinking, for what it was worth, in the cold case unit assigned to the Sandra Mohan murder. But Keating couldn't afford to take any more chances until the political situation had been resolved.

'He had to think of his career. He told me to give the key to you.'

'Keating, ha!'

'He thought you and Healy, with your stubborn ways and your long-standing grudges and your familiarity with the case, might fare better.'

'Right.'

'It's not because I like you.'

'Didn't think that for a minute.'

They reached the graveyard, a tranquil setting on a gentle slope leading down to a lake. As she passed the headstones, Joanne recited the names of the dead, relying on the inscriptions to imagine the lives they'd led. Not far from where Dove was interred, they found Sandra's grave, still awaiting a headstone. On the mound of clay above her remains were scattered dozens of little figurines made with pipe cleaners, some of people, men and women in various poses, and some of animals, dogs and horses and a unicorn.

Although neither of them was what you might call religious, both Joanne and Philip recited, in their own language, a prayer. Philip's phone couldn't have rung at a worse time. It was Healy, exhorting him to get his skates on and make his way pronto to the Phoenix Park.

'And Joanne?'

Joanne looked at him expectantly. He put away his phone.

'They have a match for the hair.'

The hair of the dog

'Just like old times, ha?' said Kevin, his nose dripping, colourful lasers lighting up the city below as it neared peak festivity.

Keating didn't reply. They were waiting at the barrier outside HQ, the pair of them hopping from foot to foot to keep warm, baby Paul asleep inside, minded by a doting desk sergeant, when Joanne and Philip finally arrived in her groaning Toyota.

'The traffic was mental,' says she.

'No harm done.'

The four of them trooped inside, Keating leading the way to the forensics lab. Nobody passed any remarks of the gurgling baby.

Karen took a long drag of her cigarette and let it rest in an ashtray. She took a sip of sherry and removed her lab coat, drawing out the suspense for all it was worth. A sort of perk of the job, Kevin supposed. She deserved her big moment.

'Who was it, Karen? Give us a name.'

She looked at each of them in turn before announcing gravely, 'Charlie O'Dowd. It was Charlie.'

It's fair to say that everybody present in Karen's office – more of a prefab, really – gasped. It was a proper, noisy, involuntary, collective gasp. Even baby Paul gasped.

'Charlie O'Fucking Dowd,' spat Philip.

The news wasn't what anybody was expecting. Nor, in hindsight, was it a complete surprise.

It's amazing, thought Kevin, how quickly one adjusts, how one comes to terms with a new reality. He recalled a Christmas long ago, on the busiest shopping day of the year, when he and his mother took the bus to Dublin. On Henry Street, he – dressed in a fake leather coat with a faux-fur collar, looking like a little mini-tsar – let go of his mother's hand to look at football boots in a shop window. When he turned around, she was gone, swallowed up in the throng of shoppers. He was upset but didn't cry. He loved his mother but, ever the pragmatist, his first thought was, *I'll probably never see Mammy again*, quickly followed by a second thought, *I better go and find a new mammy*. A kindly woman took him by the hand. *She'll do*, he rationalized, *she smells nice*, and he started to imagine a new life in somewhere like Howth, with brothers and sisters and no milking to be done. About ten minutes later he was reunited with his mother, and her distraught, in the company of a big, strapping garda sergeant who made his mother laugh and gave him a pound. That was when he decided he was going to be a guard. The new reality now was that Charlie O'Dowd, thanks to his hair, was firmly in the frame for the murder of Sandra Mohan. Where this development left Fergal Coleman, it was too early to say.

'Charlie Jaysus O'Dowd,' whistled Kevin.

Joanne wrote down the name in a notebook, although it was hard to imagine she was ever going to forget it. They all conferred for a few minutes, sipping sherry and hot chocolate, the only tipples on offer in that particular parish. They tried to piece together what they knew about O'Dowd and his relationship to the victim.

'Doesn't smell right,' said Philip, 'he's a lightweight.'

Philip's impression of O'Dowd was that he was always a wannabe, all mouth and curling lip, on the edge of things, egging others on. An electrician by trade, he had refused to speak to Joanne for her original article. Healy had interviewed him a number of times, both in the station and in his car, and although he was never fooled by the innocent act he put on, he'd never taken him too seriously. Charlie, although he was a joyrider in his youth, had no previous convictions. Keating, getting twitchy, whipped out his phone and ordered the underling who took the call to immediately arrest the suspect.

'Actually, forget it, Seán. I'll do it myself,' he said, having a sudden premonition of the next day's headlines.

Mr Bravado hung up and called the Emergency Response Unit, requesting their immediate assistance in Tullyanna, and flew out the door.

'Sorry guys, gotta go,' said the beanpole, without as much as a thank you, his Mac flapping in his wake.

'Like a bat out of hell, ha!' said Healy.

'Prick,' said Philip.

'Bit of an eejit?' asked Karen, nodding towards the door.

Kevin nodded in response, rocking the buggy and shushing wee Paul, who was getting restless, very ratty, in fact, now at the way the day was going, a fierce temper on him, not unlike his mother, it had to be said, or his grandmother, although he felt bad for thinking it.

Meanwhile, Philip, who'd known Charlie all too well, opened his scrapbook on the relevant page. From the vantage point of an innocent collector of freshly cut hair, Charlie was described as '*A show-off, thinks he's great*'. But he still managed a score of 6/10, the young and impressionable Sharkey's standards having been a good deal lower in those days. By way of a PS, Philip had added, and indeed underlined, the following, '*Never passes the ball!*', which was, in hindsight, as good an indication of poor character/borderline sociopathy as you could get. It was ironic that a strand of O'Dowd's hair – his barnet being his pride and joy, then as it was now – should bring about his downfall. In fairness, it was a good thick head of hair by any standards.

Charlie, all his hair still in the correct follicles, had been there, in JJ's bar, on the fateful night. He'd been chatting with Philip and Sandra and Dove shortly after the Evel Knievel lookalike did his party piece on the Main Street. '*A con job*', according to Charlie, who saw conspiracy and deceit everywhere, the wire being thick, the wheels of the bike being tyre-less and deeply grooved, a pole with a sequinned dolly-bird on either end providing the counterweights. Later, Philip remembered, they had argued about the respective merits of Judo and Ju-Jitsu, O'Dowd advocating the latter, sneering at Philip's martial art of choice. He further recalled Charlie approaching him on the dance floor at Shadows and instructing him to tell the guards that Coleman gave Sandra a lift to the nightclub. Philip knew better than to question

Coleman's schemes, assuming he needed an alibi for one of his patriotic sorties across the border. Besides, Philip was hammered at the time. And, what's more, he'd seen Sandra later on, to his cost. He couldn't recall seeing Charlie at all over the following few days.

Healy was sceptical about the whole thing. He had never liked O'Dowd. An *ubh dubh*, he called him, to coin a phrase in Irish, *a black egg*, but a killer? No. It was all too *convenient*. He turned to Karen, who was all dolled up and sherried for the evening.

'And the ehh . . .?'

'The what?'

'The other . . . the hair.'

'No, Kevin, sorry. No match.'

'Grand. Super. It's not important.'

After thanking his friend, Karen – a woman he'd met on a Garda Arabic course, a woman who was now running very late for her office Christmas party – he turned to Sharkey and McCollum.

'C'mon,' he says, pushing the buggy ahead of him towards the Megane, 'we'll head for home.'

Joanne took him aside. She pointed at the baby.

'About Paul. I can find out forya, if you like?'

Kevin, the mouth drooping, gave his assent.

The long drive home

It took Kevin and his grandson a good five hours to get home. The roads were slick, the Megane, no offence to the French, not designed for such weather conditions, at a crawl, sliding all over the shop, the baby bawling non-stop in the back, Ciara at home going up the walls. Mind you, unlike most other drivers out and about on that inhospitable night, Kevin, thanks to his sense memory, managed to steer clear of the ditches and avoid other vehicles, a navigational feat that did no harm to his self-esteem.

Meanwhile, in the Toyota, Joanne and Philip analysed the latest twist. Well, Joanne did, for Philip was deep in thought.

'I'm thinking,' said he tetchily.

What he was thinking about was Lonergan's key. Had the guards looked in Lorcan Lonergan's back garden? Was there a shed or a cellar they might have missed? Too obvious, perhaps. It was highly unlikely that Lorcan would keep anything of value at his own property, but Philip had to start somewhere. If that meant covering ground already covered by the guards, so be it. His job was to think outside the box, or, more to the point, to think inside Lonergan's box. Where would Lonergan keep stuff? According to Joanne, the obvious places had already been searched, which left just two options, (a) an incredibly obscure location or (b) in plain view. Philip was working on the assumption that Lonergan's ABUS storage unit – if not actually secreted at his home – was not far from his home, readily accessible in an emergency.

'A bit like Blofeld's mini-sub.'

'What?' said Joanne, trying to concentrate on the road.

'It's a *Bond* reference.'

Philip, obviously, wasn't privy to the man's movements and activities in recent years but did have the dubious privilege of knowing him previously, before he had been forced into exile at the point of his gun. Even then, although Philip was a peripheral figure in Coleman's circle, he couldn't say he ever knew Lonergan. Lonergan was either clever or very clever. But Philip was clever, too, backing himself in most battles of wit, with a touch of arrogance perhaps, in everything from the *Who Wants to Be a Millionaire?* game in a Melbourne pub to a fight to the death on White Island. He racked his brains, trying to recall every time he ever encountered Lonergan and, more importantly, where the encounter took place.

* * *

By the time Joanne and Kevin reconvened the following evening in Tullyanna, O'Dowd was in custody. He was cooperating, by all accounts. Keating popped into the Cunningham Arms, wearing his best puce-coloured shirt, the sleeves rolled up, with a salmon pink jumper hanging around his neck like a congratulatory garland.

That's where his muse, Joanne, and his old mucker, Kevin, found him, and he holding court surrounded by senior members of An Garda. As for Philip, after Joanne dropped him home the previous evening, nobody had seen him since.

In the hotel bar, in a typically grand gesture, Mr Keating bought Kevin a drink. He was loudly advising caution for all to hear.

'It's very important we don't get carried away.'

If Kevin, that most circumspect of plodders, was annoyed, he didn't show it. Rather, he made approving noises at the right times and smiled politely, going so far as to congratulate the glory-chasing goal-hanger on making the arrest. Mind you, he was grateful to be taken into Keating's confidence.

Keating filled them in. He kept looking around to make sure nobody outside the circle was listening. So far, it seemed, a contrite O'Dowd had confessed to a *limited* role in Sandra's death. When presented with the evidence, he told his interrogators what had happened.

'So,' Keating whispered, 'apparently, Lorcan Lonergan called to O'Dowd's house at about half nine on the Sunday morning, we're talking 19 June 1994. Kevin?'

'Aye, it would have been the nineteenth.' Kevin was quite chuffed that Keating picked his brains in front of the brass. He didn't have to.

'He told him, "straight out, no messing", they were going fishing and they needed to borrow his father's van. His father, according to O'Dowd, and I believe him, had no interest in politics.'

'True,' agreed Kevin, who knew the father as a gent. As if Sandra's foul murder had anything to do with politics.

'Yeah. He was blameless. Anyway, Charlie and Lonergan packed the rods and the waders into the HiAce and drove out the Dundalk Road, right. At the old school there, approximately four miles from the town, he was told to stop. You know the place.'

They all nodded. It was a derelict, one-roomed national school.

'From behind the school emerged a girl. It was Sandra. She joined them in the van, as previously arranged. She was a bit out of it, he says, but in good form all the same. They drove on a few miles. O'Dowd was saying there was a show called *Sunday Miscellany* on the radio. Apparently Lonergan loved it.'

Kevin reddened at the mention of the long-running RTÉ series. Each episode comprised a number of sentimental short stories, read aloud, in earnest tones, by writers, none of whom were household names. It was a show deeply imbued with the gloom and lassitude of Sunday mornings. The stories, separated by tasteful musical interludes, generally began with the line, '*I remember my father, thumping the table, and exclaiming, by God, Dev is dead!*' Kevin was surprised to learn that Lonergan was a fan, the man, despite in all likelihood being a terrorist mastermind, rising slightly in his estimation. Kevin, blinking away tears, was embarrassed because he had submitted, on more than one occasion, stories of his own, none of which was ever accepted.

Keating went on, his audience rapt.

'They drove for a few miles in the direction of Hallcross, until they came to a quiet spot by the Fane River. There, they rendezvoused with Fergal Coleman. Sandra literally jumped into his arms. So he says. Coleman showed her the picnic he had obviously promised – bottles of beer and a few packets of Onion Rings in a plastic bag and so on. I have it all written down. Fergal, according to Charlie, didn't waste any time. Now, look, I don't need to tell you this is absolutely confidential, and it's not pleasant.'

He was looking at Joanne as he said it, thinking himself chivalrous, giving her an opportunity to withdraw from their tight circle if she didn't want to hear any more. If Joanne was offended, nobody would have noticed.

'So, Coleman. Well, look, he injected her with heroin.'

'Fuck,' said Superintendent Hynes, his perfectly manicured eyebrows twitching.

'We have only O'Dowd's word to go on. She was a willing recipient, he says. A double or triple dose, for all he knew. Coleman then placed a plastic bag over her head and told Charlie to pin her down while she, presumably, fought for her life.

Joanne felt sick, her darkest fears being realized. Kevin caught her eye.

'Charlie objected, in the strongest possible terms, to Coleman's instructions, but had no choice except to comply. Even then, rolling around on top of her – although he knew it was wrong – he didn't think they were actually trying to kill her. It was more like they were trying to frighten her. I asked him about the hair. He thought about it for a while. And he says, at some point, Sandra must have got a hold of his hair. Despite her slight size and the anaesthetic, you know, the anaesthetic effect of the opiates and, I suppose you could say, the handicap of having two grown men on top of her, she didn't let go. Charlie conceded that he'd had to actually break her fingers in order to prise them away from his beloved hair. Anyway, the struggle continued for some time, according to Charlie, because, the fucking cheek of him, excuse the language, he wasn't trying too hard to hurt her. At one stage he even stopped to give her a drink. Now. He couldn't remember all the details but, eventually, she was lifeless on the ground.'

There was silence in the room apart from some logs hissing in the fireplace. Even the logs were distressed. Keating hesitated for a moment, aware of the effect the graphic and harrowing nature of his story was having on his audience.

'Then he said a very strange and very disturbing thing. There's no nice way of putting it. He said that Coleman *didn't* urinate on her body. On Sandra. He stressed that. Apparently, that was a Coleman thing, pissing on people. In O'Dowd's mind, that was out of respect for Sandra.'

'Fuck sake. What sort of people?'

'Exactly. Anyway. After placing Sandra's body in the van, Lonergan drove off, leaving Charlie and Coleman by the river for a couple of hours. They did actually spend the time fishing. As if nothing was amiss. Coleman caught a few trout. Being the compassionate sort, he threw them back in.'

Keating, demonstrating that the irony was not lost on him, made a big show of disgust at this part of the plot.

'Hours later, Lonergan returned with the van, which by then had been thoroughly cleaned. Putting two and two together, he, O'Dowd, surmised that Sandra's body had been stored somewhere nearby, before being moved at a later date, possibly more than once, over the years, who knows, to her final resting place on White Island where, as we know, Kevin found her.'

The Superintendent patted Kevin on the back.

'The main thing, O'Dowd maintains, is that Coleman killed her. Coleman, not him. Of course, there's no doubt Charlie, with the girl's blood on his hands, knows the score. I didn't get into all the detail as of yet, but it looks like he was initiated into the brotherhood, shall we say, at a young age. They left him alone for a couple of years, which suited him down to the ground. But he was theirs. He knew that. And he knew they'd come calling again.'

Keating paused and turned to Kevin.

'Kevin, this isn't easy. O'Dowd admitted to being the getaway driver at the Blackhill post office robbery. I think he was trying to ingratiate himself. He didn't have to tell us.'

O'Dowd knows who shot me, thought Kevin, his glass of unasked-for Chardonnay going warm. *Mind you, half the town probably knows*, he mused, the old paranoia surfacing for a second, not helped by everyone looking at him with pity. There was certainly enough there, you would think, to charge Coleman and Lonergan.

Kevin was tired. His head was in a spin, regurgitating all that he'd overheard. Onion Rings, *Sunday Miscellany*, trout. Profoundly sad, he sat down at a table on his own. He was almost crushed by the weight of it all. There was no sense of victory to be had or, God forbid, notions of vindication.

'Excellent work, Peter,' said the Super.

'I better get back to the station.'

Joanne joined Kevin and, for a long time, in silence, they looked into the fire.

The pipes, the pipes are calling

While the endgame – if that's what you'd call it, as if the game ever ends – was being engineered in the Cunningham Arms, Philip, his new bobble hat on his head, found himself in the less formal surroundings of JJ's bar, atop a high stool. There was just a Latvian barman with a gammy eye and a few hardcore Latvian drinkers for company. Philip had always got on well with Latvians, but this particular party was unruly.

Never an overly popular pub, JJ's, it was still a surprise to find it so empty and Christmas fast approaching. He ignored the patrons, two drunk men and a drunk woman, and they ignored him. It was hard to tell who or what the barman was looking at, given the peculiar roving disposition of his bad eye. Philip was in no rush, now that he'd more or less forgiven himself for all his indiscretions, petty and otherwise, over the years. The whiskey helped to absolve him. A reliable sealant for the leaky soul. There was very little in the way of tinsel or holly in the bar to herald the birth of Christ, or Santa's imminent arrival, or his own rebirth as a saint. Nor indeed, he thought, appraising the premises with a handyman's eye, was there much in the way of fixtures and fittings to acknowledge the advent of the twenty-first century.

There were only three taps, Guinness, Smithwick's, and Harp, the same choice you had fifteen years ago when you crossed JJ's threshold to sample your first ever pint. Apart from the piped music – The Pogues, 'A Rainy Night in Soho' – providing a bit of consolation, it was a dreary *mise-en-scène* by any standards. It was as if the publican, whoever that might be – and Philip had his own ideas about that – didn't *want* to attract a trade.

He didn't like the way the men were behaving towards the woman. It was unsavoury, and them making faces behind her back, and making lewd suggestions in their native tongue, Latvian or was it Russian, not that she seemed to mind the attention one bit. Who was he to judge? Given the season that was in it, he wished the threesome well, although he wasn't going to bank on their evening being a runaway success. Surely, he contemplated on their behalf, Christmas in Riga could, in no way, be as grim as Christmas in Tullyanna? Of course, Philip wasn't in JJ's for the goodness of his health or moral edification. Or in search of festive cheer.

When, finally, the rolling maul vacated the premises, it was Philip who bolted the door behind them, and Philip who wrested the baseball bat from the barman – a man by the name of Maris Kalnins – who'd crept up behind him.

'No trouble, boss. It's Christmas,' said he.

'Well then don't be threatening me with a baseball bat,' said Philip reasonably, thoroughly fed-up of violence but still, in the interests of self-preservation, raising the weapon above his head.

'I go home now, I go.'

The man, not turning his back to Philip for a moment, unbolted the door and reversed out into the snow. Snow? It was a blizzard by now. Maris, wearing only a T-shirt, was not in the least put out. He couldn't believe that his head was still in the one piece, all the features intact, apart from the gammy eye, of course, which first went south, or so he'd claimed in an earlier chat, when a Russian army plane in which he was travelling hit an air pocket above the North Sea and plummeted many thousands of feet. Philip, alone now, but still a little irate, smashed an old mirror advertising Bass and instantly felt better, never having been a fan of that particular ale.

With the place to himself and the night stretching out nicely before him, Philip proceeded to take the pub apart at his leisure. He had formed the opinion, rightly or wrongly, that JJ's, although only two doors down from the garda station, was as likely a place as any to find what he was looking for. Not that he knew exactly what he was looking for. It was a hangout of Lonergan's for as long as anybody could remember. The memory of Lonergan calling the shots the night they battered him black and blue only added conviction to his notion that this was no mere watering hole.

With a variety of screwdrivers he'd retrieved from a toolbox under the bar, he dismantled the pool table. Beneath the playing surface he found the balls, as you would expect. All of them bar the number seven stripe. He also found less expected items, things that were alien to the game. There was what looked like an engagement ring, some coins and a blackcurrant Chewit. And in a cordoned-off corner of the ball-pen itself he found various packages wrapped in clingfilm. When he removed the side panels, he found a number of similar packets taped to the inside.

JJ's wasn't exactly the Iraq Museum, and he wasn't the US army, but he felt bad all the same for desecrating such an antiquity. It was on that very table that he had learned the hustler tricks that had stood him in good stead in bar-room standoffs round the world. That said, it was high time JJ's had a makeover. And he was relieved to find something for his efforts. He was happy that his hunch was right, that his exertions in removing 450 pounds of slate with a dodgy arm had paid off in some way.

However, upon opening the packages, he was disappointed to discover nothing more incriminating than pills. There were thousands upon thousands of ecstasy tablets and methamphetamine-type narcotics, or so he assumed – not being an expert himself – given the playful logos, frogs and the like, with which they were stamped. It was not nothing. Whether it would be enough to indict characters as slippery as Lonergan or Coleman was another question, and him not knowing that O'Dowd had – by this time – already thrown them under the bus.

With a chisel, he prised away the skirting boards from the walls of the dimly lit annex, his way guided by only a single 40-watt bulb dangling naked over the pool table. Playing pool to the extent that he did in his youth, and in such a disreputable place, was either the most colossally stupid waste of his time or the best possible use of his time. He could never figure out which. What did he learn at the pool table? And what would he have learned elsewhere? It was a huge waste of his time trying to figure out such an ineffable conundrum. While planning his latest escapade, it had occurred to him that security in JJ's was lax despite the pub being – at the very least – a stash-house, if not an actual money-laundering asset belonging to former paramilitaries. He might have been wrong about that.

It wasn't a huge pub and it didn't take him long to complete his search of the pool room, or even the main bar. It must have been two o'clock when he opened the trap door on the floor behind the bar and descended the stairs to the basement. He switched on the light. Philip was impressed. The area was bigger than he had imagined possible, and well-kept too. It was neater than the bar above. In one corner, there was the remains of an old micro-brewery. It was with some reluctance, and he a traditionalist at heart, as well as a connoisseur of bottled beer, that he began to pull apart the historic plumbing. There was nothing of interest in the mash tun, no documents or photographs stored in the copper tank, and nought of note secreted in the various pumps and valves of the rusting equipment. A one-time home-brewer himself, he could imagine one day restoring the mini-plant and manufacturing his own beer, and not telling anybody about it, and just sitting down here on his own, drinking away to his heart's content until he died. It was important to have goals.

There were a few old wooden lockers along the wall, salvaged, you would imagine, from a school. Philip tried the key on each of them. Mind you, all of them were bashed and perfectly openable without a key. In one of them, there was a white puffa jacket that he presumed belonged to the barman. He found nothing in the pockets except some chewing gum and a set of house-keys and a sock with a pool ball in it. Number seven stripe. Maybe it was time to go.

Philip was fairly philosophical about his failure to find anything more specific to nail Lonergan or Coleman in relation to Sandra's murder. Searching JJ's was, he admitted, a far-fetched idea to begin with. Still, the haul of drugs would be an embarrassment at least. And perhaps Joanne could look into the ownership of the bar.

He was about to abandon the mission for the night and go and look for Joanne when, suddenly, he heard a clanging noise above him. Looking up, he saw a horizontal metal door, double-doors that opened out on to the footpath. Ever since he was a child, he'd been afraid to step on such portals himself, for fear they'd give way and he'd fall to his death on a basement floor. Somebody stepped on it again. The pedestrian, whoever he was, was clearly braver than Philip. He started to jump up and down on the door, defying the odds and/or the gods, in what was probably a crazed pursuit of 'the craic'. Or maybe it was a not so subtle attempt to give Philip a warning. Or maybe somebody was about to deliver new barrels. Either way, it was probably time to go.

But something held Philip back. He wasn't ready yet and he didn't know why. He looked around the room again. A hemp cushion lay directly underneath the steel hatch. It was there, presumably, to bear the brunt of the barrels as they landed on the floor. There were about forty steel barrels standing in storage, four of them attached to plastic pipes. Philip was reminded of the story of Ali Baba and the forty thieves. He instinctively kicked a few of the barrels, not managing to disturb any lurking thieves or sleeping *djinns*.

Thirsty after all his hard work, Philip ascended the stairs and poured himself a pint of Guinness. Something wasn't right. He was getting the yips. Where was Healy when he needed him? As a young footballer, Philip's spatial awareness was good. He once overheard a selector for the county minors saying that his spatial awareness was *'uncanny'*. His ability to bring others into play was second to none. As a labourer and, later, a foreman on sites around the world, in zones temperate and tropical, in places prone to earthquake and mudslide and other geological uncertainties, his hawk eye was a thing of legend. It was relied upon by engineers with better qualifications than him, and better instruments too.

While he waited for the pint to settle, he went downstairs again. Yes. As he suspected, the area of the basement was greater in square footage than the total area of the floor above – the bar and pool room and jacks combined. That could mean nothing, or it could mean something. Furthermore, four of the beer barrels were rigged to pipes yet, as he recalled, there were only three taps in the bar. If there was one thing Philip excelled at as well as physics, it was maths. He followed the pipes up the wall. Three of them, bunched together with plastic ties, disappeared into where he quickly calculated the bar was situated. The fourth pipe diverged away to the left towards, it had to be, the jacks!

After bounding up the stairs, he paused, took a quick sip of the stout, and then stepped into the men's toilets to test out his theory. It hadn't changed much. The old porcelain ditch was still there, along one wall, but was no longer in use. It was usurped by a stainless-steel bucket full of lurid yellow macaroons of eye-watering disinfectant. Opposite the piss-pot there were two cubicles. Both were heavily graffitied and without locks. And both toilet bowls, bereft of seats, were, per the usual small-town custom, stuffed full of bog roll.

One thing was certain. There were no secret compartments behind the cubicles or Narnian-type gateways to another world. More prom-isingly, though, in Philip's mind, and he in full *Hardy Boys* mode by now, there was a door to a cleaning cupboard. It was a fairly redundant cleaning cupboard, it being clear that cleaning wasn't a priority. Philip took the mysterious Lonergan key from his pocket and tried it in the lock. It didn't fit. Oh well. He was considering forcing the door with his good shoulder when he heard a commotion out in the bar. That's it, he thought, not without relief, there goes the plan to screw Coleman once and for all. There goes all his plans, probably.

He left the jacks stoically to be confronted by the barman, Maris, and two other sailors, stocky men well-salted by the Baltic Sea, all of them armed and in a position to inflict pain.

'No trouble, boss. We just want our stuff.'

Philip, calmly fondling the number seven ball, still wrapped in the sock, that he'd slipped into his trouser pocket as a precaution, was slightly surprised at the respect shown to him by the Latvians. He was assuming that they were assuming that he was one of Coleman's crew. He smiled. How quickly the world turns? He figured out that *they* had just figured out that their little arrangement with the local *mafiosi* had been unilaterally terminated. As far as they were concerned, the 'lease' of the pub – legally binding or not – was up, and the licence to deal – illegal and only within their own community – had been abruptly revoked. That was plain enough to these plain men. Philip speculated furiously while they went about their business. These hardcore realists, he decided, had provided a buffer, a layer of migrant fat, a front, for want of a better word, for the real owners of the bar.

More importantly, they had maintained a silence *vis-à-vis* the comings and goings of Lonergan and his men, a silence not enforced by fear but borne out of genuine ignorance and disinterest in the neo-Republican cause. There was no danger whatsoever that curiosity would get the better of those fellows. The likes of Maris were old enough to have lived in the Soviet Union and to have served in the Russian army and were well-trained in the arts of inscrutability and looking the other way. Maris recognized *Power* when it walked into a room and knew to cower accordingly.

Oddly, the men didn't bother with the pool room or the contents of the disemboweled pool table. Maybe they were in a hurry. Maybe it was more trouble than it was worth, or maybe it wasn't theirs. Once they'd gathered up their 'stuff' – clothes, money from the safe, and as many bottles of spirits as they could carry away – they wished Philip a *Happy Christmas* and left the pub.

Joanne spills the coffee

The callow Garda O'Loinsigh had been on foot patrol – no mean feat in the icy conditions – that night when he spotted Maris and his pals breaking into the pub at about three in the morning. He radioed for back-up. Obviously, he could have walked the approximately five yards to the Garda station for help, but being the diligent young officer he was, he wanted to keep his eyes on the prize. He was soon joined by two other uniforms and a bleary-eyed Detective Sergeant Peter Keating.

'Hit me! What's the score?'

O'Loinsigh brought his superior up to speed and personally arrested the intruders when they emerged from the premises.

'Good man, what's your name again?'

'O'Loinsigh, sir.'

'Good work. I'll keep an eye out for you. Here, leave the big moody lad alone.'

The youthful officer of course recognized Philip and removed his handcuffs. A short while later, alerted to the incident, the former detective Mr Kevin Healy *and* the former journalist Joanne McCollum turned up. It was all very unethical in O'Loinsigh's opinion, but who was he to argue with Keating?

Keating ordered one of the uniforms to run back to the station and get gloves. The other one, he ordered to stay outside and call for help immediately if she noticed any suspicious activity.

'Anything at all. A fucking . . . fox. Anything.'

332

You could tell he was nervous. Philip outlined his thinking about the possibility of there being a secret room and led them to the cleaning cupboard.

Keating was sceptical.

'Lonergan's a careful man.'

But Kevin, utilizing the theodolite in his head, figured there must be *something* behind the door. They couldn't find a key to fit and sent the fella who'd just brought the gloves to go and look for a drill. Within minutes, Philip had the door open. It was just a cubby-hole, full of mops and buckets, cans of bleach and old rags

'You see?' said Keating. 'Nice try, Philip. Right, fuck this for a game of soldiers, what we need now is some serious kip.'

'Wait!' said Joanne, pointing at the back wall. 'Look! There's a gap there between the top of the wall and the ceiling, do you see it? An inch or two, is that usual?'

'Plasterboard,' says Philip, rapping his knuckles on the back wall. He, balancing on an old tin of paint, ran his fingers along the top of the panel. 'Hooks. The fucking thing is hanging on hooks.'

'Take it down,' said Keating.

Philip gave him a baleful look. What did he think he was doing? Joanne smiled. He eased the false wall off the hooks and placed it to one side.

'Jaze,' exclaimed Kevin.

'Fuck me,' said Keating, staring at a steel door.

'You see?' said Philip, with just a hint of sarcasm.

It should go without saying that JJ's had been raided more often than any other pub in the town, for all sorts of reasons – its history, its clientele, and, to be harsh, the sheer laziness of the gardaí next door who'd be afraid of missing the second half of a Champions League game if they ventured much further afield. Nobody had ever suspected such a room existed. Unfortunately, Philip's key didn't open it.

Keating, reasserting his leadership, on the one hand, and undermining it, on the other, called Dundalk for the assistance of a specialist unit.

'You'd want to get a warrant, too,' suggested Kevin.

'I was about to fucking do that, Kevin. I am actually still a guard, you know, no offence.'

'No need for that, Peter. We're all in this together,' said Joanne.

Keating was rattled.

'Sorry. Could be anything in there. We're as well off waiting for Dundalk.'

Within the hour, they had the warrant. The specialist unit arrived with their specialist welding equipment along with some tedious specialist unit banter, all *stand back, girls* and this sort of craic. With some difficulty, they torched open the six-inch-thick door.

Joanne, Philip, and Kevin exchanged a series of looks, all the various permutations between them represented, a psychological triangulation that helped stiffen their resolve before entering the room.

From the doorway, they could see the room was about ten foot by ten. To their right was a work surface with a fridge, a washing machine, and a sink. There was also a kettle, cold to the touch, and a catering-size tin of Maxwell House coffee. On the left stood a safe and a number of filing cabinets and cupboards. In the middle of the room, there was a table. On the table sat a lump of TNT, two kilos at a guess, a light general purpose machine gun, and a matching tripod. As well as that there was a large quantity of ammunition and some fully assembled detonators.

'Don't touch anything!' snapped Keating.

The others bit their lips.

Later, apologists for the Party would audaciously claim that these items had been *confiscated* – in the interests of public safety – from an upstart terror group. After being photographed with the munitions, Keating helped himself to a pint of Harp from a tap – connected to the fourth pipe – that had been set up in the strongroom. Healy had never seen him so nervous.

As well as the military cache, the team found bags of cash and files containing the names and addresses and car registrations of various notables, among them many gardaí and a High Court judge. The specialist unit from Dundalk wasn't able to open the safe, so Keating had to call for an even more specialist unit from Dublin.

'Better bring in the big boys, so,' he sneered, sticking the knife into Dundalk.

There was great excitement, as you can well imagine, due to the extent of the haul, and no little trepidation, as they waited for Dublin. The hubbub subsided a bit when Joanne, who'd been making herself a coffee, noticed something odd about the catering-size tin. Although it was a huge tin of coffee by any standards, it felt *heavier* than it should have. In the heel of her hunch, she upended the tin, spilling the coffee all over the counter.

'Jesus, Joanne, I told ya not to touch anything.'

They all thought she'd lost the head. She held up the empty tin, showing them the false bottom that was halfway down the container. Using a knife to lever away the top half, she soon discovered a small strongbox in the bottom half. Philip, at this point, stepped forward to open it.

Kevin beamed with pride at his protégés. They had all come a long way.

Philip turned to Healy. 'It's an ABUS alright.'

From the box, Philip removed a VHS tape and some photographs and placed them on the table. It was Healy who spotted the picture of Sandra Mohan. The air was sucked from the room. Apart from Healy, Joanne, Philip, and Keating, everybody else left the room.

The moustachioed man in some of the photos was a paramilitary commander. One of the Untouchables. He had been close to the Leadership and played a key role in selling the Peace Process to the 'army'. Now a community activist, mass-goer, and family man, the last photo Kevin had seen of him had been taken by a local paper in Belfast about two years ago. He'd been pictured at a fundraiser – minus the moustache – for a two-year-old girl in need of a heart transplant.

Joanne, all the colour gone from her face, covered up the photographs with her scarf. Philip held her hand in his.

'Why didn't she ever *say* anything?' Joanne said.

Keating slumped on a chair.

Healy knelt down on one knee to say a prayer. No prayer would come. His hotline to heaven had been well and truly disconnected.

His mind, a bird – or a drone – flew away from Lonergan's secret chamber, out of JJ's, and high above the town. He looked down in despair into all the bunkers, the nooks and crannies, into all the false walls in people's homes and the secret compartments in people's hearts. He surveyed in despair all the secret places. And all the secrets people keep. You can find the arms dumps and blow them to bits, but how the hell do you decommission the hidden caverns in people's minds? Healy was at a loss.

Apart from that one photograph of Sandra – the eye mascara running in all directions – Healy didn't see any of the other pictures that were taken in the bunker. Nor did he see the multitude of other pictures that weren't taken in the bunker. He never saw the videotape either. Or the contents of the safe. Later, he was invited, sensitively, to do so if he so wished. But he didn't want to. His heart was weak. And he didn't have the stomach for it. Of course, cops will talk. They'll make inappropriate jokes, too.

Copper in the well

Next day, Fergal Coleman presented himself at a garda station in Sandyford, county Dublin, of his own accord. Having resigned his newly won seat, he vowed to clear his name. With the avalanche of evidence – not least the testimonies of Charlie O'Dowd and Noeleen Sheriff, Sandra's diary, the postcards, and the material from Lonergan's panic room – even he would find it hard to do so. Although in this world, Kevin stroked his glabella philosophically, you could never be sure.

Joanne, using all her connections and her *mettle*, tried to visit Coleman in prison. She wanted to see his reaction when she called him a rapist and a murderer to his face. In this endeavour, she failed.

History, as you would expect, carried on regardless.

So. Sheriff was dead. O'Dowd was in custody. Macker was neither dead nor in custody. Tommy C was dead. Lonergan was missing. And Coleman was in custody, brazening it out. Well, that is to say, he *was* brazening it out, until he was found hanging in his cell at Mountjoy Those who knew him, and many who didn't, found it very hard to believe that he would do such a thing. There was talk the Organization had place-men and women everywhere, planted in garda stations up and down the country, and in schools, and government departments at every level. Countering that sensational claim, others argued it was the *deep state* itself that had infiltrated the institutions of the more *regular state* that everyone knew and loved. Either way, they said, Coleman had help. A few lone voices, not least his wife Teresa, refused to believe O'Dowd and insisted her husband had nothing whatsoever to do with Sandra's death.

Macker – who had no charges pending and, as he said himself, nothing to apologize for – was tipped to stand in the by-election called after Coleman resigned/died.

Nobody was charged with Tommy's murder.

Lonergan was never seen again, well, not in Tullyanna anyway. Legend has it that he was cursed to wander the world, Lestat-like, for the next thousand years or more. God help the other vampires, Kevin feared for their well-being, and them all shadows of their former selves, all cheekbones, moody and misunderstood, and metaphors for all sorts of minorities and misfits.

Peter 'Bad News' Keating was promoted to the rank of detective inspector, cited by the commissioner for his doggedness and, in particular, his bravery in bringing Sandra Mohan's killer to justice. Healy had to laugh. If he bore a grudge, it was just a little one.

Kevin disagreed with Joanne's idea that it was Coleman himself who sent the key implicating Lonergan. Mind you, their *folie à deux* was bound to be ruptured as the whole conspiracy crumbled and a desperate Coleman scrambled to distance himself from the fallout. No, he had his eye on Macker, one of the rising stars of the local set-up. He was not an *unelectably* squeaky-clean. He had *form*, but as one of a newer breed, he was not quite as tarnished by the past. He was also well-got in the region. Could it have been Macker who provided Dove with the address on White Island? It was a theory Kevin kept to himself. Leave the loose ends to the historians to fight over in fifty years' time. He'd done his bit.

* * *

Philip spent a few months in Tullyanna, keeping himself to himself and playing Scrabble with his mother. One day, there was a knock on the door. When he went out to answer it, there was nobody there. There was, however, a package on the doorstep. It contained Dove's graphic fiction, *Brouhaha*. Philip had two more copies made, which he presented to Kevin and Joanne. To no one's surprise, Philip didn't settle and was soon beset with the old wanderlust.

A week or so before he departed, Philip and Joanne joined Kevin at his house. Joanne pulled Kevin aside.

'I have a name.'

Kevin thought about it for a second.

'Thanks, Joanne. Sorry you went to the trouble. But it's none of my business.'

'I hear ya. Rest assured. He's not from around here.'

'That'll do.'

He brought them down to the den, where they dismantled his shrine to Sandra. They took their time, looking at the photographs, reading the bits and pieces of evidence, poring over the paraphernalia. They shared memories and stories. When they were good and ready, Philip wheeled three or four barrowloads of the material out into the garden. Kevin poured kerosene over the pile and set it alight. Their faces warming on the conflagration, they toasted Sandra with whiskey. After a while, Kevin judiciously took his leave.

* * *

'So where you off to this time?' asked Joanne.

'South America,' replied Philip.

'I'd say they really need you there?'

He ignored her teasing and, not lightly, he asked Joanne to go with him.

'Sure, I'll just get me coat.'

'I'm serious.'

Joanne, by this time, had been offered her old job back at the *Chronicle*. She levelled with Philip.

'I'd love to go, but I can't. I feel I've no choice but to stay here, where I belong. You're going to laugh, but this place has a lot going for it.'

Philip looked dubious.

'There are good people here, Philip, any amount of good people. They just need a bit of encouragement.'

'Is that what you call it? And you'll *steer* them all in the right direction?'

He was thinking of Brouhaha and the balm made from the rendered bones of the ancient elk.

'I'll do me bit. Let me know when you make it as far as the Amazon. I'll come and visit.'

'You'll bring the Tayto?'

'I promise.'

He smiled at her, relieved she'd said no. They hugged. Kevin and Sheila watched the pair of them – silhouetted by the fire – from the kitchen window.

* * *

A few days later, Kevin rounded up his immediate family – his wife Sheila, daughter Ciara, son Shane, grandson Paul – and without protest they accompanied him to St Dymphna's Well. They all crossed the stream that led to the well. The stones were fierce slippy, but they didn't lose anybody. A thin layer of ice covered the well itself. Kevin broke the ice with a stick. He handed out old two-pence pieces to each member of the party and each of them in turn threw the copper coins into the water. He didn't explain why he'd dragged his family all that way to perform the ritual – or why they were doing it in the depths of winter – because he wasn't quite sure himself.

Sheila, who knew the story of St Dymphna, probably thought it was a gesture, Christian or Pagan – it made no odds – to thank the saint for her intercession in solving the case and/or restoring her husband's sanity. Ciara and Shane assumed it was for luck. Luck had nothing to do with it. The copper in the coins purified the water. It was as simple as that. It cleansed the water of all sorts of micro-organisms, moulds and fungi and algae and bacteria, as it had done for centuries. Or maybe that was just a superstition, too? Kevin hesitated, the old self-doubt never far from the surface, before he cupped his hands and drank from the well.

His mother, during the summer months, used to put copper coins in a bag of water and hang it from the kitchen ceiling to keep the flies away. As a boy he'd stare at the bag for ages, as it twirled slowly in the breeze coming from the window. The story he was told was that the flies were afraid of the bag. The coins, magnified in the water and reflecting the sun, looked to them like the eyes of bigger insects and frightened them away.

They drove the thirty miles home. Kevin was tired, and a bit sad, but satisfied that he'd done his bit to repair relations between the living and the dead.

Ensconced in his bedroom, he put pen to paper and wrote down, in freehand, in his own idiosyncratic and idiomatic way, a little bit every day, in neither hope nor despair, his unvarnished version of events.

Quoted Materials

'Some Kinda Love', written by Lou Reed
'Are you Lonesome Tonight?', written by Turk Roy and Handman Lou
'Born to Run', written by Bruce Springsteen
'I Want to Break Free', written by John Deacon
'The Lake Isle of Innisfree', written by William Butler Yeats
'The Man Comes Around', written by Johnny Cash
The Return of the King, written by J.R.R Tolkien

Acknowledgements

I'd like to thank Conor Nagle at HarperCollins Ireland for taking a chance on this enterprise. His ambition for the book matched my own. Not for a moment fooled by his charming manner, I was all too aware of his sharp mind and firm hand and hungrily accepted his suggestions. Thanks also to the rest of the HarperCollins Ireland team – Patricia, Kerri, Tony, Jacq, Ciara and Catherine – and to Paul Erdpresser and Fionnuala Barrett in HarperCollins UK. My no-nonsense editor Rachel Pierce was a godsend and I'm hugely grateful that she lent her forensic superpowers to this novel. As well as identifying problems in the text, she was hyper-creative in offering solutions. It would be a far lesser work without her input. Nervously, I showed a chunk of the novel to Faith O'Grady at an early stage in its evolution, trusting her judgement on the material and her advice on publishing matters. With her *imprimatur* I had the confidence to proceed. Authors are guilty of all sorts of indulgences, not least burdening their friends with work-in-progress. Among the people I put in such an awkward spot on this occasion are Helen Carey, Martin Hughes, and Martin Doyle. All three of them generously gave up their time to read a first draft and provide expert and invaluable criticism. My brother Shane was a great help in making sure none of the characters bore too close a resemblance to any of the living or the dead. Gratitude also must go to my parents, Rory and Teresa, and family and friends whose constant encouragement and goodwill are never taken for granted. To this list, I'd like to add my former agent Dawn Sedgwick, who's been in my corner for the last twenty-five years, and her assistant, Isabel White. Finally, and especially,

Ardal O'Hanlon

I'd like to thank my wife, Melanie O'Hanlon, who has been tremendously supportive of this endeavour from the start, wading through it time after time, dispelling my own doubts about its merits, and inflating the fragile ego when necessary. Apart from the book, she has always been incredibly supportive in every way imaginable.